"Fans of Lackey's epic Valdemar series will devour this superb anthology. Of the thirteen stories included, there is no weak link—an attribute exceedingly rare in collections of this sort. Highly recommended." —The Barnes and Noble Review

"This high-quality anthology mixes pieces by experienced authors and enthusiastic fans of editor Lackey's Valdemar. Valdemar fandom, especially, will revel in this sterling example of what such a mixture of fans' and pros' work can be. Engrossing even for newcomers to Valdemar." *—Booklist*

"Josepha Sherman, Tanya Huff, Mickey Zucker Reichert, and Michelle West have quite good stories, and there's another by Lackey herself. Familiarity with the series helps but is not a prerequisite to enjoying this book." *—Science Fiction Chronicle*

"Each tale adheres to the Lackey laws of the realm yet provides each author's personal stamp on the story. Well written and fun, Valdemarites will especially appreciate the magic of this book." *—The Midwest Book Review*

"The sixth collection set in Lackey's world of Valdemar presents stories of Heralds and their telepathic horselike Companions and of Bards and Healers, and provides glimpses of the many other aspects of a setting that has a large and avid readership. The fifteen original tales in this volume will appeal to series fans." *—Library Journal*

Anything With Nothing

Anything With Nothing

All-New Tales of Valdemar

Edited by
Mercedes Lackey

DAW BOOKS
New York

Cover art by Jody A. Lee

Cover design by Adam Auerbach

DAW Book Collectors No. 1952

DAW Books
An imprint of Astra Publishing House
dawbooks.com
DAW Books and its logo are registered trademarks of Astra Publishing House

Printed in Canada

Library of Congress Cataloging-in-Publication Data is available upon request

ISBN 978-0-7564-1873-1 (trade paperback)
ISBN 978-0-7564-1874-8 (ebook)

First edition: November 2023
10 9 8 7 6 5 4 3 2 1

Contents

A Herald's Bag of Magic
Phaedra Weldon   1

Suffering Knows No Borders
Dylan Birtolo   20

Needs Must When Evil Bides
Jennifer Brozek   33

In Memory's Vault
Kristin Schwengel   49

Look to Your Houses
Fiona Patton   60

What You Know How to See
Dayle A. Dermatis   78

Good Intentions
Stephanie D. Shaver   90

Beebalm and Bergamot
Cat Rambo   112

The Stable Hand's Gift
Ron Collins   123

Warp and Weft
Diana Paxson   140

An Enchantment of Nightingales
   Elisabeth Waters   158

Where There Is Smoke
   Brenda Cooper   171

What a Chosen Family Chooses
   Dee Shull   188

Enough
   Louisa Swann   206

Both Feet on the Ground
   Paige L. Christie   224

Once a Bandit
   Brigid Collins   238

Wooden Horses
   Rosemary Edghill   256

Intrigue in Althor
   Jeanne Adams   269

A Day's Work
   Charlotte E. English   289

Old Wounds
   Terry O'Brien   303

Anything, With Nothing
   Mercedes Lackey   322

About the Authors   339
About the Editor   345

A Herald's Bag of Magic
Phaedra Weldon

"Take me with you!" Luke yelled up at the Herald seated upon his Companion. Luke loved the magical horse, and delighted in the Herald's white garments that gleamed in the early morning.

Herald Aramis had spent well over a week in Luke's village. He'd come to settle an old argument between feuding families, and done his job well. Peace now seemed possible between the two neighboring villages.

Aramis told stories by the fires at night, listened as the villagers sang songs, and spoke privately with anyone needing council. Luke had never seen anyone work such magic. In a place where fighting was how people said good morning, this was sorcery indeed.

Aramis looked down at Luke and smiled. He was a young man, maybe a year or two older than Luke's own brother, who had died during the last skirmish between the villages. He had dark hair that brushed his shoulders, and green eyes. His skin was slightly tanned. "Take you with me? Why would you want to leave such a promising place?"

"Promising?" Luke looked to his left and right. They were at the village's edge, just past the first building, the blacksmith's forge, which happened to be owned and operated by Luke's father. No one else was around. "What's promising about it? There's no adventure here. I want to do what you do! I want to learn magic and see the world. Karse, Hardorn, and the Pelagirs Forest!"

Aramis laughed. "You are well learned in geography, Master Luke. You enjoy reading?"

"I have read every book in the village. Which is why I want to travel for more books. But I want to learn magic most of all. I want a Companion, I want Gifts—I want to be the best Herald in the world and travel everywhere!"

"Such bold words for someone so young," Aramis said. "You are fifteen?"

"Yes."

"And you think you can accomplish these things by becoming a Herald?"

"Yes."

"And there is no other way?"

"Heralds are looked upon with respect and awe. I want that."

The horse made a whinny noise, but it could also have been a snicker. She was looking at Luke, and he met her gaze without flinching.

Aramis got that faraway look in his eye, the one Luke assumed meant he was talking to the horse. To hear a horse talk in one's mind was indeed something to strive for.

The Herald dismounted, gathered his Companion's reins, and turned her back toward the village. "I'll tell you what, Luke. I have time before I am needed back at the Collegium, and with winter fast approaching, I do not look forward to traveling in the cold. What if I stayed here for that time, and I showed you what it is to be a Herald?"

Luke's excitement threatened to overwhelm him. "You . . . you would do that?"

"Yes. I will speak to the town elder and seek his permission. Once I have my answer, and have set up a place to live, I will call upon you."

"I can help you."

Aramis leaned his head to his shoulder and gave Luke a crooked smile. "Yes, you could. This should be very interesting."

"And you'll teach me magic?"

"Of course."

* * *

Within a week, Aramis had secured a nice cottage between the two villages. There was a field in front of the house where his Companion could run and graze. Behind the house was a forest, with several fruiting trees and a lake shared by several farms and the two villages.

Luke waited for what felt like years for Aramis to call on him for his first lesson. But when he arrived at the cottage, which had been cleaned inside and out, he didn't recognize Aramis at first. The Herald had removed his white robes and donned clothing similar to the villagers. His dark hair he kept pulled back in a small leather tie.

He met Luke at the door and together they had tea.

But Luke was too excited for small talk, and wanted to know what his first magic lesson was.

"First, you have to know the basics for survival as a Herald. You said you wanted to travel as a Herald—well—Heralds travel on their Companions. They travel through every possible weather condition, and often have to sleep without shelter."

"They don't just stay at inns and taverns?"

"There aren't as many of those as you would think. And many times, small holds and towns and especially hamlets don't have them. So you either hope someone will give you a room, a shed, a place in a stable, or you camp outside."

"That doesn't sound very fun."

"It is the way," Aramis said as he smiled. "Colds, fevers, bug bites, snake bites, wild animals, all of these have to be contended with. So a good knowledge of the available plants is a good idea." Aramis stood. "Follow me. Oh, and grab those sacks on the counter. There should be about twenty of them. And pick a walking stick from those at the door."

Luke had no idea how this was going to show him magic, but he went along with it. He grabbed the bundle of sacks, then grabbed a stick at the front door and joined Aramis, who had what looked like one of his saddlebags on his shoulders.

"What's in there?"

"Magic," Aramis said as they took off walking from the back of the house and into the woods.

For hours Aramis looked around the forest, poking at things with his walking stick. He plucked snails and put them in a bag at his hip, along with different varieties of wild onions.

He told Luke which plants to pull, showed him how to pull them, and told him what they could be used for. Luke sorted them into different bags, and kept them all in a larger bag Aramis had pulled from his saddlebag.

At first, Luke was bored. What did any of this have to do with magic? But as they approached the lake's edge, he found he was famished and wanting water. Aramis cleared out a natural flat area at the river's edge and set the saddlebag down.

"Are you going to teach me magic now?"

"Hand me the sacks," Aramis said. Luke watched as the Herald reached into the bag and pulled out what looked like a stack of wood, each piece an inch thick. It looked like it was bound in leather straps, but when Aramis unfolded it, it became a tabletop, held in place by two pegs and the straps.

"That's . . . where did you get that?" Luke asked.

"I made it." Aramis placed what now looked like a small plank of solid wood on the ground, creating a solid surface to work on. He untied the sacks, reached into the bag, pulled out two rocks, and handed them to Luke. "As a blacksmith's son, I assume you can make us a fire?"

Luke snorted. "That I can do. There's no magic in that."

He found a good dry spot, dug a shallow hole, gathered up twigs and branches, stripped off bark where needed. He found some dry grass, made a nest under the stacked sticks and wood, and used the flint to spark a fire.

It took about twenty minutes, but eventually he had a nice fire going.

"How's that?" he said to Aramis as the Herald walked over.

"Now, that's magic. You made that out of what you had and two rocks. Now let's do some fishing."

"We don't have anything to fish with."

Aramis held up two of the sacks. "Most of what you picked today is medicinal. These, however, are magic. Now watch."

Luke followed behind Aramis as he waded into the lake to the edge of the shallow shore. He pulled plants from one bag and then the other, then handed the bags to Luke. The Herald bundled the plants together and then scattered them on the water.

"Why'd you have me gather those and then throw them away?"

"Just wait." He pulled a wad of something out of his pocket and unfolded it.

It was a net with tiny weights on the edges.

Within a minute or two, fish popped up on the surface. They lay sideways and didn't move. Aramis threw the net out over them and then gently pulled most of them to the shore. There he pulled them as far from the water as possible, emptied the net, and went back to the edge where Luke stood, open mouthed, as more fish bobbed up and lay flat.

"How . . . what . . . it's magic! It's magic! How did you do it?"

"By rubbing two plants together that are mere weeds when separate, but when you combine them, make a very potent drug in the water."

Luke watched him haul in another catch of fish. "You drugged them? With plants?"

"Yes."

"That's not magic."

"Why not?"

"Because it's not."

Aramis waited until the fish stopped bobbing up and grabbed up the rest of them and dragged them to the shore. Once there, Luke counted close to twenty-seven fish, three different kinds. "Why is this not magic?"

"Because it's not." Luke was impressed, but he wasn't . . . impressed. "You said that bag had magic in it."

"It does. Watch." Aramis reached into the bag and pulled out a small pot, a small frying pan, a small box of jars, and a pouch of some kind. He also pulled out a grate and set it on the fire, poured the contents of the pouch—which Luke assumed was water—into the pot, and then dropped in several things from the jars.

He pulled out a folded strip of leather that, when opened, revealed six different-sized knives and a sharpening stone. With skilled ease, he began gutting and cleaning the fish.

"Take the fish I don't use and hook them together using this." He handed Luke an oversized hook. "Keep them in the shallow water until we're ready to head back. I have salt in the cottage, so I can teach you how to cure them."

Luke huffed as he started carefully putting the fish on the hook. "None of that is magic, Aramis." Though he had to admit, the aroma coming from the boiling pot was heavenly.

"Why isn't it?" Aramis filleted three of the fish, removed the pot, and set the pan on the fire. He took a ladle from the bag, dipped it into the pot, and emptied it into the pan before he put in wild onions and the fillets.

"This is just cooking."

Aramis sat next to the fire and tended the cooking fish. "Why isn't cooking magic?"

"Because it's not."

"You keep saying that."

"And you keep not using magic. Are you really a Herald?"

Aramis laughed. "Aoibheann would argue for me."

"I can't say that word. Is it a name?"

"It is the name of my Companion, whom you so carelessly call a horse. She is far from it." He pulled two smaller plates from the bag and set the fillets on them. He pulled another pouch from the bag, and two cups carved from wood, and poured water into them. "I'm afraid I haven't had time to remake my utensils. Those were stolen during my last set of travels. I'm afraid I was careless, and got captured."

"Captured?" Luke plopped down and blew on the hot fish. He downed the water and Aramis refilled his glass. "By who?"

"Whom. And it was Karse soldiers. Though I was lucky, because I wasn't in my Whites and Aoibheann had hidden away.

They took me with the intent to sell me, and then confiscated my things."

"And you used magic to escape, right?"

Aramis shook his head as he set his plate on the ground and pulled a dagger from his side. Luke gasped—he hadn't even known it was there! "I received this from a blacksmith on my very first Circuit. He said I would need it, wearing clothing so white. It's crafted to be sewn into a strap or a belt. Not seen or noticed until it's too late."

"That's ingenious. Can I look at it?"

Aramis handed it to him. "No spell crafted that blade, nor did a spell or magic or power force that blacksmith to give it to me. That man's own knowledge, experience, and thankfulness manifested that blade for me. I call *that* magic." He gestured to the entire spread. "He made everything you see here, and taught me to make the wooden-slat top. He possessed far greater magic than I."

Luke was looking at the knife, at the perfect connection between hilt and blade, and the way the hilt was flat enough to appear ornamental. It was an ingenious design. "You said 'possessed.' Past tense."

The Herald blew out a breath. "He was killed. Thieves, looking to steal his creations and not pay for them." Aramis took his blade back, and hid it once more. "They were dealt with. But I am no blacksmith or crafter, naught but a simple Herald, and I fear these items of craft have seen better days."

Luke finished his fish, making happy sounds. "That was good. Those things you added to the water, they cooked into the meat."

"And tenderized it as well as cleaned it. Some cook fish with oil, but that is for days spent in leisurely pursuits. You and I still have a walk back to the cottage."

Aramis cleaned all the items thoroughly and set them into the bag. Once it was on his back, and their sticks in their hands, Luke picked up the remaining fish and the two of them set back at a brisk pace.

*   *   *

It was midafternoon by the time they returned, and Aramis took everything out of the bag and set it on the counter, putting all the cooking items into the sink.

There was so much more inside the bag, and Luke was too curious not to have a look at everything. He might have to agree with Aramis about the bag itself being magic for holding so much, but he figured the secret out very quickly.

"Everything's smaller than standard," he said. "That's how you hold so much in there, and it's all light and simply made. It makes it seem like magic."

"Why is it not magic?"

"You keep asking me that."

"Because you haven't answered the question once. I say it's magic, you say it's not. Why are you right and I am wrong? Who is to say that the combination of the skills to come up with the idea of the bag, setting the sizes smaller, and designing them to fit together isn't magic? It came from thought, did it not, just like magic? And it was the craft of a blacksmith's hand that made it physical." Aramis smiled and gestured at the mess in his kitchen. "Magic."

Luke didn't feel like arguing. Though the fish had been good, he wanted something a bit more sustaining. He also wanted to take a look at that knife again, and those pots, and wondered if he could make a bag like this for himself.

"Aramis, do you mind if I take the bag and some of these things—not the seasonings and the knives—well, yeah, the knives too? I'd like to study them."

"Want to create your own magic bag?"

"No. I just might want to see if I can make you some better stuff."

"Yes, you can take it with you. But I must have it back before I leave for the Collegium. You are dismissed for the day. But come back tomorrow. We have more herbs to gather."

Luke groaned as he carefully repacked everything back into the bag, asked to take the walking stick, and headed back to his dad's forge and his home.

* * *

Luke spent the first week walking the woods with Aramis in the morning, learning the trees, what fruits are good, which are bad, and which could be turned into impromptu weapons.

He also helped prepare some land for gardens, built a fence around it, and helped shore up the stable behind the house.

He then worked the forge under his father's tutelage in the late afternoons, and at night, he worked on what he called his *Herald Bag of Magic*. His father didn't understand it, but he seemed very happy with Luke's newfound interest in the smithy.

Luke also worked with the tanner to duplicate the bag by making the pattern and learning how to tan and work the leather. He couldn't make his own bag yet, because there wasn't enough spare material to work with. But he had his plan, so that when he traveled as a Herald, he would be as prepared as Aramis.

A month passed, and the days grew colder as fall approached. Aramis had cured enough meats, fish as well as rabbits, and he'd planted enough in the garden behind the house to store grains and foods that would keep for the winter.

But as the winter season moved in, Luke didn't come to see him as often because of repairs needed for the village requiring the working of iron and steel. Word came from the neighboring village, the one they'd finally made peace with, that their blacksmith had passed away and there was no one in their village who could repair wheel or blade.

Luke and his father worked night and day, filling orders and making wagon parts, hinges for doors, handles, knives, swords, and blades.

Aramis was seated by his fire, reading some books Luke had brought him, when Luke came in through the door. It was snowing, and some of the powdery stuff was blown in with him.

The Herald offered him a hot cider, made from the apples they'd picked and stored in the back of the cottage.

"I didn't expect you today," Aramis said. "Is something wrong?"

"I've got an order that's got to get to the next village. It's things they desperately need, knives for cleaning, cooking, hunting, swords for fighting, and parts needed for repairing and enforcing houses. I brought your bag back, with a set of new magic inside." With that, he grinned.

Aramis looked at the bag he set on the dinner table and pulled out the contents. He marveled at the new pot, grate, pan, and knives. "Luke . . . the blades, even the handles are beautifully done. You did this?"

"I did all of it. I wanted to make my own bag, but I've not had the time, and leather's in demand. We don't have many hunters in the village, not like our neighbors."

"You have craftsmen, such as yourself." Aramis placed everything back in the bag, along with the items Luke had not taken. "So, you have these things that need to be moved?"

"Aye, they're in the wagon outside. I made new wheels and joints for it this week. There's a covering over it, to protect from the snow, and it'll take a day and night's ride to get there."

"You're not going alone, are you?"

"I'm . . . other than traveling around with you, I've never really ventured outside of the village. But no one else will do it."

"And you were wondering if I'd go with you."

Luke shrugged. "You're a Herald. You've traveled all over. I know this isn't really what you do, but I'd be happy if you would come with me. Maybe use your magic to protect us. There are wolves out there."

"And bears," Aramis said. "I suggest we travel during the day. Leave at first light?"

"Yes!"

"Let's put the horses up for the night."

Aramis took the reins at dawn, and the two of them talked on the first stretch of the journey. After crossing the river, the one that fed into the lake they'd fished from, Aramis found a nice place with trees to brace the wind and enough grass to let the horses rest and graze, and set up for a quick lunch.

Luke wanted to show Aramis that he could also make magic from the bag. He set up a fire, made some soup with a few small cut potatoes and salted pork and onions. Aramis showed him which herbs to use from his jars, and soon the aroma set Luke's stomach growling.

After finishing his second bowl, Luke leaned against a tree and looked at Aramis. "You said you were a born in a hold."

"Yes. To the north. I know my skin doesn't exactly bear that birthright, but my family was from the south. The winters were long and hard there, and I was trained to be one of the hold's hunters."

"The hold had their own hunters?"

"We went out at certain times, watching the weather, listening to the wind. My teacher taught me how to respect the natural order of things."

"Like what?"

"Like, a wolf could eat a rabbit, a bear could devour a wolf, and a man could take down a bear."

"Did you kill bears?"

"A few. Not as many as you would think. Our game was deer, though we were careful to watch the populations, killing only what was needed. We used every part of our kills, making things from the bones to the marrow within those bones." Aramis leaned back against his own tree. The wind picked up and blew his hair and his cloak. "Before Aoibheann chose me, I never thought of nature and what we did as anything but magic."

"You think differently now?"

"Oh, no. I believe it even more now. What I know, what you've seen, what we've built together, I didn't learn at the Collegium, Luke. I learned it in the hold, and while out on Circuit. I made mistakes, and like I said, got captured, and survived. But not because of magic.

"Magic has a place, just like everything else. We have those with Bardic Gifts who can calm a room with a song. Will that skill keep them warm in the wild? There are those who can find a path in the woods with no signs, but that skill won't repair a wagon wheel. None of the Gifts you call magic can replace the basic skills of survival. They won't feed you, or clothe you, nor will they be your best friend.

"In some places, they can get you killed."

Luke sighed softly. He knew Aramis spoke of Karse. "Where is your horse?"

"Aoibheann is near. She is always near, watching. But I will say this only once again—she is not a horse."

"Well, she looks like one."

Aramis smiled, and Luke offered to clean up. The Herald went to the wagon and hopped into the back. After a while he jumped out with a sword in his hand.

Finished, Luke set the bag on the floorboard of the wagon's front and then came around to watch Aramis swing the sword. He recognized the rotations the Herald went through, having practiced them himself. "You can fight?"

"I was a hunter. My preferred weapon is the bow and arrow. But I have learned a skill here and there—" His expression changed as he stood still, then turned to face the direction they traveled. He set the blade carefully back in its sheath and returned it to the wagon. "Get the horses hitched and pull the wagon into the woods. We'll need to camouflage it as best as we can."

"What's wrong?"

"We've got company—"

"Are you using magic?"

"I'm using my ears, and the smell of horses . . ." He shrugged. "And Aoibheann told me."

"That's magic."

"No, that's my Companion. Let's go."

They quickly hitched the horses and moved the wagon into faint ruts in the road. Luke took one of the shorter blades and hacked at trees and limbs and set them all against the back of the wagon.

Aramis retrieved a beautiful quiver and longbow from the wagon. Luke had seen this set on his back as he'd headed out of town. The Herald took up a position near the front, his bow ready, while Luke remained with the horses to keep them quiet.

The sound of horses galloping grew louder. Luke saw Aramis hold up three fingers.

Three riders.

But were they friend or foe? He trusted Aramis's caution. The man had traveled along lonely roads for years. He only hoped the men couldn't hear his heart thundering in his chest.

The riders galloped past without stopping. Aramis didn't move, nor did Luke. They remained where they were for a good ten minutes. Finally, Luke realized he couldn't see Aramis anymore. He panicked and moved to the back of the wagon.

Something dropped from the tree to his right. Luke immediately pulled the blade he'd modeled after Aramis's—and nearly stabbed the Herald in the gut.

But Aramis grabbed his wrist and redirected the blade. "That was good, but try to relax. I was in the tree to make sure they kept traveling."

Luke took in a very deep breath and tried to quiet his heart. He resheathed the secret blade. "Did they?"

"It looks like it, but I want to wait another ten minutes to make sure they don't circle back."

"You don't trust them?"

"I don't trust *anyone* on the road." Aramis smiled again. "Go tend to the horses. It's going to be difficult enough backing the wagon out."

The wind picked up and the temperature dropped as the sun went down. Luke insisted the neighboring village was another half day away, and wanted to keep going into the night.

But Aramis worried for the horses with the dropping temperature. He scouted for a safe place, out of sight of the road. Luke was amazed as his friend used the wagon as a block against the wind and coaxed the horses down on their bellies near the fire.

Aramis also suggested wrapping up the cargo and placing it

nearby, but half buried in snow and branches. Luke didn't understand why, but so far, Aramis's caution had been well advised.

"I'll take the first watch," Aramis said. He was bundled in a gray, fur-lined cloak. In his hand was his bow and on his back his quiver. "You get some sleep by the horses. They'll alert us if someone or something approaches."

"Will your hor—your Companion also warn us?"

He grinned at Luke. "She will. Keep the fire stoked and get as much sleep as you can. We need to leave out early."

Luke bundled himself up against a wagon wheel and immediately fell asleep.

He had no idea how long he'd actually slept when cold woke him. He stirred to the sound of voices and saw the fire was out and the horses were gone, but the wagon was still behind him.

"Oy . . . 'e's over there!"

"'e got Natty! Shot 'im right in the froat!"

Luke immediately checked to make sure his weapons were still with him. His sword was under him, and his knife still hidden in his belt.

He moved under the wagon and went still, listening. He heard the *thwap!* of Aramis's arrow. And then the clash of metal. Aramis was fighting!

But where? He tried to pinpoint where in the forest they were, but everything seemed to echo around him.

"There ye are," came a voice too close and too loud. "'Ey, Bolger—got the other in roight 'ere!"

A powerful hand grabbed Luke's ankle, and he immediately kicked out. He knew if this man pulled him out from under the wagon, he would kill him. He felt the wagon move above him and heard the steps as he kicked and held onto the wagon wheel.

"They ain't nothing in this wagon. Old Pinto lied to us about a shipment of steel and stone."

So that was it—these had to be the men they'd seen earlier. Someone had tipped them off to Luke's coming, and they planned on stealing the weapons and bits and selling them.

Still not willing to call out for Aramis, just in case he might still be in the trees or watching, Luke continued kicking, but the robber was too strong and, once he got a good grip on Luke's ankle, pulled him out from under the wagon.

On the slide out, all Luke could think of was the sword under him, the knife at his belt, and Aramis's words just that morning: *"It is not magic that forges the blade, or the center of wagon wheels, the chase of a cart or the knives needed for cooking and sewing. The fashioning, and the wielding, come from the mind, from the body, and from the soul, the true instruments of magic within us."*

Luke grabbed the hilt of the sword and allowed it to follow behind him as he was exposed to the robber. He turned and faced him, spinning as the man bent over to plunge his own dagger into Luke's chest, and with a yell, sliced into the robber's neck.

There wasn't enough force to take off his head, but there was enough to do some serious damage. The robber screamed and scrambled back, dropping his weapon and shoving his hand against his wound.

The one still in the wagon jumped down and tackled Luke. The impact knocked the wind out of him, and the robber struck him across the face a few times.

Luke fell back and coughed and tasted blood.

"I'll take it awl out of yer 'ide," he spat, and grabbed Luke by the neck.

Luke let the robber pull him up by his collar, slipped the knife from his belt, and jabbed it into the man's stomach.

The robber instantly let go and Luke scrambled out from under him. He pressed himself against a tree and used it for support as he pulled himself into a standing position. He couldn't see much in the dark at any distance, not like having the robbers up front and in his face. The full moon coming through the trees did make the shadows visible.

He had never fought real people before. Not like this. And he'd never used a sword, or a knife, to harm anyone. But the slamming of his heart against his chest alerted him to the danger of his situation.

To fight or to die.

That would be life on the road, wouldn't it?

The two men didn't move, so he stumbled to the road and looked both ways. He was shivering as he called out, "Aramis!"

There was no answer. He dove back into the forest and found the wagon. He also found Aramis's bag under the wagon. He grabbed the flints and built the fire again. He checked the bodies. They were cooling in the snow. Luke stood, walked a few feet away, and threw up what little he'd eaten earlier.

:We need your help, Luke.:

He was washing his face with snow when he heard the voice in his head. It was a woman's voice, and it sounded so close. "Who . . ."

:Follow my voice in your mind. We are close by.:

Luke retrieved his sword, the bag, and the blanket he'd been sleeping on, and followed the voice deeper into the wood.

He came to a grove that seemed to be lit directly from the moon as it peeked through the trees. There rested a white horse with a bridle of silver bells. And tucked against her was Aramis.

Luke ran to them and checked for a pulse. He heard a whinny as soon as he heard Aramis's heartbeat and he saw the horses were nearby, safe and sound.

:His wound is in his shoulder, but it was the hit to his head against the tree root that worries me. I cannot speak to him. All is dark.:

"How . . . how are you speaking to me?" Luke didn't really understand how he could see in the dark, but he peeled back Aramis's cloak and saw the wound to his left shoulder. It was deep, but did not go through to the other side.

:You trust one another. And I know you can get him to safety.:

"I can?"

:Miracles occur every day by common people, Luke. It is today that you will see true magic.:

"You . . . you're going to heal him?"

:No. You are.:

Healing. Aramis had drilled the meanings and uses of common road growth into him. He pulled the cloak from around his neck and, with his belt knife, ripped it into long strips. He went through the contents of the bag, and found the sacks with the dried and fresh ingredients of a poultice Aramis claimed had helped stanch a bleeding wound before.

Once he was done combining and pushing the poultice into the wound, with the Companion's help, he wrapped the shoulder tight, but not so tight as to cut off circulation.

He then set to finding any bumps or cuts on Aramis's head. He did find a bump on his left temple, but the skin had not been cut.

Luke dug into the bag and found the small vial of black powder. He pulled the cork and set it under Aramis's nose.

Immediately Aramis jumped, and then cried out at the wound. But he was blinking and looked up at his Companion, then looked at Luke.

He saw the bag, and reached over to feel his bandaged shoulder. Aramis quizzed Luke on what herbs he had used and then smiled when Luke answered.

"And the robbers?"

Luke replaced the items in the bag. "Dead. Or at least the two I killed are."

"Mine is dead as well. I won't go into any details of how I got into this condition, but suffice it to say, I owe you my life."

:*Oh, I wouldn't go that far.*:

"Aoibheann!"

Luke laughed, and felt his exhaustion taking hold. "I wouldn't suggest staying here any longer. You think you can walk back to the wagon? I'll go ahead and put the cargo back in."

"I can help."

:*You should rest.*:

"Don't fuss over me. I'm younger than you, you know."

:*And a tad crankier.*:

Luke laughed. "Do you two always argue like this?"

:*Yes.*:

"No."

Aramis stood with some help from Aoibheann, who also helped him back to the wagon. Aramis did regain a bit of his strength, and once the wagon was refilled, the horses hitched, and the camp stricken, the sun was rising.

Luke took the reins as Aramis rested in the back, beneath the wagon's canopy. Aoibheann strode beside them and kept a watchful eye out until they reached the gates of the neighboring village.

There, they were welcomed with open arms as the town leaders took the cargo and distributed it to where it was needed, and the town apothecary and Healers took the two of them into their sick house.

Luke recovered the fastest after a real rest and food, and helped get the local forge working. He found they were stocked with plenty of ore, as well as the compounds he needed. The tannery was also stocked with leathers—the very ones he needed.

The apothecary was interested in the medicinal herbs in the bag, and the cook at the social hall wanted to know what was in that fish soup he made on the second day.

Aramis woke on the third day, his arm cleaned and treated by the Healers. The arm in a sling, he left the sick house on his own and found Luke busy at the forge. There was a line of people with needs and wants, repairs and orders, and a pretty young woman speaking to each of them, and getting Luke's opinion on the more complicated matters.

"You look better," Luke said as he left the forge and the two embraced. "The Healers were a little worried when you wouldn't wake up."

"Head injury. But Aoibheann would know if it were something too serious. So . . . you've settled in."

Luke put his hand on his hip. "Didn't mean to, but it sort of looks that way. They asked me to stay, but I need to get back home and help my own father."

"I see." Aramis pursed his lips. "I'll stay in the cottage through the winter. As you might have noticed, I don't like traveling snow-covered roads. Too many robbers."

Luke laughed.

"But," Aramis said, "I do owe you my life. So I will make

this offer once—for you to travel back to the Collegium with me when the time comes. Learn what you can, and maybe a Companion will choose you one day."

Luke licked his lips, aware he was covered in dust and soot, and he was sweating, even in the cold. "I do appreciate it." He glanced back at the young woman. "But I think I've had my share of adventure for a bit. You taught me I have a lot to learn still about the magic of life."

"You've grown up in the three months I've known you."

"But not enough. I do thank you for all you've shown me. I adore your Companion, but unless one comes here for me, I'll make my way and maybe one day set out on that road to other places—but not before I do a bit more growing." He patted his chest. "I turned sixteen while you were sleeping."

"Congratulations."

"Oh! Come look," and he led Aramis under the forge's roof where it was warm. On a table in the back sat a bag. It was like Aramis's, but not the same.

"You made a new one," Aramis said and immediately started rifling through it with his free hand.

"I did. I also made a few improvements here and there. You'll see where I put some reinforcements in, and I put in a few lightweight braces to help it keep its shape. It's a nice tool." He gestured to it. "This one is yours."

Aramis stared at him. "No. I can't take this."

Luke smiled. "I insist. And if you'll do a bit more healing, say, for a week, I'll ride with you back to the cottage. I got a few ideas for that stable of yours."

Suffering Knows No Borders
Dylan Birtolo

Eranel's hand moved of its own accord, driving his sword deep into the Karsite's abdomen, despite his internal screaming to stop. Cold hands gripped Eranel's wrist, the fingers sending spears of ice through his skin and piercing his bones, holding him as solidly as the teeth of a bear trap. The chill spread up his arm, creeping through his shoulder and burning across his chest. He opened his mouth, but no words came out. Eranel was paralyzed, unable to tear his gaze from the Karsite before him. The barbarian's gaze, once filled with hate and rage, shifted to surprise and pain, but ultimately ended with sorrow and a wordless accusation.

Eranel opened his mouth, trying to scream, but no sound poured forth. Some part of his brain screamed to let go of the sword, to pull away, but his arm was trapped in the icy snare of his victim. The stranger's mouth opened, and blood poured forth, thick and dark in the dim light. That glow faded around them, washing out the rest of the battlefield until only the two of them remained. Even that grew dark, until all Eranel could see were the Karsite's burning eyes.

He fell, dropping into the void, stopping with a jerk as his frozen arm halted his descent. Even through the chill, his shoulder stretched, threatening to tear itself free in a shower of crystalline shards. Eranel wanted to struggle, to climb up, to do anything to not fall into the darkness where even shadows were loath to tread. But his body refused to respond to his desires. For a moment that stretched each heartbeat into an hour, he hung there, his grip locked on the sword, the only thing preventing his plunge.

The sword shifted, sliding free of the Karsite with a sickening sound that had echoed in his ears every night since he'd first heard it. The blackness reached up to claim him as the weapon pulled free . . .

Eranel shot up in his bed. He patted his chest and shoulder, relieved to find it wasn't frozen. Despite resting atop the thin bedroll, his skin was coated with a thin sheen of sweat. Reassured that he had returned to reality, Eranel pulled his knees to his chest and wrapped his arms around them, squeezing tightly as he forced himself to breathe. It was several minutes before his eyes focused and his mind registered his surroundings.

The other Healers in the tent were sound asleep, or doing their best to feign it. Five of them called this structure their home, each with a small space dedicated for their bedroll and what few belongings they carried with them. A few sacks of mostly clothing and healing tools sat on the ground, scattered about in personal piles. At the front lines of a war, field healers had little time for luxuries, and always needed to be ready to move at a moment's notice.

Eranel grabbed the thin shirt he'd been using for a pillow and pulled it on. He also grabbed his Healer's satchel, tying it around his waist. Suitably dressed, he crept toward the sliver of light that indicated the tent opening. Parting it just enough to slide through, he hoped the beam didn't wake his companions as he slipped outside. Sleep was a precious commodity here.

It was never dark this close to the center of camp. Fires burned throughout the evening, casting flickering shadows in all directions. Off in the distance, the Karsites kept their own fires burning, a beacon of the enemy as they prepared for more fighting with the rising sun.

Eranel walked toward the far end of the camp, furthest away from the battlefield. More than one of the soldiers on guard duty shook their heads as he passed, and one of them spit in his general direction. The reaction was expected, but it still caused the skin across the back of his shoulders to crawl. He refused to let it quicken his pace, instead keeping his steps measured as he approached the only tent under constant guard. Both guards at the opening turned their faces away as Eranel entered the dimly lit interior.

Inside the tent, six Karsites rested on simple mats, no more than scraps of cloth. The healthy prisoners were held some-where else—this tent was reserved for those who were griev-ously injured. A single lamp attached to the ceiling flickered, providing more smoke than light with how low its reserves had dropped.

Eranel walked over to a young man who tossed in his sleep, his bandaged arms clutched tight against his chest. Between gasps, he cried out words Eranel couldn't understand, the ter-ror carrying across the language barrier. Eranel grabbed a cleaning cloth and dipped it into the bucket of water. He dabbed it on the soldier's forehead, wiping away sweat as he rested his other hand on his patient's shoulder. The Karsite calmed be-neath his ministrations, his ravings slowing into a murmur under his breath.

Eranel kept working, providing comfort as he dunked the rag again. His fingers twitched as he heard footsteps coming up from behind him, instincts trained for years urging him to leap to the side and face the newcomer. But this wasn't a battlefield. This was the cost of one.

"Why do you come here?" the newcomer asked. The voice was thick and heavy, and carried notes of pain all too familiar to Eranel's ears.

"Suffering knows nothing about borders or conflicts," he an-swered, making sure the man in front of him had entered a less fitful sleep before placing the rag over the edge of the bucket.

Eranel rose to his feet and turned to face the stranger who asked him. The man stood a head taller than him, with arms that looked carved from stone rather than made of flesh. Eranel wasn't short, and had a wiry strength from years of military training, but the Karsite in front of him looked like he could tear Eranel apart if he was so inclined. Despite his obvious physical prowess, he shook when he stood, small tremors passing through his entire body. Out of the corner of his eye, Eranel saw the darkened bandage around the man's right leg. From the odor filling the air between them, he could tell the wound was infected.

"I'm Eranel. What's your name?"

The man stood there for a moment, making a point to measure Eranel. In another time, it would have made him eager, hungry for the inevitable battle to come. But his own experiences on the battlefield had taught him the simple truth. The Karsites were not barbarians or villains; they suffered, bled, and feared just like those he loved in Valdemar. Instead of an enemy, Eranel saw a soldier in a lot of pain standing before him, one who might not have long to live. That realization brought a sense of calm far surpassing that acquired from any battlefield training.

"Ashon," the soldier said. "I'm . . ."

His words faded as he stumbled, the effort of standing tall and imposing proving to be too much as his injured leg buckled. Eranel shot forward, catching the larger man's arm and draping it over his shoulders so he could ease both of them to the ground. Ashon's arm was warm, so once he was safely on the ground, Eranel fetched the bucket and cloth. He wrung it out over the man's shoulders, letting it cool his back.

After a time, once he had recovered his breath, Ashon broke the silence. "I've watched you, Healer. You come here most nights, despite the tired lines in your face that show how little sleep you get. Despite the comments from the soldiers. I'm sure I don't need to tell you the type of things they say."

"No, you don't." Eranel paused, hesitating before placing the rag back in the bucket.

Ashon turned, sliding in the dirt so the two men could look into each other's faces. "You have a kind soul."

"Not one very well suited to a battlefield, I'm afraid." Eranel feigned a smile, creasing the lines at the edge of his face, the exhaustion he carried deep inside bubbling to the surface for a moment.

"You are wrong. Your soul is one best suited to a battlefield. A reminder of humanity we would otherwise leave behind." The lamp overhead sputtered as Ashon continued, "You often come here in the hours before dawn. I've had soldiers in my command unable to sleep like you. They often wandered in the hours before the sun rose, avoiding sleep to hide from the nightmares they all shared. You have them too, don't you?"

"Everyone has bad dreams." Eranel tried to brush off the comment and squirmed where he sat.

Ashon shook his head. "These are the same fever dreams you dispel from your patients. Your fever is of the mind. Not as visible, no, but still dangerous, and in need of easing."

Eranel stood up, the urge to move becoming overpowering. He didn't walk away, but he rocked his weight back and forth from his heels to the balls of his feet.

"I mean no offense, Healer. But it is important to heal yourself if you want to help others."

"And what would you suggest?"

"I have no answers. Your medicine is caring for others, that much is clear. And that . . ." Ashon paused, smiling as if in response to a joke only he knew. "I could say something noble about that's why I could trust you, but the truth is, I don't have any other options."

The Karsite's tone captured Eranel's attention far more than the words themselves. He crouched down, getting close so they could speak in hushed tones to minimize the chances of being overheard.

"There is a camp north of here, not far. It's in Valdemaran lands, and was meant to be a staging site for strikes behind your people's lines. Now it is just a group of soldiers too wounded to journey back home. We have no Healers. These men have no fight left in them, and only wish to return to their families. But without aid, that won't be possible."

"Why not surrender?"

Ashon glanced around the tent at the soldiers attempting to get some rest despite their injuries. The care they received was minimal at best, almost all of it provided by Eranel himself.

Given his other duties, his ability to minister to these soldiers was limited. If it weren't for his efforts, most of them would have likely died, but even that much care proved difficult. The point was well made.

"What are you proposing?" he asked.

"I could bring you there, have you care for the men just enough to get them able to retreat to their homeland. I promise you, they have no interest in fighting."

Eranel chewed on his lip as he looked back at the soldiers here. What Ashon proposed was reckless. Not only that, but it would brand him as a traitor. He wasn't foolish enough to think he could escape with the Karsite and not have to pay the consequences of such an action. Even if they did succeed and find the camp, Eranel might find himself branded as a war criminal. No, it was beyond consideration.

"Please."

Ashon reached out and placed a hand on Eranel's arm, a motion far gentler than he thought the giant capable of. The word sliced through Eranel's will and to his core with a razor-sharp blade. The pain in that single word carried a truth that would not be denied. People were suffering, and there was no one else who could help.

"Get some rest. I'll come see you tomorrow evening."

The next day, Eranel's mind tumbled as he moved from tent to tent, caring for those he could. As he did, he was keenly aware of the stares and whispers around him. Before, these sounds had faded into the background as he focused on his work. But now, the words pricked at the back of his consciousness like an itch that sat just out of reach, no matter how much one stretched.

His position as soldier-turned-medic always earned him second glances, and had many questioning his presence, but after the conversation with Ashon, it seemed more pronounced. His visits to the Karsite prisoners continued to erode the goodwill he garnered from his other healing efforts. Granted, it was only a small portion of the army who murmured, but it was enough for him to notice.

He had just finished cleaning the bandages of a soldier with a deep gash across his chest when Healer Aelyn came up to him. He wiped his sleeve against his forehead to mop the sweat before offering a shallow bow to the Healer, who shook her head.

"I've told you before, you have more than earned your place here. There's no need for such formality." She studied him for a long moment. "I'm concerned for you, Eranel."

"I promise you, my injuries are completely healed." To accentuate the point, he stretched to the side, pulling the skin tight around the scar he'd received a couple of weeks ago. Healer Aelyn had tended to his injuries, bringing him back from the brink of death, and mending his body with impressive skill.

"The physical ones, at least," Healer Aelyn said. "You need rest. You cannot heal everyone yourself. There are none here so injured that they will not last a day or two without your assistance. Have faith in your fellow Healers, and trust them to shoulder the burden to care for the injured."

"I do. I know my skills are not the strongest, but I need to help. It won't make up for what I've done, but I have to try."

The Healer put a weathered hand on his shoulder, a gesture that reminded him of the gentleness shown by Ashon the night before. "You have a unique ability to help those scarred in their souls and minds. Save your strength for helping those no one else can."

Another Healer came forward and tapped Aelyn's shoulder to get her attention. After a brief conversation, Aelyn excused herself and strode away, heading to another section of the tent where her Gift was needed.

Eranel stood and stretched before heading back to his tent to catch whatever sleep he could before the sun set. "Help those no one else can . . ." he muttered as he crawled into his bedroll.

"You returned," Ashon said when Eranel entered the tent of wounded prisoners. From his tone, Eranel wasn't sure if Ashon was surprised or not.

He unslung his satchel from his shoulder and placed it on the ground in front of him. Rooting around inside, he fished out a small vial and handed it to the Karsite soldier. The larger man looked at it for a moment, and Eranel gestured for him to drink it as he picked up his satchel once again.

"Your leg is infected and burns when you put weight on it. If we're to have any chance of you leading us to this camp of yours, you'll need this. It will dull the pain and renew some of your vigor. I won't lie to you. It will be much worse when it wears off, but it's the only chance we have."

Ashon gulped the concoction down, handing back the empty vial. "I wasn't sure you would come."

"As I said, suffering knows no borders. Now come. If we're lucky, we have until sunrise before they notice either of us is missing."

Eranel led him to one of the sections at the back of the tent. If he didn't know what he was looking for, he would have never noticed that the section of the wall here was loose, fluttering slightly in the breeze. He lifted the edge, ushering Ashon to slip outside. Despite his injured leg, the larger man ducked under with a wince. Eranel followed, dropping the tent wall as soon as he was on the other side. He pulled the anchor ropes taut and reattached them to the spikes in the ground. The setup made it difficult for someone inside the tent to leave, but was easy enough for someone on the outside to disassemble.

The guards at the entrance didn't notice their escape, their attention lax and focused in the direction of the heart of the camp. Eranel led Ashon into the darkness, turning toward the north only when the flames from the campsite became a glow on the horizon. In an unusual twist, Eranel found himself grateful for the mistrust the rest of the camp felt toward the Karsite prisoners, as it made their escape that much easier.

"Come. I'll show you the way."

Eranel was concerned whether the valerian root would last long enough for Ashon to get them to the camp, but at this point, there was no going back.

*   *   *

The sun was starting to lighten the sky as they approached a line of trees. By now, Ashon's face was strained, and his entire body was drenched in sweat. His foot dragged through the dirt as he shuffled forward, but he refused to stop moving, driven by an energy that far surpassed any semblance of sanity. Despite having no chance of being overheard, they had given up on conversation hours ago—it took too much effort when that energy was needed elsewhere.

As they passed through the trees, Eranel saw movement ahead. He wanted to pause, but Ashon continued forward, crashing through the underbrush and destroying any possibility of stealth. A few soldiers stood and shuffled to attention, wielding swords as they came forward to greet the newcomers. Despite their show of force, it was clear they were sorely injured and in no condition to fight. One man's sword trembled in his hand as he pointed it at Eranel with a noticeable effort.

Ashon dropped to a knee next to a tree and leaned against it with his forearm. When he spoke, his words came out through ragged gasps. "He came . . . to help . . . Healer . . ."

With those words, he collapsed to the ground. Eranel threw caution to the wind and rushed forward, rolling the larger man onto his back. The other soldiers came forward, their weapons still held in weak grips.

"Do you have fresh water? Bring it. And start a fire. We need to burn out the infection as best as we can." Eranel barked orders to the soldiers as he dropped his satchel on the ground and rifled through the supplies he'd liberated from the main medical tent of Valdemar's forces. There was a brief moment of hesitation before the Karsite soldiers jumped to follow his commands.

He cut back the bandage around Ashon's leg, and saw the tissue around the wound had darkened, and the odor had progressed further. Even though he didn't have formal training, he had picked up quite a bit during his time following the Healers around camp. The unhealthy skin needed to be removed so the body could start to heal. Walking for several hours was probably one of the worst things they could have possibly done, but it had been a necessary risk. Now the real struggle and work began.

A few days passed, and Eranel only slept when his body refused to follow his commands. More than once, he retired because his hands shook and his vision started to blur. He would sleep for a few hours, then return to work. Despite the very limited nature of his sleep, it was miraculously free of the nightmares that had hounded him since his first and only day as a professional soldier.

Eranel stood up from applying a fresh bandage and walked to the edge of camp, bending his back a bit as he stretched, and took in a deep breath. He rolled his neck from one side to the other, creating a symphony of several pops and cracks. The sun was high overhead, and he was glad for the shade provided from the makeshift campsite in the woods.

The soft shuffle behind him let him know that Ashon approached. His foot dragged less today than it had yesterday, a good sign that he wouldn't lose use of his leg.

"You are making a difference. Most of my countrymen will be able to travel in a day or two. Several would not be alive today if not for you. I cannot thank you enough."

"If our situation was reversed, I'm sure you would have done the same."

Ashon chuckled with a sadness underneath the mirth. "I don't think so. No, Healer, you have a unique way of looking at people."

With those words, Ashon walked away, leaving Eranel by the edge of the campsite to his own musings. Those musings were interrupted by a distinctive whistle. To most it would have sounded like a songbird, but those birds weren't indigenous to this region. Eranel recognized the call he'd used with Taelor when they trained together what felt like a lifetime ago. Eranel glanced over his shoulder to make sure he wasn't being watched. While the Karsite soldiers had maintained a careful eye on him at first, his actions had led them to give him free reign around the camp. After all, why would a Healer go to such lengths to treat the injured if his only plan was to turn the soldiers over to Valdemar?

A short distance from the camp, some movement off to his side triggered Eranel's instinct. He ducked as a blade sliced through the air over his head. His leg shot out and he kicked at his adversary, but she jumped over the foot sweep. However, he expected that, and sprang up at an angle into her from his crouched position. His shoulder collided with her leather breastplate just as her feet landed, before she had a chance to brace herself.

She fell back from the impact, grabbing his shoulder as she collapsed and pulling him down on top of her. The momentum enabled her to roll over, tossing him to the ground underneath her as she pinned him with her knees. Before he had a chance to throw her off, a dagger flashed from her belt, the point placed just under his chin.

"You're getting slow," Taelor said, grinning and raising an eyebrow in challenge as she looked down at her friend since childhood.

Eranel considered smacking her weapon away, but decided it was better not to prolong the scuffle, especially so close to the Karsite camp. While they had accepted his presence, he doubted they would be so welcoming to an active soldier in the Valdemaran army.

"Well, I couldn't have you suffering the mental anguish of being bested by a simple field medic. How would that look to your commanding officer?"

She wrinkled her nose at him before tucking her dagger away and then getting up. She offered a hand to help him rise, then recovered her dropped sword.

"What are you doing here?" Eranel asked, hissing out the words to make sure they weren't overheard.

When Taelor turned back to face him, the mirth was gone from her face. She scowled as she closed the distance and came within an arm's reach.

"I could ask you the same thing. Desertion? Aiding a prisoner escape? Associating with the enemy? I may not have understood why you couldn't swing a sword anymore, but I accepted it. This, though? Have they bewitched you in some way?"

Eranel shook his head. "No, they haven't. They needed help."

"But they're the enemy. They are barbarians who would just as soon as kill you as they would look at you."

"Then why am I still alive?"

Taelor paused at that, but eventually shook her head as if to dismiss the thoughts before they ran rampant.

"The commanders know what you've done. They're assuming you were held hostage and forced to help the Karsite escape. They've dispatched a regiment to come here and eliminate any Karsite forces behind our lines and free you from their captivity. I urge you to stick to that story."

It might be Eranel's best chance to live freely in Valdemar. He thought of the people he loved, of the invitation to the Healer's Collegium stashed at the bottom of his satchel, of so many dreams that were still so new as to yet be given shape. He thought of Taelor's unspoken pleading as she stared at him, struggling to comprehend how this was even a decision that required any thought.

He also thought of the wounded who posed no threat to Valdemar, of the pain on their faces as he tended their wounds, and of the nightmares that had chased him for weeks. He couldn't explain it, but he knew that if he took this offer, the dreams would return.

"Go. I'll be ready when the troops arrive."

Taelor smiled and grasped Eranel's arm briefly with a reassuring squeeze before she sprinted toward the edge of the woods in the direction of the Valdemar camp. As he watched her go, he couldn't help but wonder if she had deliberately misunderstood him. He had no desire to wound his oldest friend so deeply by dispelling that illusion.

When he returned to the Karsite camp, he sought out Ashon. The Karsite noticed his dour expression and spoke before Eranel could say anything.

"We need to leave, don't we?"

"Yes. Valdemar troops will be here before long. Those who can need to head to the border as quickly as possible."

There was a flurry of activity as Ashon gave the orders. For his part, Eranel applied a last bit of splinting and doled out what remained of his medicines, getting as many soldiers ready for travel as possible. While most were capable of the journey, several soldiers were still too injured to be moved. They were somber as they realized they would be left behind, but none fought against their fate.

As the small gathering of Karsites prepared to leave, Ashon came to stand next to Eranel. "You're not going with them?"

Ashon shook his head. "I will not leave these men behind. Besides, if I leave, they'll chase me, putting everyone you saved at risk." He paused, nodding his chin in the direction of the Valdemaran camp. "You could go, Healer. You've done more than enough."

Eranel considered it, but the phantoms waited at the edge of those woods, ready to pounce on him should he leave. "No. I can't turn my back on people who need my help."

"As I said, you have a unique way of looking at people."

Eranel smiled, despite the gravity of the situation. "Look at us. It's not unique. Some people just need a reminder."

Needs Must When Evil Bides
Jennifer Brozek

Edda heard the girl's running steps long before she heard the frantic pounding on her sturdy wooden door. Still, she waited until the knock came to get out of her seat to see what was needed. It had been a long day of chopping wood along with the many, many other chores her small homestead required on a regular basis, and she would not hurry along to more work if she did not have to.

Any hope of an easy evening by the fire died as she opened the door and Blossom Gow, the Collymore estate's maid of work, stood there in tears. "Widow Vardon, please, you've got to help! They're threatening to kill everyone!" she panted as she leaned against the doorjamb, trying to catch her breath.

Edda peered at the girl. It was clear she had run the whole way through the woods to get here. Though Blossom was not quite yet a woman, Edda had never known her to exaggerate or prevaricate. "Come in. Tell me." Edda's voice cracked with age and disuse. She turned, leaving the door open as she considered what she might need. The first was information. The second was gear to travel.

"Bandits. They invaded the house. I was getting water. I saw them as I came back. They didn't see me. There was yelling, and I heard one of them swear they would kill everyone in the house. I didn't wait. I ran for help."

"Why here? Why me?"

Blossom, stepping into the small home, hesitated. She opened her mouth, closed it, glanced away, then seemed to decide something. "Because . . . you used to be someone. Everyone knows when you need something no one else can give you, it's time to see the Widow Vardon." She paused before adding, "And you're closer than town."

The Widow Vardon. That was what they'd always called her, and Edda had never sought to correct them. She hadn't been married to Dustan. He had been her closest friend, her greatest love, her only companion, but never her husband. He'd died. She'd lived. The townsfolk had just assumed she had been a guardsman or a mercenary who had lost her spouse. When she came here to hide (and eventually heal), she found a home like no other she'd experienced before—small, quiet, trusting, compassionate, and willing to let those who wanted to be alone stay alone. Thus, she allowed the town their mistake, never correcting them.

Edda nodded as she put on her boots, tough leather things good for work, and asked, "How many?"

"Three." Blossom shook her head. "Four. There were four."

"Why would they invade? We're not a rich town, this far out from Haven. What do the Collymores have that they want?" She shrugged into her warmest woolen sweater. Springtime it was, but still chilly at night.

Again, Blossom hesitated, then shook her head. "I don't know. Not really."

Edda gave her a look but said nothing.

The maid looked away. "It might have something to do with the rumor that Lord Collymore just inherited a small fortune. We received a heavy metal chest a couple of weeks back."

"Is it true?"

Blossom shook her head. "I don't know." She lifted her chin at Edda's frank gaze. "Really, I don't. I can only guess. It's not like the lord and lady consult with me on what they receive unless it needs cleaning. Please. Morwen is only five years old and they're threatening to kill her. They need you. *I* need you. Please."

As much as Edda did not want to admit it, Blossom was right. She was needed. Had she ever been able to resist the call when it came for her? No. Did she have any idea how she was going to rescue the Collymores from four armed bandits? No. Was she all that Blossom had at this point? Yes.

Needs must when evil bides, she thought as she gestured Blossom toward the door. "All right. Let's go. We'll plan on the way."

There was enough moonlight out that they did not need a lantern to light their steps as they hurried through the woods. Edda thought about what the girl had said and how she had said it. Then she considered what hadn't been said. There was something.

"Did you see what they were armed with?"

Blossom shook her head, then nodded. "One had a sword. The other two had cudgels. One of them also had a dagger."

Edda hurried on behind the girl. Bad, but it could be worse. "And the fourth?"

"He didn't have weapons." She paused before adding, "Not that I saw." She paused again, longer this time, then shrugged before repeating, "Not that I saw . . . but maybe."

"We can't take them in a straight fight. An old woman and a stripling of a girl is no match for four armed men." Edda frowned, trying to remember what she knew of the Collymore estate. She'd been there a handful of times over the decades. "Where are the rest of the servants?"

"Brannon is in town, seeing his love. It's his night off. Soren and Della are gone for the week. Her mother is ill. I've been cooking for the family along with all my other chores. It's why I was out so late."

Edda kept half an eye on the ground. It would not do to go sprawling and hurt herself before she could even get to the estate. That would not bode well for any kind of rescue attempt. "There are back stairs for the servants?"

"Yes."

"Discreet?"

Blossom nodded. "Yes. A servants' entrance and back hallways, too."

"Thought so. The manor house is big enough." Edda slowed to a stop as she saw the roof of the large home come into view through the barely budding treetops. The high moon reflected off the glazed rooftiles. She gazed at Blossom, certain there was more than what the girl had told her. The woods were silent with their less-than-quiet passing.

Blossom stopped, looking anxiously between Edda and the Collymores' home. "What? Why are we waiting? We have to help them!"

"Blossom." Edda kept her voice quiet and firm. She waited until Blossom looked her in the face before she asked, "What are you not telling me?"

The girl's face crumpled, and she turned away, but didn't say anything.

Edda turned Blossom back to her with a gentle hand. "If I am to help, I need to know everything. What else do I need to know?"

Tears spilled down Blossom's face again. "It was Rylan. He let the bandits in."

Rylan Bardot, a young man from town who cared for his ailing father. She hadn't realized the two youngsters were courting. Why would she? She hadn't been to town in a few weeks. Edda nodded. "He was the fourth? The unarmed one?"

"Y-yes. He asked me to get water for a bath. Said he wanted to feel like Lord of the Manor. He hadn't had a real one in a long time." Blossom wiped at her face with angry fists. "He just wanted to get me out of the house." She stopped and shook her head. "No. I don't know. Maybe he wanted me to escape. I don't know. I know he saw me with the buckets. He waved me back. He mouthed something to me, but I couldn't make it out. The light from the doorway was behind him. Then the bandits came. He let them in, waved me away, and followed in after. He was *with* them."

Edda could see the conflicted emotions on Blossom's face. Anger at being used by her love. Confusion at being waved away. Hope that he had done so out of care. Fear for the family she served. Guilt. Why did she feel guilty? "Did you tell him about the chest that had been received?"

Blossom looked at the ground and nodded. "This is all my fault. They could be dead because of me."

"Did he ask you about it first, or did you volunteer the information?"

The girl shrugged with defeat. "I don't know. Does it matter?"

After a moment's consideration, Edda shook her head with a sigh. "I suppose not." Whether or not the boy had been coerced was a question for another time. "The plan: we are going to rescue the family. That is it. We sneak in. We sneak them out. We flee to town and report to the guard. We do *not* confront the bandits nor Rylan. Do you understand?"

Blossom raised her chin, hope—damnable hope—brightening her face. "We use the servants' stair. And the back hallways."

"Or the flower trellis, or whatever comes to hand. What's most important is that we move about unseen, unheard." She looked at the roof of the large home. "It is possible to do so. But we will need to be quiet and patient."

"That's what a servant is: quiet and patient. I know that house like the back of my hand."

"Good." Edda smiled, encouraged despite knowing they had no idea what they were walking in on and even less of a chance of succeeding in their goal of rescuing the family unscathed. "Well then, lead the way. Get us to the back of the house without us being seen."

The pair moved like thieves in the night, darting from shadow to shadow, keeping out of the scant glow from the house and the bright light of the moon. The house felt quiet but unsettled as Blossom led Edda into the Collymore home through the back servants' entrance. They stopped after they stepped into the servants' quarters.

Edda noticed a change in Blossom's demeanor as soon as

they entered the house. Even though it was darker inside, her head came up, her shoulders straightened, and her steps were more assured. She was on familiar ground.

Instead of constantly looking back at Edda for instruction, the maid actually took charge, leading the older woman to her room, where she gathered a small set of keys. "Master keys. For emergencies only," she murmured with a small, guilty smile.

"This is an emergency indeed," Edda agreed, then listened to the house around her as hard as she could.

It had been a long time since she'd had to call upon the skills she needed now. Decades since she had used stealth, strategy, and observation. She had thought all of it had died when Dustan died. She discovered now that it hadn't; it had only lain dormant until it was once more desperately needed by those who could not do for themselves. Part of her soul cried out in anguish at the memory of where these reawakening skills came from. Part of her, the practical part, ignored the emotions teeming in her heart.

Needs must . . . It was time to get to work.

Edda felt the presence of people around them. Sensed movement. Sensed stillness. Sensed tension. "What is on this floor and the floor above us?"

Blossom looked up. "This floor's the general-purpose rooms: den, great hall, dining room, family room, kitchen, bath." She shook her head. "Just public rooms and company rooms."

"No bedrooms?"

"Those are on the second floor, along with other family rooms and the library."

"And the third?"

"Attic. Storage. There's a widow's walk we use for lookout when waiting on important guests."

Edda considered. She heard neither the wail of a child nor a woman. That could mean multiple things. She did not smell blood . . . not yet, anyway. Thus, most likely, the child was asleep and not hurt. "Can we get to the second floor without being seen? To the child's room?"

Blossom's answer was to beckon and sneak out of the servants' quarters and down the hall. They turned down another hallway to a set of stairs across from a door. Edda gestured for her to go ahead, but paused at the foot of the stairs as male voices floated to them through the door, muffled and indistinct, but coming closer.

Edda shifted backward. Her bootheel hit the wall with a distinct thud. She froze. Blossom froze with her for a second before moving to Edda's side. There, she gripped the older woman by the arm at the bicep and waited.

"—*was that?*" Gruff, older. "*You sure no one's here?*"

"*I swear, everyone's gone for the night.*" Younger, familiar. Rylan.

The world paused and listened.

"*It's the house settling. Big houses do that, Holt.*"

"*Maybe. Go check on the woman. I swear if she's gotten out . . .*"

"*She hasn't. She's locked in. I'll check right now.*"

"*Be quick about it. I'll be with Seton.*"

Edda felt Blossom's grip tighten, and didn't resist as the maid pulled her back down the hallway and ducked them both into an alcove. Edda turned the girl so both of their faces were hidden and wouldn't reflect light if Rylan had light with him. Also, she knew that people on high alert could often sense eyes on them. They both heard the door open and close, then a single pair of feet ran up the stairs without hesitation.

"We always take the servants' stairs when he's here. It's . . . better that way," Blossom said, her voice quiet and furious.

"I know. Now we know they have at least Stephen and Narah separated. Remember, we're here to get the family out. That is it." She left the subtext of not confronting Rylan unsaid, but knew the girl understood.

Blossom heaved a deep sigh and nodded. They both listened for a couple of heartbeats. "I think we can go now. Mind your feet and step where I step," Blossom said and turned out of the alcove, leaving Edda to follow again.

They hurried up the stairs on light feet. At the top, the hallway ran both left and right. There were two doors visible. On that same wall, several small holes let in feeble light from the rooms beyond.

Blossom stopped at the first door and peeked through the viewer. "He's going into Morwen's room. I think they're both in there." She stepped back for Edda to see.

Looking through the small hole, Edda saw the opened door and heard muffled words but could not tell what was said. After a moment, Rylan exited the door, saying, *"I'll get it. I'll be right back."* He stopped and locked the door.

Edda looked at Blossom and whispered, "He's coming. Hide!"

Without waiting to see what Blossom did, Edda rushed down the hallway to the left and ducked around the corner. She stopped short before she ran headlong into the end of the short hallway. Controlling her breath, she paused and listened, hoping Blossom had done the same thing she had. Rylan opened the door without hesitation and bolted down the stairs. Edda waited until she heard the second door open and close before she looked around the corner.

To her surprise, Blossom stood there, mouth opened with her own look of surprise. The girl murmured, "I froze. But he didn't see me because of the door, I think."

"Thank providence for that. Will one of your keys open Morwen's room?"

She nodded and, without being told to, exited the back hallway and hurried to the girl's room. Edda was on her heels, moving as quietly as she could. The only reason she wasn't out of breath was the fact that she'd spent most of her time fending for herself and her homestead. It was hard work, but it kept her in a sort of fighting shape.

Blossom got Morwen's door open and slipped into the darkened room with Edda on her heels.

"Relock it," Edda commanded as she surveyed the room. Narah stood next to her daughter's bed. Morwen was in bed, but also still dressed in day clothes. Both of them looked afraid and rumpled. Neither seemed hurt.

Edda lifted a finger to her lips, keeping her eyes on the young girl. "We're here to get you out," she whispered. "Do not make a sound." She probably didn't need to warn the girl to keep silent. Morwen looked exhausted, and was almost asleep as she sat there, even with a new stranger in her room.

Blossom moved to Morwen's side. "We're gonna play a game. You have to be as quiet as . . . as a flower."

Having cataloged the room in a habit she had never been able to break, Edda already had a plan in mind. She walked to the window, opened it up, and looked down. Two stories up. Not too far in the grand scheme of things. Vines grew up the wall, but nothing they could hold onto. The curtains were of a heavy satin edged in gold trim, and the girl's bedsheets looked like quilted muslin embroidered with tiny roses. "Tie the sheets and blankets together. We'll anchor with the curtains and the bedpost. You three are going out the window."

Blossom got to work without hesitation. Edda would have smiled if she had not already seen the argument growing on Narah's face. Frightened or not, the woman was used to getting her own way.

"I am not leaving without my husband."

"Do you love your daughter?" Edda asked the question in a quiet and unassuming voice.

Narah frowned, confused. "Of course I do."

"Then you will listen to me now and save your daughter while I save your husband." Edda still saw the signs of stubbornness on her face. She added, "It will go better and safer if I don't have you and your daughter here as a distraction. If you love her, listen to me and do as I ask."

Blossom touched Narah's arm. "Please, m'lady. I'll need help with Morwen. She won't go without you."

"Go," Edda urged, feeling time slip through her fingers. "Let me do my job. I'll get him to safety."

Narah finally agreed with a nod and helped Blossom tie the sheets and blankets together. Edda made certain the whole affair was secured to the bedpost and that everything was braced. After Blossom convinced Morwen to go for a piggyback ride, Edda tied the girl in place. "Narah . . . Lady Collymore . . . first, then Blossom. I'll anchor here."

Giving her an appraising look, Narah said, "I think you have earned the right to call me by my given name. Thank you. The boy will be back soon. I requested tea to help with my headache."

"I will deal with the boy when he returns. Run. Run as fast as you can to town and send the guard."

Blossom gave her a look, opened her mouth to say something, then seemed to think better of it. Instead, she shifted Morwen—who was already asleep again—to a more comfortable position on her back and said, "I'm ready."

Edda moved to the door and listened while Narah, then Blossom, navigated the makeshift escape route. As soon as Blossom went over the edge, Edda shifted between checking on the window and listening at the door. Part of her heart unlocked as Narah made it to the ground and the strain on the bedsheets visibly lessened. The woman already had her hands out to steady Blossom as the maid touched the ground. Without more than a single look back, the two of them ran off toward town.

Edda let out a relieved breath as the figures disappeared from sight. That was one problem down. The second was unlocking the door as she moved into position. Part of her marveled at how quickly the old skills that had been beaten into her had come back to life. Crouched next to the door, she knew Rylan would see the evidence of the escape. What he did next would dictate her actions.

Rylan opened the now-unlocked door and paused, a wooden tray in both hands. He blinked in surprise at the open window letting in a cool breeze that ruffled his unruly hair. His eyes darted from the window to the shifted bed as his stunned mind worked out what had happened. He rushed to the window to look out, but tripped over Edda's quick hand grab at his ankle. He fell flat with a soft *oof* as the tray—teapot and all—went flying, to land on the bed in a quiet clatter of spilled tea, cream, and sugar.

Edda pounced on the teenager, trying to pin him down, but he squirmed and flipped over. He froze when he saw who was attacking him. Eyes wide and wild, he stopped trying to dislodge her and asked, "Widow Vardon?"

Realizing Rylan was much stronger than she was and could easily best her in a physical fight, Edda moved their struggle from a physical one to a mental one. She shook his shoulders once in a single, emphatic motion, then said, "Rylan Bardot, I am *so* disappointed in you."

She got up, freeing him as his face crumpled into something so young and hurt it made her feel ashamed. That didn't stop her from closing the bedroom door with a quiet click before turning to ask, "How could you?"

The hurt expression turned haunted with fear. "I'm sorry. They were gonna hurt my da. They said . . . I didn't think . . . It was just to steal the chest!" He struggled to his feet, recovering himself as he did. He took the time to glance out the window before asking, "Blossom?"

Edda crossed her arms, thinking fast. If he'd been coerced into it, things could be salvaged. "You've hurt that girl bad. Now, you have two choices. One," she pointed to the window, "you go out the way they went, hurry to catch up with them, and see them safely to town and the guard while I finish what I came to do. Or, you call your *friends*," she spat the word at him like a curse, "in here, and I'll deal with all of you." Silently, she begged the gods above that he would just leave and wouldn't force her hand—not only did she not actually want to hurt him, she wasn't certain she could.

Rylan shook his head. "They're not my friends. They threatened to hurt my da, then kill him if I didn't help."

"Whose fault is that? What did you tell them about the inheritance?"

Rylan grimaced, guilty and rueful. He shook his head again. "Yes, it's my fault, but let me make amends. Let me help you free Lord Collymore."

"Why should I trust you?"

"Because I'm asking . . . and because I haven't called them in here yet."

An able-bodied young man on her side might do the trick, and she didn't have much time left. *Needs must*, Edda thought. "All right. Where are they keeping Stephen?"

He pointed to the left side of the room. "Two doors down. The library. It's where they have . . . have everything. The chest and Lord Collymore tied up."

"Why haven't they just taken the chest and left?"

"It didn't arrive with a key. That's what he says. Teon doesn't believe him. It's why they're here. Also, I think . . . I think they're thinking of ransom or more robbery." Rylan dropped his arms and his eyes to the ground. "I'm sorry. I didn't know they'd do this. I was worried for my da."

Edda *hmphed*. "You can apologize to the correct people once we get Stephen free and escape." She glanced between the left wall and the window. "If we can get the bandit out of the room, I can get in and free Stephen, then we can leave this way. Where are the other bandits?"

Rylan raised his head. "In the smoking room. Drinking. At least Seton was, and Holt said he was going there."

"How soon before anyone misses you?"

"I don't know, but I know how to get Teon and the rest out of the house."

She raised one gray eyebrow in a question.

"I tell them the truth." He shrugged. "I rush in. Tell Teon the woman and child have escaped, and I saw them running away. Then I lead them away."

Edda considered the plan. It wasn't much . . . but it was more than she had at the moment. "It could work," she allowed. "And keep you on their good side . . . But head toward my homestead. Blossom already laid a trail a blind man could follow. The moon is high. It will make them believe your story."

His face crumpled again at the mention of the girl. "Tell her I'm really sorry. I never meant for her to get involved."

"You'll tell her yourself. Do you think Teon will want to look in here first?"

Rylan nodded. She didn't know what he was nodding to: her comment or her question. She took it as both. "I'll hide in the room next door so I can hear what's happening in both rooms." She looked him in the face. "Are you sure you want to do this? They will be angry."

Rylan looked away, then met her eyes. "I have to. It's the only way to save Lord Collymore."

"Well, then. Let me get into the room next door. Then you . . . do what you think you need to do to whip the bandits up in a frenzy. Once they leave, I'll free Lord Collymore and get us out as soon as I'm certain we won't be seen." She hoped they could use the front door as opposed to the makeshift rope. The idea of climbing down was not appealing, and she could see herself sprawled on the ground beneath it all too easily.

He nodded and stepped aside, allowing her to take the lead. She took it, knowing Dustan would've chided her for her easy trust. She shook away the thought. This was not the time for ghosts or imaginary conversations—no matter how much she still missed him.

The house was quiet as she stepped out of the bedroom and down the expansive hallway to the closed door. At the end of the hallway, the library door was cracked open, with the flickering light of a candle leaking around its edges. She paused by the closed door and listened. Beyond the beating of her heart, she could hear Rylan in the doorway behind her, the soft muttering of a deep male voice down the hall, and the scrape of metal on metal.

The door to her hiding spot opened without a sound on well-oiled hinges. Slipping inside, Edda found herself in a combination sitting room and music room. She nodded to Rylan and left the door cracked open so she could hear what was about to occur.

While Rylan got himself and his story together, she looked around at the well-appointed luxury. Two busts of unfamiliar faces sat in alcoves on either side of the door. A small half-circle of four plush chairs sat to one side of the fireplace while a large harp, a fiddle, and a small guitar sat next to their accompanying chairs. She could imagine the tidy domestic scene of well-dressed nobles enjoying tea while they listened to music.

Outside this little fantasy, Rylan ran past the room, feet pounding. *"Teon! Teon!"* She heard him crash into the library door in his "panicked" haste and felt her own tension rise. *"They're gone!"*

"Who's gone?"

"The woman and the child. Out the bedroom window!"

"Hell and damnation. You were supposed to watch them!"

Rylan's voice took on a fearful note. *"Seton ordered them locked in the bedroom."*

"Then how'd you know they've escaped?"

"Holt heard a noise and ordered me to look in on them. I did. They were gone. But I saw the way they went. Toward the Widow Varden's homestead." He paused before adding, *"They can't have gotten far. We . . . we could catch them."*

When silence descended, Edda strained to hear what was happening. After a short while that seemed like eternity, she heard the grunt of a man and the chunk of something metal hitting the carpeted floor with a thud.

"Get that end of this thing," Teon ordered.

"What are we doing?"

"What I probably should've done as soon as I found out the key was lost—getting this someplace I can break it open in private."

"We're leaving?" Rylan's question was strained but louder.

Teon grunted his agreement. *"If they get to that busybody, it's all over. The guard'll be here in no time."*

Edda saw the faint shadow of someone shuffling past the door before she saw the person. It was Rylan, walking backward, carrying one handle of what was obviously a very heavy chest. She took a step back from the door as the second man, about Rylan's size, shuffled past, also straining with his half of the chest.

A quick inventory of makeshift weapons told her what she needed to do next. After taking one of the heavy stone busts, she opened the door to the hallway and stepped out. She kept her eyes on her target, ignoring Rylan's suddenly widening eyes. That boy was strong, but he wasn't smart.

With adrenaline and determination fueling her strength, she

hefted the bust above her and slammed it down on the back of the bandit's head. Teon collapsed without a sound.

The same could not be said of the heavy metal chest or of Rylan, who yelped as the chest suddenly dropped and was yanked out of his hands. The crash seemed to echo through the whole hall. Rylan and Edda froze, listening for signs they'd been heard.

After a count of twenty, Edda asked, "Where is the smoking room?"

Rylan pointed to the right. "Far end of the house. Thick walls and door. Did you kill him?"

Edda glanced down at the unmoving form and saw the small puddle of blood forming next to him. Probably not. She decided she didn't care if she had. "Don't know. Doesn't matter. Let's get Stephen free and out of here. You can explain to him why you're in his house on the way to town. Maybe we'll catch up to the others."

"You'll come with us?"

She nodded. "I will. I'll speak on your behalf. You helped me, after all, and you didn't do this of your own free will. I'll see to it that everything will be all right."

They headed toward the library as she spoke. Something tight, heavy, and full of grief unlocked in her heart. Edda realized she would do as she'd said without feeling pressured or like she was putting on a mask. It felt good and right in a way she hadn't felt in a long, long time.

"Of course Lord Collymore was right to be angry, but even he had to admit he could understand why Rylan had done what he'd done. Still, Rylan knew Stephen would be angry when we freed him. Knew he deserved the man's ire. I do not know what the guard will do about him, but we did make certain that he and his father were safe. I spoke for him tonight, and will do so in the coming weeks."

Back at her homestead as the sun was coming up, Edda sat on her bed feeling every second of her many decades of life. She turned from the window to look at her wardrobe. "I suspect Rylan's courting days with Blossom are done for now. They might resume. They might not. Still, despite his lack of sense, he's got a good heart. He stayed when he didn't need to, and helped me when it wasn't required. I appreciate that. Maybe I'll hire him to help around this place. Keep an eye on him."

She stood and groaned. "I'm getting old, Dustan. Hell, I've been old for as long as I can remember." Popping her back before she walked to the wardrobe, she sighed, soft, sad, wistful.

With an aged hand that now trembled with fatigue, she opened the doors, revealing the clothing within. Ignoring those, she bent and slid open a drawer—one she had not opened in a very long time—and pulled out an old white tunic. Now much too small for her, it was the only remaining element of the uniform she'd worn long, long ago. As she did, there was a quiet *clink* of metal as Dustan's bridle shifted from its spot. She hugged the tunic to herself and stared at the bridle with stinging eyes.

Gazing at the memory of her beloved Companion, Edda whispered, "You would've been proud of me tonight. I did what I could with what I had . . . just like we always did. It wasn't much, but tonight, it was enough."

In Memory's Vault
Kristin Schwengel

The wind howled around the edges of the building, seeking to drive snow deep into any cracks it might find. Gaven tilted his head to one side, listening. In his days as a traveling sword-for-hire, winter nights had always been accompanied by tales of frost demons with icy claws shredding those who had the misfortune to be in their path. It was easy to believe in such creatures when the wind shrieked like this right outside one's tent, harder to accept from the comfort of a well-built guardhouse.

He shrugged and stood up to stretch, using the long poker to resettle the burning logs in the kitchen's great hearth. In midsummer, his kitchen would get unbearably hot, but when the worst of the winter storms came through, half the Guard seemed to find reason to come to the back of the building. He didn't bother concealing his wry smile at the thought—at least he usually managed to get some potato- or onion-chopping out of the visitors while they warmed up.

Retaking his seat and turning back to the open book on the long table before him, Gaven considered his inventory. Trindon's Guard had been well stocked before winter began, but the snows had been heavier this year, and the resupply wagons from Haven were delayed. They still had plenty of root vegetables in the cool cellar, and grains and beans in his dry storage, but he didn't like the lower amounts of dried and preserved meats. The hens had nearly stopped laying in this latest cold snap, so he couldn't rely on supplementing with eggs. All of the Guard had been given instruction to take extra time to hunt when they were out on patrol, but a few scrawny rabbits wouldn't go far.

He frowned at the pages before him, trying to convince himself that his neat calculations were wrong and that they weren't going to run out of meat before the next wagons could get through. It wouldn't be worth checking in the town, either. The townsfolk would be in much the same situation, if not worse, for they didn't have the standard ration supplies provided by the Crown.

Footsteps pounded down the hall, and he looked up just as Rimmick, one of the younger guardsmen, burst through the kitchen door. "Hot water for Coulson!" he cried almost before the door was fully open. "Jer found someone wounded in the Pass!"

Gaven stood in such haste the bench he was sitting on flew halfway across the room. "Lennie, pour off what's in the kettle and take it with Rimmick. Flick, fill the great pot and add an extra log to the fire to speed it up."

His two assistants hurried into their tasks while he put a few pieces of dried beef into another pot, adding a handful of herbs and pouring in water from one of the jugs Flick had used to fill the large pot.

"Tell Healer Coulson there will be broth in a little while, whenever he needs it." Gaven bit back the urge to add "*if* he needs it." Whomever Jer had found on his patrol, he hoped it had been in time, and the poor soul wouldn't still die of injury or cold.

Gaven filled a mug from the broth-kettle and pushed it across the table to Coulson, who'd come down to the kitchen to relax after settling his patient as best he could.

"You know better than this—drink. You need it every bit as much as she does."

The Healer frowned at first, then nodded and wrapped his hands around the warm ceramic. "You're right, of course. I *do* know better. I may not have any Healing Gift to burn up, but simple exhaustion could still cost me—and my patients."

Gaven hid his own frown. Coulson's herb-and-knife healing was more than enough for a tiny Guardpost and village like Trindon, but he didn't like that the younger man clearly thought of himself as less-than for not having a full Healer's Gift.

"So, what do we know of her?"

"Not much. She's not Valdemaran, that's for sure, but I'm not sure she's Hardornen either, for all that she's dressed like most of them."

"And not Karsite, not with that coloring." When he had brought the first batch of broth up to the room Coulson had taken over for a sickroom, Gaven had seen the young woman's dark complexion and nearly black hair for himself.

"Not Trader, neither." Coulson frowned again. "Whoever beat her and left her for dead took anything she might have carried or worn that might identify her."

"There's not been bandits like that around here since I've been at this Guardpost, although that's only six—no, seven years now." He'd not been one of Kerowyn's Skybolts, but he'd come to Valdemar with one of the mercenary companies, and had decided it was time to leave off being a sword-for-hire. Fortunately, his skills had quickly secured him a place with the Valdemaran Guard, and eventually he'd found his way to Trindon.

"No, and not since my gran'ther's day at least. Trindon's too small to draw them, that's why so few Guard are needed here. Which *also* begs the question of why someone attacked her, especially in weather like this."

Gaven decided not to point out the obvious: that the stranger had been followed from wherever she'd come from. He idly tapped a finger on the table between them. "So we're waiting for her to wake up and tell us for herself."

"Assuming she knows a language one of us can speak," Coulson added. The Healer tilted his head, considering. "You know, the cold nearly killed her, but it also saved her life. It slowed the bleeding from the wounds so she didn't bleed out, and it kept the swelling down, especially from that head injury. If there's been too much swelling in her brain, her wits could be affected. But with the cold, it's likely her mind should still be intact. Jer did a good job field-splinting her broken arm and leg, too." He sighed, then drained the last of the cooling broth from his mug. "So we wait. If she's unconscious more than a day, then we worry."

"Well, she's awake, and able to drink the broth herself, but we're not sure about her wits yet."

Coulson slid into the same place he'd taken the previous evening, across the bench-table from Gaven, then picked up a spoon and reached for the dish of stew Flick brought over. He gulped down several mouthfuls, then paused mid-chew, giving his full attention to the food. He swallowed, then smiled. "Venison?"

Gaven all but beamed. "Jer got a deer, too, on his patrol yesterday. But he stowed the carcass after he discovered the stranger—he couldn't carry them both—and didn't have time to go back out for it before nightfall. We dressed and butchered it today; it was a good size, and will make for a few good meals if I'm careful with it."

"It's a treat, however long it lasts." Silence fell while Coulson savored the rest, then he pushed the bowl away with a sigh. "If only I had been Gifted, as well as interested in healing. Then I'd be able to actually *do* something for her—"

"Enough of that kind of talk! Who bandaged her wounds, kept infection away, kept her alive so that she'd have a hope of remembering? And Mindhealing is rarer even than Healing Gift." Gaven's voice was firm. "There's many a time when my company would have paid good coin for a Healer of your talent and skill. Not to mention caring. Trindon is fortunate to have you, and that young woman is lucky to have been found and brought here."

Coulson blinked, taken aback by Gaven's gruff words. "I hadn't thought . . . thank you, Gaven. Put that way . . ." He trailed off, and silence returned, broken only the crackling fire.

At last, Gaven sighed. "It has been a long day, and you need to get back to your own house. Perhaps another night's sleep will restore her mind yet further."

"Still no memories for the stranger?" Guard Captain Elina frowned, drumming her fingers on her thigh in unusual restlessness.

Coulson shook his head. As had become his custom, he had returned to Gaven's kitchen for the warmth and a hot drink after checking on the young woman's wounds, and the captain had sought him here. "She's only spoken in the Trade Tongue, but I'm sure it's not her native speech; she doesn't *look* like a Trader, and they're such a close-knit people and keep so much to their clans that their features are very regular. She doesn't respond to Valdemaran, Hardornen—surprising, considering that's where she was coming from—or even the little bit of Karsite Jer knows. She has yet to have any recollection of how she came to be injured, or by whom, or why she was in the Pass in the first place."

Elina sighed, now pressing her fingertips against her brow as though to smooth out the marks of her worried frown. "That's what concerns me most; if she was coming from Hardorn to Valdemar, in this weather at this time of year, it must have been important. And using the Pass here, which isn't the easiest way through the Kleimar. And since she's presumably *not* Hardornen, but dressed like one, she was probably engaged in some sort of spying. Which explains why she was followed and beaten, to prevent her from getting here. Which leads back to the fact that we need to figure out what she knows, so we can get a message to Haven. This can't wait for the next Herald to come through on Circuit—they normally wouldn't be out here for another three or four weeks, longer if they've been held up by the weather same as the supply wagons. And there's no guarantee they would be able to learn any more than we have. I don't know that Truth Spell can reveal what a person isn't able to consciously recall."

"And with that shattered leg, she's in no condition to travel herself, to get her to a Mindhealer. I don't even think there's one still in residence at the nearest House of Healing. She'd have to be taken most of the way to Haven just to find someone who could help her."

Gaven held his breath, waiting for yet another self-deprecating remark about Coulson's lack of Gift, but it seemed his reminder of the Healer's other abilities had taken root, and the Healer was no longer blaming himself for not being able to see into the young woman's mind.

"So there's nothing for it but to wait, and hope?" Elina asked.

Healer Coulson lifted one shoulder in a half-shrug. "I had thought to see if she recognized any forms of writing, to see if that would unlock her memory, since spoken words have not. But all of my herbals are only in Valdemaran."

"I'll see if there's anything in the Guard records that might be useful," the captain replied. "At least it's something to try."

"I don't suppose you have a Karsite cookery book or some such thing from your mercenary days?" Coulson grinned at Gaven, who chuckled.

"I spent my spare coin on the spices themselves wherever I traveled, not the instructions on how to use them!"

"And the whole of the Trindon Guard is grateful for it," Captain Elina added. "Not every Guardpost can boast a staff cook who can make the same three ingredients taste different every night!"

"One does what one can, with what one has," Gaven replied. "And right now, we've got lots of dried beans and potatoes and turnips."

"Two more meals we'll get out of that deer, if I stretch it with dried beans and more root veg from the cellars."

Flick rolled her eyes. "Beans and 'taters and 'nips again. No wonder folks are taking naps lately, with all that starch!"

Gaven shrugged. "It's what we've got most of, and it's hearty. And the ice and storms have kept things so quiet, the off-duty guards can nap if they wish." He turned and poked at the dough set aside for rising in a large wooden bowl. "Even the yeast has gone to sleep, it seems. It's plenty warm here, but it's not doubling properly."

Out of the corner of his eye, he saw Flick start, then blanch. "Flick?"

His apprentice twisted her apron between her hands. "I think I . . . forgot to divide in the starter."

Gaven walked over to the starter crock and lifted the loose lid. The sour note of fermentation hit his nostrils, and he eyed the volume of the softly bubbled dough in the container. "Aye, this looks too full to have been used today."

Flick flushed a deep red. "I'm sorry, Gaven, I've ruined the bread now. It's too late to add it and have it rise in time to bake and set for dinner."

Gaven shook his head. "Nah, it'll be fine. We still have some sour milk, and we'll just add a pinch or three of pearl-ash to give it a little lift, then cook thin pieces in a skillet instead of baking it. It's a good thing I'm putting stronger spices in the stew tonight, though—the pearl-ash gives a bitter flavor when it's used without other seasoning to balance it."

"That foreigner sure is a strange 'un, though," Lennie said, placing the empty dishes into the soaking-pot.

Gaven raised his eyebrows in question.

"She took that thin bread you made tonight an' used it to pick up th' meat pieces in th' stew, 'stead of using th' spoon. They must not even have spoons where she comes from!" The serving lad shook his head in disbelief.

"Bah," Gaven replied, "that's not so strange. I've been to places where that's just—" He broke off his thought. *Where* had he seen that? If the stranger ate like that, without thinking about it, her *body* remembered what her mind could not. If he was able to cook something from "home," would it open up other memories as well?

"Not Karse," he muttered, "except maybe in the far south . . ." Fingers drumming on the broad table, he raked through his own memories for when and where he had seen people using flatbread as an eating utensil. Rich, fragrant foods, strong spices, stews with root vegetables and dried beans that soaked and simmered for hours all sounded right . . . but *which* spices? And did he have any of them remaining in his meager store?

"I wonder if we should try music? See if that might be something she'd know?"

Captain Elina looked across the broad table at Healer Coulson, her brow arched.

"The stranger hasn't responded to the languages we've spoken, and we only have written Valdemaran and written Hardornen, neither of which she recognized. But maybe she knows how to sing or play? I wonder if that would help, if we brought her an instrument or played for her."

"Rimmick has a recorder pipe he plays in the common room after dinner some nights, and I think Delzie has a lute. Don't think there's anyone with a harp, though." Elina exhaled sharply. "It's worth a try, at least. It'll be weeks if not months before she's healed enough to move, and the weather is still too questionable to expect the Circuit Herald for at least a month. We *need* to know why she was trying to get to Valdemar."

Gaven opened his mouth, then closed it again, suddenly reluctant to share his idea of using food for the same purpose. What if he was wrong? "It is something to try, as you say. After all, do not all mothers sing their children to sleep? A lullaby might be just the thing to open her mind."

Standing in front of the locking cabinet where he kept his most treasured spices, Gaven passed a shallow bowl below his nostrils, inhaling lightly. The smell of the crushed herbs and spices conjured a memory of visiting a market in the south of Rethwellan, far back in his mercenary days. Jkathan traders were there, and they had brought their own food sellers. He remembered going from tent-stall to tent-stall, tasting everything he could afford.

Sniffing his own concoction once more, he nodded. It wasn't perfect, but it had that combination of sweet baking spices with savory herbs and a little heat he remembered. When the last, toughest cuts of the meat were cooked down with the beans and vegetables, with maybe a splash of the vinegary wine for contrast, served with the thin, foldable flatbread like the one he remembered wrapping around chunks of meat to eat with his hands in the market . . . well, it might just be close enough that the stranger—if she *was* Jkathan—would recognize it.

The slump of Coulson's shoulders told Gaven all he needed to know about how the musical test had gone. "Nothing?" he asked anyway.

The Healer dropped onto the bench and leaned his head in his hands. "I had such high hopes. After all, as you said, mothers in all households sing their littles to sleep. But, well, she winced as soon as Rimmick started to play, and even Delzie's most soothing strumming had no discernible effect."

"Her ear must be attuned to another type of music, then. Although all mothers seem to sing, they use different melodies."

"Indeed. I asked if she wanted to try her hand with the lute, but she said she did not think her hands would know what to do, even if she had the use of both of them. It must not be an instrument she grew up with, then."

Gaven looked over at the stew pot, where the rich and pungent herbs simmered with the last of the venison. "Perhaps there's something we've not tried yet."

Gaven was so anxious to see the results of his experiment, he himself brought the tray up to the room where the stranger was. Healer Coulson was still there, chatting idly in the Trade Tongue with the young woman. He raised his eyebrows to see Gaven instead of Lennie or Flick, but stepped aside to make room for the head cook at the woman's bedside.

Gaven set the tray table across her legs, then took the warming cover away, allowing the steam—and the scent—to rise up to her. The seasonings had imparted a rich, red color to the final dish, lightened with just a hint of soured cream. It looked like nothing he had made before, and the stranger stared at it in wonder.

Her face tightened in shock, and her lips moved, silently forming words in no language he could lipread. She turned and focused on him, her expression suddenly haunted.

"Bring the captain here at once," Gaven murmured to one of the Guard who was in the hallway. "She's starting to remember."

"How . . . ? Why . . . ?" Her words were halting, as though the sudden return of one tongue was crowding out the one she'd been using, and she looked back down at the dish before her. "It's like Jkathan *roghan ghosht* and *nān*, but not . . ."

"Eat," Gaven said softly, a slight smile of reassurance lifting the corners of his lips, "and remember."

With trembling hands, she tore off a piece of the thin bread and folded it around one of the chunks of venison, bringing the morsel to her mouth and closing her eyes to savor the flavors as she chewed and swallowed.

Her eyes flew open, and she looked around the room. "My . . . boots. Did they leave me my boots?"

Healer Coulson nodded, bending to retrieve the footgear from below the bed.

The stranger grabbed the right boot with her good hand, scraping at the tar sealing the inner edge of the heel with her thumb until she could work her nail in and pick out a cleverly concealed container.

Captain Elina strode down the hall just as the stranger opened the flat box and removed a folded and sealed piece of paper, still dry from its hiding place.

"This must get to Haven," the stranger said, her words halting as she struggled to integrate the newly restored memory and language into her wearied mind. "Ancar will move sooner than your Queen thinks."

Elina reached out and took the folded paper, turning it over in her hands while she thought. "Jer's our best rider, if the roads are clear enough."

"The weather-witch said there wouldn't be another storm for a few days at least," Coulson offered. "If he goes with a pair of horses to take turns riding and leading, he can get to the Old Quarry Road before then, even if he has to break through drifts on the way—"

"—And there will be Heralds stationed near the Cebu Pass," Elina finished. "He doesn't have to take it to Haven; getting it to a Herald is enough." She gestured to the guardsman in the hall.

While they were talking, the young woman had continued to devour the stew, using the last of the flat bread to mop up the final drops of the sauce. She looked up at Gaven, who smiled back.

"Thank you—" She arched a brow.

"I am Gaven," he replied, "and I once traveled in lands far from Valdemar, and tasted the foods of some Jkathan traders."

The stranger nodded. "I am . . . Akshara," she said, relief suffusing her expression as she at last recalled her own name.

"We are glad to have been of service, Akshara," he returned, "and more than glad that your memory is no longer locked away from you."

Look to Your Houses
Fiona Patton

The capital city of Haven was immortal. Its limbs, the cobbled streets through which the bustling commerce of everyday life flowed, remained forever young, its edifices, great and small, which nourished industry by day and enfolded sleep by night, remained forever venerable.

Sergeant Hektor Dann had heard a fledgling Bard sing these words his first night as constable in the Iron Street Watch, and they had stuck with him, growing in their meaning as he had grown. Now, standing in the watch-house doorway, they came back to him as he took in the ebb and flow of watchmen, young and old, changing shifts from night to day: the young sweepers and runners, weaving through the press with the self-important confidence of childhood, the awkward gait of newly minted lance constables, and the easy stride of veterans. *The watch house is like Haven,* he thought, *always changing, yet always just the same.*

Today was one of those days. Night Sergeant Jons, a constant in Hektor's ever-changing yet never-changing world, had retired after a broken foot had made even desk duty a difficulty. Corporal Hydd Thacker, next in line and next in age, had flatly refused the position, declaring he was too old to flip-flop his sleeping like that. Each senior corporal in turn had said no despite the pay increase, causing Hektor to wonder out loud if they were going to have to promote the char lady.

Walking past with her army of littles carrying buckets, she'd just laughed.

"Not that thankless job, deary," she'd said. "I'd sooner turn chimney sweep."

Finally, Hektor's old partner, Kyle Wright, had been promoted in his place. Kyle had settled in quickly, taking on some of the night sergeant's more *traditional* duties with enthusiasm, including watch-house bookie.

"All-cap'ns meetin' at the White Lily last night," he said with a conspiratorial wink as he handed over the duty roster once Hektor had found his way through the throng.

Beside him, Hektor's older brother, Corporal Aiden Dann, nodded. "What have we got?"

Kyle rustled the papers in front of him with an air of mock importance, even though there was nothing on them that related to their conversation. "Let's see. Crime's up everywhere since their days of walkin' a beat: two to one?"

"Too easy."

"Crime's down, and everythin's beer and skittles?"

Kyle couldn't help but snicker as both Danns gave him a disgusted look. "Yeah, that's a thousand to one. How about, crime's seeping into the richer jurisdictions from the poor, with a thinly veiled accusation that we can't keep our riffraff on our own side of the fence? Two to one, snide remarks; four to one, strong words; six to one, shoutin'; an' a hundred to one, actual fist fightin'."

"I'll have a pennybit on that last one," Aiden said. "I heard Cap'n Bridger an' Cap'n Whelks nearly threw down over the dessert last year."

"Hek?"

Hektor handed the duty roster to a passing runner, pointing him in the direction of the day sergeant's office. "Snide remarks. The cap'ns wouldn't risk gettin' barred from the White Lily. The wine's too good. What else you got?"

"How 'bout Banquet Seniority? That musta been a fun conversation. Who gets to sit closest to the monarch at the civic leader's dinner next month. Two to one, Cap'n Wellworth'll point out that he an' Cap'n Reedbury are nobs, so it oughta be them 'cause they wouldn't want the rest of 'em to feel *uncomfortable*. Three to one, Cap'n Ashwood'll say his patch is right up next to the Palace so it oughta be by proximatey, an' by that he'll mean by richest, an' four to one, if he's had too much to drink, Cap'n Whelks'll say Water Street is the biggest an' dare anyone to make a comment, an' our cap'n'll have to soothe his feathers."

"Almost like he had a spy in the room," Aiden noted.

"Almost like a nephew waitin' tables," Hektor agreed. "Besides, it'll be up to the Palace whatever-he-is, arranger, to do the seatin' at the dinner, not them."

"The Earl Marshall," Kyle supplied.

Both men blinked at him.

"What?" he demanded. "I know stuff."

Hektor shrugged. "Fair enough. Anyway, Cap'n Campion's the fella's cousin. No bets."

"Fine," Kyle sniffed. "Budget, then."

Aiden groaned. "Is it time for budget?"

Eyeing the piles of reports on his desk through his open door, Hektor sighed. "It's always time for budget. What have you got?"

"There's the usual: overtime, outfittin', outsourced expenditures like maintenance and canteen."

"Canteen?"

"The overall decrease in the quality of the tea and biscuits," Aiden offered.

Kyle gave him a dark look. "The quality of my Auntie Nessa's tea and biscuits is without peer, Corporal," he growled. "I meant supplies and wages."

"They come out of each watch house's own pocket," Hektor said. "They wouldn't be discussin' that at an all-cap'n's meetin'."

"I'll take overtime, though," Aiden said. "There's nothin' they love more than tryin' to figure out how to get more work out of us for less money."

"Left it as is for now or slashed to the bone?"

"Depends on what else they talked about, don't it? But I'll take slashed to the bone anyway, on account of the grim set of your jaw."

"I gotta learn to control that, but that brings us to the more imaginative cost-saving brainstormin' over brandy part of the event. Cap'ns love discussing that. Manpower Sharing was the main one last year. Think it was brought up again? Four to one?"

"It's been shelved," Hektor replied. "Turns out, the richer watch houses don't wanna come our way, an' they *really* don't want us comin' their way."

"They think we'll nick *their* tea and biscuits," Aiden added.

"More like their spoons an' mugs," Kyle corrected. "But if you don't fancy that one, how about my personal favourite, Civilian Cooperation Initiative? Pretty fancy words, that."

Hektor shook his head as Aiden laughed out loud. "That turned out to be more civilians complainin' than civilians helpin' us for free like they wanted."

"Could've told 'em that," Aiden pointed out.

"Some things have to be experienced to be truly understood."

All three men snickered.

"That leaves the only slightly different Community Outreach," Kyle continued. "Meanin' officers takin' tea in fancy houses in the rich nicks an' constables buyin' tea for outta-work drudges an' pot-boys in ours."

"That one," Aiden declared.

"Two to one."

"Figures."

"That about covers it then, an' there's the bell. Let us know what the cap'n says, Hek."

"Will do."

It was late afternoon before Hektor was to meet with Captain Torell, and by that time, most of the watchmen had put their bets in. He'd made a half-hearted attempt to clear up some of his paperwork, then made his way, under the vigilant eye of those gathered, to the captain's office.

The door was closed, but whether that was a good sign or a bad one was anyone's guess.

"By now, I'm sure you're all champing at the bit to know what was discussed at the White Lily last night," the captain said in a dry tone once Hektor had taken the indicated seat. "We'll go over the less pertinent items later. There have been some allegations of less than exemplary watch-house behavior recently, which need to be addressed first."

Hektor's eyes narrowed. "Allegations by who, sir?"

The captain frowned. "That is immaterial, Sergeant. Regardless of by whom, this must be taken seriously." He raised a hand as Hektor made to speak. "I understand that the people we oversee are often our friends and families, but we have a responsibility to remain steadfast and stainless in order to do our duty. Wrongdoing is wrongdoing, irrespective of the perpetrators or the severity. To this end, we, in each watch, must look to our own houses with clear and unbiased scrutiny of our conduct. I am not suggesting that our people are engaged in illegal activities," he added at Hektor's increasingly thunderous expression, "but we at Iron Street have become somewhat lapse in the required day-to-day minutiae, for example."

"Mi . . . ?"

"Details, Sergeant. Such as the timely completion of relevant reports which would help shed light on any challenges we might have faced regarding the general public and the proper, authorized distribution of watch-house stores.

"Now, I am equally to blame for this," the captain continued, "as I have not insisted on as strict an adherence to deadlines as I should have done. This will change. The reports from each shift are to be on your desk no later than noon the next day and on mine by the beginning of the next week. I also want a full inventory of all stores and their allotment by the end of this week. If there are any discrepancies to be found, even those that may seem harmless or insignificant, I expect reparations to be made and those discrepancies to cease. And any unauthorized use of watch property is also to cease. At once. Do you understand my meaning, Sergeant Dann?"

Hektor maintained a strictly neutral expression. "Yes, sir."

"Good. Now, I understand that every watch house is unique,"

the captain unbent, "with its unique challenges, such as the cost of replacement uniforms, bells, or lantern oil, but we must be exemplary. Everything must be accounted for."

"Yes, sir."

"Yes." The Captain set his expression with a look that suggested the difficult part of the conversation was still to come. "To facilitate this process, I will be filling two new positions."

"Illegal activities?" Aiden demanded an hour later when Hektor began to explain the meeting's particulars.

Hektor sighed. "Close the door if you're gonna shout, brother."

Aiden did as he was asked with barely controlled force. "What does he think we're doin', runnin' some kind of crime syndicate from the privy?"

"No, he thinks we're fudgin' the books so lance constables like Evan and Gazer can keep decent boots on their feet."

Aiden snorted, but said nothing.

"He wants a full inventory by next week. Of all stores, even the smallest. An' lists of every allocation. With signatures."

"Goin' back how far?"

"I . . ." Hektor slumped. "I've no idea. Let's just work our way from today an' see how far we get before we run outta time."

"Fair enough. So, what'd the cap'n mean by fillin' positions?" Aiden asked, suddenly changing the subject.

"You won't like it."

"Tell me anyway."

"We're gettin' a lieutenant."

Aiden's eyes narrowed.

"From outside. But the rest better be told to all," Hektor added quickly as Aiden opened his mouth, possibly to shout at him. "Get the corporals together at shift change in the storeroom. They'll all wanna hear it firsthand."

Hydd Thacker summed it up best a few hours later.

"This new lieutenant better not be anyone's nephew," he

growled to the general agreement of those gathered. "I'm too old to put up with that kinda nonsense: struttin' about like he's lord of the nick an' gettin' in everyone's way. I'll not put up with it."

"Me neither," his partner, Corporal Bren Sacklin, put in, his chin thrust out in belligerent agreement. "I'll quit afore I take any sass from some tripped-out youngling in his uncle's uniform. We've never needed no lieutenant afore this. Yer da, Ethan, did the day sergeant's job full out, an' his da, Tomar, did it afore him."

"There's only ever been one outsider at Iron Street," Hydd added, jerking his head in the obvious direction of the captain's office. "We don't need another."

"Well, he's comin'," Aiden said bluntly, ending the discussion with a chop of one hand. "So get used to it."

The gathered subsided, grumbling. Hektor might be sergeant, but Aiden had the legendary Dann temper, and when he said something was ended, it was ended.

"Hek's new clerk's comin' from outside too," Chief Runner Padriec Dann, the youngest of Hektor and Aiden's brothers, pointed out in an attempt to change the subject.

"That don't matter so much," Bren snapped, taking the bait. "He won't be in charge of nobody."

"But he better not be cuttin' into anyone's hours for his pay packet," Corporal West Lunbridge warned.

"That's right," Hydd agreed, warming to the new attack. "Jus' cause you can't do your job . . ." He stabbed an accusatory finger in Hektor's direction, "'an fill out yer paperwork on time ain't our problem."

Hektor gritted his teeth. As a contemporary of his father, Hydd had never quite come to grips with the younger man's authority and now, with his face turning a dangerous red, he looked to have forgotten it entirely.

"Half my job is chasin' you lot down to fill out yours," Hektor retorted, his own temper rising. "If you weren't late, I wouldn't be neither. But . . ." He gave the older man a dark smile. "My new clerk'll fix that. Outside don't mean outside

Iron Street, it just means outside the watch house. Call it . . .
community outreach if you like."

An ominous silence fell.

"Who?" Hydd demanded.

"Holly Poll."

A general groan rose up.

The meeting broke an hour later, with each corporal charged
with sorting out any *discrepancies* they might know about. As
Hektor headed up the stairs, Hydd fell into step beside him.

"Yes, Corporal?" Hektor asked in an attempt at a neutral
tone of voice.

"I just thought that, since you was havin' to make a list of
everythin', you might wanna look to the cell door keys, Sergeant."

Hektor stopped, one foot raised. "Why?"

"You know how Jaz Poll used to jus' let himself in rather
than go home after he'd had a snoot full?"

"Yeah?"

"Well, we never did get the key back. You might wanna have
a chat with yer new clerk about where he mighta left it. Oh, an'
there's the watch-house key as well, now that I come to think
about it."

"What watch-house key?"

Hydd gestured toward the main door. To the left was a large,
ornate, brass hook that had been empty of keys for as long as
Hektor could remember.

"But the watch house is never locked," he protested. "We
don't close."

"True enough," Hydd agreed. "The key always was more
symbolic than anything else. Like a lot of things around here.
But with the new lieutenant comin' in . . ."

"So, where is it?"

"Not sure."

Hektor's jaw tightened. "When did it go missin'?"

Hydd scratched thoughtfully at his beard, making a show of
considering the question carefully. "Durin' your granda's time,

I think," he said, waiting just long enough for Hektor's eyes to narrow in warning, but not long enough for his temper to snap. "You might wanna ask Cam Marble. He was night sergeant afore Jons. He lives in Mosswall Court these days. Better take a jug of somethin'," Hydd added, his eyes twinkling. "He does like to talk, an' he builds up a powerful thirst doin' it. Now here's my missus, come to collect me. Evening, Sergeant."

With a snicker, the older man slipped past.

Three other watchmen approached Hektor as he made his way through the main hall. The first had lost his notebook and was unsure of how many reports he hadn't written, the second was concerned about the number of cautions he'd given out rather than arrests, mostly to his cousins, and the third had lent his boots to his brother so he could go to Waymeet with a load of scrap iron and had—maybe—said he'd outgrown them to receive a new pair.

By the time Night Constables Jakon and Raik Dann, Hektor's middle brothers, fell on him when he finally made it out the door, casting a jaundiced eye on the empty hook, his mood was distinctly sour.

"Hey, Hek," they said in unison, each trying, without success, to look as if this were an innocent encounter.

"Hey yourselves," he growled. "What?"

"Oh, nuthin'. Just, um, we heard there was a new lieutenant comin' in," Raik said.

"Yeah. And?"

"Any idea when he's startin'?"

"Nope. Why?"

"Well, um, you don't figure he's gonna be spendin' much time on night shift, do you?" the younger man replied evasively. "I mean, he'll be tight with the cap'n mostly, right?"

"I expect so. Why?"

"Well, we heard you said the cap'n wanted a full report of inventory and the use of watch property, an' so we was wonderin' when the new lieutenant would be here an' when he might be readin' any reports that got made, that's all."

"Again, why, Constables?"

His brothers shared a nervous look.

"Well, so," Jakon began, "you remember how we told you that on the full moon a couple of months back Bennett an' Jensen Miller were horsin' around in the street outside the watch house, knockin' a ball back an' forth, an' Jensen gave it a mighty kick an' it caught Constable Rams right in the gut?"

"Yeah?"

"An' how they took off runnin', like, you know, you'd expect they would, 'cause even though it were an accident, Rams's got a right temper on him?"

"Yeah?"

"An' how he came on, limpin' and shoutin' right behind 'em?"

"I remember. He lost 'em." Hektor glanced from one to the other. "Didn't he?"

"Oh yeah, he did," Jakon said quickly. "'Course, they did have a bit of help with that."

"What kinda help?"

"Well, they come racin' around the corner, toward the back, see, an' we were on break, so Raik here sees 'em an' sings out, 'Millers, to me!' an' they dove behind the wall just in time."

"The four of us were crouched down tryin' not to laugh, as he went by, blowin' like a spent horse," Raik added with a snicker.

"Anyway, once the coast was clear, we coulda sent 'em on their way, but you know how he holds a grudge, an' he might of been just around the corner, so we kinda hid 'em," Jakon finished.

"Kinda hid 'em how?"

"We tucked 'em in the storeroom for a bit, just until he went off shift. He never goes down there if he can help it. He don't like the stairs," Raik explained.

The faint smile he'd been trying to suppress during the narrative lightened Hektor's expression slightly.

"Can't see much harm in that," he allowed.

"No, we didn't think so neither, but see, well, Kassie and Kira Allslip were already down there."

"Why?"

"The cells were full that night, an' so was the canteen on account of the student riots. Well, not really riots, more like end-of-lesson celebrations. Remember, it were all in the reports, how they met up with a bunch of apprentices and fightin' broke out, an' how all the masters an' parents had to come an' bail 'em all out, so when Kassie an' Kira came in with their baskets of biscuits, like they do every week, Sergeant Jons didn't want the whole lot gobbled up so he told 'em to set 'em down in the storeroom."

When Raik paused for breath, Jakon took up the rest of the story. "The four of 'em started talkin', an' Jensen had a mouth organ, so Bennett was showin' Kassie how to dance a reel when Nessa came down . . ."

"She was waitin' on goin' home until the streets quieted some . . ." Raik interjected.

"An' then her two, Opal an' Sam, came to walk her home," Jakon continued, "an' old Rink Parcel was with 'em. He'd come to chat with Sergeant Jons, only he was in the privy, so Rink went down to the storeroom with 'em, an' he joined in the dancin' with Nessa cause he'd been sweet on her years ago . . ."

"An' the whole thing kinda became sort of a social club," Raik finished. "They meet once a fortnight."

Half expecting to learn the story's end revolved around a wedding and a funeral, Hektor blinked slowly. "Once a fortnight," he repeated.

"Yep."

"In our storeroom."

"Yep."

"In the middle of the night."

"Not as such," Jakon corrected. "More like eightish. Some of 'em are old, you know, they don't like being out too late."

"We kinda figured it was like a community outreach program," Raik added.

"How?"

"Well, some of the watchmen come by on their breaks. Sergeant Jons was all right with it, so Sergeant Wright went along with it, too."

"An', well, that'll be why the tea an' biscuit numbers won't even close to workin' out."

"Those old folk can really tuck in when it's free."

"But we figured we could get a whip-round to buy new tea an' biscuits if we had enough time, so we were just wonderin' if we did. Have enough time, I mean."

Hektor sighed. "I've no idea if you've got enough time," he said truthfully. "So you better get that whip-round sorted out sharpish."

"Right. Will do."

"Thanks, Hek."

Noting a lance constable nervously waiting his turn to speak with him, Hektor shook his head. "Sure. You're welcome."

The next day was a continuous rendition of "No, I don't know who he is, no, I don't know when he'll get here, no, I don't know what his duties'll be, so stop askin' me."

The reasons for the questions had been as varied as the openings had been the same:

"I know my uncle's cart ain't supposed to park there, but Toni shouldn't've started shoutin' at him in the middle of the street . . ."

"The milk woulda gone bad by mornin' an' old Miss Winnie's hard up since her man died, an' it weren't all that much, but it was watch-house property an' all . . ."

"So I let 'im sleep it off in the cells, jus' like ol' Jaz used to do, but he did pack a lot more breakfast away than I thought he would . . ."

"We stay longer 'cause there's sometimes fights at closin' time, so that makes it watch-related, don't it, but the new lieutenant might not see it that way, on account of it's our auntie's pub . . ."

"The warehouse door was unlocked, see, an' one of us had to wait while the other found the owner, an' he was so grateful that he gave us breakfast an' that put us past our shift's end, an' we kinda forgot an' added that into our overtime . . ."

Finally, Hektor sent for his little brother. The youngest chief runner in watch-house history, Paddy Dann knew everything that happened in Iron Street and everyone it happened to. If anyone could learn who the new lieutenant was and when he was coming, it was him.

Eyes sparkling with the challenge, he grinned widely. "I am on it, Hek," he declared.

"Well, that's one thing checked off the list," Hektor breathed, as Paddy practically skipped out of his office. "Better be keys next."

He headed across the main hall, but Holly Poll's first official attack to the tune of "Don't you take that tone with me, Constable Grant Woodyard, or I'll have words with your mother at our next quiltin'. You march yerself back into that canteen an' finish that report. I know full well you can read an' write," spun him around toward the back door.

He bought a jug of ale at the Rose and Key, then made for Poultry Row. At the far end, a narrow set of stone steps known locally as Old Stair Hill led toward the river. Halfway down, a passageway had been created when one of the buildings had been destroyed by fire. This opened into a courtyard surrounded on three sides by two-story tenements and closed off from Old Stair Hill by a stout iron gate. Beside the gate, an old man sat, smoking a pipe and carving a wooden puppet out of what looked like a watchman's truncheon. He nodded as Hektor approached.

"Lookin' for Cam Marble," Hektor said.

The old man took a long draw at his pipe. "An' you is?"

"Hektor Dann. Ethan's Dann's son."

"You got passage?"

Hektor held up the jug, and the old man's face split into a wide grin. "Well then, you best come in." He stood. "My Bessie don't like me smokin' in the courtyard," he confided as he pushed open the gate. "Say's it's bad for her chucks. But she's off visitin' her cousin in Hoop Lane, so I reckon we're safe."

He led the way into a small, hard-packed yard where a half dozen birds sat roosting on a fence attached to a small, neatly built chicken house. The man took a seat on a wooden bench and invited Hektor to do the same.

"You Cam?" Hektor asked, passing over the jug.

The man took a long pull before giving a loud guffaw. "I look that old to you, boy? Never mind," he added at Hektor's non-plussed expression. "When yer young, everyone else looks old. I'm his son, Albie. Cam passed a month back."

"Sorry."

"S'all right. He was in a lot of pain by the end. What did you wanna see him for?"

Hektor explained about the key, and Albie chuckled.

"I remember that night," he said. "Buncha young girls came into the watch house with a long tale about needin' a key to learn who their future husbands were gonna be. 'Parently, if they threw it over a shoulder on a full moon, it would point 'em the right direction or some such nonsense. Course, they were awfully pretty an' awfully persuasive, so Corporal Vic Thacker gave 'em the watch-house key, on account of how we never use it anyway. He an' a couple of the other lads went off with 'em, but I stayed behind, as I already had an understandin' with Bessie." He took another pull at the jug.

"Do you know what happened to it after that?" Hektor asked.

"One of the girls, Annie her name was, kept it. She married Len Munbridge, one of the lads that had gone with 'em, and always said it was a good-luck charm. Her granddaughter, Joyce, has a yarn shop in Loom Street. She might know what happened to it."

He passed the jug back and, after a moment, Hektor took a pull of his own.

"Word is you made sergeant after yer own da passed," Albie noted. "How're you findin' it?"

Hektor mulled over several answers, then just shrugged. "It gets a bit hairy," he admitted. "I can't get nothin' started before I get pulled away a dozen times over."

Albie chuckled. "That's what it means to be sergeant," he

said, not unsympathetically. "Settin' shifts and tellin' people what to do are part of it, sure, but smoothin' the way between the men and the officers an' the way between the watch and the folk at large is the main thing. Yer da did it pretty well, yer granda did it better. If they're comin' to you every hour of the day, then yer doin' it right. They trust you. That's important."

Hektor took another drink. "Yeah," he agreed.

"You gonna cradle that jug all day?"

"Nope." Hektor passed it over and stood. "Thanks."

"Gate's always open."

The yarn shop was halfway up Loom Street between two weavers. Joyce was just about to close when Hektor arrived. He made his request as succinctly and politely as possible, but she still frowned at him in suspicion.

"That were a long time ago, an' yer jus' askin' for it now?" she demanded. "Gran passed five years ago, an' Mam a year after that. You think I keep everthing they had jus' layin' about?"

"No, but the way I hear it, it was a precious family heirloom."

"It was, too. Gran always said Vic Thacker gave it to her, an' the whole watch knew she had it. It ain't stealin' if you're given it, you know?"

Hektor decided on honesty. After all, gossip was often the best currency, and it was possible Loom Street hadn't yet heard about the changes at the watch house. Joyce would be the first.

"I know," he said. "An' ordinarily I wouldn't be askin' at all, but we're gettin' a new lieutenant, an' everything has to be shipshape an' in place. If he's sees it missin', there might be all kinds of trouble. It would still be yours," he added. "We'd jus' be borrowin' it."

She raised an eyebrow at him, then unbent slightly as she spotted two of her neighbours in the street beyond. "I'll see if I can find it," she said. "Wait here. Don't touch nothin'."

It was nearly shift change when Hektor finally got back to the watch house. He returned the key to its hook with a sigh of relief, then turned to find Nessa, laden with a huge tea tray, right behind him.

"Here, let me get that," he offered.

"Thank you, dear." She smiled at him. "I were just takin' it down to the storeroom. If you wanna carry it for me, we could have a little chat on the way."

"Sure."

"It's about the tally, you see," she started as they navigated their way past a number of watchmen who just happened to be passing.

"Get yer fingers off that biscuit, Lance Constable," Hektor growled. "It's all right, Nessa," he said. "Jakon an' Raik are havin' a whip-round. That'll sort it out."

"Thank you, love. That's a load off my mind."

"So, why is this goin' to the storeroom instead of the canteen?" he asked, eyeing the cellar stairway with some trepidation.

"Oh, it's for the poll arrangement, of course."

"The what?"

"It was Holly's idea, s'why we call it that. There was a bit too much work for one clerk, so she pulled in a few favors. It's goin' to be a regular thing, she says, once a week at least."

The noise swept over him before they reached the bottom of the stairs, and Hektor gaped at the scene spread out before him.

The back shutters and cellar doors had been thrown open to allow a rich shaft of golden light from the evening sun to mingle with the dozen candles and lanterns around the room. Tables and chairs had been scattered about, and at each one, a watchman and at least two other people, sometimes old, sometimes young, bent over a sheaf of papers. Nessa's son and daughter weaved in and out, handing over mugs of tea and plates of biscuits, occasionally glancing down and offering bits of advice or encouragement.

"What—What's all this?" Hektor sputtered.

"I told you." Nessa accepted the tray back, giving it to her son as they moved more fully into the room. "Holly and Hydd got into it, you see," she began. "She said her grandchildren could write better than some of the drivel your men were handin' in, and he said, then why don't you bring 'em in to do it, only he said it somewhat less politely than that, an' she said maybe she would . . ."

They passed a table where Constable Zach Stile was laboring over a report while two of his nieces offered advice on spelling.

"An' so she did," Nessa finished. "Hello, Holly, love, is that for the sergeant?"

Hektor turned to see Holly Poll holding out an official piece of paper like it was a dagger. "Sign this."

"Um, what is it?"

"It authorizes this—biscuits an' all." She waved her hand at the room. "The Civilian Cooperation Initiative."

"Seriously?"

"Do I look like I'm jokin', Sergeant Hektor Dann?"

"No, ma'am."

"Good boy. Those there are the finished reports." She pointed at a large pile of papers on a table beside them. "You can work on 'em right here. You need help, jus' sing out. Oh, an' there's this." She passed over a brass key. "T'were in Jaz's coat pocket," she explained, her voice softening. "Hangin' up behind the door. I hadn't even looked at it since he died."

"Thanks."

She nodded, then, stabbing a finger at the pile of finished reports, waited until he took a seat, then moved deftly to block the passage up the stairs of two constables who were trying to sidle past her.

Hektor picked up a pen, his expression still somewhat stunned.

"Hey, Hek—I mean, Sarge."

He looked up to see Paddy standing in front of the table, grinning from ear to ear. "That mean you've got an answer for me?"

"Yup."

"That was fast."

Paddy tried to look indignant, but soon gave it up. "It's Uncle Daz, Hek," he said, leaning over the table so that only his older brother could hear his words. "You remember at the Rose Fair how he said he got promoted to lieutenant at the Cheese Court nick, an' how Alana said she'd be happy to move back, an' how he said he would too? Well, he is."

Hektor suddenly felt a huge weight lift from his shoulders.

"Uncle Daz?" he repeated.

"Yup. It won't be for at least a fortnight, but he's comin'. We can take orders from Uncle Daz, right, Hek?"

"We can."

And they could. Daz Browne knew how a watch house worked: how overtime was justified and how leftover milk was given away, how notebooks got lost and keys got found, how all of that was the province of the sergeant, not the lieutenant, but how to step in when the lieutenant was needed. How to be trusted. How to be part of the never-changing, always-changing ebb and flow of their world.

"Hek? Sarge?"

Hektor forced his attention back to Paddy. "What?"

"You wanna tell everyone?"

Hektor's gaze swept across the room, noting the unusually peaceful and diligent levels of activity going on. A pair of littles set a bundle of finished reports on the table, blushed at his thanks, then darted away to fetch more. By the door, Bennett and Jensen Miller chatted with Kassie and Kira Allslip not ten feet away from where Constable Rams was deep in conversation with Corporal Sacklin over what looked suspiciously like a proper duty roster.

Picking up a mug of tea that had suddenly appeared at his elbow, he shook his head. "Nope," he answered.

What You Know How to See
Dayle A. Dermatis

Thestry stoked the fire in the kitchen stove, grateful for the heat on this icy late-winter morning. The old biddies complained about their joints in the cold, and she was starting to feel that in her hands—although she wasn't quite yet ready to think of herself as a biddy. She was just grateful for the warmth all over the three-story house, in fact, generated by some internal system developed by Master Artificer Qualla.

She didn't need to understand how it worked. All she had to understand was how Qualla worked.

She'd been employed by the engineer for going on twenty years, responsible for the household. She oversaw the cook who made suppers, the handyman, the woman who came in every few weeks to do the deeper cleaning Thestry had no time for. She managed Qualla's calendar, saw that her clothes were laundered, and handled a myriad of other small tasks as needed.

She also wrangled Qualla's apprentices, who were in and out during the day, their fingers constantly stained with ink or charcoal, as they took instruction and worked on projects under Qualla's tutelage.

Qualla was good at what she did. Thestry was good at what she did. There was little overlap. The thought made her smile.

Thestry wrapped up the still-warm half loaf of granary bread that remained from her and Qualla's breakfast, then tucked the cloth-swaddled package into its box to keep it fresh. She covered the sticky-sweet honey and put the pot in its place on the shelf, and was putting the knives and her own plate and cup in the sink when a bell jingled.

Qualla had set up that system, too, allowing her to call for Thestry no matter what room she was in. Thestry glanced at the board to see which bell was chiming. Right now, Qualla was in her workshop on the third floor.

Thestry frowned. Qualla was a normally late riser, staying far into the night at the Compass Rose, a tavern that served as a gathering place for artificers and engineers. The apprentices ate, laughed, and worked on their inventions, often debating ideas and suggestions, while in the back room, Qualla and her fellow Master Engineers held court.

It hadn't been that long ago that Thestry had sent up Qualla's breakfast of honey-drenched bread and a pot of tea, plus a carafe of milk and a small bowl of sugar cubes, using the chute with a box and system of pulleys so Thestry didn't have to balance a tray on the stairs. She'd expected Qualla to sit in bed reading while she ate and gradually woke up.

Although . . . Thestry pressed her lips together. Qualla hadn't been reading as much of late.

With a final wipe of her hands on a dish towel, Thestry headed up the two flights of stairs.

The house was laid out simply. There was a front room, with bookcases stuffed with tomes and more books piled on the floor and chairs. Behind that, a dining room, and then the kitchen, which opened out to a back area for a small herb and vegetable garden. On the second floor, four bedchambers, one each for Qualla and Thestry, and the other two for apprentices who needed a place to stay for a time.

Qualla's workshop covered the entirety of the third floor. It wasn't quite as messy as the front room—Qualla needed organization—but it still felt a little overwhelming to Thestry even now. She wasn't allowed to clean in here save for dusting and sweeping, provided she didn't move anything.

There were more bookcases, along with cabinets with wide shallow drawers for storing large drawings and schematics, and tilted tops for examining the paperwork. Other large paperwork—the apprentices' projects—were rolled and tucked in tall baskets. Multiple wooden tables bore the memories of experiments and stains of ink. Wooden models of various inventions sat on shelves between the books and hung from the high ceiling.

Windows on all four walls provided light during the day; even now, the bright morning sun made lamps unnecessary except for the most detailed of work.

The air smelled of ink and dust and paper.

Qualla stood before one of the shallow-drawered cabinets, her white hair in its customary two thick braids down her shoulders. Her hands gripping the cabinet edges, she peered closely through her wire-rimmed spectacles at the paper before her. Then she shook her head, removed the spectacles, and pressed her thumb and forefingers against the bridge of her nose.

Even in her concern, Thestry smiled at the sight of her.

She and Qualla each had their quirks, to be sure, but their relationship was a friendly companionship more than anything else—despite rumors to the contrary. Neither had been interested in having a partner of either persuasion, and they were comfortable with each other. Thestry was proud of the work she did, because it meant Qualla was free to use her amazing knowledge and understanding to better, well, all of Valdemar, really.

She cleared her throat. "You called for me?"

Qualla quickly replaced her spectacles as she turned. "Ah, yes, Thestry. Thank you. I was hoping you could assist me with something."

"Of course."

She explained that she was looking for a particular schematic, that she must have misfiled it. That was unusual for her. Thestry wondered if one of the apprentices had made the mistake.

But Qualla wouldn't make excuses for them. And Thestry had heard the anxiety in her voice.

Qualla described the shape of the drawing and several pertinent details that made it unique, different from the others. She didn't bother to explain what the device was or how it worked, because Thestry wouldn't have understood anyway.

Thestry looked at the paper on the cabinet, and quickly saw it was similar to what Qualla had described, but not the same.

Methodically, drawer by drawer, she pulled out a stack of papers, brought them to a table, and went through them one by one. Several times she had to ask Qualla for an additional description or detail. But in the end, the missing schematic wasn't to be found there.

Thestry suggested she check the rolled paperwork in case the drawing Qualla was looking for had gotten mixed in with the apprentices' work, and at Qualla's agreement, examined those as well.

Still, nothing.

"Perhaps you left it at the Compass Rose?" Thestry suggested.

Qualla sank onto a stool, frowning, her brow furrowing. "I don't recall taking it there, but it's a possibility."

"When the apprentices get back from Collegium, why don't you send one of them to the Rose to check?"

Qualla hesitated, clearly making a decision before speaking.

"There's a mistake in it," she said finally, not looking at Thestry. "One even a new, wet-behind-the-ears apprentice wouldn't make. I don't want any apprentice noticing that." Under her breath, she muttered something about needing new spectacles.

Thestry leaned against the table. It was time for the truth. "It's more than just your spectacles, isn't it?"

Qualla's head whipped around to stare at Thestry. She looked stricken. "How did you know?" she asked. "For how long?"

"I know you, and I keep an eye on things," Thestry said, adding a quick shrug to make her words less weighty. "You've been reading less. You have an apprentice escort you to and from the Rose—which, mind you, isn't a bad idea with the roads so icy. But still. Other small things that I've noticed."

She'd noticed Qualla would miss parts of her plate when she ate, although she'd gotten good at scraping food around until, Thestry assumed, she could see it. She turned her head slightly to one side or the other when going up and down the stairs.

"Do you think anyone else has realized?" Qualla whispered, her eyes closed.

Thestry shook her head. "I don't think so." She was confident that the apprentices didn't, unless they were very, very good at keeping their counsel. She couldn't say about Qualla's peers at the Rose . . . although she imagined they would be honest and tell their fellow artificer their concerns.

"Have you been to see the Healers?" she asked.

"Of course I have," Qualla snapped. Then she put a hand on Thestry's. "I'm sorry. I know you're concerned. This is beyond the Healers' capabilities, although they've been able to slow the progress. It's a black spot in the center of my vision . . . I can see around it by looking sideways, but I know I've started to . . . miss things."

She looked past Thestry's shoulder—although Thestry realized it meant Qualla was looking at her.

"I'm not ready to retire," she said. "I know I have more to contribute. I must keep this a secret as long as possible."

Her mind was still as sharp as ever, Thestry knew. To lose her eyesight would mean losing her position. She could still instruct, but without being able to draw or examine work, she could no longer have apprentices.

She took both of Qualla's hands in hers and squeezed. "One thing at a time," she said. "Let's find your missing schematic, and we'll worry about the rest later."

Thestry laced up her fur-lined boots and tucked a scarf around her neck before shrugging into her warmest coat.

The clear, icy air snatched her breath away. The center of the cobbled streets was clear of ice and snow, thanks to the dirt that has been scattered to help defrost the stones, and to the tromping of many feet. The sides of the road still bore clumps of dirty snow, where the sun and shovels hadn't reached.

The Compass Rose wasn't open for the midday meal yet, but it would be soon. The door was unlocked, and Thestry pushed it open, calling out to the proprietors as she did.

Cosa, tall and lean, was unstacking the chairs that had been propped on the tables so the floor could be mopped. Thestry's mouth watered at the scents of meat pastries, a dish easy to eat with one hand while sketching designs with the other. She stripped off her gloves and hat in the warmth as bald-headed Anders, Cosa's spouse, appeared from the kitchen, wiping his hands on his food-spattered, formerly white apron.

"We're not yet open, but you're welcome to have a drink while you wait," Cosa said.

The proprietors knew Thestry because of her relationship to Qualla, as well as their affection for Qualla's apprentice Kya, who had worked at the Rose under the name Burrow while hiding from her parents, who didn't want her to study at the Collegium.

"Thank you, no," Thestry said, and explained her mission.

"Of course," Anders said. "Take all the time you need."

That gave Thestry access to the back room, where the Master Artificers held court in the evenings. They gathered there to have their own conversations and debates, only emerging when there was an emergency or their presence was otherwise requested, or when they wanted to honor a particularly promising student with an apprenticeship, as Qualla had done for Kya.

The room smelled of fresh lavender; Cosa and Anders kept it as clean as they did the rest of the Rose. Sunlight streamed in from windows on the far wall, giving the room an extra warmth as well.

Thestry first examined the plans and drawings and notes that papered the walls. Then she moved to the sturdy wooden rectangular table with accompanying chairs in the center of the room where the Master Engineers gathered, and finally, she checked the side table as well.

Her hopes were dashed with each failure.

She left the back room with a frown, then paused. By the

door was a box of drawings and ideas abandoned by the nightly students. Every few days, Thestry knew, someone would pick them up and scrape them so the parchment could be used again.

Thestry scooped them up, perused each one.

Her hopes sank further.

There was nothing remotely like the design Qualla described there.

Back at their residence, the apprentices had returned from their morning classes at the Collegium.

Thestry had left a hearty barley stew, filled with leftovers from last night's beef and vegetables and redolent with herbs, simmering on the stove, and she served that along with today's remaining bread.

She took a tray up to Qualla's room rather than using the box and pulleys. She suspected, rightly, that they would need to talk.

She practically had to force food into Qualla's mouth, even as the stew cloyed on her own tongue.

Qualla paced, her bootheels a rhythmic tattoo on the wide oak planks, muffled when she trod over a woven area rug between her bed and her green-shot, marble-topped washstand.

"I know it existed, and I know I didn't have the paper reused or put it in the fire," she fretted.

Thestry knew a comforting gesture would be unwanted at the moment.

"If not the workroom, and not the Rose, then where?" she asked. "You don't keep your work here or anywhere else in the house. And it's highly unlikely it was stolen."

No one could have entered the house and made it to the third floor without *someone* hearing. As for the apprentices . . . Qualla—and Thestry—trusted them implicitly. They might not have been Herald or Mage trainees, but they were held to the same standards, and not a one had shown any action to prove differently.

Qualla thrust her hands into the hair at her temples, dislodging white strands. "No, there's . . ." She stopped in her tracks, lowered her hands. "Oh no."

Thestry went to her, pressed a morsel of bread into her hand in the hopes that she'd automatically bring it to her mouth.

"What is it?" she asked.

"There's one more place . . ." Qualla dropped into the washstand chair. "The Palace. It might have gone with a package of schematics for the Queen to review."

Thestry sank onto the bed. "Oh."

Qualla took a deep breath. "The package was sent yesterday, so it's likely the Queen hasn't yet seen it."

"She wouldn't notice the mistake, surely," Thestry said.

"No, it's a small error, but crucial," Qualla said, and Thestry could hear the concern in her voice. "If the device were made and used, someone would be injured. Plus . . ." Now she choked. "I can't let anyone know . . ."

Thestry rose and went to her, took her hands. "No one will know," she said. "Tell me how to get it back."

Truth be told, the idea of going to the Palace was daunting. Thestry had never been, and hoped she knew the correct etiquette. She didn't even know whom to approach or speak to.

Her nervousness wouldn't stop her from doing what needed to be done, of course. It was important—crucial—to Qualla, and so Thestry would do it.

"Take Kya with you," Qualla said, and Thestry's shoulders loosened. "She needs experience dealing with the Palace. She has my authority, of course. You both do."

"What shall I tell her?"

"Fetch her for me, will you?" Qualla asked.

Thestry brought Kya down from the workroom. The slender girl was wide-eyed at being allowed in Qualla's bedchamber, which was otherwise completely off limits to the apprentices.

"Kya, I need you to escort Thestry to the Palace to retrieve one of the schematics that were sent yesterday," Qualla said. "She knows which one, and I would prefer it if you didn't ask questions about it. Just help her find the batch of schematics and let her do the rest."

And so in short order Thestry was bundled up against the cold again and walking down the street, this time with Kya at her side. The young woman's white-blond hair stuck up in all directions around the fur-lined muffs she wore. She looked like a pale hedgehog . . . well, a pale hedgehog wearing muffs.

Thestry chuckled. They wouldn't be admitting *her* to the Bardic Academy anytime soon.

The afternoon sun slanted, blocked by buildings so more of the street was in shadow. Thankfully, it wasn't a long walk.

After a few minutes, Kya spoke. "It's her eyes, isn't it?"

Thestry stiffened, but didn't stop walking. "That's not for me to discuss."

"Oh, come on, then," Kya said. She planted her feet on the road and Thestry was forced to turn. "You know I can keep a secret, good as anyone. Better, even."

"I don't question that," Thestry said.

Kya's parents hadn't wanted her to come to Haven; they'd planned a life for her as their heir, docile and complacent. Her sharp, analytical mind was no use to them; indeed, it was something they had tried and failed to discourage.

So she'd gotten a job at the Compass Rose and paid attention to what the apprentices were working on, doing her best not to call attention to herself. Eventually, her work on the students' discarded drawings was noticed by the Master Artificers, and Qualla had taken her on.

Since then, Kya hadn't grown bigger, but to Thestry's eye, she took up more space now that she had been accepted and recognized for her talents. She no longer had to hunch and hide and try her best to go unnoticed.

Qualla was pleased with her progress so far.

"I must be good at keeping secrets as well," Thestry continued, "in order for Master Qualla to do what she does."

Kya looked down, chastened. "I'm sorry, you're right. It's just that I've noticed things . . ."

"Things you've kept to yourself."

Now her blue eyes met Thestry's, and she stood straight. "Of course."

"Then we can let this go now."

Thestry began walking again, and Kya paced her in silence until they got to the Collegium and the Palace.

From there it was something of a blur for Thestry as she let Kya navigate her way through successively more important people until they came up against someone who wasn't going to be helpful at all.

They had been ushered into a small antechamber that contained a few scattered chairs and tables, and a welcome fire crackling in the hearth. The chairs and tables were the finest Thestra had ever seen, with intricately carved wood and teal upholstry that felt like—and probably was—silk.

Her Majesty's Secretary looked as though he considered everyone beneath him, between his pressed lips and the ingrained parallel frown lines between his eyes. Of average height and slender, he sported a short, pointed, going-to-gray beard.

"You cannot simply *paw through* the Queen's papers willy-nilly," he said.

"Our apologies," Thestry said. She'd expected to be overwhelmed at the Palace, but she'd dealt with self-important officials before. That he worked for the Queen made no difference. "That is not our intention. Master Artificer Qualla accidentally included an unfinished schematic when she sent her most recent suggestions. All we wish is to retrieve that single schematic."

"And why isn't Master Artificer Qualla here herself?" the secretary demanded.

"She is a very busy woman, as I'm sure you can imagine," Thestry said, surprising herself by wanting to smack the officious man. "She sent us in her stead."

"And you are?"

They'd already introduced themselves to multiple people, but Thestry bit back her annoyance. "I am her assistant."

"And I'm one of her apprentices," Kya added.

"She sent us," Thestry continued, "because she trusts us to do what she asks and nothing more. The Queen trusts you, does she not?"

The secretary sputtered. "Of course."

"Then we are all here to do the bidding of those who trust us," Thestry said. She guessed she shouldn't call them equals; he was the sort of man who would take umbrage at that. "We can certainly go back and have the Master Artificer write directly to the Queen, but . . ."

But time was of the essence.

And such a letter would look poorly on the secretary.

He huffed air through his nose, clearly not willing to admit that she was right.

"Very well, then," he said finally. "Come with me."

They followed him to an office full of paperwork. He was clearly organized, because in short order, the stack of diagrams, not yet seen by the Queen, was in their hands.

The stack was thicker than Thestry expected, so it took her distressingly long to find the right one. When she did, she rolled it up and tucked it into the tube that Kya had thankfully thought to bring.

They quickly made their way back through the lengthening shadows and growing cold.

That evening, the apprentices went en masse to the Compass Rose, where they ate supper, but Qualla took her own supper in her room. She sent a message with her students to the Masters that she wouldn't be joining them this evening. A short time later, she came down to the front room.

Thestry had spent part of her own evening shelving books, so some of the furniture made for sitting on was actually clear.

She made tea for them both, and they sat in companionable silence for a while.

Finally, Thestry spoke. "Kya has guessed," she said. "It might not be a bad idea to let her know the truth."

Qualla breathed out a long, slow sigh.

"In time," she said finally. "I know I can trust her, but it's still hard to admit to anyone. You're my closest friend and companion, and it still took this. And I trust you with my very life." Her voice quavered at the end, and she paused to sip her tea. "But perhaps I'll ask Kya specifically to escort me to and from the Rose. These icy roads—I could slip, you know, and then I'd be no use walking up and down these stairs."

"For anything and everything else, you know you always have me," Thestry said, affection warming her heart. "I will be always your eyes, for whatever you need."

Good Intentions

Stephanie D. Shaver

Khaari had been promised a boring ride to Briar's Rock.

She should have known better.

"Ride west, then north. Should take you two days," Herald Challen had told her. Challen had an unusual Gift that let her "Hear" across vast distances, and at Khaari's request had found the people she'd been hoping to meet up with: Herald Wil and his company of friends. "They had an unshielded Bard with them, and from what I Heard in her thoughts, they are definitely headed that way. They're a week or so out."

"Excellent," Khaari had said.

"There *is* a Waystation between the town and here. I wouldn't be surprised if your Herald stops there, but you'll be better off at the Briar's Rock inn. Aesha calls it a 'last chance town,' because it's all you get before the Northern territories start." Challen gave her one last hug. "Take care, Scrollsworn."

"You too, Herald."

"And please remember, for all intents and purposes, I'm still dead."

Khaari clapped her on the shoulder. "You seem very alive to me."

"Yes, well. I'd like to stay hidden here with Aesha." Her eyes sparkled. "I'll make my return soon . . . but not just yet."

So Khaari left Sweetbark, the High Hills fully exploding in the green leaves and buds of spring, following Challen's directions. And at first, the journey was every bit as unremarkable as she'd been promised.

Until the morning she got to Briar's Rock, where the snow-line started.

And the screaming began.

Snow blanketed the road before her. If not for the rock cairns piled up at intervals, she wouldn't have been able to stay on course. Over a candlemark, spring vanished.

Then came the screams—a distant skirl of rage and grief that bounced off the landscape of tall pines and rocky outcroppings. Khaari couldn't place its origin: human or animal, possibly a twining of both. The pack mule she'd acquired in Sweetbark bleated in distress. Her battlemare, Toecrusher, did not spook, but did announce her annoyance with a snort.

"I agree," Khaari said. "This has veered off from *boring*."

By late afternoon the road bent, and suddenly a palisade, watchtower, and gate confronted her. Briar's Rock, she presumed.

She drew to a stop and waited.

The gate remained shut.

"Heyla!" she called.

"Heyla back to you," someone in the watchtower replied.

"Are you going to get the gate?" Khaari asked.

The figure called down, "We don't let in OutKingdom."

In the distance, that strange, unsettling scream. It didn't sound too far.

Khaari struggled to parse what was happening. There must be a misunderstanding here.

"I am no enemy," she said.

"Sorry," the person replied. "Go somewhere else."

The inanity of the request—*There* is *nowhere else!*—confounded her. Surely, no one could be *this* stupid.

She worked her mind furiously, and then said, "By chance is there a Herald Wil here?"

Logically, she knew he could not be. But she didn't have anything else. And the screaming kept getting closer. Any minute now, she'd be finding out what could make such a terrible racket.

"Herald *who*?"

"Herald Wil," she said, forcing a calm she didn't feel. "He's on business from the Queen. Did he get here before me or—"

Something heavy *clunked* in front of her. The gate swung open. A young man in Blues frantically ushered her through. "Get in!" he yelled.

Both her beasts surged eagerly forward—just as one final scream tore through the air. Looking back, Khaari saw a mass of fur and muscle bearing down on her—

The gate crashed shut, shuddering as that *something* slammed into it. Khaari heard vigorous swearing from the tower.

"Get the brace on!" a man shouted, sliding down a ladder and helping roll a log up onto a pair of brackets attached to the gate. The gate shuddered again, but held.

Both men turned toward her.

"Meeting a Herald? Here?" said the older one, also in Guard Blue.

"I am," she said, matter-of-factly.

The look he gave could have curdled fresh-skimmed cream. She got the sense he did *not* believe her—but he saved most of his ire for the younger man, grabbing him and hauling him a little ways off.

Khaari didn't hear the full heated exchange, only a few words, mostly from the younger. "—can't again—" and "—cursed—" in particular caught her notice.

Finally they came back. The elder guard pointed to a large, rambling house off the entrance. "Go stable your beasts there. You're stuck here now, with the rest."

"Stuck?"

"What the sergeant means," said the younger man, "is welcome to Briar's Rock, ma'am. I'm Darvin." He put a hand out.

"Khaari shena Pretera'sedrin." She shook hands awkwardly from the saddle.

"And I'm Prince Darenwatsisbals," the other sneered.

Khaari lifted a brow at him. "Strange," she said, "I thought you'd be taller."

He rolled his eyes. "Sergeant Beck." He glowered at his subordinate. "We'll talk more later, Private." Then he climbed back up the ladder.

Khaari looked over at Darvin. "What *was* that thing on the road?"

He stared at her blankly. "Oh, that." He smiled, very slightly. "That's the curse." He nodded. "Yeah. That beast's been killing us all winter."

Much later, after her animals had their stable and Khaari had something resembling food—a hard biscuit studded with desiccated fruit she had to dunk in tea to make edible—she ruminated on what had passed. She came to the uncomfortable realization that Sergeant Beck would have been content leaving her to die on the road.

She did not sleep easily. Her thoughts drifted back to the Plains and Kata'shin'a'in. It felt like a lifetime since she'd seen sunlight on the grasslands.

At dawn, she wandered off to check on Toecrusher before adjourning to the inn's common room for tea and more biscuit-shaped objects. Darvin happened to be in the inn's common room with a young woman. Aware that she towered over them, Khaari affected her most pleasant smile and lowered herself into a seat.

"You showed me my room last night," she said to the woman. "But I didn't catch your name. I'm Khaari."

"Jolie," she said. She bumped Darvin's shoulder affectionately. "His sister."

"Nice to meet you." Khaari touched her forehead in the guard's direction. "Thank you for saving my life."

"I just opened a gate." He looked away. "That's . . . what we're *supposed* to do."

Neither of them met her eyes. *Embarrassed?* she thought.

"You said this beast is killing you?" she said.

"Ever since the last big blizzard at Midwinter. Six of us, total." He looked intently at Khaari. "Were you being honest? About the Herald?"

She nodded solemnly.

"Okay." Darvin reached for his coat. "I need to get to the tower."

"Maybe I can join you?" Khaari asked.

He hesitated, then shrugged. "Sure."

The village's defenses consisted of a mix of stonework, earthworks, and hardened wood. A rickety ladder was the only access to the tower, with enough room at the top for four bowmen. Recurve bows and racks filled with arrows stood to one side. A stove in the middle cast feeble warmth.

As soon as they came up, a woman in Blue ("Morning, Salli," Darvin said.) came down, though she side-eyed Khaari before sliding down the ladder.

A pot of the ubiquitous tea sat on the little stove, and Darvin filled a mug, cradling it for warmth. With a weary sigh, he fished a biscuit from his pocket and dipped it in the tea.

Khaari asked, "Is there anything for breakfast other than rocks?"

Darvin chuckled. "The big meal is lunch. Beck has us all on rations. When this all started . . . we herded everyone into Briar's Rock. But we didn't think to grab food, just people. Can I . . . tell you something?"

"You've already told me many things."

He laughed. "I have. I barely know you."

"Among my people," Khaari said, "I have a calling as a good listener. They call us Scrollsworn. I suppose your equivalent is an Archivist? Maybe a Bard. A . . . Bard-chivist? But I do not go around playing a gittern to crowds." She patted the hilt of her sword. "As you noted, I come armed."

He nodded. "So the thing is—I think Beck assumed we were going to all be together . . . one, two days? But it's been months. And the question we all have is—how *hard* can it be to kill *one bear*?"

Khaari looked confused. "Did you say a *bear*?"

"A big one—well, you saw. Pelagirs-touched, probably. But it's a bear. And it just keeps—out-thinking us." He held up his biscuit. "We're down to nearly nothing. We've tried raiding homesteads to get supplies, sending messengers for help. It drives us back, or worse. We've started slaughtering our breeding stock and mounts. But if we kill it all, we'll have nothing come summer and thaw."

"And when you go hunting . . ."

"It hunts our hunters. They were the first to die . . . after my parents."

"I'm so sorry," Khaari said softly.

"Yeah." Darvin leaned out from the tower, his face to the wind. "No love lost between us, to be honest. My da . . . not a perfect man. I just wish Jolie hadn't had to go through that."

"A bear." Khaari peered down at the sweeping landscape of rocks and snow-tipped trees. She could see clawmarks in the snow—trampling over Toecrusher's hoofprints—from yesterday's encounter. "Where is it *coming* from?"

"Darvin!" a voice shouted below.

They peered down to see Beck—with a saddle on *her* mule.

"Sir?" Darvin called.

"Get down here!" He squinted. "What is *she* doing up there?"

"Enjoying the view," Khaari said, cheerfully. "Excuse me, why do you have my mule?"

Darvin slid down the ladder, a maneuver Khaari knew would be a disaster if she tried it. *No doubt comes from years of practice.*

When she arrived at the bottom, she found Darvin in the mule's saddle, his face ashen. The mule flicked its ears in annoyance, but otherwise took the load without complaint.

She caught the tail end of Beck and Darvin's conversation. "—ride fast," the sergeant said.

"Y-yes, sir," Darvin said.

"Sergeant," Khaari said. "That's *my* mule."

Beck ignored her. He and Salli lifted the log from the gate and opened it up, sending Darvin through.

"Good luck," Beck called after, before turning to smile at Khaari. "You should be *happy*." His lips peeled off his teeth, which were clenched around his words. "I've sent him to find your 'Herald'!"

She stared for an uncomprehending moment, before it occurred to her: he still didn't believe her.

I am graduating this man from stupid to actively malicious, she thought.

"I'm *sure* they'll meet up," he continued as Salli hauled the gate shut again. "And bring help! Then Darvin can be the big hero he's always wanted to be."

"But you took my *mule*," she said. "You didn't *ask*."

"Only because your damned horse nearly bit my face off," he spat.

She buried a laugh in her belly. *Good job, Toecrusher.*

"If you wanted to find Herald Wil so badly, you could have sent me," she said.

Beck put a hand to his chest, feigning distress. "No, no," he said. "I can't send a civilian to do a guard's duty."

"What if I *want* to leave?"

Beck laughed. "But you worked so hard to be under *my* protection."

You small man, she thought. *The last thing I want to be is associated with you!*

She felt that keen ache again, for the Plains, for her people. She took a deep breath of the northern cold, letting the icy air calm her down. She'd known a few like this in her life. People who *needed* to exercise their power over others to feel proud.

Part of her wondered, *What threads in your tapestry twisted you this way?*

But another, angrier part just wanted to headbutt him so hard she squashed his nose into a perfect, flat oval.

She recognized the bad intention for what it was. Satisfying in the short term. A poor outcome in the long run.

And they might try to eat Toecrusher.

Beck leaned forward so he spoke in Khaari's ear. "I'm the only thing keeping these people fed and cordial," he said. "Remember that, OutKingdom."

She touched a knuckle to her forehead. "I will, Sergeant."

* * *

Toecrusher greeted Khaari's gentle pats with an appreciative snort. She showed no sign of harm.

The same could not be said for Jolie.

Khaari found her in the kitchen, standing over a table covered with flour and half-rolled biscuits, her face in her hands, her shoulders heaving.

The Scrollsworn touched her lightly. The young woman looked up, her face snotty and wet, and then she collapsed into her embrace, sobbing.

"Beck's killed him," she said.

And kept repeating it. The hopelessness touched a thread inside Khaari. She had no consolation. She simply held on until the storm diminished, and then she passed a floury rag.

"I'm sorry," Jolie mumbled, dabbing her eyes.

"Tch. You're fine." Khaari smiled. "We will think good thoughts for your brother. Now, let's go wash up."

Khaari had not done much cooking *en masse* over the years—not since she'd sworn her oath to the Crone—but she wrapped her long braids into a high bun and settled in to help Jolie.

To conserve resources, most of the village took their meals at the inn, eating a stew of meat and cellared vegetables at lunch time and picking up their daily ration of biscuits, tea, and honey. Beck's guards—six strong—oversaw it all and kept people from taking too much.

No one seemed surprised to see her, but if village life mirrored clan life at all, every detail of her arrival had already been shared and spun about twice over within two candlemarks of her arrival. Anything to keep the boredom at bay.

Later, after the tables were cleared, she sat down at one and unrolled her maps to study the topography. Escarpments and caves surrounded them. She found the Waystation to the southeast, as well. And east—the High Hills and Sweetbark, where Challen and Aesha would be.

But her eyes lingered on those caves.

Where bears sleep.

"That's a lot of maps," Jolie said, rousing her from her studies.

"Maps, histories, the odd hagiography. Anything to get a sense of where I'm going."

"Valdemar?"

Khaari gestured. "All of it. Some Northern tribe knowledge, too."

"Why *are* you here?" Jolie asked, a cup of tea in one hand.

"The Herald I know is hunting a criminal."

"A bear criminal?"

"No." Khaari laughed. "But I'm curious. Your brother said something about a curse?"

Jolie snorted. "My brother has a way with words."

"Why *those* words?"

The innkeeper shrugged, but didn't meet her eyes. "The way it keeps coming and going. The way it screams . . . Beck doesn't believe it. But some of us do. What else could it be?"

"I am reminded of a story among my people," Khaari said. "A *true* story. Many generations ago, during a very cold winter—colder than usual—a strange old woman came to the Dhorisha Plains. She asked for shelter. In our kindness, we gave it to her."

Jolie listened intently, her tea forgotten.

"But we were fools. You see, she cast off her human skin that night. And in her place—a snow demon."

"Oh."

"She killed half the clan as they slept." Khaari put her chin in her hand. "But—that's something I don't know happens in Valdemar."

Jolie drained her cup. "Khaari, I want you to know . . . I don't blame you."

"Blame me?"

She met her gaze. "Beck sent Darvin away because he let you in. Darvin truly believes you know a Herald. And for what it's worth, I do, too."

"Well, thank you."

"Anyway, I need to sweep," Jolie asid. "If you'd like more tea, there's a fresh pot in the kitchen. Even has honey."

She watched the innkeeper walk away, her skirts swishing across the floors.

A howl of rage and anguish woke Khaari that night.

She rolled out of bed, grabbed her sword, and went outside.

Torches illuminated two figures in the watchtower. She climbed up.

"—been a while," Beck was saying as she got to the top. When he saw her, he glowered. "You."

"I wish to help," she said.

"You're not a guard."

"I'm in blue."

Again, the curdling look. "This isn't your job. Go back to bed."

She peered down, but the glare from the torches prevented her from seeing much. She closed her eyes, breathing in the cold stillness.

"What are you doing, OutKingdom?" Beck asked. She ignored him.

The beast screamed again, very close, and she cocked her head in the direction of the sound.

And then—before they could stop her—she picked up one of the bows, drew, and fired several arrows.

In the distance, she heard a new scream. Surprise. Pain.

She opened her eyes to find the guards staring at her, slack-jawed.

"Hunting is part of life on the Plains," she explained. "Learning the bow comes early. Trick shots come later. Like shooting blind." She lowered the bow. "I just hope it was not a grazing shot."

The howls faded off eventually. She remained in the tower for a candlemark, waiting to see if the beast returned. No one spoke. Sometimes the other guard looked at her, but Beck refused to. His jaw stayed clenched the whole time.

"Good night, sirs," she said eventually, climbing down the ladder.

She got halfway to the inn when someone tapped her on the shoulder.

She turned, and just barely ducked the swing Beck took at her head.

"OutKingdom *misbreed*," he snarled.

She jumped back, one hand on her sword hilt.

"Don't you *ever* pull a stunt like that again!" he said, and to her relief he did not close the distance she'd made between them. "I am the *wolf*. You are the *sheep*. Do you understand?"

She stared into his face. The mental image of his nose as a perfect, flat oval returned, unbidden—but she did not act on it.

After a moment, he walked back to the tower.

This man despises challengers. He alone must hold all the power.

Which means he should have none.

"Star-Eyed," she whispered skyward, "what have I gotten into?"

Toecrusher still hadn't been stolen or eaten the next morning, so Khaari came back to help Jolie with food preparation.

As they worked, Jolie said, "So . . . you haven't turned into a snow demon and eaten us."

Khaari blinked owlishly at her. "Did you take my story as a threat?"

"No! I—I'm sorry." She blushed. "I meant that as a joke."

"Ah. To be honest, I had not thought of it that way, but I can see how you might interpret it so." She folded some dough into thirds. "Your sergeant did talk a bit about wolves and sheep last night. Can he turn into a wolf?"

Jolie laughed in surprise. "Oh, yes, Beck and his *wolf* talk." She lowered her voice into an uncanny imitation. "'I'm the wolf, you're the sheep, don't you forget it.'"

"Ah, so he is *fond* of this allegory, I take it."

"It's probably why he hates that bear so much," she said. "First time he's been at the mercy of something else. Agh!" She shook her head. "It didn't used to *be* like this. Before the war, Heralds came *regularly*. But they cut Circuits back, I think because they lost too many? And . . . we still get them, just not as often, but it's not the *same*. My parents. Half the village. They all . . . got worse. And Beck's right there, leading them down this . . . *path.*" She looked pleadingly at Khaari. "It's probably why he doesn't believe you. Our next Herald isn't due until Midsummer."

Again, I am challenging him, Khaari thought. *Heralds only come in Midsummer. How* dare *I suggest otherwise.*

Jolie stared down at the pile of cut biscuits. "The truth is, it's not that we took someone in. It's that—"

Behind her, Khaari heard the front door to the inn slam open with a *bang.* Beck yelled, "OutKingdom! Where are you!"

"In here," she called.

Beck appeared in the kitchen door, glowering. "You're coming with me. I need you to show me where you shot those arrows."

Khaari looked at Jolie, but the innkeeper had her eyes firmly fixed on her biscuits.

Later, she thought. *I hope we can talk later.*

Beyond the gate, Khaari took a moment to get her bearings, and then led Beck and four other guards down an embankment, into the forest below the village.

They found two spent arrows and the blood trail immediately. It led toward the hills, and then stopped—

At the body of a bear.

"Lucky shot," Beck said. "Looks like you nicked a vein and it bled out."

Khaari frowned and knelt by the body, touching the fur. It looked like an ordinary she-bear.

Star-Eyed, she thought, half-praying. *Something is not right here.*

A wind from the north stirred up, blowing through her, as if in answer.

What am I missing? she thought. *It is not a demon, nor magic-twisted.*

"You going to kiss it, OutKingdom?" Beck asked above her.

"Have you ever stopped to ask, Sergeant, *why* this is happening?"

The other guards shifted, looking uncomfortable.

"You talking about that stupid curse?" Beck snorted. "All I see is a crazy bear killing my people. Except now, we eat bear steaks." He gestured to the others. "Let's get it back to the village. I'll open up the ale barrels."

Everyone cheered. Everyone but Khaari.

The guards whistled and laughed all the way back to the village.

Khaari couldn't stop looking back over her shoulder.

The bonfire crackled merrily. The guards hauled out benches and announced the good news. Khaari's unease wouldn't let go.

Jolie sat beside her, equally sullen.

"No sign of Darvin?" she said.

"No," Khaari said. "I'll go look for him tomorrow."

They watched as villagers made themselves sick on greasy bear meat and too much ale. The sun sat low on the horizon.

"I share Darvin's confusion," Khaari said. "No ordinary bear should have done this much harm."

"It seemed as tall as the inn, the night it attacked my family." Jolie fiddled with the hem of her skirt. "The gate didn't have the log across it back then. Just a simple bar. It broke through. Killed my father—he was the mayor—and stepmum. Then it came for me."

"Where was Darvin?"

"On patrol."

"And you escaped?"

"I didn't. It caught me sleeping. Sniffed me all over. Then it left." She took a small sip of ale. "Didn't tell Beck that. Told him I hid under a bed."

Khaari knuckled her forehead. "Your secret is safe."

Jolie gazed into the fire. "Khaari, you should know. *Your* people let a stranger in. My people—we locked five of them out. In a snowstorm, right before Midwinter. This woman and her children. They came begging my parents for a room. They had nothing—nothing at all. I slipped her some food, all I could do without anyone knowing. But . . . my parents . . . because of

Beck . . . turned them away." She rubbed tears out of her eyes. "Back into the blizzard. Because they were from the Northern tribes. OutKingdom."

"And that's why you think you're cursed?"

"Who *does* that to children? To the needy?" She drew her knees up. "But yes, I think it is—*was*—their spirit in that bear. They were all wearing bear-carving necklaces."

"Bear carvings?" Khaari said, surprised. "As in—Bear Clan?"

"The Bear Clan?"

"I'm surprised you do not know this about your neighbors," the Scrollsworn said. "The Northern clans all have totemic animals that guide them. Not dissimilar from my own people. Maybe theirs was a bear."

"You seem to know a lot about them."

"I am Scrollsworn," Khaari said. "And I live in a city with access to vast troves of knowledge. My maps were not the only research I did before I hied off to Valdemar."

Jolie raised her cup. "Well, here's to being the smart one in the room."

"Except when you're in the wrong room," Khaari said archly.

Jolie laughed. "Don't I kn—"

Something inhuman screamed just outside the gate.

The mood in the village changed instantly, as if someone had taken an hourglass and slammed it over.

Mugs crashed to the ground. Beck bellowed to *"brace the gate!"* but too late. Khaari leapt to her feet, sword flashing, as Jolie scurried away. And then the beast came roaring in, a monster equally as large as the one on the spit, all black fur and claws. It howled and lashed out at a guard in the way. Blood sprayed. Chaos erupted as people ran for shelter.

Khaari whistled a particular set of high notes. She heard a *crack*, and then Toecrusher came crashing out of the stable. She mounted and sent the mare running past the beast.

She slashed across its shoulders, a shallow, stinging cut. The beast spun, screaming, but Toecrusher had already cleared its reach. The bear's eyes blazed with a mix of rage and intellect. Toecrusher spun and backed up.

"Come," Khaari yelled. *"Come!"*

It charged.

Toecrusher danced and avoided it, wheeling and leaping past. The bear swiped—missed—and shambled after horse and rider, down the road, out the gate.

Beck yelled, *"Close it!"*

Khaari nudged Toecrusher into an all-out run. The beast screamed its impotence as it failed to catch them. After a while, it stopped in the road, sides heaving. Behind it, the gate had shut. Slowly, Khaari turned Toecrusher around.

"I'm not your enemy!" she yelled at it.

The bear growled and snuffled. Now that she had a chance to examine it outside the heat of battle, she realized it was *not* as large as the first. A juvenile.

Khaari tried another approach. Her studies on the Northern tribes had not been limited to their culture.

"I am not your enemy," she said again, in the Northern tongue, and hoped her pronunciation and dialect weren't *too* off. "Please. I mean you no harm. I can help."

The bear took a step back. And then, to her astonishment, it howled—a piercing note—that she *swore* sounded like *"No!"* in the Northern tongue.

It charged down the embankment, back to the forest. Gradually, its howls diminished, leaving Khaari and Toecrusher alone on the road.

"So much for *boring*," she muttered.

Then she rode away from Briar's Rock.

They rode all night, until they came to the branch in the road that led to the Waystation. She brought Toecrusher to a halt.

I could just keep riding, she thought.

She could already see the snow diminishing the further south she went. A few more weeks, and she'd be in Rethwellan. And then Kata'shin'a'in, with her sisters and brothers and the Webs of Time again.

She could leave *all* of this to Herald Wil. He could handle it—she knew he could.

But no matter how much she missed the sunset on the Plains, she'd curse her days if she didn't see this through.

With a twitch of her knees, she sent Toecrusher plunging down the path toward the Waystation.

When Khaari got there, she was not surprised to find it occupied—but rather by *who* occupied it.

Her mule greeted Toecrusher with a snort. Khaari knocked on the door and waited.

Darvin emerged in nothing but a nightshirt, his hair rumpled.

"Swordlady?" he said sleepily.

She looked him up and down. "You live."

"I figured—if I had to meet a Herald, this would be the place." He rubbed the sleep out of his eyes. "What are you *doing* here?"

"Put on a pot of tea and I'll tell you."

While the tea brewed, she got Toecrusher settled, and checked her over thoroughly. No cuts or scrapes, her hooves and ankles looked good. She threw a blanket over the mare and set her up with the good feed of the Waystation; Heralds knew how to treat their Companions.

Inside, the snug cabin smelled of cedar, and she settled into a chair and told Darvin what had transpired.

"*Another* bear?" He looked defeated.

"Mm." Khaari rubbed her chin. "Why aren't you dead?"

"I . . . I don't know," he said. "I heard it howling. It definitely *knew* I'd left Briar's Rock. But then it just—stopped coming."

"I wonder how this curse works. What do you know of the Northern woman and her children?"

Darvin sputtered tea.

"Jolie told me," she said.

"Of course she did." He pressed the heels of his hands to his eyes. "I was on watch that night. *I* let the strangers in." When his hands came down, his eyes were red. "I got the sense she was running from something, just not sure *what*. Beck . . . my parents . . . they insisted she was a 'spy.' A vanguard for some sinister force. They shoved her and her four children back out the gate." He looked up at the ceiling. "You know, I think I'm going crazy, because I swear I heard them while I was riding out here."

"The children?"

He nodded.

"Hm." Khaari sipped her tea. The night of riding had come due; she felt a great lassitude come over her. "How safe is it here?"

"Like you said, I'm not dead," he said. "So, what comes next?"

She raised her cup in salute. "Breaking a curse."

Khaari made a crude ink from the fire's ashes and used a stick to draw with. Nothing durable, but she didn't need this to last. Then she set to recreating her maps on the tabletop.

She gestured. "There are caves all along these hills, close to Briar's Rock. Tell me, if you were looking for shelter in a storm, where would you go?"

Darvin pointed. "Here."

"And where would bears sleep for the winter?"

"Any of those."

"The one I shot was headed *here* before it bled out." She indicated a section. "We'll start there."

"Our hunters already *tried* to track it back to its cave."

"And what happened?" she asked.

"I told you. Most of them got scared back to Briar's Rock. Some of them got mauled to death."

"The ones that died—were they part of the group that ran the woman and her children out of town?"

He nodded.

"Interesting. Darvin, do you speak any of the Northern tongue?"

"I can say 'hello,' and that's it." He studied her. "You seem to be thinking something."

"Just suspicions." She pursed her lips. "I need to prove them now."

They stayed in the Waystation a full day. During that time, she wrapped Darvin in her shirt and pants.

"Why?" he asked.

"I need to smell like you tomorrow," she said.

That night, she meditated on the Moonpaths. Being outside of walls meant she could finally ask advice from the *leshya'e Kal'enedral*.

Her teacher smiled as she approached. "You decided to stay."

It shouldn't have surprised her that he knew she'd wavered, but it did. "Yes."

"Good."

She put forth her theories, and he nodded. "The dyheli king stags have a Gift not unlike what you're describing. It may also be the work of a totemic spirit."

"And if I'm wrong and I'm bear food? What happens to Toe-crusher?"

"Aesha will come get her."

That answer brought her some peace, and she went to bed without trouble.

She and Darvin started their day before dawn on foot. Once or twice, they heard the beast howl in the far distance. They stayed on the road only a few candlemarks before turning off into the mountains.

By afternoon, her nose picked up the smell of woodsmoke, and she silently signaled a halt. Eyes shut, she listened.

"You hear it, too?" Darvin whispered.

She did.

Children chattering.

They scrambled up a hill, across soft scree that took them to a cave. Soot blackened the roof from a small fire. Three children sat around it, wearing what looked like oversized, fur-lined hide coats and boots. Darvin gasped.

The children looked at them with round, black eyes. The oldest stood up. He had a thick stick in his hand, which he bared menacingly.

"No," Khaari said in the Northern tongue. She gestured to Darvin, then herself. *"Friends."*

"Hello," Darvin said, in the Northern tongue.

The boy looked nonplussed. He wet his lips. "Help?" He pointed to the back of the cave.

Away from the light, stretched out on a thick blanket, she found their mother. The woman's cheeks were sallow, her pulse thready. A carving of a bear on a leather thong hung from her neck.

A few feet away, a child lay curled on her side, fingers outstretched to her mother's. It took Khaari a moment to realize that the child did not sleep.

"Mother does not eat," the boy said. "She is—bear."

"I know," Khaari said.

She picked the woman up, straightened, and turned—

And saw the flesh-and-blood bear standing at the cave's mouth.

The children showed no fear. Darvin backed up against one wall. The beast advanced on Khaari on all fours.

"Sorry I hurt you," she said to it. "Let me help, now."

The bear growled, a low rumble. In her arms, the woman growled as well.

"Let me help," Khaari repeated, addressing them both in the Northerners' language. "Sister, for *them*, let go. Let the bear sleep. You are safe now. You have my word."

The bear stepped forward—

And then continued past her, deeper into the cave, before lying down and going to sleep.

"Can we *go*?" Darvin whispered.

In Khaari's arms, the woman sighed.

"Go," she said.

They took the children and the mother back to the Waystation. Sometime on the second day, Herald Wil showed up.

"Khaari?" he said.

"So good to finally see you, Wil," she said cheerfully. "And Grier! I need a Healer. Can you confirm something for me?"

"Sure?" said Lord Baireschild, in the entry.

She pointed to where the Northerner lay stretched in the boxbed. "I believe *this* woman has Animal Mindspeech, as you

Valdemarans call it. But it's a bit *more* than that. She seems able to *control* the animals. Specifically those of her clan's totem, the bear."

"I'm not sure I can confirm *any* of that," Grier said.

"Can you at least Heal her?"

"*That*, I can do." He went to kneel beside the bed.

"Thank you, Lord Longhair." She turned back to Wil, eyes sparkling. "Herald, there is a sergeant in Briar's Rock we must have words with."

"I guess?" Wil said. "But first maybe you can tell me *what is going on?*"

From behind him, a woman in Scarlet peeked over his shoulder, saying, "Heyla, I don't know what's happening either, but I'm *ready* to write a song about it."

Wil agreed to Khaari's plan, with one change: he went to Sweetbark first and came back with a complement of guards.

When they rode into Briar's Rock, Beck met them with a mix of forced gregariousness and confusion. Wil's company consisted of five guards, including Darvin, Khaari on her mare, and one over-eager Bard.

"Greetings," the Herald said, "I am here to give you the good news that your bear problem has been resolved."

"I-It has?"

"Yes. Are you Sergeant Beck?"

"I am!"

"Excellent." For a moment, Beck lit up, but only a moment. "I have the confession—under Truth Spell—of one of your men, as well as an emissary of the Shin'a'in."

"I—"

"On behalf of Her Majesty, Queen Selenay, I am issuing you a reduction in rank, Beck of Briar's Rock. You will be brought to trial for gross negligence and abuse of authority."

Beck looked bewildered. "You—*what*?"

Khaari approached and dismounted. Stunned by Wil's words, Beck barely registered her. His face was wide open. She had the perfect shot. Her forehead *twitched* at the thought.

She breathed in the cold northern air. She held the intention in her head—

—and breathed it out.

Khaari patted him on the shoulder. "I am sure you meant well in the beginning, Sergeant. The path to disaster is paved with good intentions. Learn from this."

His face twisted. *"You!"*

He balled his fist and swung at her head. And once again, she dodged it, easily.

The difference this time, though, was Toecrusher. Unfortunately for Beck, she saw him as a threat to her partner.

Lucky for him, she only flattened his feet.

The morning of the funeral, Khaari, the bear mother—whose name was Teeala—and her children all set out together to the cave on foot.

They arrived in silence. Khaari helped Teeala construct the funerary pyre out of seasoned wood they'd brought from the village. And then Teeala took her child from the cave to her final rest.

The Scrollsworn had explained to the mother that, among her people, she was a Goddess-touched priest. Teeala had asked her to say some words.

Each of the children lit a corner as Khaari sought words within her, taking the northern wind's stillness into her lungs.

"Mother," she said, "cradle this child in your warm embrace."

The wood popped and crackled.

"Warrior, protect her on her way."

Teeala's remaining children gathered around her, and she stretched her arms around them, the fire dancing in their eyes.

"Crone, let her story not be forgotten."

A wind circled Khaari's ankles, moving across the rocks.

"Maiden—"

A spring wind suddenly roared around her, fueling the fire to furnace-hot temperatures. A column of flame burst up, consuming the small body inside.

For a second, the image of a bear seemed to blaze within. Teeala gasped.

Then it died again, the body burned to nothing.

"—dance with her in your fields, ever blooming," Khaari whispered.

She could not tell if it was the heat of the blaze or her own sorrow that caused the wetness on her cheeks.

Once more back at the inn, Khaari sought out a cup of tea—and found the Bard waiting in ambush.

"Amelie, is it?" the Scrollsworn said.

She nodded. "You've had quite a week."

"And I'm ready for it to stop."

"Care to tell me about it?"

"In time."

"Why do you keep rubbing your forehead? Do you have a headache?"

"Tch." Khaari put her hand down on the table. "No, just a memory of a bad intention."

"Er—what?" Amelie said.

Khaari chuckled. "Don't worry, I kept it in line."

"And what do you get for that?"

"I remain the better person."

"Well, *that's* boring," Amelie said.

Khaari raised her hands in a gesture of praise. "At last! The long-awaited boredom. I guess the power was within me all along."

The Bard looked confused.

"Tea?" Khaari asked, and poured them each a cup.

Beebalm and Bergamot
Cat Rambo

Beebalm and bergamot, Deirdra sang to herself as she worked in the garden. *Lavender and moneywort, tarragon and tarrytime.* Her herbal lexicon, committed to memory at her grandmother's knee, evoked every time she stooped to pluck a leaf and inhale its fragrance as it had been since her childhood, and through the five decades that had followed it.

Two of the hives in the apple orchard overlooking the river were restless, on the edge of swarming. She could hear it in their hum when she went down to collect frames of honeycomb, deep amber and smelling faintly of rose and apple. Normally their hum was soft and lazy, but now there was undertone to it, something ready to be unleashed.

She'd have to figure out where the new swarms could go; she had no skeps ready, but last year she'd made up plenty of her grandmother's bee lure recipe. Wherever she painted a swab, the bees would be drawn. Keep them in the orchard to scent their honey with its rosy sweetness? But there was a bed of thyme she'd been cultivating, and she was curious how those blossoms might spice the bees' output.

She mused it over while she decanted the dripping honeycomb in her back garden. Bees rose and swirled around her, pausing to light on the herbs and flowers nearby before taking to the air again. She held a bottle of golden liquid up and admired it. Honey was like stored happiness, moments you kept to savor later. Each drop flavored with the flowers harvested to make it. Each one different, each one precious.

A sharp whistle from over the rose hedge caught her attention, and she whistled back. Seconds later, a familiar face poked itself over the garden gate. Hair as graying as her own, but sharper features and a long scar across his eyebrow.

"Morning, sunshine," he said. "Is there tea ready?"

She waved a sticky hand at him. "You know where the kettle is, Kal. Put it on yourself, and I'll be there shortly."

Grumbling something to himself, he withdrew. Deirdra grinned to herself. She and the retired soldier had become fast friends a year or so after her return to the village, and she knew he was aware of where everything in her kitchen was, and would provide commentary on the disorder if he felt anything was out of place.

When she came into the tidy little kitchen, there was a steaming mug already waiting for her on the table. "Thank you," she said, as she sank into the chair opposite him. "What's the gossip?"

"Alou left sudden, they say. Took her kids and went off elsewhere."

"She was never the same after Tom died," Deirdra said. "Some people are like that."

He grunted at her and she raised an eyebrow. "What's got you in a mood?"

"All sorts of new folk in the village," he said. "Up to no good, I would say."

She snorted. "You always think people are up to no good."

He crossed his arms. "And haven't I been right, once or twice?"

"A few times," she admitted. "But you scowl at the innocent as fiercely as the guilty."

"If they didn't feel guilty, they'd scowl back."

She threw up her hands. "Not everyone is like you!"

"That," he said with satisfaction and a sip of tea, "is true."

"New folk," she said musingly, and let the words linger too long. He leaned forward.

"You should go meet them," he urged. "Show them our humble village has a distinguished herbalist."

She froze in her seat.

"They are only from a city, they are not a walking replica of it," he said gently, his eyes searching her panicked face. "But if it is too much, it is too much."

After he had gone, she looked at the honey jar sitting on the table. Stored happiness. She had stored so much of it in her early years, she had never thought it could run out. And then she had been sent off to the city to learn, and learn she had, become an expert. And then she had found herself moving in high circles indeed!

And then, at the height of her career, it seemed, had come the summons to serve the nobility.

The Sweetsprings court had been a pleasant place at first. Some of the girls and a few of the boys came to her for herbal scents and remedies. There were so many faces, so many names and stories and tastes. There was such a variety of people, including Heralds, dressed in their whites, circulating with the nobles but always managing, somehow, to keep to their own. So many people interested in meeting her, giving her gifts. She'd accumulated jewels, the most treasured a great green jewel given her for her service. It had been exhilarating at first.

But she had always been anxious, something that had driven her onward in her studies. Day by day in the court, that anxiety had grown, driven by cruel sarcasms and the witty barbs that seethed there. Only the Heralds were kind, and so few followed their example. It had finally been too much. It was as though her soul had grown knives that were flaying her from the inside. Five years ago, the Herald Rishi had found her crying in a closet. Kneeling beside her, he had comforted her, and then, gently, suggested that the court was not the right place for her.

She had resisted the suggestion at first, outraged at the thought. But then, day by day, she had realized he was right. And so, finally, she had retreated here. Trying to heal. Trying to refill the sweetness that had once filled her soul.

Bit by bit, she had been replenishing it. Her day-to-day interactions fed it. Marnie from the inn bringing her seeds coaxed from traveling merchants and unsolicited advice about her love life. Jun from the forest, bringing her a baby fox to be nurtured back into health before he was able to re-release it. Louan, who'd come so shyly to admit an infirmity she held private, and had been so grateful when a tincture chased it away.

She tapped her fingers on the table. "But if it is too much, it is too much," Kal had said. Was it too much? She was, after all, still an herbalist, and one who had gained more than a little renown for her cures. After she had withdrawn to the village, many had come seeking her. Trying to lure her back. But she refused, in those first few years, to treat anyone who was not of the village itself, and thus the flood of pursuers had ebbed, and become a trickle, and then, eventually, gratefully, dried up. Nowadays no one would have heard of her.

She did not think it was exactly too much, to go see them. A challenge, perhaps, for which she would have to steel herself. Kal was surprisingly understanding of her fears, but at his heart, did he not think her weak and feeble, he who had faced so much in battle?

And so, finally, she rose and drew on her cloak. Slowly, as though armoring herself, and she tucked a few leaves of bergamot in her sleeve, so she could smell it if her resolve faltered.

The market was not very large. A cluster of stalls set up around the square bordered by the village's most impressive feature, a large house built a century ago by a mayor who had wanted to be lording it over a much larger place, and had built a domicile to match. Now it slumped unused except for a few lower rooms, one for the schoolmistress, another for the village's scant archives.

She spotted the newcomers as soon as she stepped onto the square. Hard to miss them, flashy fresh-dyed cloaks and an air of arrogance about them that seemed as much fashion accessory as attitude. A tall woman, flanked by two lackeys, their power relationship immediately signaled by the way they stood back a little from her, unobtrusive but at hand if needed. She was speaking with Jun, who had laid out his usual small piles of furs. Jun was a trapper and a good one, and Deirdra appreciated the way he managed to coexist with the animals he lived on, trapping carefully and prudently, never letting the animals die out due to excess culling. And it was he who made sure that wolves didn't descend on the village during the harshest moments of the winter, including its outlying areas, like her orchard-surrounded cottage.

The woman gestured, and her minions scuttled forward to heap their arms with furs. She dropped several coins in Jun's hands, and turned to inspect the next stall. It was mostly turnips. Despite their purple and white gloss and the neat way Pati had stacked them in pyramids, with a little vase of marigolds to the side, this clearly was not to her liking. She tossed her head with a sniff and moved on.

Deirdra stopped beside Jun. "Bought you out?"

"Entirely," he said.

"Why so sour?"

He glanced at the woman's back. "Drove a hard bargain, that one. Don't know that I came out much ahead. Said buying in bulk merited a decrease, and was talking at me so fast and hard I just started nodding like a fool."

"Cheated you?" Deirdra said, but Jun shook his head.

"Skirted the edge of it," he admitted. "Waltzed right up to the line, as I see it, but I did agree to it."

"Hmph," Deirdra said. More loudly than she had meant to, for, a few stalls away, the woman turned to look at her. Let her eyes sweep up and down, then back up from Deirdra's worn (but comfortable) shoes, her rumpled (but serviceable) skirt and apron, the perpetual edge of dirt under her fingernails no matter now she scrubbed, and finally to Deirdra's face. Deirdra had washed and made herself presentable before coming out, but now she felt utterly inadequate.

This was one of those sharp-edged people that she had known at court. The ones who flayed you with their presence, who said nice things with knives under the words, backhanded compliments and insults dressed up in pretty clothing. Her tongue locked in her mouth and she felt unable to draw breath.

Worse, the woman was marching toward her, followed by

one of the minions while the other carried both armloads off to some unknown destination.

The woman drew herself up in front of Deirdra. This close, Deirdra could see the fineness of the lace at her cuffs, see the satin-stitched lines of embroidery on a jacket that only the wealthy could afford, the gilt and blue stone (sapphires? Surely not, but it certainly looked like them.) buckles on her boots.

"Brickleboro's herbalist, I take it," she said, pale blue eyes lingering on the state of Deirdra's hands. "They say you were trained in Sweetsprings. And now here, of all places."

"I am Deirdra," she managed.

The woman paused as though interrupted, but then re-launched her flow. "I am Leyna, here to oversee my master's investment. You may prove useful to the operation."

"Useful?" Deirdra said. Well, at least that raised her contribution to the conversation to four words instead of three. And then, "Operation?" Up to five words.

"There is to be a great investment in this village," Leyna said. "A stillroom, to produce scents for the wealthy and those trying to smell wealthy. It will be placed just where the river bends. You will come and speak to me, tonight, at the inn, and I will interview you to determine your suitability."

Without waiting for an answer, she turned away.

Deirdra released the breath that, she realized, she'd been holding all along.

"A right bitch, that one," a voice said at her shoulder. She jumped.

"Dammit, Kal!" She didn't mind when her friend kept his skills sharp on the townspeople, but she was another matter. "I'm not a target to be snuck up on."

"And good thing you weren't," he said. "Standing there without watching around you. Anyone could have gotten at you."

"We're in Brickleboro," she said patiently. "Not some frontier or war zone."

He pursed his lips. "Doesn't refute my point. Bad habit. Anyhow, are you going to go be 'interviewed'?"

"Not for all the money in the world," Deirdra said. "I don't want to get tied up in anything like that. Stillrooms can be ugly places."

"Stillrooms are places that make money," Kal said. "Plenty will be looking first and foremost at that. She must have bought or leased the land—that's Alou's family property. Want me to find out?"

"It's not a spy mission," she said. Then, "But yes. Just because I'm curious."

She didn't expect him to report back as quickly as he did. Nor with a sheaf of papers in his hand. "Should I ask how you got those?" she asked.

"Probably not," he said, shoving the pot of honey aside in order to unroll the first on the table. "Let's see. Here's a drawing of the building they intend."

It was complicated, and Deirdra struggled to make it out. "There are boiling vats," she said, tapping one spot, "but what are these?"

Kal squinted. "Looks like they take boil-off and take it here, to be dumped in the river."

The river? But the flow would take anything from the stillroom and carry it along the entirety of the space the village occupied. And then the border of her apple orchard.

Kal was rustling through more papers. "Here's a supply list." He looked a little sheepish. "Let's go through these quick, eh? So I can replace them on the, er, location I found them."

Forbearing comment, Deirdra flicked through the handful he shoved toward her. "This can't be right," she said, scanning through names of ingredients. She raised a stricken face to Kal. "This is why they've chosen this place. They want to pollute our waters, rather than the ones closer to the city."

"And bought it outright in order to do so," he said, pushing a bill of sale. "No wonder Alou and her family left so sudden-like after selling it. She must have had some sense to know they wouldn't be popular once this operation started running, for being the ones to have opened the door to it. And they would have had enough to set themselves up elsewhere, and do it in style."

"We can't let this happen."

"Deirdra, progress rolls along," Kal said. "If not here, they'll move elsewhere."

She pointed at the bill of sale. "And double their costs in doing so? No, merchants calculate profit margins. If we make it expensive enough for them, they'll rethink their plans. Maybe find a way to make their perfumes without destroying wherever it is they're making them."

Kal was rolling up papers, readying them to be returned. "The question," he said, "is how, though?"

And so, despite herself, Deirdra went to the inn that evening. She'd taken care to scrub her fingernails, and she wore what had been her healer's outfit in the city, neat and subdued and orderly, but also easily cleaned.

Leyna had reserved a private room for the interview. As Deirdra sat down, one of the minions scuttled forward to pour her wine.

"No, thank you," she said, "but water would be welcome."

It took visible effort for Leyna to refrain from rolling her eyes, but she got straight to the topic.

"You are an educated woman," she said, with a flick of a look around that said, *unlike everyone else here.* "You might serve the stillroom in some capacity."

"Your stillroom will destroy this area," Deirdra said. "The off-flow into the river will kill the fish and plants downstream for at least a few miles, if not more."

Leyna's chill blue eyes narrowed. "You seem to know a lot about it."

Deirdra's words couldn't seem to come out. She wished, desperately, that Kal was there. He always knew what to say.

Leyna waved her off with a hand. "If you cannot assist the stillroom, you can assist the workers. I am sure your scruples would not extend to refusing treatment to someone who was ill."

"Are you," Deirdra said somehow, "planning on having many sick workers, then?"

She heard one of the minions smother a gasp. Leyna ignored it and simply looked hard at Deirdra.

"I can see," she said with a haughty sniff, "that further conversation will be of little use."

"I came to persuade you not to build the stillroom," Deirdra said desperately, but Leyna just laughed.

"And how," she sneered, "would you have any hope of that?"

How indeed. This wasn't a problem that could be solved by the Heralds on Circuit. She couldn't wait for months, and what's more, commerce wasn't against the law. Only the town could fight this fight.

For the next few hours Deirdra's thoughts sizzled and popped, trying to figure out angles of attack. But it had been so long since she'd planned something like this, and it meant dealing with people, and people like Leyna, to boot. She shivered despite the kitchen's warmth, and went out to the bees for solace. The hives were sleeping, but if you stooped close enough to put an eye to one of the woven skeps, you could just hear the humming.

They are so good, the bees, she thought. *They work together. They cooperate.* No bee went and seized extra honey for itself. No bee fought its fellows or quarreled or said cruel things.

She wished, so much, that she was a bee.

And then she thought of the hives readying themselves for flight within the next day.

The half-built stillroom squatted on the river's edge like a toad surveying its surroundings with complacent apathy. By the time Leyna arrived, though, the place glistened and moved. Across the walls, bees crawled, flying in and out. Five hives had been ready to move, it turned out, and five swarms of bees were sufficient to make any habitation uninhabitable for anyone but bees.

And near the entrance was Deirdra.

She'd dressed in her court clothes, high enough quality to never seem dated. At her throat swung the great green gem. The only thing she'd kept of her court gifts, but Leyna didn't need to know that. All she'd see would be the gem's worth.

"I take it you are somehow . . . responsible for all this," Leyna said. "You think it will dissuade my plans." Her voice was full of mocking glee. "Bees? We can smoke them out."

Her expression, her tone, the way she stooped her face condescendingly at Deirdra, all made the familiar anxiety stab at her. But this struggle, unlike the court back-and-forths, was worth it. She raised her chin. "I have plenty of bees."

Leyna simply rolled her eyes.

"She also," said a voice, "has plenty of friends."

Kal, stepping up the path. Behind him, what seemed like the entirety of the village's population. Marnie, Louan, and Jun in the forefront.

"Perhaps her not wanting you here," Kal said to Leyna, "is not enough. But none of us wants you here."

"Won't serve you and your workers at the tavern," said Marnie.

"Won't treat your dray or messenger horses," said Louan.

"Won't sell you anything," Jun said. He spat and muttered, "Won't sell you what they're worth, no how."

"Going to drive up your costs considerably," Kal said.

"I can't just tell my masters they've wasted money here!" Leyna protested.

Relief held Deirdra where she would have sagged. She drew herself up to her full height. "You can and you will," she said. "And you'll tell them that likely enough the same will happen anywhere you go. You may find a greedy fool here and there willing to sell you their land and move away, but they got neighbors. Out here, everyone's neighbors."

After the wagons had stripped whatever they could salvage from the building and trundled away, after Leyna's last tart but ineffectual imprecations, after the villagers had straggled back to Brickleboro, Kal and Deirdra returned to her garden.

"The bees might as well hive there as anywhere," Kal said. "That land will lie fallow till the merchants figure a way to sell it back."

"As to that," Deirdra said, "Leyna was able to find a purchaser, it seems."

She fingered the chain at her throat where the green gem had once hung. She had prized it for so long, had kept it as a memory of one of the honeyed moments at court, among all the sourness, all the sharpness. Now it was gone, along with all the other moments. They had lost their power to panic her.

"A pretty price," Kal said.

"Yes," Deirdra said, and added more honey, scented with beebalm and bergamot, to her tea. "And yet, totally worth it."

The Stable Hand's Gift
Ron Collins

The cold shiver that froze Maizy tonight came from more than just the night air.

Everyone considered her the manor's most capable stable worker—something she thought was because she saw details others couldn't. She cared about the animals in ways others didn't. When the operation to capture Nwah had succeeded, it was only natural Maizy had been tasked to tend to the kyree as she recovered from the baron's ministrations, and to ensure Nwah was capable of withstanding additional questionings as needed for the baron to obtain his information.

She had been the obvious choice.

She sighed and stretched her fingers toward the warmth of an oil lamp whose flickering flame colored the stall's closed-off planks.

At least her assignment meant the baron allotted fuel for that.

She felt different as she waited for the baron's men to bring Nwah back to her stall. Uncomfortable. Oddly disjointed from this place where she had spent her entire life.

The hour was late. The stable vacant. The aroma of straw, oats, and manure was thin, and the rhythmic bumping of the animals moving in their stalls came low and disquietingly normal. She sat on the hard ground, knees wrapped in arms, still unable to shake words the kyree had spoken last evening when Maizy, who had been administering to her wounds, asked why Nwah continued to suffer the baron's torture.

"The baron doesn't enjoy it either," Maizy had noted. "He says so himself. It would go so much easier if you simply told him what he wants to know."

Baron Haffti was a hard man. Maizy knew that. He had his own form of the truth, but his truth was easy to decipher. And he was consistent. If one kept to the right of the path, everything remained fine.

Nwah held silent for several beats.

:Your baron is a bad man.:

Nothing else. No effort to defend the words. No attempt to persuade Maizy to think in Nwah's fashion. They were simply words left hanging there in that startling Mindspeech Nwah had, which in that moment felt as strong as any river current Maizy had ever swum in.

"I see," she replied. But she hadn't seen anything at all.

Baron Haffti was her lord. The only ruler her family had ever known. Life was hard, but it was hard everywhere. And for all its rules and punishments, the baron's manor was a place of refuge. She could ask for no more.

Nwah's words stuck in her thoughts, though.

Growing more anxious as her waiting continued, Maizy stretched to glance at the manor doors, still locked shut. The interrogation was going long tonight. Did that mean the kyree had finally broken? She gritted her teeth and, with only a hint of surprise, realized she was now worried about Nwah.

Though she hadn't known what to expect from the assignment, the stories she'd heard came with a mixture of excitement and wonder. Nwah was a Gifted kyree, newly running with the wild pack in the northland woods. Some said she had been trained in Valdemar by none less than the wicked hand of Darkwind himself.

Who wouldn't be interested?

That first night, Maizy had examined Nwah closely. She admired how the wolflike form of the animal's head and shoulders merged with the lithe, feline frame of her body. She marveled at the kyree's strong jawline. She loved how Nwah's pelt took a soft fluff after being cleaned. It felt so plush against her palm.

When clean, the kyree smelled of a faint, loamy confidence that Maizy could not describe beyond how it made her feel.

As the nights passed, Nwah shared other thoughts through that startling Mindspeech, a form of communication more intimate to Maizy than any other.

The kyree, Maizy had decided, was strong of heart and clear of thought.

Between the cracks of their conversations, Maizy had begun to see things differently. She didn't doubt Nwah had information the baron coveted, but tonight, for the first time, Maizy was questioning the baron's methods. And—as dangerous as such could be—if even his descriptions of Valdemar were proper to begin with.

:Your baron is a bad man.:

Over those words came those of Baron Haffti: "*Hardorn is for Hardornens.*"

Though the baron's views were at odds with those of Hardorn's current leaders in Shonar, he remained adamant in his stances. Ancar, he said—though reviled by many—had been right. The usurpers from the east were illegitimate. The victorious but degenerate reprobates of Valdemar had unjustly destroyed Ancar's reputation. The raiders who occupied Hardorn today were savage, ruthless animals—evil people capable of the foulest deeds humans can perform.

The days of Ancar's ascendency would return, Baron Haffti said, and when they did, the baron and his people would be there to take control.

Maizy believed it, too. As did the others. Why would they not?

So committed to this stance were the baron and his loyal gathering that rumors within the servants' hall said they had already created plans to return power to Crown City when the time grew right.

But . . .

Nwah did not seem violent. She did not seem depraved, nor did she seem inclined to scheme against the barony. When Nwah spoke of her companions, they did not sound manic or fiendish. Instead, using her Mindspeech so warmly that Maizy couldn't help but feel her closeness, Nwah spoke of Kade, her lifebond. She told stories about how she had traveled to her new pack in the woods to the north, and about Darkwind, who escorted her without a second thought. She said he was a kind if moody mentor. His sense of humor was surprisingly dark and deftly wielded.

Last night, Nwah had told of her admiration for Maakdal, the pack leader she had traveled so far to join. Though the two remained apart due to aspects of the pack's expectations, Maizy could tell Maakdal loved Nwah as much as Nwah loved him in return. It was only a matter of time before they gave in to each other.

The allure of that romance filled Maizy's mind.

She wanted it to be true.

"Maakdal would come if he knew she was here," she said to the empty evening.

Maizy admired the kyree's ability to put herself into others' thoughts. She wished she could do that. It would be good to calm animals when they were fearful, so useful to communicate in ways that went beyond tone of voice or soft but firm touches.

Maybe Nwah could teach her?

This new yearning was something different in Maizy, too.

She had never been interested in a life beyond the stable—not even service inside the manor. Though young enough to marry, the idea of a husband seemed foreign. Better to work with animals, whom she found easier to understand than men. Or women, for that matter.

Her discussions with Nwah had ignited new sensations in her, though.

In quiet moments, she had begun to wonder what it might be like to live outside the borders of Lord Haffti's manor. Found herself imagining what it might be like to have a spirited presence as strong as Maakdal's to build her life around. The vision of a life lived in the wild stretched her heart in ways uncomfortably painful.

Examining the dirt-lined rings of her fingernails, however,

reminded her she had no such talents and no such romance. Maizy might well be the best stable worker in the manor, but she was nothing more than that.

She pulled her threadbare jacket collar tight against her throat, thinking of her sister, Prim, and their mother, huddled together in their tiny nook of the servants' hall. Winter was still a month away, but the gusting wind made the stable's rafters rattle and pop. Across the stalls, one of the baron's finest horses nickered anxiously.

Still finding no movement at the baron's door, she glanced at the padlock that hung in the latch, gleaming, open, and catty-wampus.

It was her job to ensure the gleaming lock was set each night as she left.

The iron brace reminded her of the baron's sorcerer, who had placed his magic on this stall before Nwah arrived. She asked what the casting did, but the sorcerer grunted dismissively. "You'll pay it no mind, girl."

It was another stable hand who had later explained that the casting damped the effect of certain magics in the area, hence deadening it to scrying so others would not find Nwah once she was here.

Staring hard at the lock, Maizy felt nothing different in the stall.

Another reminder of her lack of anything resembling a Gift.

Annoyed, she wondered if the baron had decided to keep Nwah inside tonight, and simply forgot to inform her of the change.

At that thought, the manor door clapped open, and the laboring clatter of bootheels rang out on the flagstone path.

Maizy pressed nervous palms down her pant legs.

A pair of guards grunted and strained with the weight of Nwah's body, which lay across the stretcher they bore. When the baron's men arrived at the stall, Maizy saw Nwah was, again, muzzled and magicked into a deep sleep. She lay on her side, reeking of blood and the harsh, smoke-touched remnants of the sorcerer's spellwork. Her front and back paws jutted from the stretcher like turkey legs off a plate. Her tail, dark and matted, fell limp as rope down the stretcher's back edge.

The men staggered into the bay, then dropped the kyree hard onto the floor, raising thin curls of dust and dirt. Nwah's only movement was the rise of her solar plexus as she slept.

"Same time tomorrow," the bearded man commanded, standing taller and grimacing to stretch his back.

Maizy suppressed a wry grin.

Nwah had not broken.

"I'll have her ready," she replied.

The men returned to the mansion house, their boots hammering the hard walkway, their complaints and conversations fading into the autumn nighttime until the doors shut behind them.

Alone again, Maizy turned to her work.

"Good evening to you, Nwah," she cooed. She placed her hand on the kyree's brow, hoping her simple touch would relieve pain.

The fur along Nwah's wolflike jawline seemed to relax.

Using clean cloths and water warmed by the lamp, she cleaned the kyree, humming gently as she worked, taking care to rinse the dirt and soot from the roots of Nwah's pelt while addressing her wounds. Rot grew in untended places. Letting gangrene take hold would bring beatings.

She massaged Nwah as she worked, knowing contact brought blood to the surface, and that blood brought its own form of healing. She spread ointments into wounds, then wrapped them in firmly placed bandages.

Nwah's body radiated warmth.

Her solid muscles were firm in the way of animals who lived on the land.

When Maizy finished grooming Nwah, she grunted with satisfaction.

The kyree's fur glowed in the dim light. Her wounds were salved and bound. Though her eyes remained closed, movement rippled the thin sheaths of her lids to let Maizy know she was conscious.

:Thank you.: Nwah's voice came through as Maizy washed the remnants of the apothecary's oils from her hands. The kyree was weary. *:I enjoyed your music. You have a lovely tone.:*

Maizy blushed. Her humming was mostly involuntary.

"I'm sorry they hurt you."

:Their harms are not your doing.:

Maisy shrugged, but couldn't make herself feel that was right. Nwah opened her eyes and turned her wide gaze onto Maizy. A disquieting sense of assessment came over her.

"Are you well?" Maizy said. "Can I get you water?"

:You remind me of someone.:

Maizy smiled hesitantly. "Who would that be?"

: She was good with medicines, too. Her name was Winnie. For a time she was interested in pairing with my lifebond.:

"Kade?" Maizy said. "The Herald."

:Yes. Which is why it didn't work out.:

Maizy nodded. Heralds were elite members of society. They required equally elite pairings. "It is not done," she said in a knowing tone.

:It is done, but it can make things hard.:

The answer confused Maizy. Matches between Heralds and those without Gifts? She wanted to ask how that could work but, didn't know what to say. Instead, she sat at Nwah's side.

"Tell me about her, then?"

Winnie was the daughter of a sheriff in Oris—a city not far away to the east and south. Nwah and Kade had visited because it was the home city of another human to whom Nwah had been lifebonded before Kade. Winnie had wanted to be a Healer—like Kade. She took a fancy to him, but like Maizy, had no Gift. She could nurse, but she could not Heal. She had followed Kade and Nwah back to Haven, but eventually, after Kade was Chosen, left the city to return to Oris.

:Your demeanor reminds me of her,: Nwah finished with a calm sigh. The kyree rolled onto her stomach, then tenderly groomed a forepaw. Her tongue was pink and feline in its roughness.

A sense of admiration came over Maizy. "I can't imagine leaving her manor like that. Traveling that distance."

Nwah chuffed.

"What?"

:*Kade and I came from the Pelagirs before that.*:

"You were not born of Valdemar?"

:*We were not.*:

A frown crossed Maizy's face.

If Nwah wasn't born of Valdemar, how could her blood be tainted as the baron's enemy?

"Well," she said, "I could never leave home." When Maizy felt disagreement in Nwah's gaze, she added, "I couldn't leave my mother and sister behind."

Nwah cocked her head. :*Den mates need to live their own lives, too.*:

Maizy hesitated, feeling the weight of discussing a future that couldn't happen. Talking about it made the option seem possible. "The baron does not take kindly to defectors. If I left, he would make their lives horrible."

:*I understand.*:

"I need to go now," Maizy said, still feeling Nwah's judgment.

:*Sleep well,*: Nwah said.

Maizy smiled. "You, too."

In her bed of straw, Nwah closed her eyes.

Maizy left, closing the door, and setting the lock in place with a solid clank.

When the baron's men came the next evening, Maizy met them at Nwah's stall.

The sun had not set, and the stables still bustled with activity.

She stood before the locked stall and peered at the guardsmen who held the stretcher between them. The nearby sorcerer glared daggers at her unexpected presence.

"Please inform the baron the kyree's wounds have not yet closed," Maizy said, fear edging into her chest. "She is not ready for another interrogation."

"Then it's a good thing you are not the judge of her readiness," the bearded guard said.

The younger guard presented the key, but Maizy stepped before him.

"Be careful of your belligerence, young stable hand." The sorcerer's expression was something between a smirk and a sneer.

"The baron tasked me to help her recover," Maizy said.

"Do not twist words. The baron said only that you were to keep her alive."

Maizy's jaw gaped, then shut. The sorcerer was correct. Baron Haffti had expressly used the phrase "keep the kyree alive," but, like other things, Maizy had changed it in her mind.

"I see," she replied.

And this time she did see. Or, rather, she felt.

She stepped back.

The sorcerer chanted the magics that made Nwah into their docile prisoner. Then the guard opened the lock, and the two pushed the kyree's dead weight onto the stretcher.

Maizy watched them cart the defenseless animal away— Nwah's pink tongue lolling to one side. As their boot steps faded, the clamoring din of stable work returned, accompanied by a sense of unease she could not deny.

:Your baron is a bad man.:

Maizy pressed her lips together, knowing she had to do something.

By the time she finished tending Nwah that night, Maizy had decided what that something was.

She wrapped the rags she'd used to tend Nwah into a packet that felt as tight as the ball of anxiety filling her throat now. She placed the wad into a burlap sack she looped around her belt.

Maizy closed the stall door and latched the lock.

Then, rather than return to the servants' hall, she slipped into the darkness of the north woods.

A tenuous fear rose as she picked a path through trunks and under the shadowed canopy of trees that were nearing readiness to drop their dry leaves. Moments later she felt a new strength rise inside her, though. The woods seemed to be alive, filled with a vivid cacophony of sounds.

Night scavengers scurried through the underbrush.

Breeze rasped through the leaves.

She stopped often to listen intently, her breathing coming hard as she tried not to imagine predators looming in every cave, or around every copse—a wildcat or bear, or worse, one of the dangerous brigands who roamed the wild. At each stop, though, she also experienced a sense of excitement.

She was here. In these vibrant woods. Doing something.

Stopping so often was a problem, though.

Offhand comments from the guards said Maakdal's pack would be about two hours north. Two hours back gave her little leeway to return in time for morning feeding and shoe checks. She noted the moon's position and remembered her mother's lessons on how to judge time by its movement across the sky— one span per hour.

Pressing the package of wrapped cloth against her thigh, she pushed on, trying to conjure the same strength as the girl named Winnie, and thinking about Kade and Nwah as they crossed the roads from the Pelagirs to Oris.

Her thoughts made her feel like she had companions.

As her vision adjusted, the moonlight tinted the bramble with a silver glow she found quite lovely. The air grew sharper with the smells of damp wood and peat moss. Each of her steps in the crackling undergrowth made her feel like she was a part of the world in ways she hadn't felt before.

Her spirits buoyed.

Two moon spans later, Maizy reached a clearing the size of the baron's corral.

She was out of time. She needed to turn back.

Fatigued from her intense focus, and filled with anguish at not having met Maakdal's pack, Maizy lifted the sack of Nwah's bandages, knowing they held her scent, but now despondent she wasn't going to be able to use them.

She pulled open the sack and considered leaving a trail for Maakdal to follow.

There weren't enough rags, though.

She would never be able to leave a trail to the baron's manor this way. Over several nights, maybe?

Maizy laughed at that. Her legs ached from the hike, and her breathing felt heavy. Her thoughts dragged, too, her brain so muddled she was losing track of things. Another night without sleep would put her under.

She hefted the rags. Maybe simply indicating a direction would be enough?

If he came across Nwah's scent, would Maakdal follow their path even after that path faded?

A gruff snarl came from the clearing ahead of her.

Then again, low and rough, accompanied by a thick form that loomed in the shadowed woods.

Maizy froze.

"Maakdal?"

At her voice, the beast lumbered forward, cautiously at first, then growing swifter. She clenched her jaw and held out the sack of wadded cloth, but something felt wrong. Maakdal should move with more grace than power, and this animal was the opposite.

It breached the clearing, and moonlight glinted off its rounded pelt and exposed fangs.

It was a bear, not a kyree. Huge and muscular, it ran at full pace now.

Maizy dropped the sack and turned to flee.

The pounding of the bear's rambling gait ripped through the open grasses, its weight thundering against the ground. The heat of the beast's enormous size seemed to burn behind her as she ran. Knowing she could neither outrun it nor best it, Maizy yelled wildly. Her eyes searched for a tree to climb.

The bear roared. Its huge forepaws piled into her shoulders, sending her flying forward to impact the ground so hard her breath left her body.

The bear advanced on her, smelling warm and rancid, its pelt matted with bramble and grasses.

Despite panic that came from starving for breath, Maizy scrabbled backward. Her eyes teared as she gasped for air. The movement helped a single breath come with a mix of stabbing pain and blissful relief.

The bear grunted.

She kicked at it.

A sudden flash of moonlight on pelt flared behind the bear, as, with a ferocious growl, a second animal leaped into the fray.

Teeth flashed. Foreclaws slashed.

The bear rolled to avoid the new attacker.

The second animal landed lithely amid the gnarled roots of a tree.

Maizy felt a third presence in the woods then, and another, then more outlines that moved with silent confidence.

She recognized their profiles.

Maakdal!

The kyree was huge and muscled. His forepaws extended to reveal sharp, wickedly curved talons. He braced into a hard posture in the moonlight, bared his teeth, then growled.

Unable to control the fear and relief surging inside her, Maizy burst out crying.

She managed to roll to her feet, and with a deep, gasping breath, grasped a fallen branch as she stood.

The bear turned its attention on Maakdal.

It lunged, but Maakdal was too fast for it.

A second kyree launched from one side. The bear swiped a massive paw to send the yelping creature flying.

Others closed in, and the bear halted in a posture Maizy read as contemplative.

With a resigned grunt, it stepped backward, then sideways, peering at Maakdal.

The pack leader gave a final, guttural growl, and the bear turned and rumbled back through the woods.

Maakdal stood taller, his breath coming as ragged as hers.

Maizy stepped instinctively to where the second kyree had

managed to sit up against the tree trunk. It was panting, obviously in pain. As she drew closer, Maizy heard the rest of the pack move to surround her.

Heart pounding, she stood an arm's distance from the wounded kyree.

It was important that the animals felt commitment from her, even when she felt fear.

"Thank you for your help, kyree. It was very brave of you. I don't know your name, but I can help you if you would let me try."

:Your bag carries the scent of Nwah.:

Though she'd never heard the voice before, she instantly knew it was Maakdal's.

She turned to him. "I have news of her. But I would provide aid to your packmate first if she will have it."

:You are a Healer?:

"Alas, only a well-meaning soul. But I am good with small comforts."

The injured kyree whined low.

:Her name is Bree,: Maakdal said.

"Thank you," she replied. Calmer now, Maizy knelt to examine the kyree.

Bree was small, certainly young. The bear had gouged her shoulder, which was bleeding, but not profusely. She seemed unable to put any pressure on that leg, though, and that would be a problem.

Maizy ran her fingertips over the shoulder blade and down the leg. Either the bear's battering or the fall against the roots had pulled it from its joint.

She had dealt with this before, after one of the baron's calves had fallen. "This is going to hurt," she said to Bree. "But if I do it well, you should feel better soon."

She turned to Maakdal. "Did she understand?"

:Yes. Proceed.:

She took hold of the leg just below the joint, then braced her other hand above the shoulder.

Bree yipped as the joint slid back into place.

"All right, little lady. I'm going to move you into the moon-glow where I can see you well enough to clean that wound."

Bree huffed and put her muzzle on Maizy's shoulder.

Maizy lifted her.

"Can you bring me the sack of rags?" she said to Maakdal.

Then she got to work.

Later, Maizy joined Maakdal in the clearing.

The kyree stood firmly, his pelt darker than even the shadows. His eyes glowed with golden flashes against the wooded back-ground. The sound of his breathing came from somewhere deep and primal. The sight of him, strong and proud in the open space of the wild, laid further truth to the depth behind Nwah's words.

Maizy had been wrong. She had listened to the baron, and she had been wrong.

:*Speak,*: Maakdal said, wielding his Mindspeech like a sledge.

"Nwah is . . ." Maizy said. She should have practiced something. ". . . as well as she can be, given her situation."

:*I have no patience for double talk.*:

"I'm sorry. I'm nervous." She paused. "My name is Maizy. My baron is holding Nwah. He thinks she has information regarding Valdemar. She is still alive, but he is . . . not being kind."

:*How do you know this?*:

"I have tended her wounds each night since her capture. Hence the bandages."

The leader's stare sharpened, and the fur on his collar bris-tled. :*She will not break from her friends,*: Maakdal replied with a gruff rumble.

"I know that now. She is very strong."

:*Where is she?*:

"I can show you. And I can help retrieve her. But I want your help, too."

:*My pack does not bargain in these matters.*:

"I'm not attempting to bargain. I'm asking a boon."

:*What do you ask?*:

"I want to leave the manor, but my leaving would be a risk to my family. I want to take my mother and sister with me."

:Can they travel on foot?:

"They can walk."

As Maakdal contemplated, the call of insects rose over the woods.

To her left, a kyree yipped, causing her to start.

Then another behind her. And another, and another, until the entire pack clamored in the darkness.

In the past, hearing such sounds in the distance had made her shiver, but here, in the silver-toned lighting of the woods—each voice rising, each blending into the mix, each a member of the society in ways that felt familiar, yet so distant—she felt the pack's power as she hadn't before.

The hair on her arms rose.

Then the pack went silent.

Maakdal stepped forward. *:I give our word. Help us retrieve Nwah, and we will escort the three of you.:*

Maizy's chest filled with a newfound joy.

Maakdal had presented the idea to them, she realized. The response gave her another sense of strength. It was all she could do to keep from crying again.

"I am honored."

:So where is Nwah?:

"I have a plan," Maizy said.

The next night, physically dead on her feet, but so filled with anxiety she might burst, Maizy whispered directions into Nwah's ear.

This time, as she left the stall, Maizy left the lock unlatched.

Keeping her pace in check, she returned to the servants' hall as she always did, but now, rather than fall exhausted into her straw, she gathered her sister to her.

"Come," she said, explaining everything. "We have to go."

Together, they addressed their mother.

"I'm not leaving the manor," she said firmly.

"If you don't come with us, the baron will make you suffer."

"I don't care, Maizy. If the baron takes his frustrations out on me, I will bear it."

"But—"

"I will not leave my home."

"Please come," Prim begged.

"No," Mother replied, eyes pleading. "You should stay."

"I can't," Maizy said.

"So you'll ruin your life and Prim's, too?"

"She's not ruining my life, Mother," Prim whispered, tucking the tail of a shirt into her trousers to prepare. "Everyone knows what Maizy says about the baron is true, even if nobody says it."

An iron cast came over their mother's face. "I should scream now. That's what a good mother would do."

"No, Mother," Prim said. "That's what a mother who *wanted* her daughters' lives ruined would do . . . and you are not that mother."

"We'll come back for you if we can," Maizy said, saying her goodbyes.

Then they were gone.

As they left the hall, Maizy tossed a bag of bandages into the manor yard.

Noting the sign, Maakdal's pack struck, yipping and braying, causing commotion to the south and west, tipping over water barrels, and bringing other animals to their unique forms of ruckus.

As guards dealt with the distraction, Prim and Maizy made it back to the stalls and helped a fragile Nwah onto a thick blanket. A moment later, each supporting one end, they dragged Nwah out of the stables and across the open corral. Maakdal's commotion had died by the time they made the woods, but it was enough. Maizy had latched the lock this time. No one would realize Nwah was gone until the morning. Getting her through the underbrush in her injured state would be tough, but properly escorted, they would make it.

:*Thank you,*: Nwah said as they pulled her farther into the woods.

Prim's gaze swung to Nwah, and her expression beamed with delighted surprise.

Maizy laughed. She would enjoy watching her sister grow up.

"No," she replied. "I need to thank you. You've given me a new path. That's a gift far greater than I could have imagined."

Nwah chuffed at that. *:Where will you go?:*

"I understand there's a courageous young woman in Oris I might be able to learn from."

:Yes,: Nwah said. *:I think you may find a compatriot there.:*

"I hope so. Either way, it's time we expose the baron for what he is."

Nwah's answering huff felt warm and generous. *:That would certainly be a fine gift.:*

Maizy smiled, dead tired, but filled with determination. She thought about her mother and her other friends, still under the baron's thrall, then she looked at Prim. Addressing the baron would be a dangerous, difficult fight, but she felt the sense of rightness that came with the idea.

"I can live with that," she said.

She hefted the makeshift stretcher again, working with her sister to pull Nwah to safety.

Warp and Weft
Diana Paxson

Deira hooked the end of the warp thread around the last peg at the base of the weaving frame, pulled it taut, and looped it around the string to knot the end. The thread was medium-weight bleached linen, as white as a Companion's coat, but when she had finished spinning the skein, she had given it a random mottling by twisting, knotting, and swirling it through a dye bath of her favorite blue.

Blue for her, and white for Andry.

Strung across the frame, the threads suggested the dappling of sunlight on a lake. Deira had considered warping the loom in alternating bands of blue and white to symbolize equality in marriage, but she suspected that whatever their union brought them, it would be nothing so predictable.

She looked around what had once been a warehouse, half workroom, half living space, where a table covered with the books and papers for the accelerated classes that were boosting Andry through Herald training bore witness that she no longer lived here alone. He had a room in the Collegium, but her lodgings were home. Racks with yarn in various stages of preparation lent color, and a kettle of stew simmering above the hearth sent a welcoming aroma through the room.

In the first delirious moments after Andry had been Chosen by Lochren, Deira had relinquished him to the Heralds, abandoning the dreams of returning to his farm they had so briefly shared. But despite the support he drew from his Companion, Andry, coming to this new identity in his forties, still seemed to need her as well. She set her hand on the weaving frame. Her own certainty was in her craft. On the other side of the room, the narrow-frame loom on which she would weave Andry's scarf leaned against the wall. The one she was warping now, wider, was for her wedding shawl.

In Westerbridge, where she was born, it had been the custom for a bride to weave matching scarf and shawl. Deira had never even been betrothed, though for a few ecstatic weeks she had been the lover of Herald Aldren. He had meant to come back for her, but by the time he could return, Westerbridge was ashes and she and their child refugees. Aldren was dead now, like Andry's wife and the children she had borne him, while Deira's own daughter, Selaine, would graduate from the Healer's Collegium soon. Deira had no need to prove her fitness for marriage by showing off her skill. Her work hung on the walls or covered the floors of half the highborns in Haven. Scarf and shawl were an affirmation that both she and Andry could start anew.

And as if her thought had summoned them, she sensed Andry and Lochren were near, the awareness diminishing as the Companion settled into his comfortable box stall in the stable next door. She cast a quick look in the mirror and smoothed back her still (mostly) dark gold hair, knowing that in a few moments she would hear Andry's step on the stair.

"Something has happened!" she exclaimed as he came in. His gray tunic was unlaced at the neck, and perspiration sheened his brow. "Are you all right?"

Andry paused, and as always when he stopped to look at her, there suddenly seemed to be more light in the room.

She had found him attractive when they had met the year before, his muscles strong from outdoor work, and only a few strands of silver in his dark hair. The weapons-work that was part of Heraldic training had broadened his shoulders and given a balanced grace to his stride.

"Yes—maybe—I don't quite know. I just got out of an unexpected meeting with Elcarth and Talamir."

She tensed, looking up at him. "But you did well in the last examinations, you told me so—"

"It wasn't about my work." He swallowed. "They've received a letter from home."

For a moment she did not understand.

"From Denorsdale," he added. "When Herald Galen was on his last Circuit, he met one of my neighbors at the market in Thornton, and told him I am a trainee here. There's some problem about my farm."

"Who wrote the letter?" she asked, reaching for a cup and the pitcher of cold tea.

"It was signed by my neighbor, Valdon Wiganson. He didn't tell Galen what the problem is. I was stunned to learn he's still alive. I thought the bandits would keep coming back until they killed everyone. It's not an offer to buy the farm. He just says my presence is needed there."

"What are they like, these people of yours?"

"Sturdy, stubborn, linked to the land."

"Like you." She smiled.

"I suppose so. All of us are related in some way to old Denor, who built a cabin up by the spring back in King Restil's day."

"Can't you just send a letter back?" she said, her gaze going to the weaving frame. The end of the summer break was when they were planning the wedding.

"Elcarth says I should resolve any issues from my former life before taking on the responsibilities of a Herald. I didn't know there was anything left of my old life . . ." The kitchen chair creaked as he sat down. "They said I should go. The Midsummer holiday is coming, so I won't miss too many classes."

"I suspect," she said slowly, "they want to make sure that it *is* your *former* life. What does Lochren say?"

Andry sighed. "Lochren wants to go . . ."

"Why am I not surprised?" Deira poured tea into the mug and pressed it into his hand. "What do *you* want to do?"

"That life is *over!*" Andry exclaimed. "It was over when I found a place with the Gold Grass Valley Rangers! And *that* life was over when they packed me into a wagon and carted what the fighting had left of me to the hospital here. *That* life ended when I met you, and then I was Chosen, and another life began. How many lives do I have to lose before I can settle down?"

Deira sighed. From the stories told by the Heraldic, Healer, and Bardic Trainees that gathered around her dining room table every Seventh-Day, stability was not a notable characteristic of a Herald's career. Especially not now, when every wagonload coming up from the border might bear what was left of one of those bright young boys or girls. She had accepted that once Andry completed his training he would be under orders, with no choice regarding what parts of his life he could share. And she would be alone with her looms, wondering when, or if, he would return.

But he was not a Herald yet.

Unbidden, words came. "I want to come with you—"

"What?" Tea sloshed as he set the mug down.

Deira grabbed a napkin and made a show of swabbing up the spill, avoiding his gaze. "When you put on your Whites, you will often be away with the army, or riding Circuit if peace ever comes again," she spoke with careful calm. "This journey might be my only chance to learn a little about your past, and what a lot of your future will be."

"But the danger—" he began.

"Right now the fighting is to the west, well away from the Jay Song Hills. What you didn't learn about fighting when you were with the Gold Grass Rangers, Alberich has beaten into you," she said bracingly. "You and Lochren should certainly be able to handle any bandits still skulking around there. There's a tradition of sending a new couple on a bridal trip, is that not so?"

"After the wedding," he observed dryly.

"The wedding is only a formality." Deira glanced at the weaving frames, the blue and white warping threads waiting hopefully for the weft that would fill them with meaning. "If our love can survive three weeks of travel out and another three back with who knows what challenges in between, we'll hardly need a ceremony!"

"And if we return, the Heralds will know if it's possible to turn a forty-year-old farmer into a proper Herald . . ." Andry said grimly. "Do you *really* want to do this?"

She was about to say "of course," when it occurred to her that Andry was not the only one whose approval was required. "What does Lochren say?" she said then, and waited as his gaze went distant. After a few moments, his focus returned.

"My Companion—" his tone held resignation, "—thinks it will be *fun.*"

By the time Deira and Andry started down the Southern Trade Road, he on Lochren, she on a placid piebald mare with an equally somnolent packhorse bobbing along behind, it seemed as if half the Collegium had expressed an opinion. Loudest was Deira's own daughter, who was not enjoying having to worry about her mother as Deira had worried about her. Lying awake at night, Deira could admit the truth of Selaine's arguments, but by now, making the journey had become a matter of pride.

Constrained to the plodding pace of the two horses, they had plenty of time to appreciate the well-tilled countryside south of Haven. From time to time, other travelers passed them, all going the other way. The weather was getting warmer. Now low hills varied the landscape, with clumps of wilder country between the farms. Beneath the haze on the southeastern horizon, she could see the darker blur of the mountain range they called the Comb. That way led to Evenleigh, her former home.

That way led to the war.

A week and a half of travel brought them to the bridge at Daryville, where they crossed to the eastern side of the Terilee. That night, they lodged at one of the Waystations about which her daughter's friends among the Heraldic trainees had told so many tales.

Wincing, Deira sank back on the mattress in the bed box, whose hard stuffing of straw Andry had tried to cushion with a layer of ripened meadow grass. This Waystation was one of the better built ones, but she thought longingly of that last hot bath at the inn at Daryville. Through the open door she glimpsed the pale shape of Andry's Companion, who was enjoying the cooler air outside.

"Still hurting?" Andry murmured, arranging the sticks on the hearth so they burned most strongly beneath the pot he was heating soup in. "It takes a while. I still have scars from the saddle sores I got when I joined the Rangers." He ran a hand along the inner seam of his breeches, eyebrow lifting as if waiting for her to ask him to take them off so that she could see. That the image stirred barely a flicker of interest was a measure of her fatigue. If Andry had been looking forward to a romantic interlude, he must be disappointed.

Was he, too, wondering why she had come?

"I believe you." She sighed. Fortunately Selaine, once convinced that no pleading would make her mother abandon the journey, had provided her with Healer-approved padded tights to go with the padded saddle the Heralds had found for her quiet cob. It was her aching back that tormented her now. "If you can't distract me in a way that we would *both* enjoy," she said tartly, "tell me more about Denorsdale . . ."

"Valdon Wiganson is my nearest neighbor. His land begins at the outcrop beside my house." He stopped, smile fading. "Where my house used to be. I meant to repair the roof after harvest. Don't suppose there's much left of it now." He pushed the chunks of wood that still smoldered to the back and scraped ashes forward over the hearthstone and began to build up a landscape out of dead charcoal and half-burned branches. "Denorsdale's more a canyon than a valley. Ground rises to cliffs on either side. There's five holdings, set t'either side of the stream, with the land below the cliffs divided into barley field and pasture. My land is across from the spring at the head of the canyon, on the western side. Valdon's below me, and since he wrote the letter, I guess he's still alive. Reval Ormundson's farm is beyond him." His gaze went inward, angular features easing as he brought up memories. "Old Nannie, Ormund's widow, lived by the road. She kept bees and a garden."

"Sounds as if Ormund was the biggest landowner. Is his house the largest as well, and if so, why was Nannie living by herself in a hut by the road?"

"Ah, well, she was Ormund's second wife, ye see, so Reval got the greathouse and lives there with his wife Kima and their brood. Or did. They was breeding like rabbits, so some must have survived."

"But it was Valdon who wrote to the Collegium. Who lives across from him?"

"That's Bestry. He has—had—the only stretch of land on that side big enough to farm, but 'tis on the dry side of the dale. Beyond it, there's another outcrop what comes all the way down t' the road."

Deira noted with amusement that Andry's country accent, worn thin by years in Haven, was returning as he talked about his home.

"And the land at the top, across from you?"

"Too small to support a family, and mostly rocks. There's a hut, though, beneath the wooltrees, for them that come t' make offerings at the spring."

"Trees that grow wool?" she raised her brows. "I thought you had sheep for that."

Andry laughed. "When the seed pods pop, the air's full of fluff that floats on the wind. In a good year, it piles up in drifts like snow. I hated pickin' out the seeds, but the cloth my mother made from it was fine as bleached linen." He glanced at Deira and laughed. "What? Ye look like Lochren when he sees me eatin' a pocket pie."

"I could spin it . . ." she said slowly, ignoring the snort from outside. "If enough fluff could be gathered, I could spin it and set a fashion. Children could collect it and sell it to the traders."

Andry nodded thoughtfully. "'Tis an idea. When the war's over, an' the roads secure . . . People ought to welcome anything that'll bring a little money to these hills. Those that's left." He shook his head with a sigh. "I wish Valdon's letter had included more of the local news."

* * *

They slept two more nights at Waystations, then turned east toward the border with Hardorn, following a track that wound upward through hills where sandstone outcrops striped in bands of russet and cream poked through the red clay soil. The air held a dry heat that sucked moisture from the skin. The grass here had already ripened, and patches of brush furred the higher ground, with an occasional tree whose spiny needles gave off an aromatic scent when they laid a branch on the fire.

Wheel ruts showed that this road was still in use, but the occasional horse droppings were several weeks old. Where the ground flattened, they glimpsed an occasional building and the regular shape of a planted field, but the only house near the road was a burnt-out shell. There were not even any Waystations, only a campsite where water seeped from between two boulders to create a small pool. Andry showed her the Heraldic sigil scratched into the rock above it that told them the water was good, and they made their bed beneath the stars. In the morning they filled their bags brim full, for at the top of the ridge they were climbing there was no water at all.

As they journeyed, Andry had grown silent. That night, she held him, feeling the tremors that shook his lean frame. Lochren was awake as well, his white coat seeming to reflect the starlight as he stood, head raised to scent the wind. *Everyone said the bond with a Companion met all his Chosen's emotional needs, but maybe,* she thought, *the times Andry needs me are not when he's being a Herald, but when he's only a man.*

"We are close, aren't we?" She felt his grip tighten.

"We'll be there by tomorrow's sunset. This is the last ridge. Denorsdale lies at the bottom of this hill."

"Goddess preserve us, 'tis Master Andry himself, thin as a whip an' ridin'—" the old woman's voice cracked as her gaze slid across Deira and the packhorse and focused on Lochren, who had posed as if on parade, neck arched and tail high. "'Twas true, then, what that Herald said, not just old Valdon tryin' t' cheer us wi' tales."

This must be Nannie, Deira thought. The old woman stood in the garden, talking to a boy who was thinning young carrots there. There were scorch marks on the wooden fence, but the cottage was of fieldstone, and the roof was tiled. It would be hard to burn. Beyond the vegetable garden, she could see flowers.

"I've yet to finish my training," came Andry's quick response. The further they traveled into the countryside, the harder it had seemed for people to distinguish between his faded gray trainee uniform and the grubby Whites of a Herald long in the field. "This is my Companion, Lochren."

Nannie's eyes widened as Lochren favored her with a regal nod. She bobbed a sort of curtsy in reply.

It was curiously peaceful here. The stream that came down through the canyon freshened the air and lent its music to the humming of insects in the garden. The Jay Song Hills had their own arid beauty. She was beginning to understand how Andry could love this land.

"Sir, ye be most welcome!" Nannie's gaze moved on to Deira. "An' this be yer good lady, aye?"

Heralds did not lie. "This is Deira, and my lady she will always be . . ."

Deira blinked, realizing he had neatly avoided admitting they were not yet wed, and returned his smile.

Nannie nodded, then gestured at the small boy. "Barni! Take up them young carrots ye plucked and giv'em to Master Lochren. Then git yerself up the road an' tell yer da that Andry's come home!"

"We are very glad to see you," said Deira, since Andry sat silent, looking back and forth—*drinking in*—the land. "Andry feared you'd all been killed."

"Some were," the old woman said grimly. "After ye left, them reivers came again, burnt Bestry in his house. His brother came last year, and is buildin' it up again. Two o' Reval's sons got killed. But we ha'nt seen hide nor hair o' the bandits for nigh on a year now, only refugees . . ." She glanced sideways at Andry.

"And my place? Is the house still standing?" he asked.

"Oh yes," said Nannie, "they fixed it up."

"They?" Andry's face became very still.

The old woman's wrinkled cheeks creased in a grimace. "The refugees . . ."

Long ago, when the climate here had been wetter, periodic floods had filled this rift in the hills with soil. The crops that needed water were planted on the flats near the stream, shaded here and there by wooltrees. Beyond them, the land sloped upward in rocky pastures, giving way to low cliffs in whose crevices bushes grew.

As they traveled up the little valley, Deira and Andry passed Reval's house with its long porch, but no one was in the fields. On the right, they could see the unfinished skeleton of Bestry's. Recalling the map Andry had made on the Waystation hearth, Valdon's should be the house they were coming to now.

Lochren halted, head up, ears swiveling forward as the door opened and people streamed into the road. Andry stood in the stirrups, shading his eyes with his hand. They shouted his name, but he was looking past Valdon's farm at the whitewashed house on the next hill.

"It's Andry!" they cried. "Look, he's riding a Companion! The Herald spoke true!"

The crowd surged around them, recoiling as Lochren stamped, ears flattened in warning. Deira's pony shied, and by the time she had wrestled it back under control, mothers had snatched up their children and the older folk were gathering in front of the Companion, who looked down his nose at them and whisked his tail.

"Andry, 'tis grand t' see ye!" A tall man in a frieze coat who must have been Valdon pushed through the crowd. He reached for Lochren's rein, thought better of it as the Companion showed his teeth, and stepped back again. "We heard ye'd gone to the wars and thought ye dead. Yer adventures have clearly done ye no harm—" He paused, but Andry was staring up the road. "And then, Lady be praised, th' boy comes runnin' to say yer here with yer wife and all . . ."

As his words trailed off, Andry finally turned. "There's smoke coming from my chimney," he said in a still voice that somehow made all the others quiet down as well.

"Aye, well, that's the other reason I wrote the letter," said Valdon. "We need a Herald. There's strangers settin' up there. Squatters. We didn't know what t' do."

Andry shook his head. Deira did not need Mindspeech to know what he was thinking, but acting like a Herald might be the only way to solve the problem here.

"Who are they?"

"Call themselves Wellerans, from Kleimar," growled a heavyset older man who must have been Reval.

"How many of them are there?"

"Too many," muttered one of the other men. She thought it was the Bestry brother.

"There's a man and woman and their children, ranging from littles to a girl who's near grown," said a young man with broad shoulders and waving dark hair who looked like a younger version of Valdon.

"A nest of vermin," muttered someone behind him.

Deira closed her eyes. She herself had once been a refugee. It went hard to think these people might be forced to take to the road once more, but with the neighborhood set against them, they could not survive here.

"We were meeting to discuss some action, but with you here, our path is clear—" Valdon said briskly. "Everyone get ready. Tomorrow we'll deal with this once and for all." He turned back to Andry. "Come up to the house an' settle in. My younger boys can sleep in the barn."

Deira shook her head. "Children need their own beds. The weather is fair, and we have our camping gear."

"Is that hut up by the spring still there?" Andry asked suddenly.

The young man shrugged. "Nothin' t' loot. There's been no pilgrims since the wars began. Not much left of it though," he added. "No pilgrims, no repairs."

"Nonetheless, that's where we'll sleep."

"That's settled, then," said Valdon. "My son Marl will take yer—mounts," he corrected quickly, meeting Lochren's eye, "to water. You come on up to the house with me."

"If there's a field where we can put the horses, we'd be grateful," said Andry. "Lochren, of course, goes where he will."

Deira stood on the porch of the Pilgrim's Hut, the broom she had borrowed from Valdon's wife in her hand. The temperature was finally beginning to drop as the sun sank beyond the western hills. Long rays gilded rock and tree. Lochren, grazing the dry grass on the hillside below them, was a figure in silvergilt upon a field of glowing gold.

Light shimmered in the dust motes she had been sweeping, though there had not been as much as she'd expected. Derelict the place might be, but someone had been taking care of it. She had not found the abandoned nests of mice and rock-hoppers she expected, and the grass that filled the bed boxes was no more than a season old.

It had been late afternoon by the time she and Andry reached the spring. Valdon's wife had given them a good dinner, and his sons had offered Lochren a measure of grain to supplement the grass he would find on the hill. She looked up as Andry came around the corner, a tangle of sticks in his arms.

"This should be enough wood an' we want tea," he said, dropping it beside the hearth.

"We'll surely not be needing it to keep warm!" The bench on the porch creaked as he came back out and eased down at her side. They sat in silence as cool shadows gathered in the folds and furrows of the land below them, spreading rapidly as the last light faded from the western sky. The only sounds were the chirrup of hoppers and the music of the spring.

"What am I going to do?" Andry said at last. "I'm *not* a full Herald. I have no authority here."

"But how often does a Herald need backup to enforce his decrees?" she replied.

"With the whole Herald's Circle behind him, he doesn't need soldiers. I dread to imagine what would happen to anyone who tried an imposture!"

Deira shuddered, picturing a tidal wave of white Companions stampeding toward her, eyes blazing with wrath. "You have the authority of legal ownership," she said then.

"Oh, yes—I can rally my neighbors and drive the squatters out, and what will that say about the kind of person the Heralds admit as a trainee? Or I can refuse to act, and be responsible for anything my neighbors do to those poor people when I am gone. I'll be betraying someone whatever I choose."

The first stars were kindling in the fading sky. Deira set a hand on Andry's shoulder and got to her feet. "We will sleep and ask for guidance," she told him, "and see what counsel comes with the morn. In the meantime, you light the fire, and I will make tea."

They sought their beds early, but neither Deira nor Andry slept well. The frame of Andry's box bed creaked every time he turned. Whoever had built the hut had not expected couples, or perhaps they thought that married pleasure would distract from the spiritual purpose for which they had come. Would Andry be more at ease if she lay by his side, or would her own anxieties resonate and amplify his? Perhaps she should have told him to go sleep with Lochren.

Her own bed creaked as she turned over, lips twitching as she tried to imagine the kind of counsel Andry's Companion might give, then sighed. Certainly *she* had nothing better to offer. Alone on Lochren, Andry could already have journeyed here and returned to Haven again. She had been nothing but a drain on his time and energy. Selaine had been right. She should not have come.

Most trainees were Chosen young. Growing up in Haven, they developed their identities as Heralds as they grew. As they came south, she had noted Andry's changing response to the countryside. And *here* . . . he trod this earth with a certainty he had never had at home. Would he be able to tear himself away?

And if he did, could he function both as Herald and husband? Did he even need a wife when he had a Companion? Was she making it harder for him to fulfill his destiny?

She threw back the thin blanket and sat up.

This was going nowhere. She would not find sleep watching the bar of moonlight that came through a gap in the roof, inching across the floor. This place had been built as a shrine. Perhaps there would be counsel from the spirit of the spring.

Moonlight dappled the stone path and filtered through the twisted branches of the resin tree that grew by the water, sparkling on the pool. Deira paused at the edge and poured out the rest of their dinner wine in offering. When they had first arrived, Andry had made a formal prayer. She kept having to remember that he was the native here. Town-bred, she knew the charms for the hearth-hob and the wight that guarded the door, and of course the words to say when you started a new project on the loom, but she was just beginning to understand the depth of Andry's connection to his land.

The shrine had been built where water flowed from a seam in the rock. It filled a pool before flowing through the dale. To bathe here was said to bring healing. She and Andry had done so that evening, and if it had not healed their spirits, the cool water had certainly brought their bodies ease.

She had started toward the stone bench when she heard a sound that was not water. Was it Lochren? She peered around and saw that what she had taken for boulders bright with moonlight was the Companion, lying with limbs tucked under him on the slope above the pool. His head was up, but if he sensed danger, surely Lochren would be doing something by now.

Again—it was a voice—a girl's voice. Deeper tones answered, murmuring her name. Deira eased back into the shadow of the porch, listening. The girl seemed to be pleading, the man reassuring, though he did not sound very sure. Beneath the tree she glimpsed movement, shadows merging for a moment in a desperate embrace. Then the smaller shape fled down the path, followed after a few moments by the other, whose footsteps dragged with despair.

"Did you hear them?" Deira ran toward Lochren.

The Companion nodded, then sighed. Deira reached up to scratch behind his ears, where he sweated beneath the headstall on warm days. The mare who foaled him had died with her Chosen in the Tedrel wars. Deira wondered sometimes if Lochren found consolation in her affection.

"Andry has enough to worry him already," she murmured. "Let's keep this our secret for now."

For a moment, Lochren did not move. Then he nodded once more. She put her arms around him, breathing in the clean, faintly spicy scent that was not quite that of a horse, sensing, for a moment, something of the comfort Andry must get from their bond.

At noon, the sun's blaze bleached all color from the land. Lochren's white coat was almost too bright to look upon. It was easy, seeing Andry and his Companion approaching, to believe in Heraldic power. Certainly everyone else was watching them, hope mingling with anger and fear. Most were armed with spears or cudgels. Reval and Bestry's brother both had swords.

"Everybody here?" shouted someone. "Let's get 'em!" and suddenly the mob was in motion, tramping across the pasture and past the wooltree to the road.

How quickly they seemed to be moving. In moments they reached the path through the pasture and began to climb toward the house on the hill. The door opened, and seven figures stepped out—two adults, three littles, and a boy of about fourteen and his older sister. They had stout sticks. The younger children were holding baskets of stones. Their mother clutched a kitchen knife and looked ten years older than her probable age. The father was leaning on a staff.

Andry had dismounted and sent Lochren to the rear, then moved to join Valdon and Bestry's brother, a silent emanation of Heraldic power.

When they were twenty paces from the door, Valdon held up his hand. "Wellerans!" he called. "We've let ye be till now, but the land's true master is returned, and you must go. Gather yer gear and come peacefully, and in peace ye may go."

"And if we do not?" came the reply.

A feral growl rose from the Denorsdale men. Deira shivered despite the heat of the day.

"Resist, and we'll turf ye out with naught but the clothes on yer backs and harry you down the road. Fight, an' yer blood will water this ground."

As the mob moved, Deira found herself carried forward. Now she could see the faces of their prey, fierce, obdurate. The face of the young woman showed a desolation that struck her unshielded soul as if the girl was beside her—no, that intensity of feeling was coming from somewhere closer—turning, Deira saw a matching grief in the strong features of Valdon's son.

The lovers I heard at the sacred spring! Suddenly the solution was clear. But there were too many people between her and Andry. She whirled and pushed through the stragglers to get to Lochren.

"Look at Marl Valdonson and that girl! They're the ones we heard at the spring. Tell Andry they're in love! You don't want to live here, do you? Let the young ones have it. Tell him to give it to Marl and the Welleran girl."

Lochren tossed his head, and she followed in his wake as he pushed through the mob.

"Silence!" Andry's command cracked across the gabble as if he had summoned lightning, and suddenly everyone was still. He might still be wearing trainee gray, but with Lochren looming beside him, no one doubted that a Herald was standing there. His gaze searched the crowd.

"Marl Valdonson, stand forth!" He turned back to the house. "Alissa Welleran, come down!"

For a long moment no one moved, and then, slowly, with faces ashen and burning eyes, they came. When Andry spoke again, his voice was soft, but everyone heard.

"The folk of Denorsdale have asked me for justice as a Herald, but I speak to you as a man, bred and born and nurtured by this land." He bent suddenly and scraped up a handful of soil. "Hold out your hands!"

Uncertain, they did so, and he poured the dirt onto their palms, clasped them together, and held them closed. For a moment his face tightened, then he spoke again.

"I give it to you. I give you this earth, and you are wedded one to the other, and both of you to this land. I give it to you and your heirs after you. Ward it well!"

He stepped away, arms stretching as if to embrace house and hill, and then he let it go.

The next day Andry and Deira set out for home. Andry had made it very clear to everyone in the dale that there would be consequences if anyone challenged his will, but he did not think it likely. Valdon, for one, was well pleased.

The journey back was uneventful, but both of them were grateful when the green hill of Haven rose up before them. By the time they reached Deira's house, it was late.

"Will you stay with me tonight?" she asked as Andry set her gear bag down.

"Oh, yes." He sighed. "Elcarth will be wanting a report, but nothing I have to say can't wait till morning. This was not an official journey, after all." He paused, looking around him as if expecting something to have changed.

"You asked me once what it is you do for me." He turned to face her again. "At Denorsdale . . . I was so afraid of not living up to what they expected of a Herald, but it wasn't Herald magic or Heraldic authority we needed there, only some compassion and common sense."

But those are no small things . . . thought Deira, smiling as he headed back down to settle Lochren and the horses for the night. Their journey might have been unofficial, but if Elcarth was as good at his job as she had heard, he would realize that the trainee who had ridden out had undergone that invisible transformation that made a Herald, even still wearing gray. It seemed to her that Lochren had grown too. She might not have

Mindspeech, but she and he were communicating remarkably well.

And herself?

Deira picked up the frame that she had warped for her wedding shawl. In the lamplight the mingled blue and white of the thread glimmered enticingly. On this journey, she and Andry had strung the loom well. Now it was time to pick up the shuttle and weave in the weft—blue for their home, white for the Heralds, and a rich brown for the earth of Valdemar.

An Enchantment of Nightingales

Elisabeth Waters

Stina took a seat opposite Mother Felicity in the Abbess's parlor and tried to hide her nerves. Being nearly illiterate, she found it intimidating to face the head of the Sisters of Ardana, an order devoted to reading and copying books. The fact that she wanted to ask the woman for a favor did not make things easier.

"I was wondering if I might be permitted to visit my sisters. They're both Novices here."

"Annika and Carina?"

"Yes, Mother Felicity."

"So you're the missing sister." Mother Felicity looked thoughtfully at her. "I understood that all three of you were to come here, and I am very glad to see you safe and well. I've been wondering for years what happened that night and where you disappeared to. While our novices often come with books from their families, your sisters were the only ones we received packed into the crates *under* the books. Your mother's explanation was incoherent and brief, and the note we found stuck into one of the books wasn't much better. At least she did tell us that they had been drugged, so we had some idea why they didn't wake up when we unpacked them. Do you know why your parents did this?"

Stina grimaced. "Yes. They were terrified. You knew they were in debt, right?" Mother Felicity nodded and motioned

Stina to continue. "We'd been trying to keep up appearances so our creditors wouldn't all pounce on us at once, but part of that was that all three of us attended the Midwinter parties. I was fourteen, so I attended the afternoon parties, but they were nine and eleven, so our mother took them to the children's parties in the mornings. Then we spent the evenings swapping around the trimmings on our dresses so that they would look like different dresses the next day." She sighed. "Anyway, they were out in public enough for one of my parents' creditors to see them. That night he came to the house and told my parents he would forgive a large part of their debt if they gave my sisters to him. He added that I was too old to interest his particular clients, but that he could recommend someone who would take me if they wanted to sell me as well."

Stina shuddered at the memory. "He left, Mother had hysterics, Father said we would need to smuggle them out somehow, and I packed them into the boxes under the books after he drugged them. I put Carina's stuffed lamb in with her because she always slept with it, and I hoped you would allow her to keep it until she outgrew the need for it."

Mother Felicity smiled. "We let her keep it. She may be sleeping with it still; I have made a point not to ask. In addition to the bruises left by the books—" Stina winced, "—they were troubled in spirit."

"They'd have been a lot more troubled if they had heard that horrible man and the way he talked about them. Back then, I wasn't totally clear on what he wanted them for, but I knew *I* didn't like him. The fact that my father was willing to drug them and pack them in crates full of books only confirmed my belief that he was a bad man. I padded them as best I could, but I told Father they'd get bruises when the crates were moved, and he didn't care about *that*, so the alternative must have been horrible."

"Let's just say that they are better off here and leave it at that. But what happened to you? Why didn't you come with them?"

Stina was surprised. "My sisters didn't tell you?"

"No," Mother Felicity replied. "They said you were supposed to come here but you didn't want to, and that they had no idea where you were—or where your parents were."

"I can't help with the last part; I haven't seen my parents since they drove off to bring the crates to your temple. Father told me if I wasn't willing to go with my sisters, I had better find a good hiding place on my own before morning. My best friend lived next door with his mother, but he spent most of his time at the Temple of Thenoth, Lord of the Beasts. We had played together for years, so I knew all the hiding places in his mother's garden. I hid there the rest of the night, snuck in at dawn when the servants unlocked the back door to let the tradesmen in, borrowed some of his old clothes, and went down to the temple. I had kept back a bracelet my father gave me when we started selling jewelry, so I gave that to the Prior and told him I liked animals and was willing to work hard. He agreed to take me as a Novice, so I spent several years at the temple in Haven and in the daughterhouse in the country—the Prior sent every female he had there when it was created—and then I came back to Haven with Lord and Lady Lindholm this past winter when the king required them to be formally received at court. They'd been married for a year, but almost nobody knew that, and he wanted it to be public knowledge. All four of us are Perpetual Novices of the Temple of Thenoth, but Lena—Lady Lindholm— hired Sven-August and me so we could get married. His mother had remarried, and her new husband wanted to marry Sven-August off to the highest bidder, but we had planned to marry since before my parents lost their money . . . and I'm babbling. Sorry."

"So you prefer animals to books?"

"Yes. I understand them better. My sisters love books; they were always library mice. I can't believe they didn't tell you I can't read, especially considering how often they called me stupid for it. Well, I *can* read a bit if I really try, but the letters wriggle when I look at them, so I didn't think I'd be much use to an order that works with books."

Mother Felicity smiled. "We would have done our best by

you if you had come here, but I think you made a good choice. You chose a temple that suited you, made a good home for yourself there, and found friends who valued you. You are now married to a young man you have known and loved for years, and are gainfully employed in the bargain. I don't believe anyone could call you stupid."

Stina sighed. "My sisters probably will, but they are still my sisters, and I want to know that they are well and happy—not that I'm doubting your word," she added hastily.

"Of course you want to see them yourself," Mother Felicity said. "I'll send for them now." She stood up and came out from behind her desk—Stina hastily bounced to her feet, knowing better than to remain seated when the Abbess was standing—and went to the door. "Please send Annika and Carina to me."

"Yes, Mother," a voice replied, and footsteps receded down the hallway.

Mother Felicity returned to her chair and gestured to Stina to be seated. "Are they doing well here?" Stina asked. "I know we didn't send them with much of a dowry . . ."

"They have both learned to be good copyists, and I'd say Annika has a true gift for it. We would have taken them with no dowry if necessary, but several of the books your parents sent were ones we did not have in our library, and we were able to get a good price on many of the duplicates. We consider them to have been well dowered, and they are assets to our order."

"I'm so glad," Stina said. "I wasn't in a position to do anything to help them, but I've prayed for their safety and happiness every day since then."

Mother Felicity smiled. "Prayer has more power than most people think."

There was a tap on the doorframe, and the girls stood there, looking at their Abbess. "You sent for us, Mother?" Annika asked.

"Yes. Please come in, close the door behind you, and have a seat." She gestured to a bench at the side of the room, from which they could see both her and Stina. "Your sister has come to see you."

"You're back." Annika's voice was flat. "Do you happen to know where our parents are?"

Stina shook her head. "I haven't seen them since the night you came here."

"And it's not as if they could write to her," Carina said.

Stina wondered if the snide tone in that remark escaped Mother Felicity's notice. From a quick glance in that direction, she suspected not. "They could have written to Mother Felicity," she pointed out. "I think they were afraid to contact any of us."

"So where were you all these years?" Carina asked.

"I went to the Temple of Thenoth," Stina said.

Annika started snickering. "You mean you went chasing after Sven-August—as if Mistress Efanya would ever permit you to marry her precious son after we weren't rich anymore."

"I served there as faithfully as you have done here," Stina said calmly. "As for Sven-August's mother, we knew she wouldn't agree to our marriage, so we didn't ask her. Once we were old enough and had jobs that would support us, the Prior married us."

Carina gaped at her. "You're joking!"

"No, I'm not. I'm really married to him."

"He must have found a good job to buy you a dress like *that*," Annika remarked. "Or is he just living off his mother's money?"

"Actually, she remarried. Her new husband is highborn and avaricious, so the only thing Sven-August got is some land his father left in trust for him. Lord Crane, her new husband, even had someone sneak Sven-August's horse out of the stables to sell him at the horse market by the fairgrounds. We live with our employers, who also belong to the Temple of Thenoth, and they were seriously annoyed that someone raided their stables. Lady Magdalena had us escort her to the market to buy him back." She grinned at the memory. "Don't ever make somebody with Animal Mindspeech angry. Lena told Jasper to act uncontrollable—not that I think he needed much urging—and she got a really good deal on him after convincing the sellers he was unmanageable. As for the dress, it was a Midwinter gift from her and her husband."

"I guess she must really like you," Annika said.

"She's been a good friend," Stina said, "and she lived at the Temple from the time she was ten, so she's not at all snobbish. Most of the time we all wear Novice habits, but since I was coming here, I dressed up." She turned to Mother Felicity. "Speaking of holiday gifts, it's almost the Equinox. Am I allowed to give gifts to my sisters?"

Mother Felicity looked dubiously at Stina's dress. "We live very simply here—" she began.

"Oh, I wasn't thinking of fancy clothes!" Stina assured her, wincing as she realized she had interrupted a Superior. When Mother Felicity didn't say anything, she went on. "I was thinking of things like flowers or sweets."

"As if we'd want anything from *you*," Carina sniped. "If you really cared about us, you would have come here with us—or at least kept track of where our parents are!"

Stina sighed. "If I had tried to track them, I might have led their creditors to them. Believe me, their creditors were *not* nice people."

Annika bit her lip. "I remember there was a man who was always watching us when Mother took us to parties. Was he one of the creditors?"

Stina nodded, and looked uncertainly at Mother Felicity.

"Yes," Mother Felicity said calmly. "He was the reason your parents sent you here packed in crates of books—and you can thank your sister, Carina, for remembering to put your lamb in with you—and the reason we kept you in the infirmary and out of public view for so long. I'm reasonably sure he's the man who attended our public services shortly after you arrived, claiming to be a friend of your parents, and asked if you were here."

"What did you tell him?" Annika asked anxiously.

Mother Felicity smiled faintly. "While, in general, lying is wrong, there are some times when it *is* the right thing to do. I told him your parents had sold us a couple of crates of books—

he might have had spies who saw the delivery—but I told him I hadn't seen you. It *was* true that I hadn't seen you yet that day."

Stina tried in vain to stifle a giggle.

"With regard to gifts," Mother Felicity said, returning to the original question, "we prefer that they be made to the Order, rather than to individuals. I hope you can understand."

"Absolutely," Stina said. "Our Temple is the same way; our favorite gift is food for the animals."

"What if somebody gives you the wrong thing?" Annika asked.

Stina grinned. "We haven't received anything yet that something in our care won't eat."

"It doesn't work that way here," Annika informed her. "We need specific types of paper, ink, and pens—not just what somebody feels like giving us."

"I realize that," Stina said. "If you're making a new book for someone, those details matter."

"Besides," Carina said, "the only place we put flowers is on the altar, and we grow those ourselves."

Stina kept a smile fixed on her face as she rose to her feet. "I'm glad to see that you are well. If you ever need me for anything—" she ignored a snort from Carina, "—the Temple of Thenoth will know where to find me. I'm currently living at Lord Keven and Lady Magdalena Lindholm's house; it's on the hill near the Palace in Haven." She bowed respectfully to the Abbess. "Thank you for permitting this visit, Mother Felicity."

"You are welcome, Stina." The Abbess rose to her feet and made a sign with her right hand. "May the goddess bless and keep you."

Well, at least they're happy there, Stina thought, as she mounted her horse and headed back to Haven. *And Mother Felicity thinks I did the right thing not coming here with them.*

She was glad to get back to Lena's in time to soak her sore muscles in a hot bath before everyone gathered for supper. Jade, the new horse Lena had given her, saying she needed something that could keep up with Sven-August's Jasper, was lovely and well mannered, but she and Stina were still getting used to one another. Stina hadn't yet reached the point where she adjusted automatically every time Jade moved.

"Did you get to see your sisters?" Sven-August asked at dinner.

"You have sisters?" asked Lady Sara, Keven's younger sister and his and Lena's ward.

"Yes. They went to the Sisters of Ardana when I went to the Temple of Thenoth, so I hadn't seen them in years. Carina is about your age, and Annika is a couple of years older." She turned to smile at Sven-August. "Mother Felicity was kind enough to allow me to visit with them briefly in her office—and in her presence, of course. She seems fond of them, and they appear to be thriving. That was definitely the right order for them. Unfortunately," she added, "I am not permitted to give them Spring Equinox gifts, though I suspect Carina would throw anything I gave her back in my face. She seems to blame me for our parents' disappearance."

"Bratty, was she?" Keven, the only other one of the group with siblings, asked with a smile.

"Not *quite* enough to force Mother Felicity to take formal notice of it," Stina said, "but I wouldn't be surprised if they got a lecture on manners and courtesy to guests as soon as I mounted my horse and started home."

"I hope you're right about that," Lena said, "because the Sisters of Ardana are one of the options we're considering for Sara's education."

"Mother Felicity seems very nice," Stina said, "but it's a bit of a ride. She'd probably need a new horse."

"No!" Sara's anguished protest startled everyone, and it took Stina a few seconds to realize how her words had sounded.

"Not instead of Brownie, Sara," she said quickly, "in addition to Brownie. If ever a horse deserved to live peacefully with a loving family for the rest of her life, it's Brownie. I wouldn't dream of trying to send her away."

"None of us would," Keven said firmly. "You and Brownie are both safe here with us."

"Speaking of the Sisters of Ardana," Sven-August said, "Lena was kind enough to help me find me a lawyer of my own to deal with my mother's lawyer. My property is now out of trust. It's a small farm, and it's right next to the Sisters of Ardana. You may get a chance to see your sisters more."

"I'm not going to sneak around behind Mother Felicity's back," Stina said. "That would be stupid, not to mention ungrateful, after she was kind enough to let me visit them."

"Superiors, especially if they're looking after children, do tend to get touchy about that," Lena said. "Our Prior is very easygoing, but I don't think he ever forgot that the King would be the person inquiring about anything that injured me. Even when I was off performing with a traveling show, I had two Companions and a Herald Trainee to watch me."

"I wasn't suggesting sneaking around," Sven-August protested. "I was thinking we could attend their public services whenever we're down there. Of course, only when we're not needed here; I'm not forgetting that we have responsibilities to our gracious employers." He grinned and bowed to Lena.

"Sven-August, you truly are the little brother I never had," Lena said, making a face at him. "Still, I think things are sufficiently under control here that we could give you a week off to inspect your new property. Keven," she turned to her husband, "can you think of anything we need them for in the next week?"

Keven shook his head. "Besides, they'll know if you want them. When a flock of birds starts flying in circles around them, one of them will come back here to see what you need."

"It does give a whole new meaning to the concept of messenger birds," Stina agreed.

They found the farm easily, following the map the lawyer had provided. As advertised, it bordered the Sisters of Ardana, with a chest-high hedge on their side of the boundary line. Apparently, however, Sven-August's mother had taken no interest in property she could never own—or perhaps it was her dislike of animals—so the property was severely run down. While the house could probably be made habitable with a little work, the stable, while small, was in much better shape, and Jade was new. Sven-August knew what to expect from Jasper, but Stina decided she would prefer to sleep in the stable, both to protect the horses and to reassure them.

No novice of Thenoth had trouble sleeping in a pile of straw in an empty stall, but Stina woke in the hours before dawn when the stable door creaked and soft footsteps rustled past her to the stalls occupied by Jasper and Jade. She rose silently and peered over the side of the stall. To her astonishment, she saw her youngest sister's face, illuminated by the candle she was holding.

Stina put a hand over Sven-August's mouth to make sure he woke silently, nudged him awake, and then carefully snuck up on Carina, who was starting besottedly at Jade, and took the candle away from her.

"Carina," she said calmly, "never, *never*, carry an open flame in a stable—or anyplace else where your surroundings are flammable."

"I wasn't going to hurt anything," Carina said defensively. "I just wanted to pet your horse. How was I supposed to know you were sleeping in the *barn*?"

"Where I'm sleeping isn't the point. You are welcome to pet Jade if you have Mother Felicity's permission, but I'm reasonably certain you are supposed to be asleep in your dormitory now."

Sven-August had lit a proper lantern and joined them, so Stina blew the candle out. Carina looked at them both and said, "You weren't joking about living in Novice habits." She sighed. "Are you going to tell on me?"

"I don't think we need to," Stina said. "You'll confess it at the Chapter meeting tomorrow when they see the scratches on your face."

Carina winced. "At least I look better than the bird stuck in the hedge. It's got blood dripping from its wing."

"Show me where the bird is," Sven-August demanded. "Stina—"

"I know. Towels and your instrument pouch. I'll be right behind you."

She grabbed a few towels, the pouch, and another lantern and followed them to the hedge. A very unhappy nightingale was trying to thrash its way out of the hedge and only making matters much worse for itself.

"Here." She slapped a towel in Sven-August's hand and took his lamp and held it so he could see to grasp and remove the bird. "Can you manage out here?" she asked him. "The horses won't like the smell of blood, and even I can smell it."

"I need more light."

"It'll be dawn in another hour," Carina said helpfully.

"The bird will be dead by then," Sven-August said grimly. "It can't afford to lose as much blood as we can."

"Let me take the bird," Stina said, "and you can light the extra lantern I brought and set up your instruments."

Sven-August gingerly transferred the bird to her. "Careful, don't squeeze him. Remember, he needs to be able to breathe."

"I may not have your gift for dealing with birds," Stina replied, "but I do have enough training to hold him without squeezing him to death."

He rapidly spread out the largest of the towels on the ground, lit the second lamp, placed a lamp on each side of him, and pulled out a pair of forceps. Stina knelt next to him, passed the bird back, and carefully stretched out the wing he unwrapped.

"Hold the wing steady," he ordered. "I think it's more than one feather." He took up his forceps, gently slid them up to the root of a broken feather that was bleeding steadily, grasped the root firmly, and pulled the feather out with a quick tug. He repeated the process on a second feather, and the bleeding slowed to a trickle. "I think that's it."

"Should we check the other wing?" Stina asked.

"Yes. I don't like the way it was thrashing around."

Fortunately, however, the second wing had no broken blood feathers. "If you've got him," Stina said, "I can escort Carina back to her dorm."

"That won't be necessary," a voice from the other side of the hedge said calmly.

Carina looked up and winced. "Good morning, Sister Anice," she said meekly.

"Novice Mistress?" Stina asked, receiving a nod in reply. "I'm Stina, and this is my husband Sven-August. He inherited this property, and we're just moving in. It's nice to meet you."

"I was under the impression Mother Felicity allowed you to visit with your sister yesterday, Carina. What are you doing here now?"

Stina kept quiet to allow her sister to answer for herself. When the silence stretched out, she said, "I don't think she should be thrashing through the hedge again. We've got birds nesting in there. I can get my horse and bring her around by the road."

Sister Anice looked at the injured bird in Sven-August's hands and sighed. "I guess you had better. I will meet you at the font gate, and I expect you to go straight there."

"Yes, Sister," Stina said meekly. "Come on, Carina."

The bird survived the night, and the next morning they went out to examine the hedges. "If we trim it here where there are no nests," Sven-August said, "and give it just a hint of a break, people who are determined to come through it will hopefully use that one place, and not shove through at random, harming anything in their path."

"It was kind of you not to tell Carina that she was the one who nearly killed him," Stina said, locating the nest where her sister had stepped on the edge of it.

"I wasn't in the mood for an explanation of what blood feathers are and why it's important that they not get broken," Sven-August said, gently settling the bird in its nest. "He'll be all right now. With any luck, his songs will attract a female nightingale, and we'll get babies here."

"That would be nice," Stina agreed. She looked around at their surroundings. "Given that we both have jobs and don't have to make this property earn a profit, we can keep a lot of it wild enough for a bird sanctuary. If we let the hedges at the field boundaries grow instead of cutting them back, this would be a great place for birds. You might even tell Brother Thomas you can take any birds he wants to release to the wild."

"You know Brother Thomas will insist on inspecting the place, and probably demand improvements."

"Of course he will," Stina said, "but it would be nice to be able to give back to the Temple that sheltered us, even if it's on a much smaller scale than Lena did."

"Not everybody has enough land to build an entire second Temple." Sven-August looked around. "You're right; this could make an excellent habitat for wild birds—and I agree about giving back what we can. We can probably make a butterfly garden as well. That would give the Sisters next door some beauty to enjoy."

"That's a great idea, and it wouldn't take much more than planting the right kind of flowers. We'd get beauty and birdsong. You know," Stina added, "Carina may have inadvertently helped us with a Spring Equinox gift for their Order. I don't think Mother Felicity will have any objection to the gift of music."

Where There is Smoke
Brenda Cooper

Merilee laughed with pleasure as her five-year-old daughter, Annabelle, snuggled closely against Gideon. The retired guard dog easily outweighed Annabelle by a factor of three or more. The ball of dirty white fluff turned his head to regard the child he had so clearly grown to love.

Gideon pleased Merilee. He didn't add nearly the safety and protection of her late husband, Liano, but for the first time since she had been widowed two years ago, she felt like someone else in the house could help protect her and the two children. After all, he had protected herds of sheep for years. Sometimes she felt like a ewe, all alone out here on the edge of tiny Johnsbarn with the children and her tiny flock of animals.

Gideon huffed lightly and settled his square head down on his front paws. Annabelle appeared to feel safer as well. The first year after her father died, the child hadn't napped at all. Now she snuggled up to Gideon every afternoon, back curled against his ample belly, her fine, dark hair mixed with his gray and white mane, and snored.

Leaving the two to their nap, Merilee went to the hearth and stoked the fire. She took out a large wooden bowl and spoon and began to mix goat's milk and some of her last flour together with a little salt and dried rosemary. Her bag of flour was nearly empty, but both of her goats were producing well this year. Maybe she could trade some goat's milk for a little more flour.

She began chopping up an onion and two of her last dozen or so potatoes. Soup would go well with the bread. Her son,

David, would start home from the fields soon with their tiny flock. She wanted the house to smell like warmth and happiness by the time he came in.

As the peppery smell of the soup began to fill the cabin, she opened the door and peered outside, checking for any sign of David or their ten sheep. The town of Johnsbarn filled the narrow valley below her own small farm. The single cart track travelers and farmers used wound up from below, turning to a footpath a few farmsteads short of her house.

No sign of him yet. But then, the clear blue sky had just begun to deepen with late afternoon. The first shoots of spring grass were starting to brighten the lower meadows, and he had mentioned taking the sheep there.

He was young to be alone. Just eleven. Smart and steady. Merilee began to hum as she turned to finish her afternoon's chores, tidying the single room they shared for cooking, cleaning, and animal care.

Merilee startled as Annabelle tugged on her smock. "I'm going out to wait for David." Merilee glanced outside, blinking in surprise. A candlemark had passed while she puttered, lost in her daydreams.

She smiled down at her daughter. "Don't go far."

"I won't."

"I'll be right there. We can feed the chickens together."

"Okay, Mommy." Annabelle tugged the heavy door open with a small grunt. It had started sticking last year, when the stones around the wood frame settled. "Mommy?" Annabelle's voice, high and curious. "What is that?"

Merilee stepped toward the door. She smelled it immediately. Smoke. Bitter smoke. Not woodsmoke.

She rushed to peer through the door. Down valley, black smoke rose from the Rossy's barn. The richest and most careful farm in the small town. What could have happened? She checked the wind, testing to see which direction a fire would want to spread.

Movement in the corner of her eye; she turned her head and

stared. A tendril of smoke rose from the smithy, quickly thickening and becoming dark.

Two fires? She blinked through a moment of confusion, then shivered with sudden fear. Bandits?

Johnsbarn had been attacked once before, when David was Annabelle's age and Annabelle had barely been conceived. The townspeople had narrowed the path into the valley and pooled extra food and nails from the smithy to pay mages to obscure the entrance by placing spells to attract passers' attention to a pile of rocks beyond the turn. But spells didn't last forever, and neither did luck.

David! The fires blazed between her and her son. Heart hammering, she fought the urge to run toward the grazing meadows. Her mind raced as she swallowed fear. She had drilled her son in the need to protect himself and his charges. He had a dog with him. Three-legged and pregnant Sasha. She would have smelled the smoke before David, and alerted him to the danger.

Merilee took in a deep, shaking breath, forcing her feet still. She hadn't been able to save Liano, or anyone else ever. But she would save Annabelle.

She threw water on the fire to erase her chimney smoke, set the soup pot aside, and pulled the nearly baked bread out of the oven, its heat a brief shock to her bare fingers. Her hands shook as she wrapped the loaf in a hand towel.

Annabelle stared upward, eyes wide. Merilee knelt and laid her hands on her daughter's shoulders. She looked directly at her. When she felt certain of the girl's attention, she spoke slowly, keeping an edge of command in her voice. "Something very bad *might* be happening. I need you to put on your coat and boots and roll up the blanket on your bed tightly. Can you do that?"

Annabelle nodded, looking quite solemn. "Will David come home?"

Merilee swallowed. "David will hide, just like we will." At least, that was what she had drilled into him, over and over.

Safety. They all had to be safe. No more losses. She couldn't help David right now, but she could save Annabelle.

The little girl glanced around. Her face scrunched up in confusion. "You won't fit under the bed."

"We have to hide in the woods."

Annabelle stiffened and glanced back toward the door. The door Merilee carefully closed every night and locked with a wooden bar, telling both children they'd be safe if they didn't open the door.

"Yes," Merilee whispered. "Trees will keep us safer than our house." Her heart pounded in her chest and her breath slammed through her lungs. She forced her voice to stay low and soft. "We have to go now. Put your boots and coat on. Get your blanket."

Annabelle stood, frozen. Merilee glanced at the dog, who had limped to the door and stood at quiet attention, tail rigid and ruff raised. "Gideon will go with us. Hurry."

Annabelle squeaked and scrambled for her coat. Merilee grabbed her own coat, tucked the rolled-up towel with the bread, a flask of water, some kitchen rags, and a wide metal cup into a basket, then slid her shoes on. She glanced longingly at the pot of soup, still warm even though the fire was out. But she didn't have enough time or enough hands.

If they lived, they could eat tomorrow.

She pulled Gideon away from the door, tucked a rope around the bulky dog's collar, and gripped it and her basket in one hand. She opened the door again and reached a hand toward Annabelle. Annabelle solemnly added her worn-out doll to the basket, clutched her blanket roll tightly, and took her mom's free hand.

Merilee led her charges out the back door and closed it behind them. "Stay safe, little farm," she whispered as she hurried up the thin path that led toward the woods. Her two goats bleated for her attention from their pen. She hardened her heart. Without David to help, she couldn't afford to worry about the goats or the chickens. The goats would follow them and give away their position, and the chickens would be safer in the coop than free. Bandits *might* find the farm, but predators *would* find the chickens.

The air reeked of smoke, tasting of burning oils and greases . . . and, maybe, flesh. It clogged her throat. Liano had been lost to bandits, not here but on the way out of town: his wagon turned over and looted, the one horse they'd owned simply gone, and poor Liano dead of knife wounds by the side of the road. She hadn't been able to help. She hadn't even known anything was wrong until he missed supper.

She ended up with Annabelle's blanket tucked under her arm, hampering her hold on the basket. As soon as they climbed high enough, she turned to look behind them. Liano's parents' old farm was on fire as well, the thatched roof glowing with flames. They had died a few years ago, but she knew the family who lived there now. The Hastings. She and Annabelle had breakfasted there just a week ago. She couldn't think about them, or anyone else. She had to focus. She paid careful attention to her footing, to Annabelle's grip and steps, to moving as fast as she could. She couldn't help anyone else. Not against what must be brigands. Worse, brigands with a mage or two to help them pillage and burn.

She *could* save her daughter. She was not going to lose another family member.

Gideon hobbled right beside Annabelle, threatening to trip Merilee as the rope crossed behind her and slapped her calves. She shifted it and started softly singing one of Annabelle's favorite songs. After a while the child started singing along, her voice thin and soft.

By the time they neared the woods, their shadows stretched out long on the cold, stubbly ground. Way up here, a few plants sprouted tentative buds, but nothing yet flowered. Despite the gnawing cold, relief formed a tiny coal of hope in her heart as they began to walk between trees. The brigands would want food and valuables most, but women were always at risk from outlaws. Even girls. They couldn't be caught.

Annabelle began to sob. Merilee found a boulder to rest on

and offered the water flask to her. The child took a long drink, and then glanced at Gideon. "He needs some!"

Merilee finished half a cup and splashed a little into the cup for Gideon. He gazed at her with a look that indicated he would help himself when he was done with his work for the day. She petted his head. "Thank you, big boy."

"Isn't he thirsty?" Annabelle asked.

"Maybe. But he knows we aren't safe yet. You drink his water now, and he can have some of your share later."

Annabelle complied, her face streaked with tear tracks. At least her sobs stopped. The fading light spurred Merilee to move. This spot was too exposed; darkness alone would not keep them safe. Merilee tucked the child on her hip and kept walking.

Her stomach could smell the soup they had left behind. Poor Annabelle. They would need more water. Had there been a sweet little stream burbling in the next ravine?

By the time they reached the top of the next rise, it had become too dark to see the smoke clearly, but it still tickled Merilee's nose. She glanced down. The side path down to the stream looked steeper than she remembered, and rockier. If she fell and broke an ankle, Annabelle could die. She spotted an animal trail—much flatter—that led into a small copse of trees and bushes. She glanced back at the trail down to the stream. Which to choose?

Gideon tugged toward the downward trail that led to water, so she followed him. He was probably right. After all, he could probably smell whatever animal had made the other trail, and all she could see was hoofprints that spoke of the possibility of wild pigs. Or deer. Or both. Why hadn't she learned more woods-lore?

Gideon had more trouble than she expected on the trail. He took it slowly, retracing his steps twice. But he was twelve—very old for a pasture protection dog. His previous master, Farhah Rossy, hadn't wanted to put him down, even though he had fully trained his younger dog. He'd made a deal with Merilee that showcased his generous heart. She gave Gideon a safe place to spend his final years, and the farmer brought enough meat for both the dog and humans regularly. But now the Rossys' farm was burning or burnt.

Merilee winced and forced herself not to think about it, or David, or their own beautiful, small farmhouse. Or the vegetable stew. She had this moment to keep Annabelle alive in. And then the next. One thing at once. Her mother had taught her that, and it helped.

Merilee clambered down the steep bank just ahead of Annabelle in case the girl slipped . . . Annabelle yelped as her tired feet caught a dusty root. Merilee caught her before her own heart had time to skip a beat. "Careful, sweetheart," she said gently, trying to sound calm, unworried. Gideon waited for them beside a rock shelf a few feet above the stream and just off the path. She patted his head and leaned over to scratch an ear, silently thanking him. As soon as she set her basket down and started laying out Annabelle's blanket and doll for her, the dog started for the stream.

The tree trunks and leaves around them had all faded to shades of gray. She shook the water flask, decided they had enough for the night. She tucked Annabelle into a comfortable seat, folded her arms around her knees, and assessed. Overhanging branches obscured most of sky but offered some shelter, maybe warmth as well. The woods were quieter than she expected, the stream loud enough to hide any sounds they made from human ears.

Gideon clambered back up from drinking and settled himself next to Annabelle, the child sandwiched between them. Merilee handed out the bread, sharing an equal amount with the dog and giving the girl most of their water. Then she wrapped the extra rags she'd brought around Annabelle's thin hands. She tucked the kitchen towel under her own head since Gideon clearly planned to be Annabelle's pillow.

A few night birds called softly to each other. A squirrel rushed by overhead. The poor wild things probably also smelled the smoke and knew horrible things were happening in town. A ridge of hard stone dug into her lower back. She shifted uneasily. Still uncomfortable, she stared up at the stars winking through the covering of evergreen branches spread out above them. Hopefully David huddled similarly, against a tree or inside a rock cave.

Merilee finally dozed, fitful, but trusting the dog to alert them to any danger. And unable to quiet the voices in her head. *One thing. Worry about now and not David. Not yet. Soon.* Owls woke her, but exhaustion pulled her back into her half-doze. *One thing. Keep Annabelle safe. Get water first when you wake.*

The howls of a wolf pack plucked her free of sleep. They sounded far away. Still, cold and worry kept her awake. *Keep Annabelle safe.*

Just as she drifted back to sleep, some smaller predator yipped close by. Gideon stood for a moment, waking Annabelle, who cried and clung to her for a long time.

Dawn birds woke Merilee next, singing up the light. She stretched, hungry, thirsty, and very stiff. She allowed herself a small worry about David, a hope that he had found his own shelter. She lay with her arms wrapped around her sleeping daughter, and listened. All around them, birds. A chorus of frogs.

She laid Annabelle down gently against Gideon, pillowing the little head on the dog's furry shoulder, and rose. She pushed out of the little safe place under the trees, her limbs stiff with cold. The dog watched, quiet, as Merilee took care of morning business and slid down to the stream to refill the flask, drink, and fill it again.

Was it safe? If she was hungry, Annabelle and Gideon would be starving when they woke.

She climbed back up, crouched in the center of the trail where she could watch Annabelle sleep, and pondered. They would be hungry soon. The woods were too barren for much. She hadn't brought a knife or any kind of weapon. She'd been in too much of a hurry. Maybe too focused on that moment.

Brush above them crackled. She looked up to see a deer standing at the top of the trail. It turned, stared at her with wide, brown eyes, and then leaped casually away. Perhaps the woods, at least, were safe.

That decided her. They could turn around if the town looked occupied. But brigands didn't usually stay. If they wanted to be farmers, well, they'd be farmers instead of brigands.

After two candlemarks of creeping through the brush, halting to listen every few feet, Merilee finally stopped Gideon and Annabelle at the edge of the woods. She couldn't see their cabin from here, but the air over Johnsbarn was crisp and clear. Did that mean it was over? She let out a long sigh of relief and stood, watching and listening.

Carrion birds wheeled through the sky.

Somewhere below the birds, a dog barked. Not Sasha.

Gideon's ear pricked forward, and his tail flagged.

Merilee told Annabelle, "Wait here. I'm going to see about our house." She drew in a deep, steadying breath and started down the path. As she topped the ridge that overlooked their little cabin, she whispered, "Let it be okay."

She peered over, heart in her throat, and then her knees gave way and she sat down hard in the middle of the path, breathing heavily. Eyes closed, she rubbed her cheeks, then looked again.

I was right. I made the right choices. I kept us safe. So far.

The one wooden wall and most of the thatched roof were charred black or gone to ash. The stone walls and the chicken coop stood, and the tiny barn. The fence had two holes in it big enough to see from a distance. Probably more. Neither chickens nor goats in sight. She took a deep breath, then another.

She watched awhile longer. No sign of movement. No bandit's horses tethered outside, no leftover tendril of smoke.

They could rebuild.

Now she could find David.

The rest of the town must be worse than this. Hers would have been the last place found, the last place torched.

She cursed, stuck between the damaged house, her missing boy, and Annabelle and Gideon. She turned back to her daughter.

Annabelle cried inconsolably as soon as she saw the house. Merilee desperately wanted to join her, but now she had two things to do: feed Annabelle and find David.

She started with the chicken coop. She found three eggs and Annabelle found a fourth. It felt like a triumph, no matter how small. The side wall was gone, and the beautiful, thick front door Liano had so carefully crafted to keep them safe . . . burned. The kitchen table and chairs had been thrown into a pile and burned beyond use. The three stone walls stood, so the fireplace remained. So did their dresser, apparently untouched. A pile of blankets lay neatly, just the way she'd left them, in one corner.

Her half-cooked stew still stood upright, a thick layer of ash coating the top. She took it out and tossed it far from the house where ants could have at it. Then she rebuilt the fire and broke the eggs free of their shells, mixing in two potatoes so there'd be enough to feed Gideon. They might not have anything to eat tomorrow. But for now, one thing.

This was how she'd survived losing Liano. Beautiful Liano. Her breath hitched; she remembered him hanging the door with help from his father. He'd cursed all morning. They'd redone it three times before getting it to open right. Both men had died in the last few years. And now the door. A corner of it had fallen and remained on the ground, its edges charred. She picked it up and set it carefully on the stone hearth.

David!

Annabelle sat on the floor to eat. Merilee took a few bites, but split most of the meager meal between Annabelle and Gideon. Then she once more gathered the rough rope in one hand and her daughter's soft palm in her other hand. Annabelle clutched her doll in her free hand as Merilee led her tired family toward the smith's workshop. It was the town's most common gathering place.

They passed a burnt house on the way, a dew-spangled field of carrots, and two rabbits.

Every wall of the smithy had been stone, and still stood. The wooden roof was gone, and the benches. She spotted two adults outside, too far away to make out faces. No David.

When she got close enough, she saw the people were the smith's mother, Old Jacqueline, and Hardy, a taciturn man who lived in his own shack at the edge of town and also raised sheep. She'd gotten Sasha from Hardy, the three-legged, pregnant herding dog with David now. In turn for her keeping dog and pups safe, he'd get the pick of the litter and a second pup she picked for him, and she could keep or sell the others. One of the small ways the town had helped her since Liano died, let her be more than a near beggar. Maybe he knew something?

"Hardy," she greeted him. "Mrs. Jacqueline." Then she realized she didn't know what else to say.

A wide smile split Hardy's lined face. "Merilee! You're well! And the wee one. We were worried."

She nodded, her question about David suddenly frozen in her throat. Hardy's sleeves were stained dark with blood. She coughed words out. Stuttering. "H-have you. Seen my boy. Seen David?"

Old Jacqueline glanced at Annabelle, shook her head slowly. She seemed to choke on her answer. "No news."

Merilee whispered, "Who else? Who else is still okay?"

Hardy's face lost the smile her appearance had sparked. When he spoke, his usually warm voice sounded cold and flat. "There's ten of us so far. Twelve with you. Us. Two children, I think; one of Rossy's youngest and one of Sue Carmichael's, although Sue is just . . . gone."

Merilee closed her eyes, swayed. Sue had still been pretty, even though she'd had three children. Tall, with long legs and a ready smile.

Hardy kept counting out his list. "All three of the Fillon men are okay. They're out looking for scattered stock." He brightened briefly. "Maybe they'll bring back word of your boy."

Merilee held Annabelle close. The girl squirmed against her chest, half asleep. "What about your sons?" Jacqueline had two. Twins. They worked the smithy. Brought in the only outside income the tiny town knew, other than whatever crops they sold or bartered.

She regretted her question immediately. The old woman pointed toward the hill the town used as a graveyard. It wasn't visible from here, but it was the only thing of note in that direction. "We buried them this morning. I told them to run, but they tried to save this place."

"I'm so sorry," Merilee said, panic rising in her. "I'm so sorry."

Old Jacqueline's lips were a tight line. "They had mages."

That explained so much. It told her, again, that she was right. Especially if David was okay.

Hardy hadn't had anyone to lose, not immediate family. But he looked pale and sounded shocked. "They killed my sheep in the barn, took one carcass, and let the others lie. Just left them. Even the ewes set to lamb any day." He held out his arms, his story explaining the blood that soaked his sleeves and had clearly splattered his pants as well. "I butchered them best I could to save the meat."

She wanted to ask about more details, but finding David mattered more. "Where are the other littles? Who is watching them?"

Hardy answered. "They're at Rossy's. The horses are gone, but the fence is standing. So's the barn. They're in there, keeping as warm as they can."

If there were only ten—twelve—people alive, that left five more living people besides her, Annabelle, Old Jacqueline, Hardy, and the three Fillons. So far, she told herself. After all, she'd just shown up. Maybe others had hidden, too. There had been close to fifty people in town, enough that she'd lost count.

"All right. I'm going." She tugged on Gideon's rope and heaved Annabelle back into her arms. With a growing knot of worry in her throat, she started the long trudge to Rossy's place at the end of town. It was the first place she'd seen the fire, and the first place any attackers would come across. That meant it was closest to where she'd have to go to find David.

Surely if he was alive, he'd be back already. It was almost

midday. In spite of her exhaustion, she picked her feet up, moving as fast as she could go with the tired dog limping beside her and the increasingly heavy child in her arms. She had done her one thing. They were all alive. The three of them.

She found two adults and three children sharing stew in Rossy's barn. After a few bites, and more news—none of it good, but none of it about David—she left Gideon and Annabelle behind. Safe.

One thing left. Find David and the sheep. And Sasha. She began to jog.

Her son often used the middle pasture this time of year but might have chosen the lower because of the greening grass. Probably had. If so, he'd have been close to the path the bandits had used. She took the turnoff to the pasture without slowing, and then stopped, studying it. Sheep had come through here. A dog. A boy. And footprints that were too big to be David's. Bandits? Or the Fillons looking for stock?

She didn't dare call out. The bandits were probably long gone. But just in case, she moved quickly and silently. The lower pasture was cleared, but rolling hills and uneven ground slowed her down. She stubbed her toe once, fell once. Drank half her water and kept going. No sheep, no David, no clear tracks. But unlike the path they'd taken down to the stream yesterday, the pasture was in full sun and dry. Ten sheep, a boy, and a dog weren't enough to leave much trail. The air smelled lightly of dust and dried sheep dung.

To get to the second pasture, she ascended four switchbacks. At the top, she stopped, breathing hard. In front of her, a dead cow lay still in a pool of its own blood. The bandits had hacked its two back legs off. Flies buzzed around the carcass, and a crow sat between her and the dead cow like a warning.

Unbelievable waste.

Beyond that, two men walking in the field, far away. Some other animals on the ground. She squinted. The men moved familiarly. Not David. The Fillons?

She raced toward them.

The closest man turned toward her. Sami. He might be the youngest of the brothers. When she came close enough to keep her voice under a yell, she slowed, caught her breath, and called, "David. My son. Have you seen him?"

Sami shook his head. "Some of your sheep." He pointed toward the animals. They weren't the only ones who had sheep, so she jogged up to the dead animals. Two sheep. Theirs. Pregnant ewes. Killed and just left to rot. Her gorge rose as she imagined the young lambs she would never see.

"Can we eat them?" Sami asked.

She'd been taught to clean meat as soon as it was killed. "I don't know. Everything else dead in town has been butchered. Take the carcasses back to town and ask. Maybe if you cook the meat right away. It was a cold night."

"But they're yours."

It took a second for the unasked question to penetrate. "Everyone will be hungry."

Sami picked up the carcass of the youngest sheep. David had named it, but damned if she could remember the name right now. Sami's brother Dell lumbered up. He was, if anything, less bright, although just as kind. "I'll help you look for the others," he offered.

She let out a long sigh. "Thank you. Where is Jules?" The middle brother.

"He's checking up the road, making sure they are gone."

"By himself?"

"We wanted two of us to look for stock. We didn't find any alive. Not yet."

There weren't enough people to do each thing safely, but everything needed to be done. She felt grateful for Dell's help. And still desperate. "Have you looked everywhere in this pasture?"

He nodded and started up the thin path that led to the high pastures. Merilee's mind raced. *Would David have come here?* The bandits had caught two of his sheep. And someone's cow. So he had been up here. Probably.

There was no sign of anyone, no human sounds, no sheep bleating. No dog.

Just silence.

Two candlemarks later, Merilee leaned on Dell's sturdy frame for balance. He looked grim, and even though he steadied her, his steps had grown shorter and slower. They stopped on a small rise, and Merilee feared he was going to say they needed to turn around. Then he straightened and pointed. She knelt, gazing at sharp-edged cow and sheep prints on a trail in the south side of the third high pasture. She spotted two sets of shoe prints. One *could* belong to David. She took a deep breath and called out as loudly as she could. "David! Daaa . . . vid!"

A bark answered her. Sasha!

Relief pushed her feet forward along the thin path. Brush obscured the view ahead. She called again. Sasha barked back but didn't come. She didn't sound stressed; her bark had been a friendly, excited response.

Why wasn't the dog racing to meet her?

Just as she and Dell climbed up yet again, they broke into a clearing. There, across a stream, she saw Sasha sitting on a rock, watching three of their sheep. Merilee's heart fell. No David. Five missing sheep. Maybe he was after them? If he had told Sasha to stay with the sheep, that explained why she hadn't raced to Merilee's side.

She leaped across the stream, Dell beside her. Sasha came to her then, pasting herself to Merilee's side, white-tipped tail thumping in the dirt. Merilee leaned down, cupping the dog to her. Sasha was no bigger than Annabelle, and Merilee scooped her up and buried her face in her fur, smelling dirt and the sweet sweat of a working animal. "Where is he?" she murmured.

The dog, of course, didn't answer. She did twist, requesting to be put down. Merilee noticed one of the sheep had made it partway across the creek, and let the dog hop away to retrieve her charge. She had become ungainly with pregnancy and with the missing foreleg. It made Marilee smile. Such a game little creature.

"Mom!"

Merilee turned. In front of her, a cow wedged its way into the clearing, followed by four sheep. And, behind them, David. He looked fine. Not hurt. His brown hair was a wild mess, his shirt stained, with a rip in one arm. A splotch of blood covered the right knee of his pants. But he had all his parts, and a wide smile for her as well. He looked . . . wonderful.

The relief that flooded her nearly brought her to her knees.

Behind him, one of the Jossy girls, Amara, a teen who must have had charge of the cows. She also looked a mess, but the four of them—her, David, Amara, and Dell—raced toward each other as soon as the way was clear, collided and clung to one another, wordless relief washing over them all.

When David let go, he looked at her. "Is Annabelle okay?"

"She is. But we lost the goats and the chickens."

"I lost three sheep."

Together, she and Dell said, *"We don't care."* In this moment, one thing mattered. Two more children were safe. It would be all right. Somehow. The first smile she'd worn since she smelled the smoke warmed her face, and all of them were smiling. Hurt, and tired, and with more pain to go. But smiling.

Dell glanced at the sun, gliding way too close to the horizon. "We should go back."

Merilee turned to David. "Is there a path that will get us home before dark?"

"I know one," Amara said. "It's a little steep, but the cow can make it."

"Then I will, too," Merilee said.

They left the sheep in a pen Hardy had hastily repaired for the purpose, with Gideon staying behind to watch them. The communal stew, far thicker with meat than it should have been, fed her and the children.

As soon as they finished, Merilee used the last of the light to lead her children and Sasha home. David stiffened at the damage.

She took his hand. "We're okay."

"We are," he said.

The fire could be built up, and they could wrap themselves in every scrap of material they could find and be warm enough. Before she let David rummage for enough wood for the fire, she set the scrap of the old door she'd saved in an empty sack in the nearly bare pantry. *Liano*, she thought, *would be proud*.

She would keep the door scrap until she'd done the next thing. Rebuild.

What A Chosen Family Chooses
Dee Shull

"So why are we going to Hartsbridge again?" Hesby said just loud enough to reach everyone's ears. The Avelard Family Circus wagons were still a candlemark out from the town, midday sun casting sharp shadows on the road behind them, but everyone seemed more cautious than usual.

Ronnet shrugged, the strongman's shoulders flexing his leather vest and tunic. "Why do we go to any town with a reputation like theirs? At least we're traveling with traders—they'll make us seem more acceptable."

Those traders were further along the road, carts mostly full of goods for Hartsbridge and towns further along their route. In the last town, the Avelards had set up just as Mathias and his crew had rolled in, and the two groups struck up a comfortable working relationship rather quickly. Mathias was the one who'd warned them about Hartsbridge, shrugging when Hallen said it sounded like a town in need of entertainment.

"Jus' keep it nice and tame, mind. They're wanting for entertainment, surely, but some places, well, mebbe it's not worth the coin or time."

The night before Mathias planned to leave, the family got together and voted. Go on with Mathias to Hartsbridge, or continue on the way they'd planned. Nine people, nine votes.

Ronnet continued, "Besides, you voted aye, just like the rest of us." He chuckled, deep and rumbly and warm. "We all know what it's like in places like that. Sure as anything there's someone there who needs out."

Ella piped up from the wagon to the right, tugging on her brown braid, "And if there's not, well, we know to stay away in future." Hallen was driving that one, and he looked off into the distance for a moment before focusing again on the here and now.

Hesby laughed, a bit darkly. "And depending on how things go, we may need to stay away regardless." He shook his head, black hair gathered in a short horsetail wagging behind him.

"So do we need me to be a boy or a girl this time?" Zanner didn't sound thrilled, but the way Mathias described the town, they'd stand out like a raven in a flock of magpies. For the moment, they were in the back of the wagon Ronnet was driving, practicing a bit of juggling.

"What will you be more comfortable as?" Hallen called out gently, since they all knew how little Zanner liked playing one or the other in towns like this.

The juggler thought a moment, balls briefly flying and falling with gentle pat-pat-pats inaudible over the sound of the wagon wheels. Eventually, Zanner said, "I think a girl. Better gossip, different expectations. It's unfortunate my hair's short, but not much to be done about that."

In their tents the night after their first performance, with curtains hung and small chimes rustling in the wind, Zanner said, "It's worse here than we thought."

They'd arrived and set up in a square clearly meant for entertainment. The square had risers for the people to stand on so everyone could see, a few boxes for the clearly wealthy folk, and space enough for their wagons and a private area, backed up against the town wall.

Ella nodded slowly. "I don't think Mathias expected that. He's talking about leaving the day after tomorrow, right?" She looked over at Hallen, who'd formed a quick bond with the trader.

"The man's spooked, to be sure. And everyone laughs at the right places, applauds at the right times, but . . ." Hallen trailed off, combing fingers through his shoulder-length brown hair.

"They all waited until the mayor and her cronies laughed or applauded." Lisbet, the newest family member and the one still closest to her escape, put down her sewing project. "It's like it was back in my town, where you'd see a gaggle of girls all in charge and everyone knew it. Only here it's the town." She hugged her knees to her chest, looking nearly as lost as she had when the family had rescued her.

"It'd be less eerie if they all dressed alike," Wenn said, his voice shaking a little. Ronnet reached out a solid hand and gently gathered the young man to his side, then reached for Lisbet. She shook her head, breathing slowly and carefully.

Wenn sighed a bit as he relaxed into the strongman's side, and continued, "But we've got an audience to entertain and coin to make. Weird way to do it, though, with them passing a bowl for coin."

Conna, practicing some sleight of hand for the next day, shook her head, beads clicking in her braided reddish-blond hair. "Nah, that's so everyone sees what you put in, and if you put in less or more than you're supposed to, bam, gossip and looks and the like. The ones as put in too little today are gonna make up for it tomorrow." Despite her knowing words, her tone was glum.

"And too much? Well, they might miss tomorrow altogether, seeing as they've clearly gotten more than their coin's worth from us." Finn sighed. He'd been the one to stand guard over Lisbet while she got over her nightmares, and he'd quickly taken that back up once they saw how the townsfolk were. "I'm going to ask a vote, though, and say that we keep our acts only to those of us who're more comfortable out front. Keep the rest making music, behind a curtain at that."

Round they went, newest to the longest in the family, and every one of them voted "aye."

The next morning, Conna and Zanner were out in front of the curtains, fussing over the stage setup and murmuring to each other about how they might circulate around Hartsbridge to look for someone who might need a way out. The family had quickly agreed they'd give it a day or two more of performing, then leave after that; if they hadn't identified anyone by that point, it wouldn't be smart to stick around and draw more suspicion. Besides, three days of performing was usually enough for any town.

"We do need some goods from the market here." Conna was in charge of cooking for the family, even though the actual duty rotated every few days. "They're not likely to have anything all that special, I'd guess, this being spring and all."

"We've made do with plain food before, we will again." Zanner turned and bounced up some stairs between the bench seats, wandering back and forth before they nodded. "The stage looks ready enough for the day's performance."

"Um," came from one side of Zanner, back toward the entrance to the square. They spun and saw a young woman who could easily have been Lisbet's sister, save for the fact that the stranger's vivid red hair was pulled tightly back, presumably into a horsetail. A dull brown skirt, plain bodice, and modest tan undershirt served to highlight the teen's hair and pale expression.

Zanner curtsied elegantly, skirts swirling as they moved to intercept the stranger. "All apologies, but we're not open to the townsfolk until later this afternoon." They pitched their voice just high enough that the teen ought to take them for a girl.

The young woman blushed and nodded. "I wouldn't be here, except . . ." She paused, hands tightening and loosening in her skirts. "My mother, Marje, is one of the councilors, and she's got some . . . requests."

Conna called out, "We'd be happy to take requests, but we can't guarantee we can make them happen. I'm Conna by the way, and you are?"

"Oh! I'm sorry, I'm Kaylan." She curtsied far more awkwardly. "I'm sorry for all this. Mother decided she'd have me come to you, since she's busy with the council right now." Kaylan shrunk down a bit. "And I'm sorry to say she wasn't really clear on what she specifically wanted?"

Zanner patted a bench seat and said, "Come, sit. Tell us and maybe we can puzzle this out with you." As the young woman nodded gratefully, Conna came over and arched an eyebrow at Zanner, who responded with a very slight shrug and a loaded look at the clearly uncomfortable Kaylan. Conna nodded in return while Kaylan was distracted, and soon enough the three were settled, with Kaylan facing the Avelards.

"See, all she told me really was 'fewer scares, more fun,' but . . . I saw the performance, and I don't know what she meant?" Kaylan never really looked directly at either Conna or Zanner, and from her tone it wasn't just from shyness.

Zanner said, "She might have not liked the knife juggling. It does look dangerous if you're not familiar with it."

"But she liked that, even said so afterward at home. But . . ."

Zanner continued with a wry smile, "Maybe it was me, then? I don't look like the kind of person you'd expect to see juggling knives." Conna put a hand gently on Zanner's back, reassuring her sibling that they'd only need to play pretend for a few more days.

"I just don't know." Nervously, more quietly, she continued, "In one breath she praised you, but in the next said it was a shame you'd chosen something so dangerous."

Before Zanner could say anything, Conna interjected, "What it sounds to me is like she doesn't exactly know what she wants out of us, and maybe we'd be best off going and asking her?"

Kaylan looked up, hope written clear across her face. "Would you? Oh, would you please? I'm no Herald to be reading her mind, not that I would if I were, because everyone knows they don't, but she seemed to think I should know what she wanted."

Zanner nodded. "Conna's the best at getting things clear for us. You want me to come along?"

"Um, I . . . probably not? Mother's a bit traditional when it comes to, well, looks." Kaylan stood suddenly, turning toward the entrance with a worried look on her face. "And she won't be best pleased when I bring you, but I don't know what else to do that won't get her upset." Both Conna and Zanner could almost hear the unspoken, *"at me."*

"Well, then, we shouldn't keep her waiting." Conna smiled, all professional and reassuring. "And don't worry about anything. I've experience with people who just need a little help figuring out what they want."

Kaylan, clearly hesitant and relieved by turns, just nodded, already halfway back to the entrance to the square.

"Bet you we've found who needs help," Zanner whispered to Conna right as she left.

"No bet."

On the way back to the wagons, Kaylan couldn't stop gushing about how well Conna had "handled" her mother. Marje had started upset about how nobody understood her clear and simple instructions, and ended by thanking Conna for taking time out of "her busy schedule" to work with her to make the evening's entertainment "just that much better for the citizens of Hartsbridge."

"I didn't bring the purse, so I'll have to come back to market for some goods," Conna said during a quiet stretch between buildings.

Kaylan looked around warily, but there wasn't anyone else in the narrow street, and no sound from the windows either. Still, she said quietly, "Mostly it'll be roots, greens, and some smaller game, not much in the way of spices or anything else fancy."

Conna had her suspicions as to why, but still asked, "A town like this, next to the river, I'd have thought would get more custom?"

Kaylan practically flinched. "Hush!" she whispered. "People don't like coming here anymore. Mathias is practically the last one who comes for springtime, with maybe a couple of people toward autumn." After a quick and furtive glance around, she said more loudly, "I'm glad Marje told me to stay with you and help your troupe out with whatever you need. Having a local guide helps ever so much, wouldn't you say?"

Conna knew when to pick up a dropped hint. "Oh that it does, thank you! You've been so very helpful, Kaylan, and if you'd spare us the time, we can even review our plans for to-night with you. Make sure we're suitable for everyone."

"Oh, could I? That'd be the *best*."

And back at the wagons, protected by curtains and the sounds of softly chiming bells, Kaylan told the family every-thing while they practiced in front of her. Several years ago Marin, the luthier's widow, stood up to be mayor, and installed all her friends as councilors. How quickly they turned the town into a place where neighbor watched neighbor, everyone "be-haved" the way Marin expected, and anyone who didn't fit was either shunned or asked to leave. And how the only people left were the ones who liked it, or the ones who *couldn't* leave.

"Mother was complaining the other day that nobody new comes to Hartsbridge, and I barely kept from telling her it was because everyone's scared of the town now." Kaylan kept clenching and unclenching her hands in her skirts, practically at the point of tears. Lisbet had plopped next to her, mending and sewing, and they looked so much like sisters that more than once Hallen gave Ella and Ronnet a thoughtful look.

"A town like this," Finn said slowly as he walked upside down on his hands and feet like a crab around the open area, short black hair hanging loose, "I bet it's all stuff like 'be a good neighbor' and 'make sure we're all doing our part,' right?" He kicked off with his feet into a handstand, and continued hand-walking, "Like it sounds good in theory, but people don't like that kind of pressure."

Kaylan paled. "You just about took the words out of my mother's mouth. She's happy as a pig in a wallow because she's important, and Marin, well, I just try to stay out of her way."

"And you said nobody leaves?" Zanner was juggling small wooden pins back and forth with Conna, dressed for the family in a tunic and pants. Kaylan hadn't even batted an eye.

"Some did, early on, but they didn't have much to lose. Later on, though, some families just packed up and left in the dead of night. The mayor put a stop to that by closing the gates at sun-set, not like there's any chance of a war or bandits hereabouts.

She said it wasn't 'civic-minded' for people to leave just when everyone was working hard to make the town a better place." Now the tears started falling, a slow drip down Kaylan's face.

"Which friend did you lose?" Lisbet asked quietly, leaning over to offer a cloth.

"Oh, his name was Robin, and he sang like one, and I think he might have had Bardic inclinations or something, and I hope he got to Haven safely with his family." She took the cloth and rubbed at her eyes.

"Well, our daughter's in Haven now, learning how to be a Healer," Ella said with a smile. "We could always send a letter up there, for just in case." A brief pause as she looked around the family, gauging expressions and finally nodding. "Or a person."

As Kaylan started sobbing, Zanner and Conna began bantering while Hallen *just* happened to lean against one of the curtain poles, making the chimes sound without the wind. Lisbet hugged the teen fiercely, and Kaylan returned it in kind.

After Kaylan had calmed, Ronnet said to Kaylan, "We've done this before. Nearly everyone here, we've rescued from one situation or another, but never from a town where everyone watches everyone else. And most particularly, not someone with a parent as important as your mother. Doesn't mean we won't try, but we need to be clever and careful and cover all the angles. But the real question is, are you ready to leave all this behind? Family and friends and anything you can't carry in a simple bag?"

After a few long, shuddery breaths, Kaylan answered, "This isn't my home. I've no friends my age anymore, thanks to my mother. I'd rather be a server in a tavern than stay. Yes, I'm ready."

Hallen chuckled. "We'll not make you do that, but life on the road isn't easy. Let's get you there first, which means it's time to ask: Is everyone here willing to try to get Kaylan out of Hartsbridge?"

Nine votes around the family, and nine ayes.

*   *   *

The evening's performance was a bit short-handed, as Lisbet
had walked Kaylan back to her house, and not returned yet.
Even still, the audience laughed and cheered at all the right
places, and the mayor and councilors nodded and smiled and
even came up after the show to say how much they appreciated
the Avelards being willing to adjust their performances.

The only moment of concern was when Marje asked, "Have
any of you seen my daughter Kaylan? She ought to have been
here." The woman's hennaed hair hung in neat curls that likely
took hours to maintain, surrounding a face sharp enough to put
Zanner's knives to shame.

"One of ours escorted her home, Councilor Marje," Ella answered. "She complained of aches and other symptoms, and it
made sense to not let her go alone."

Marje frowned. "I do hope my daughter isn't malingering, or
taking advantage of your good natures."

"Oh, Havens, no!" Conspiratorially, Ella whispered, "My
daughter had symptoms like that during her worst courses, so
best not to risk anything, right?"

The woman paled and nodded. "Well, then, thank you for
your concern. I should get home and see to her needs. I *do* hope
my husband Wilton's been caring for her properly." With that,
Marje turned and hurried off, leaving Marin and the other two
councilors to finish offering thanks.

Later that night, townsfolk up late marked a cloaked figure
heading toward the square where the traveling show had set up.
It seemed a bit odd to them, but enough had seen one of the
performers, cloaked and hooded against the sun, escort a
woozy-looking Kaylan home that nobody thought to say anything later to the girl's mother.

The next morning, Mathias came to say his goodbyes. "I've
done all the trading here I can for the time, and there's plenty
of towns along the road as need the pots an' cloth an' flour from
here." He glanced sourly around. "Don't stay too long here,
they don't like it. An' be safe, y'hear?"

Hallen smiled. "We'll be leaving tomorrow, most likely. Probably won't catch you up on the road, so thank you for everything."

Mathias just shook his head. "Weren't nothin'. Us folk who travel gotta watch out for each other, yeah?"

"That we do."

Meanwhile, Conna and Hesby went to the market for food, supplies, and a healthy dose of the town gossip. They made a big show of praising the town's goods, more than enough to make merchants desperate for any kind words share news about the couple who'd started courting over the winter, or the blacksmith who'd been so glad to see Mathias and some fresh iron, or the new rules about window-box planters only having certain kinds of flowers.

On their way back to the square, they chose a route that took them through some of the more important neighborhoods, though behind the houses for a bit of privacy. All the goods they'd purchased were stacked in a rolling wagon built for the purpose. During a quiet moment, Hesby murmured, "Havens, this place is boring."

Conna replied a bit later, after they'd needed to reshuffle the goods a bit, "'Cause they're all too afraid to do anything that'll mark them out. We're safe enough, because we'll be leaving. After, they'll gossip about us."

A few streets later, the square in sight, Hesby said, "Then we'll make sure they have something to talk about for the next several months." A very faint grin played across his face, and Conna matched it. Then the family came out and took over unloading the small wagon, Ronnet ostentatiously hefting the largest sack over his shoulders while Zanner, Finn, and Wenn scurried back and forth, transferring the smaller things to the wagons while the sun heated the square.

"Lisbet!" Ella called. "You're to stay under the awnings. No use you getting yet another sunburn on account of your fair skin."

A sound of noncommittal agreement came from the vicinity of the wagons, followed by Hallen calling back that the girl was, in fact, being mindful of the sun. And once the family had emptied the wagon and collapsed it into a neat pile of boards and wheels, they bowed all around the square to the people watching at the windows, and disappeared into the area behind the stage.

That evening, the Avelards pulled out all the stops on their performances. Nothing too scary, just as Marje had asked, but one act had Zanner, Hallen, and Conna juggling pins and Finn jumping between them all, eliciting gasps and roars from the crowd each time the pins nearly hit Finn. Another act had Ronnet lift Finn easily over his head, then flip the acrobat end over end as the strongman juggled a person as easily as the others had juggled the pins.

Then Conna came back out again, this time doing stage magic like scarves from her bodice, cutting rope then restoring it, claiming a coin from an audience member then cutting open an apple to reveal that coin, and finally a trick where she called Marje down and had her put a fabric doll into a box, then lock it, only to produce the doll even though Marje herself held the key.

"Well, I never!" Marje was heard to remark amusedly as she returned to her seat, only to frown again at the seat where her daughter should have sat. The townsfolk knew better than to say anything, as they knew Kaylan on occasion suffered from powerful headaches and cramps. But everyone could see the councilor was not pleased, even with the distraction of the traveling show.

Finally, Zanner and Hallen came out with Ronnet carrying a plank of sturdy-looking wood. The two jugglers waited while Ronnet lifted the board to waist height, then climbed up on either end, and while Ronnet carefully raised and lowered the board, Zanner and Hallen tossed cloth balls back and forth. The trio made it seem effortless, balls arcing across the space between the jugglers, and then Ronnet began turning in place, the jugglers keeping their balance and losing not a single ball.

When all was said and done, Conna and Finn came out and

the five performers bowed to thunderous applause from the townsfolk while the musicians behind the curtain played an upbeat farewell.

"That's all for the Avelards this night! May you sleep well, for I know we shall!" Hallen bowed again to the audience, gestured to their musicians, and at last the curtain dropped on the third and final night of the Avelard Traveling Show.

The next morning, the wagons packed, mules hitched, and lastminute arrangements underway, Hallen held up a hand for attention. Everyone stopped, and the echoes of a very strident voice came bouncing their way. And the voice wasn't alone; there were rumblings of uncertainty and discontent from what sounded like a sizable crowd.

"Well," Hallen said with a tight smile, "it seems we've a sending-off to attend. Everything important packed?"

"Aye," Ella responded instantly.

"Zanner, to the mules. Keep an eye on them."

The juggler was already in motion, soothing the mule teams with treats and kind words.

"Everyone else as can be up front, be here. We'll keep you safe." And like that, the rest of the Avelards finished what they were doing and moved into position flanking Hallen and Ella, Ronnet standing protectively over Wenn and with a kind hand on Conna's shoulder.

By that point, the main voice carried clear through the air. "—and when I went to her room this morning to check on her, her bed was empty!" Marje stalked through the archway gesticulating to the mayor and the crowd of townsfolk following along. "And there's only these folk from outside our town, our lovely Hartsbridge, who don't know our ways, who don't know my daughter, and probably convinced her the world outside's better than staying here!" The crowd following along made noises that were noncommittal to downright suspicious.

Hallen stepped forward, bowing politely. "What seems to be the issue, Councilor Marje, Mayor Marin?" He looked at the two, then at what seemed to be most of the rest of the town.

The mayor, blond ringlets looking too similar to Marje's, stepped forward with an imperious smile. "My dear friend, Councilor Marje, seems to think that you've witched her daughter with tales of the world beyond the walls of Hartsbridge. And seeing as how the girl is not to be found this morning, well, she insisted we search for her here."

"Begging your pardon, Mayor," Ella said, looking up slightly at the woman, "but as you can see, it's just us here, making ready to leave. Now, yes, Kaylan did come to us a couple of days ago, but we returned her with an escort, good as you please. Aside from us being strangers, why accuse us?"

Marje sneered. "We know she spent several candlemarks here with your *little* show, then came home complaining of pains and a terrible headache. And nobody's seen her properly outside my house since."

"Begging your pardon, Councilor, but she did complain of cramping in ways that would have a Healer order her right to bed," Ella said with a bland expression. "And we've had those discussions with a Healer, in fact the very one training my daughter. An escort was the least we could do for Kaylan, seeing as how my daughter's a trainee in Haven." The crowd murmured again, more doubt coming to the fore.

"People saw a cloaked figure come back to the square, yes," said Marin, "but at night, when there's no real call for having a hood over your face." She nodded as if scoring a point.

"Lisbet was being perhaps a bit cautious in what is clearly a very safe town," Ella said politely, "but as she was attacked not so long ago, I suspect she didn't want to draw attention to herself."

"She's the one my Wilton said brought Kaylan home, looking enough like my daughter to be her sister?"

"That's her, all right." Hallen spoke up this time, a fond smile on his face. "She's a good part of the show, just a bit under the weather at the moment."

Marin said, "Bring her out here. Let us ensure that no trickery is afoot."

Before Ella could say anything, a voice called out from one of the wagons, "Fine, if you must." And with that, the same cloaked and hooded figure people had seen that night carefully descended the stairs to the cobbled square, and moved gingerly forward.

"Take down that hood," Marin demanded.

Carefully, the figure shifted the hood back, revealing Lisbet's rather sunburnt face. "My apologies, Mayor. I overdid it yesterday, and have been resting since."

Marje frowned, counting up the nine Avelards in the square facing her and the townsfolk. The muttering briefly surged with a tone of sympathy for the young woman, before fading as Marin turned to glare at her people.

"Might I go back to lying down? I don't feel at all well." Lisbet managed a tiny bow.

"Fine, fine. Except." Marje glared. "How do we know you don't have my daughter hiding in your wagons?"

Ronnet sighed, and the crowd leaned back a pace. "As you can see, they're just big enough for the nine of us, our gear, and a few other things. If you truly think we've managed to secret your daughter somewhere inside, then please, let us unpack— just for you—and show you she's not there." He grinned. "Oh yes, and our supplies cart, you should certainly search that as well, though we've mostly got goods from your town and some of our props in it. Not really enough room for a young woman along with everything else, but let's be thorough about this."

For a moment, Marje was taken aback, then the sneer reappeared on her face. "Oh, I'll search every inch of your wagons and cart. I don't believe for a second you don't have anything to do with my daughter's disappearance."

And for the next half a mark and a bit more, the Avelards opened their wagons to the increasingly upset Marje. They opened cupboards that couldn't have hidden a dog, much less a person, removed the flooring of the wagons to reveal more storage, unpacked their storage cart, including a hefty bag that Ronnet demonstrated held only flour from Hartsbridge, and did so with such grace and manners that by the end, the crowd had started grumbling about how this was taking time from their busy day.

"Well, if she's not here, then you helped her escape! Over the wall, or through the drains, or some such!" Marje looked fit to burst a vein, Marin looked colder than the Forest of Sorrows, and the townsfolk had quieted as they watched what some were beginning to realize was another show put on by the Avelards. In fact, by this point, nearly everyone who'd been to the performances was there watching.

As the Avelards started putting everything to rights, Hallen said curiously, "Over the wall? In full view of everyone around?" Before Marje could even sputter a response, he said, "Ronnet, Finn, let's show these fine folk just how this wouldn't work." Finn grinned and grabbed a good length of rope, then Ronnet tossed him up and gently toward the wall. The acrobat scurried up in full view of the houses around, and when he got to the top and dropped the rope down, it was clear Kaylan couldn't have been smuggled out that way. As Finn clambered down the wall, Hallen continued, "Your daughter isn't trained to climb, so she'd need to have been hauled. And that makes noise too, and it would have been obvious."

Once Finn rejoined the rest of the Avelards, he bowed to Hallen. "It's a good wall! All the stone's sturdy, and even though I could find handholds, I don't think an amateur could." He bowed more formally to the mayor. "It's a most excellent wall, definitely good for keeping people safe inside."

The crowd murmured again, and Zanner, focused mostly on the mules, heard the subtle change as more and more of the townsfolk shifted from supporting their leaders to supporting the Avelards.

"What about the drains?" Marin asked coldly.

Ronnet sighed then. "Well, it's true there's a spot here we had to set up around, big enough for maybe one or two people, but . . ." He walked over to the rectangular grate, and waggled the sturdy lock keeping it in place loudly enough everyone could hear. ". . . that lock's not been opened for years is my guess, and you'd need a key for that, I think." He bowed to Marin. "I expect you're the sort to keep the keys on you, though, so if you'd like to unlock the grate, we can prove we didn't help her out through the drains."

Glaring, the mayor strode forward, hands reaching to the ring of keys at her belt. One by one she sorted through them, frowning and muttering until she found one specific key, which fit the lock but wouldn't turn until Hesby ran and got some lamp oil.

"The lock clearly hasn't been opened in a long time," Hallen said matter-of-factly, "and even if it had, well, Ronnet?" At that, the strongman pulled on the grating, which gave a loud groan as it moved. He put it off to the side with a clearly audible clunk.

"Hesby?" Hallen continued. "Can you tell us what's in there?"

"Sure thing!" He leaned over and reeled back a bit. "Seems like outflows from privies, would be my guess. I hope you don't mind if I don't stick my hand in it? Looks kind of shallow, though."

"I think we've proved our point, Mayor Marin, Councilor Marje," Ella said. "Kaylan's not in our wagons, and we couldn't have helped her escape otherwise. If you please, we'd like to get going. We ought to have been on the road long since, and while I understand your concerns, I suggest you search the town, in case she's had an accident." Ronnet put the grating back, fastened the lock, and moved up to be with the rest of the Avelards.

And to the sounds of upset and indignant screeching, along with a crowd that had turned quite against the two in charge, the Avelards drove their wagons out of Hartsbridge.

A ways from town, Hallen called out, "Hallo the traveler!"

At that, Kaylan, a kerchief on her head and a bundle across her back, turned, then stepped off the road and waved at the Avelards. "Hallo the travelers!"

The family paused long enough to get her into the back of the lead wagon, and Zanner asked with a grin, "How did it go?"

"Oh, Havens, it went so perfectly! My dad's going to be in trouble if Mother ever finds out he helped me escape, but he got me out last night, and I waited just like you suggested until the whole town went off to watch the morning show. Then once the gates were clear, I just walked out with nobody to see me or stop me!" Tears started flowing down her face as she hugged first Zanner then Lisbet, smearing some of the red dye they'd used to mimic a sunburn. "And he handed me a pouch with coin, said he'd been saving it for me in case one day I could leave."

"He sounds like a better man than your mother deserves," Hallen called back from the front of the wagon.

"I asked him to come. He said it would look too suspicious, but he also said he expects Marje's going to kick him out in the next month or so. At which point he'll head for Haven, find a job and a place, and be ready for me." Kaylan's eyes shone. "Haven! Both literally and metaphorically, that is."

At that, Hallen laughed. "Mind you, we're on circuit at the moment, so we may not get back there until closer to autumn and the harvest. We cross paths with other folk who'd get you there faster, though."

"Oh, no, I'm going to pay off my debt to you all first. You didn't have to get me out of there, you know." Kaylan sniffled and wiped her eyes on her sleeve.

Zanner took Kaylan's face in their hands and smiled. "No, we did, because each of us knows what it's like to be stuck in a bad place. And we're not about to let someone suffer if we can help. Even if all we are is the distraction!"

At that, every single one of them cheered. Kaylan helped Lisbet wipe off the rest of the dye, and soon the two were chattering and giggling while Zanner practiced juggling, and the rest of the Avelards discussed the next town, and what they might find along the way.

Ella leaned into Ronnet's arm and sighed. "We did a really good thing here."

"It's what you, Hallen, and I all agreed on when we started out. Find the ones we could save, and save them. And look at our family now, with all these good folk who need a place like ours. Even for a short time."

Ella nodded, and the family moved on down the road.

Enough
Louisa Swann

Blasted bard.

Riann pushed up on her elbow, scowling as an unseen rock bruised her bony hip. Fortunately, the ear-numbing *snort, snort, wheeze* that refused to let her close her eyes seemed comforting to Lil Beebee. The louder Darl snored, the deeper the babe slept.

She gazed down at Bee, breathing in her sweet scent. Lil Bee pursed her lips and made sucking motions, and Riann's heart flipped over.

"Happy ta see someone's gettin' a few winks." She resisted the urge to boop the babe's nose, not wanting to wake the little one. Between the snoring and the pressure in her bladder, she wouldn't be getting back to sleep anytime soon.

A shiver ran up her spine, leaving a trail of goosepimples in its wake. There was something in the air tonight. Something she couldn't identify.

Not a vision coming on. It wasn't that kind of feeling.

Just . . . something.

With a quiet sigh, Riann slipped out from under the heavy quilt the bard had loaned them, careful not to disturb the babe. The fire had long died to embers after an evening spent learning how to navigate using the stars. Riann thought about stirring those embers to life again, but one look at the stars told her morning wouldn't come anytime soon. Might as well take care of business and get back under the quilt before the mosquito bites outdid the goosepimples.

No use worrying about boots or cloak—the rain had stopped

two nights ago, and the woods had mostly dried. Plenty of water everywhere, though. Even Darl admitted he'd never seen so much rain.

A loud grunt followed by another of the bard's snorts chased away all thought of sleep.

"Don't ya be grumpin' too." Riann wrinkled her nose at the surly goat glaring at her from the other side of the fire. "Be back inna flash."

Miz Goat chewed, the grass stalk in her mouth bobbing up and down as her chin moved from side to side. Not only was the goat Lil Bee's only source of milk, the four-hooved nuisance had pushed and butted Riann into Darl's camp during a torrential rainstorm two nights ago. Half starving and soaked clean through, Riann had accepted the bard's hospitality, reveling in the warmth of the fire and hot food in her belly.

The next morning, she and the bard had agreed to travel together for as long as their paths converged, a relief as far as she was concerned. Not only was the bard the biggest man she'd ever seen, he was strong and smart and capable.

Everything Riann wasn't.

Made for a perfect partnership, in her estimation. For a little while, anyway.

Darl's little friend Gnash, the rat-weasel Changeling with red eyes and fangs, chittered as she headed out of camp.

"Ya stay where ya are now," Riann said, glaring at the tiny creature. Caught in a Change-Circle transformation, the little guy was neither rat nor weasel, yet still a little of both. Sensitive to the moods of those around him, Gnash also read minds and could find a gnat in a nest of mosquitoes simply by following his nose.

He was also more curious than a cat, always poking his nose in places it didn't belong. She gave him another glare, then cautiously pushed through the brush and around trees to find a spot to answer nature's call, thankful for the bright quarter moon. Night dew clung to her bare feet while spring grass tickled between her toes. The smell of damp earth and budding plants filled the air.

Along with the whine of what seemed a thousand mosquitoes.

She'd made it about four wagon lengths away from camp when the earth trembled and shook and the dirt beneath her feet dropped away with a roar, carrying Riann with it.

Her stomach slid into her throat as she half slipped, half fell amid a torrent of dirt, stones, and mud. She tried to grab something—roots, rocks—anything to stop her fall.

And failed, managing to break a few fingernails before tumbling into empty space.

She squeezed her eyes tight, not wanting to see what was coming . . .

And plunged into water so cold she thought her heart might stop.

Riann's first coherent thought after plummeting into an ice-cold river in the middle of the night wasn't about her life or her family or her imminent death.

No, *after* the initial mind-numbing, heart-pounding confusion of being dunked in the drink, her first thought was about the baby—who was going to care for Lil Beebee if Riann got sucked into the bowels of the earth?

The thought wriggled away like a slippery eel as she thrashed about, caught in a nightmare of utter darkness, swept into a vortex of watery death with no way out.

She opened her eyes—only to find her eyes were already open.

Something had swallowed the light.

Water in her eyes, her nose, her ears, she struggled against growing panic. Her woolen tunic dragged at her shoulders and neck and tangled about her legs every time she tried to kick, pulling her into the depths.

Deep under water.

Where monsters lived.

And demons.

And ghosts. And ghouls . . .

A scream bubbled from her lips, taking a bit of precious air with it as something tickled her cheek.

She flailed, trying to shove away whatever insisted on clinging to her cheek. Her thick woolen tunic pulled at her, dragging
her down like an anchor. She tore the wool off one shoulder,
then the other, thankful she'd worn a sleeveless tunic over a
loose linen shirt instead of a full dress. Growling deep in her
throat at the fabric tangling her legs, she gave one last kick,
freeing her ankles and feet. Thank Vkandis she'd left her boots
in camp.

She reached upward . . .

Only to realize she didn't know her up from her down.

Riann faltered, confused. Her head felt funny. She had to
breathe. Had to . . .

"Watch da bubbles," her mum's voice whispered in her mind,
the voice that taught her how to swim and dive almost as soon
as she could walk. A voice dead more than three years.

How on earth was she supposed to "watch da bubbles" when
she couldn't see a thing?

"Watch da bubbles."

She grabbed hold of that thought. Took a heartbeat to pic-
ture bubbles rising in a pot. Then, pressing her eyes tight, fighting the scream lodged in her throat and the suffocating desire
to breathe, she let a tiny bit of precious air escape her lips.

The air tickled the right side of her nose and drifted up her
cheek before being swallowed by the churning waters.

Riann clawed the water, chasing the bubble-path and praying to Vkandis to guide her back to the surface.

What if there isn't a surface to get back to?

The thought seized her heart. Blood thundered in her ears.
What if the entire tunnel wasn't a tunnel at all but a tube filled
with water?

She felt herself sinking again, only it wasn't her body this
time. It was her mind; her soul.

"Kick," her mum whispered. *"Kick!"*

Riann kicked and clawed, struggling to calm her racing
heart. She focused on coordinating her arms with her legs, her
strokes with her kicks, the hem of her linen shirt tickling her
knees as she was swept along by the current.

She ignored the debris brushing past her legs, the sensation decreasing as her legs grew numb.

Gotta keep movin'. Gotta. Keep. Movin'.

Just as she'd done her whole life.

Riann clenched her teeth and kept clawing, pulling herself upward like a cat climbing a tree.

Reach, pull. Reach, pull. Kick.

Kick.

Without warning, she erupted from the water, gasping air and struggling to see. Waves slapped her chin and splashed her cheeks, icy fingers of death threatening to drag her back under.

She smashed into something rough and hard, pain shooting down the left side of her head into her shoulder and arm. Her head spun, though she couldn't tell if it was from the pain in her skull or if she was actually spinning. Shivers wracked her body.

Cold. So cold.

She choked in a breath, spluttering at the watery taste of fish and dirt. Her right foot brushed something and she screamed, kicking frantically to drive away whatever had bumped her, praying to Vkandis she wouldn't feel teeth sinking into her flesh . . .

She struck at the water, splashing and spinning, imagining hundreds of snakes swimming toward her, mouths open, teeth glittering, twining themselves around her arms, tangling her legs, dragging her down again, deeper and deeper . . .

A shudder raked through Riann, shaking her from head to toe. She clenched her jaw. *No snakes*, she told herself. *Just debris—*

Her stomach dropped as the water fell, not in a waterfall kind of way, but a slippery move that reminded her of sliding on ice. Arms flailing, she reached out, searching for something to grab hold of.

Something to keep her from being swept into the depths of Hell—

Swept through lightless cracks in the earth like Miz Podahl the shopkeeper swept trash between the boards outside her shop . . .

Kick.

Riann kicked, barely able to feel her numb legs. Her hands were as numb as her feet and she was tired, so tired.

Something snagged her sleeve, tugging and pulling before letting go. Her rational mind—what was left of it—wanted to believe she'd brushed against a branch or brush or something equally as innocent. But fear grabbed hold of her heart and squeezed tight.

What if she wasn't the only one to fall into this underground river? What if she was swimming in a sea of corpses?

She swallowed another scream, forcing herself to take a deep breath—

Only to get a mouthful of water instead of air. She gasped, coughed, gasped again. Struggled to pull free of the fear threatening to turn her into a blubbering blob.

It was the dark, she reasoned, kicking and paddling, keeping her head above water. She hated the dark. Blamed that hatred on the town bully who'd lured her into a copse of dead trees when she was six. Three of his friends—wearing masks so hideous they once scared the butcher—jumped out of their hiding places and chased her back to town.

Proving to her the dark *was* scary, no matter what anyone said.

Scarier, even, than death.

Eventually, she learned to control her fears—of darkness, of the town bully. All she had to do was focus on what she could control—like leaving a candle burning at night . . .

Her feet suddenly dropped, spinning her in a half circle, whirling her into what felt like a rock wall. For the second time, pain exploded through her left shoulder and into her neck.

Taking away any thoughts of control.

Havta get outta here. Get back ta Lil Bee and Miz Goat—

But what if I can't get outta the water? Can't lie down and get some rest? Can't eat? How long will I last before joinin' the sea of invisible corpses?

Despite being soaking wet, the hair on the back of her neck stood on end as she realized that the sound echoing off the walls had changed. What had been a constant roar was more of a howling moan, interrupted by . . . hiccups?

She gasped, focusing on the sound of roaring water, forcing the fear and the pain and the ever-growing exhaustion to the back of her mind as the current carried her sideways.

A shadow appeared to her right, so brief and insubstantial she thought she'd imagined it. A strand of sodden hair lifted from her cheek, dropped against her skin, then whipped across her eyes.

She blinked, then blinked again, startled to see the vague suggestion of walls as she slipped past. Another heartbeat, and the vagueness sharpened into rough rock mixed with polished stone.

Her teeth chattered with cold; her arms and legs felt like logs. But somewhere up ahead there was light. Not bright enough to be sun. Moonlight, then.

The moan deepened, combined with a hushing, shushing undertone that made her grind her teeth. What on earth was making that sound?

Riann hadn't been out in the world before; had never seen more than the little river running past their village.

But she'd heard plenty of stories, all of which circled around waterfalls or whirlpools.

Stories or no, if she couldn't get out of this river, she'd plummet—or be whirled—to her death.

Riann had seconds to react after spotting an enormous tree jutting out of the water. She'd been swept around a corner into moonlight just bright enough to cast her surroundings in a twilight gloom—and found herself face to face with a tree.

Not a normal wrap-your-arms-around-the-trunk-size tree. A massive nightmare of mangled roots and gnarled limbs leaning at an odd angle.

The rock and dirt ceiling had slumped into the river along with the tree, leaving behind a gaping hole as big around as the Brinleville mayor's house. The hole looked to be as far away as the tip of the church steeple and through that hole, beyond the jagged edges of torn earth bracing the top of the monster tree, the darkness sparkled.

Stars.

Lodged in the river, the tree redirected the current in a wild array of crisscrossing waves. A body length or so beyond the tree was the source of the now thunderous roar . . .

Whirlpool.

Thank Vkandis there was light.

Riann shoved all thoughts of the whirlpool from her mind, focusing on one thing: that tree.

Roots or branches, she didn't care. She had to find something to hold onto. Some way to get out of the water.

Or she was dead.

Ignoring the exhaustion dragging at her arms and legs, she stopped struggling and started swimming, keeping the tree in her sight.

Choppy waves and a cross current that seemed to come from nowhere slowed her down. She kicked harder, forcing her numb feet to move. She lengthened her stroke, reaching out, pulling at the water, praying to find something to hold onto.

She couldn't feel her fingers. Couldn't feel her toes. How was she going to catch hold of anything . . . ?

Yer gonna fail again. Yer not strong enough. Not tough enough.

She didn't need to be tough. *Just need ta keep puttin' one foot 'n fronta the other.*

Her left hand hit something hard and rootlike. She grabbed, forcing her fingers closed, then drove herself forward, kick, kick, kicking into the ball of tangled roots. She caught another root in her right hand and held fast, struggling to catch her breath.

The current shifted, dragging her legs away from the tree. Her right hand lost its grip and slid down the slick root. Her legs swept sideways in the current, angling her body toward the whirlpool and certain death. Pain throbbed in her left side and her head felt like it'd been stomped by a mad bull.

Mud splashed into the water just beyond her nose. She

watched in dull fascination as the mud floated toward the whirl-pool, spinning slowly round and round before sinking into a watery grave.

Why hadn't she seen the earthquake in a vision? She could have stayed in camp. Stayed with Darl and Lil Bee.

Was she so weak, so unimportant her visions had deserted her?

Perhaps they had. Perhaps her Gift had decided to move on.

Maybe she should move on too.

In a haze of pain and swirling water, she wondered what it would be like to just let go. Let go of the pain. Let go of the hunger. Let go the sense of being alone even with people all around and the responsibility that being alone carried with it.

Responsibility to herself. Responsibility to the memory of her mother.

Let go of the failure. Of not being enough. Of never being enough.

Not big enough. Not strong enough. Not smart enough . . .

Darl would care for Lil Bee and Miz Goat.

It would be so easy to just . . .

Let . . .

Go.

The roar of the waterfall faded. Her right hand slipped again. The water—dark and deadly—beckoned like a long-lost friend.

The whirlpool enticed, cajoled, entreated, its caressing wa-ters loving as a mother's arms . . .

The song of the turbulent river wove around and through the whirlpool's thunder, soothing instead of threatening . . .

Into the song slipped a counterpoint so soft she almost let it slide by. But the new note refused to be let go, growing, then nearly disappearing only to slip in again, teasing her senses, tantalizing her curiosity.

The heartfelt song.

Of a baby's cry.

Startled, Riann tore her gaze from the whirlpool and searched the shadows, straining to hear the sound one more time.

Had she imagined it?

Or was there a baby caught in the same mess she found herself in?

"Beebee?" she called, softly at first, then louder. "Lil Bee!"

The whirlpool's thunder swallowed her voice and echoed in her ears.

But the baby's cry—real or imagined—was gone.

Riann didn't know whether to be relieved or disappointed. Relieved that the babe hadn't been dumped in the drink like Riann; disappointed that she might never see the little one again.

Her ambivalence faded, leaving behind a flame that burned brighter and brighter.

Yes, she had been alone, but she was alone no longer. She had someone who depended on her. Someone she could love. Someone who wouldn't care if she had magic or not.

She and Lil Bee had started life in different towns with different people, torn from their families too young.

But now they had each other.

They need never be alone again.

All she had to do was get out of this hole.

Riann clenched her teeth so tight her jaw ached almost as much as her head. She grabbed at the root again.

And missed.

Her other hand started to slip.

"Nononononono!"

She'd never make it. She'd die in this river, swept into oblivion.

She'd fail Lil Bee, just as she'd failed her mother.

"*Yer not ta blame fer my death*," Mum whispered in her mind. "*Not responsible fer what others have done.*"

Riann swallowed a moan, her mother's death hitting her square in the gut, even though she'd been dead more than three years. Mum had been a simpleton, but she'd believed in Riann. Trusted her to do what needed doing. Trusted her more than Riann trusted herself.

Her eyes burned. She knew in her head she wasn't responsible for Mum's death. But her heart told her otherwise.

Besides, the babe *was* her responsibility, her companion, her *salvation*. She should be back at camp with the babe, the bard, and the goat—staying warm beside the dying embers of last night's fire instead of swirling and twirling like a cockroach stuck in a rolling barrel.

All because she'd had to pee.

"Believe in yerself," Mum's voice whispered again. *"Ya be strong enough ta do anythin'. Tough enough ta handle life's battles."*

No matter how many times the townsfolk had knocked Mum down, she always got back up.

Time to follow her lead.

Riann tightened her grip on the slippery roots, eyes burning, mouth dry. With a grunt, she flung her right hand at the root held in her left, wincing as her numb fingers slapped ragged wood. She clutched the root tight and took a deep breath.

She could do this, just as she'd left her home in Brinleville— a chicken shed without any chickens—because of a single vision. Not only had she wanted to do something about the impending danger, she'd had to get away from the priests. Had to leave before they found out about her visions.

Before they put her in the burning fires.

If she could leave home without a compass, she could climb trees.

Haven't been struck by any visions since gettin' up ta pee, she reminded herself. She frowned at the realization, then decided it didn't matter. Hand over hand, she dragged her body upward, ducking her head to keep from being poked in the eye by smaller roots extending from the larger ones like tiny daggers.

She drew her knees up, shoving her feet into the tangle of roots.

Over and over . . .

On the third try, her left foot caught and held.

Heart in her throat, she put her full weight on her foot and stood, rising partway out of the water.

Holding her breath, expecting the roots to part or break at

any moment, she lifted her right foot, seeking a foothold slightly higher than the left.

And failing.

No matter how hard she shoved her toe into the roots, she couldn't seem to find a foothold. She was just about to give up—arms quivering, legs like soggy bread—

Not strong enough.

—when her right foot found a spot that held, though she had to keep her foot slightly turned.

She slid her right hand, then her left, up the roots she'd been clinging to. Then put weight on the right foot. Her ankle ached at the odd angle. But the roots held.

She straightened her right leg.

And rose completely out of the water.

Hope swelled in her chest, a tiny ember hesitant to burst into flame. She gazed at the stars twinkling impossibly far overhead . . .

Too weak . . .

Riann wriggled her left foot free. She found another foothold and lifted herself higher, then repeated with her right foot.

Over and over. Slide hands, pull, step, slide hands, pull, step . . .

The smell of wet dirt gave way to wet, mangled wood. Her eyes could see the change, see the enormous trunk rising like a wall above her.

Her hands couldn't feel a thing.

Shivers wracked her body over and over, leaving her weak as a wet rag, clinging to the tree.

Clinging to life.

Just as Beebee had.

Riann had always felt like an outsider, taken in by a kind-hearted man married to a shrew of a wife, in a village more concerned about their standing with the priests than the people who needed help.

For too many years she'd *felt* alone, without anyone who really cared whether she lived or died.

Falling in the river left her truly alone.

No bullies to make life miserable. No priests to threaten her with fire.

Except . . . she had Lil Bee. The sole survivor of the poison or disease that had killed her entire family, the babe clung to life, refusing to give up.

Riann wouldn't give up either.

She drew in a deep breath, tasting the sweet scent of grass and wildflowers tangled among the stench of mud and fishy water.

Reveling in the surface smells.

Smells that spoke of campfires and bard songs. Of waking to the sun's gentle caress, Lil Bee's soft lips suckling goat milk from a glove. Of sipping hot cider on a crisp winter night.

Roots gave way to branches, muck and mud to bark and pitch.

The gentle breeze stirred her wet hair, kiss of warmth, promise of the day to come.

All she had to do was climb . . .

This . . .

Tree.

Below, the water churned, dark and dangerous. Above, stars twinkled as though dancing to a song only they could hear. Riann turned her back on the water and climbed, using the short stubs of broken branches and the slant of the tree as best she could. Her bare toes dug into broad crevices in the bark while her hands sought branches thick enough to support her weight.

Bark scraped her palms and the soles of her feet as feeling came back to both, an agonizing burn in her fingers and toes that made her wish they'd stayed numb. Between the pain and the lack of branches, she made as much progress as a frozen slug.

But the further up the tree she went, the closer to the surface she came, the easier the climb.

Halfway up, she realized she could actually feel the bark beneath her hands. Her body was still wracked by shivers, her linen shirt plastered to her skin like a wet, icy blanket, but her feet were no longer numb blocks of wood or burning bits of coal.

Now they just hurt.

Her right foot slipped, a chunk of bark breaking off just as she reached the bank supporting the tree trunk. Bark tore at her palms as she fought to hold onto the branch she'd just grabbed, praying the branch would hold, that she had enough strength to hang on.

Too weak.

A soft splash drifted up from below.

Riann didn't look down.

Her legs shook as she wedged her toes into another crack in the bark. Her back burned almost as much as her arms. She hugged the branch, checking and double checking her foot-holds before reaching for the next one. Pain shot through both feet when she straightened, but she gritted her teeth and climbed on.

To her right, layers of rock and dirt gave way to dirt and roots, dirt and roots to grassy stems. The soft breeze caressed her cheek, tickled her hair.

The trunk had narrowed during her climb, no longer as wide as a wall, though it still presented a challenge as far as getting to the ground. Riann moved diagonally as she neared the ground's surface, her heart skipping a beat as first the crown of one tree, then another slipped into view.

She climbed and climbed until she found herself looking down at solid ground, fearful her weight might send everything crashing down. A space little more than the height of a tall man stood between her feet and the ground.

All she had to do was jump.

Suddenly that space felt like an impossible distance. What if she missed? What if she jumped back *into* the hole instead of out of it?

Think of Lil Beebee. Think of your babe.

"*Ya don't deserve her,*" a voice whispered in her mind, slid-ing into her thoughts like a river eel.

Miz Burdock. The woman whose husband had sheltered

Riann and her mother, then made Riann sleep in a chicken shed and fed her kitchen scraps after Old Man Burdock and Riann's mum were dead. *"Yer a lazy brat, not worthy of owning a hat. What think ya doing with a babe like that? Can't even save yerself."*

Riann ignored the voice and studied her surroundings, trying to figure out the best way to the ground. The tree she'd climbed had once stood at the edge of a broad meadow. Trees skirted the meadow to the left; grass stretched undisturbed to her right. The sweet scent of wildflowers drifted on the night breeze that persisted in tickling her cheek.

Her gaze drifted to a limb beneath her. Thick as her arm, the limb stabbed the ground like a shovel without a blade. A ladder of sorts. Without any rungs.

Holding her breath, she inched downward, feet clinging to the limb. She kept hold of any overhead branches as long as she could, then half slid, half jumped as the ground drew near.

The jump proved too much for her tired legs. She crumpled to the ground, tears burning her eyes, and thanked Vkandis for his help.

Exhausted, she closed her eyes.

And slept.

The sky had lightened to a steel gray by the time Riann moved again. She shivered uncontrollably, teeth chattering, neck stiff from sleeping on the ground without padding. She struggled to her feet, legs quivering, and scrubbed at her arms in an effort to warm up. Anxiety tightened her stomach in a knot as she glanced one way, then the other.

No telling how far the river had carried her or in which direction.

She peered at the sky, noted the lengthening shadows, the mountain peaks in the distance.

The peaks.

Darl had pointed them out. The road they'd been following the previous day wrapped around the base of the first peak, then wound up a pass.

They'd been headed toward that pass. *That's where Darl will be,* she decided.

Darl and Lil Bee.

What happened to them? To Darl and Beebee and Miz Goat? Had the earth opened beneath the camp, too? Had they plummeted into another river?

Or had they been buried in rubble from a crumbling cliff?

Surprised she hadn't given a thought to what happened to the others during the quake, she struggled to remember if there had been a cliff over their camp . . . and failed. Their first camp—the camp where they'd met—had been located at the base of an enormous boulder.

But this camp—where Gnash and Darl and Lil Bee and Miz Goat innocently slept while Riann slipped off into the bushes— wasn't near a cliff.

Was it?

Cliff or no, the same thing that happened to her *could* have happened to them. No use thinking she was special—

"Ya ain't no more special 'n a slug being squished by a boot," Handehl the bully's voice broke into her thoughts. *"Fact is, that slug ain't worth the leather it just ruined. Just like you ain't worth spit."*

Once more, Riann shoved the memories—and the fears—to the back of her mind, wiped her blood-streaked palms on her damp shirt, and started walking.

She'd survived the underground river. Climbed a giant tree.

A little walking wouldn't hurt.

The sun was midway to noon when she stopped to bind her feet. Took her teeth and a lot of tugging to rip strips from her shirt, now dry from the sun. No longer shivering, she wound the strips around each foot and ankle as best she could, a little embarrassed at the shortened length of her shirt.

Between what felt like hours in icy water and the rough tree bark, any calluses she'd had last night were gone.

Her feet were a bloody mess.

But she wouldn't give up.

Not now. Not when she'd survived the worst.

She gritted her teeth and walked on. After spending all that time in the water, she was more than a little surprised how thirsty she was. Perhaps she'd run across a stream—

A light chittering filled the air, weaving through the trees like birdsong. The trail curved hard to the right, then stopped, dead ending at a road.

Riann glanced around, searching for the source of the chittering. It sounded like—

She screeched as a creature leaped onto her shoulder, teeth glittering in the sun. Tears burned in her eyes when she recognized the creature.

Gnarl.

The little rat-weasel patted her hair as though trying to soothe her. He chittered and bobbed up and down, then leaned in and nibbled her ear.

Riann sobbed, scooping the tiny creature in her hand and holding him close. "How did ya find me?" she finally managed to choke out. "Are the others—? Did they—?"

She couldn't say the words. Couldn't ask if Lil Bee was still alive.

Gnarl's red eyes sparked. He leaped from her hands, disappearing into the trees.

Before she could follow, something shoved her from behind. Riann grimaced, pain shooting through her feet, her back . . . seemed like everything hurt.

She turned, hand held up to stop Miz Goat's next charge. "Happy ta see ya, too."

Miz Goat stalked up, her amber eyes accusing. She nudged Riann's leg, then rubbed her nose on her thigh. Riann scratched the wiry head, then leaned down and gave the goat a big hug, reveling in the stink of goat. Miz Goat leaned into her for just a moment, then ducked her head and slid free.

"Well, little miss. Seems ya been on a bit of adventuring!" Darl strolled up, Lil Bee safe in his arms. "Good thing Gnarl here's good at finding. Folks, things—he finds whatever needs finding."

Riann stifled a yelp as she hurried toward the pair, holding out her arms.

Darl grinned. "She be well 'nuf. Never passed up a chance to let me know she be missing ya, though."

Riann smiled as she gathered Lil Bee in her arms, smelled the sweet baby scent, felt the babe's warmth.

"Missed ya, too, Lil Bee," she murmured. She smoothed the babe's hair, glancing in wonder at the cuts and bruises on her own hands.

Then she straightened her shoulders. She'd done it. Even without her visions.

She'd survived an earthquake. Survived a fall to beat falls. Survived being tumbled about by an underground river. Survived climbing a giant tree.

It took strength. It took persistence.

Despite all odds, she'd made it.

"You are strong," Mum whispered in her mind. *"You are tough."*

Lil Bee smiled, that sweet baby smile that always brought a smile to Riann's face.

"You are more than enough."

Both Feet on the Ground
Paige L. Christie

Seated with a fork half-raised to her lips, Teig froze and stared at Delvin. "You want me to *what*?"

The chatter of fellow diners and the clink of flatware and crockery filled the dining hall. The fact that the young Palace Guard had come in full uniform and during duty hours to join her for lunch had warned her that something was brewing. But she certainly hadn't expected this.

He cut another bite of his baked chicken and ate it before replying. "It's not me that wants it. The head guide for the region is sick, and they need someone who knows that area."

Since their wild ride two years ago to escape assassins hired to kill him, they had become fast friends. It was, in fact, his gratitude and influence that had helped earn her the interview with the scholarship committee that allowed her admittance into the Collegium to train to wear the deep blue of a Palace Guard. Which was probably why he'd been sent with this ridiculous request now. Not that she minded things being ridiculous—she was often at her best in such times—but this . . .

"Del, I'm a Guard trainee, not a trail guide. And the land north of Sweetsprings isn't exactly wild territory. Even if it was, there must be a dozen Heralds and trackers who know it." Despite often sneaking away to go adventuring as a child—to the irritation of Mero and Wilhem, her adopted guardians—she wasn't trained for guide work.

The whole thing made no sense. Which made perfect sense. Foolish. Perhaps vaguely dangerous. Absurd. Yes, indeed. When a situation was all those things, whose name but hers would leap to mind? She shook her head and continued her meal. "Wait, don't tell me. None of them wanted the duty."

"Well," he agreed with a grin. "It is kind of pointless."

"Thanks for that. Did you pick me out?"

He chuckled. "Well, no. Kella asked for you by name. When she was informed that she couldn't go without an escort, she said you were the only one she wanted."

Teig put down her fork and looked hard at him. Kella of all people. Proud, dark-haired Kella, who hated being contradicted—especially when she was wrong. "*Please* tell me she's not in charge of this?"

He winced a little.

Now it made even more sense that he had been the one sent to tell her of this assignment. Delvin was aware of Teig's discomfort with Kella, the most junior of the Healer trainees. Not six weeks past, Teig had the misfortune of cutting her hand on a storage rack while helping clean the armory, and she'd been sent to Kella. While the interaction had begun pleasantly enough, Teig's forward nature had soon changed that. Years spent in the kitchen of the inn with Wilhem—who often served Sweetspring as much as a Healer as the innkeep—meant her knowledge of herbs and their uses was a little greater than most people's. So she had quickly seen that Kella's choice of tincture for disinfecting the wound was one Teig was allergic to. To say the Healer had taken exception to Teig's protest against the mixture—and her suggestion of an alternative—was an understatement. And something about Kella's anger had reminded Teig too much of herself when she was frustrated. Loud. Sulky. *But at least I'm never mean*, she thought, "Del . . ."

"Apparently the flower used to make that medicinal is extremely rare, and needs a special process to harvest. And there's something about the book telling how to do that being damaged . . . I admit I didn't listen to the whole thing. Anyway, she asked for you, so it's you she'll get."

Teig blew out a breath, whiffing loose strands of hair out of her eyes. All this because Kella had discovered, when she went to look for the medicine, that the apothecary was nearly out. Back home, Wilhem always had some in his herb collection. Teig never would have imagined it was rare enough to send an entire expedition after. "She doesn't need me. I'll be useless if I'm the only guard. And as a guide. What's really going on?"

His lips pressed together for a moment before he answered. "Mother and the lead healing trainer say Kella needs to learn a lesson, and apparently you're the right person to deliver it."

Teig threw up her hands and sat back in her chair. "What lesson? Why me?" Kella was legacy-born to her trade, just as Delvin was to his. "It's not my fault I knew something she didn't. Just because someone is country-born and raised doesn't mean they're stupid."

He just looked at her.

"Damn it," she said, and put a hand over her eyes briefly before lowering it to look at him again. "Right. That lesson." Even if they found the flower, how was this possibly going to go well?

Even though Delvin didn't seem to think it was important, the first thing Teig did after lunch was head to the apothecary section of the library and ask for the book he had mentioned.

"The information has already been copied by the expedition leader," the librarian said.

Teig nodded and explained her role, after which the man shrugged and went off to retrieve the book. When he returned from the reference collection, it was clear "damaged" was far too mild a word for the state of the book. It was warped and stained from a long-past encounter with moisture, and the pages that weren't stuck together were worm eaten and torn. A narrow ribbon marked the place where someone, probably Kella, had looked up the rare plant. Teig frowned as she carried it to a table and sat down to learn what she could.

Not only was it extremely rare, but it only grew in one region and only bloomed for a few days very early in the year—almost before winter could even be considered to have really ended. A detailed map even showed the exact location where the plant could be found.

Staring at it, Teig realized she knew the spot. It wasn't but a half day's walk from old Belton's house. She frowned, visualizing the area, steep sloped and mostly rocky. What flower could they possibly find there?

The real mystery was that the book said the flower was extremely hard to retrieve—but when she turned the battered page to read why, half of the next section was stained so badly it was all but illegible. She made out a few words: "*—you will definitely need—*" and, a few smeared words later, "*—most special of Gifts will win the cause.*"

Well, at least Kella couldn't ask much of Teig. She was the least Gifted person in the Collegium. Maybe in all of Haven. She frowned and squinted at the page, trying to decipher more of the ruined writing. She studied a rough image sketched in the margin. It almost looked like a spear, but she couldn't really make it out.

After several minutes of struggling to discern more, flipping pages to different angles and holding the book in different lights, she gave up. But something about that partial image nagged at her as she returned the book to the main desk and trudged back to her quarters.

The clues were too vague. They could mean anything. Then something leaped to mind as she walked, something Wilhem had told her when she was a tiny girl, just come into his care. *"Never assume you know what's in any of those jars in the pantry. You ask me before you touch anything. Never assume anything about a plant, good or bad."*

Well, she'd learned assuming was a dangerous thing, all in all. With that in mind, she needed to take her title of guide and guard as seriously as she could. And that meant she had to prepare for everything she could think of.

The line of wagons clattered over the road, every bump amplified by impact with hard ruts. A few inches of dirty snow lined the roadside, the last remains of winter clinging stubbornly against the promise of spring. Though the last days had brought enough warmth to begin the seasonal melt, the ground remained frozen, and the much-abused road surface jolted the wagons with every turn of their wheels. The landscape crept by at an aching pace, the mules trudging along, carefully placing their feet as they leaned into the traces.

Teig sat on the tailgate of the last wagon, kicking her feet to keep her blood moving. Despite her heavy clothing, lack of real activity drove the cold to her bones. She sighed. She was missing weeks of training by being here, and that soured her mood day by day, despite her resolve to do her best on this trek. It would have been easier to make the best of things if Kella hadn't been so *tense* from the very start of the trip.

At last, one lurch too many punched up Teig's spine. She did a quick mental calculation of the cost of disobeying orders versus feeling broken for the next month, and shoved herself off the wagon, landing awkwardly on the uneven ground.

"What're you doing?" a worried male voice asked.

"Easing my back," she answered as she caught her balance. With a shake of her head, she looked over her shoulder at the shivering young man driving the wagon. "Slow as we're moving, I'll be safer walking." *And warmer,* she did not add.

At sixteen, Calth was two years her senior, but his face held the wide uncertainty of someone unused to traveling beyond city boundaries. Even this simple adventure was so far outside his experience he might as well have been a child on his first day at school.

A glance up the line at the three other wagons drew a sigh from Teig. Even the most senior of the people in this small caravan were city dwellers. In fact, she was the only one who had grown up in the countryside. Which was probably the other part of why she had ended up on this trip in the first place—the sad combination of lived experience and some weird, petty retribution.

Ahead, on the lead wagon, Kella swayed, doing her best to look comfortable despite the painful jostling. Teig shook her head as she stood and stretched.

"Get back on." Calth's voice was low and urgent. "She wants us all riding."

Under less harsh road conditions, Kella's order would make sense. But, between the cold and the painful, unpredictable jerks caused by the rough road, the idea that walking would be more tiring was—Teig tried for a kindness her stretched-thin patience did not wish to access—*not well thought out.*

Kella was in charge of the expedition, and, despite bringing Teig on as a supposed guide, she had relegated her to the back of the wagon train. Was that to make her feel slighted? As though the road to Sweetsprings wasn't obvious, a clear, wide line drawn south, impossible to lose day or night. The only way to get lost was to plan to get lost. And Kella hopefully knew she would be out of her depth if she ventured too far from the main road. The woman was smart. She was just unable to be wrong.

Teig followed behind, placing her feet carefully among the ruts, easily keeping up, and glad to be moving. The little train of novice Healers, all Gifted in some way, and Teig's still-in-training guard self, must have made the oddest sight.

"Teig!" Calth's urgent not-at-all whisper pulled her from her musings. One by one, the wagons halted as Kella glared back from the lead position.

Teig held back a sigh and said, "It'll be dark soon. We should find a place to camp. We've got to go off trail to the west tomorrow for most of the day. Rest would be good for the mules." *And the rest of us,* she didn't add. She'd done her best to follow Kella's lead for the last weeks, but today was the end of that. Everyone sat half-stiff from the long ride. Teig had been brought on as the guide for this journey—and everyone here knew she had—and now that they were about to travel off the road for the first time, she meant to act the part, no matter Kella's need to be seen as leader.

The dark-haired woman pressed her lips together and glared, her shoulders rising as though she would speak, but then her gaze left Teig and swept over the people seated on the other wagons. They huddled together, some looking anxious, some grim.

Kella drew a breath. "Yes," she said, but her eyes narrowed as they focused again on Teig. "It is getting late."

Kella's tone held an unpleasantness Teig knew she'd have to face sooner than later, but at least everyone would soon warm up and get some rest.

Kella chose silence over argument, but it only lasted until after dinner, when she interrupted storytelling around the fire. Sitting huddled within a circle of tents, the pleasure of laughter across dancing flames offered sparse enough warmth that Kella's crisp tones quickly chilled the whole group.

She tapped her spoon against the tin bowl in her hand to silence the talking and get everyone's attention. "If we're to retrieve this flower tomorrow, we must go over everyone's appropriate position and order of participation."

Seated on the far side of the fire from the Healer, Teig watched everyone else's shoulders slump a little. Gifted in a variety of ways, to make up for the fact that no one knew exactly what the special skill needed in harvesting the bloom would be, they had been over and over how they would attempt to assist in picking it. Not one night had passed without this conversation taking place.

No one spoke. Calth, especially, looked a little frustrated, which was rare. He was usually too cowed by Kella to offer anything but weary compliance.

"Calth—begin." Kella's voice was brusque with demand.

Why was the Healer so unpleasant? Calth was pale, clearly exhausted. This was the last thing he needed. This was not going to be a good evening. Unless . . .

"One thing I still don't understand," Teig said into the strained silence. "How does a flower offer enough resistance to being picked that it requires all these skills? I mean . . . it's a flower." Even as she spoke, Wilhem's voice can again in her head. *"Never assume, and never underestimate what a plant demands for its survival. There's a reason that things are rare."*

Kella set down her bowl and spoon and pushed her dark hair back, even as she offered Teig a look that on an older face might have been stern. "It's the same reason the plant has medicinal value, I'm sure. It's likely toxic. We need to mask against the poison, or ward against something it casts off. Or it might have a more . . . magical . . . defense system. We'll know soon enough."

Why would any but the last require a mind Gift to get around? Teig left the question unasked. Not for the first time since the library, the washed-out drawing tugged at her thoughts.

"Calth?" Kella demanded again. Her voice was almost strained.

Heat welled in Teig's chest and thickened her throat. For a moment she thought it was anger, then, like a lever moving, her heart remembered—the weighty combination of fear and frustration she had felt in the year she had tried and tried and tried and failed to get into the Collegium. The terrible idea she was not good enough. The frustration that she would never be understood, or allowed to learn how use her imagination and her skills to help others. Only in the last year had she begun to let go of those feelings. And now they were back.

But why?

Because of the way Kella looked at her, at *everyone*, as though they were a lock to be cracked, whatever the cost. Teig found herself glaring at the other woman. But then she noticed something. Everything about Kella was tight and unwelcoming, except her eyes, which were too bright. Was she holding back tears? Suddenly the mirror of Teig's own emotions bounced understanding at her, halted the angry words forming in her throat.

Despite being so much older and having the advantages of living in a city full of knowledge, it suddenly became clear to Teig that the same doubts about proving herself ruled Kella.

The difference was Teig had mostly kept them to herself, only letting those closest to her see how she hurt. Kella . . . Was that what this was? The Healer using her own uncertainties to control others? Why? Did it make her any less afraid? Any less angry? Or was it simply enough that she felt superior to those around her when she made them feel small?

What if all the attempts to harvest the plant failed? What would happen if they couldn't find the flower? Who would

Kella blame? But Teig knew. That was the *real* reason the other woman wanted her along on this adventure. Perhaps Kella was even counting on *not* finding the plant. *Wouldn't that be a mess . . .*

Teig did not much like these new thoughts. But if she'd learned anything these last years in Haven, it was that asking herself hard questions wasn't optional. The real curiosity was how Kella seemed to have avoided doing so.

Calth half-stuttered through his response, and before Kella could ask anything more, Teig interrupted. "Healer Kella, cold is tiring. It's a good thing you've talked about this enough that an early night for everyone can be called for."

"Novice Teig, I don't—" Kella stopped as she flashed her gaze around the group. All there was to see were slumped shoulders and expressionless faces. Displeasure marred her expression, pulled her eyes into a squint, but Teig could see the calculation happening there.

Kella's lips twitched, but she straightened and nodded. "True. I've made sure we're prepared. I was going to suggest we sleep soon." She pushed to her feet and pulled her cloak tight around her. "Good night." She left the fire and disappeared into her tent.

Around the fire, sighs and quick glances. Then everyone rose and headed to their own shelters. Teig sighed with relief and did the same.

They turned off the main road onto a much narrower track Teig remembered from her childhood. She was only a few hours ride from Sweetsprings, and Kella's annoyed remarks and demands throughout the morning pushed the idea of just riding away to visit old friends across Teig's mind more than once. But the strange familiarity of Kella's reaction last night not only held Teig to her duty, but helped her hold her tongue as well.

Was any of this really about a plant?

The terrain grew rougher, steeper, as they rolled through a thinly forested landscape. Once farmland, as so much of the region was, this area had been reclaimed by the wilds when the rocky ground became too frustrating to work. Finally, the way narrowed and the stones in the trail were too many and too boulderish. They left the wagons and proceeded on foot.

Teig dug her pack out from the bed of the last wagon and hefted the overlarge bag onto her back. It was twice the size of anyone else's, and the weight of it slowed her over the ever more difficult terrain. She wasn't the fit country child she had been, despite regular training. Half her days were now spent in study. But those with her were even less used to physical activity. She led the way by the time they crested a hill and the spot she had remembered when she first looked at the map appeared before her.

She stood panting as, one by one, the others scrabbled up to join her. A minute later, Kella heaved for breath as she reached the crest. She was actually in a much better state than the rest of the group. The woman was tougher than she looked.

"Hard climb," Teig said, still breathing heavily. "You made it up like you've done this a hundred times." She glanced behind at the three people still struggling up the slope. "You're strong."

When she looked back to Kella, the young woman's expression was a strange mixture of arrogance and surprise. She pushed sweaty hair from her eyes. "I spend a lot of time outside looking for herbs and roots."

That was not something Teig had considered. And yet she should have. How many times had she followed Wilhem on his treks to find medicinal plants? She'd spent many a day tripping over roots as she carried his basket of cut stems and dug mosses. Knowing where to look for what was needed to keep everyone well must be a big part of a Healer's training. And probably of healing work everywhere. Somehow, she had assumed Collegium Healers just had everything brought to them. And *that* meant she'd assumed that this entire trip was some prideful journey designed by Kella to avenge some imagined slight.

An uncomfortable thought followed. She mulled it over for a few seconds, then asked, "Did I . . . seem arrogant the day I came into the infirmary and told you what medicine I needed?"

The dark-haired Healer actually pulled back a little, her eyes widening. She didn't speak for a heartbeat, then nodded slightly. "Yes. You did, a bit." Her eyes narrowed slightly, and she tipped her head the slightest bit in what might be puzzlement.

"I'm sorry," Teig said. She gestured to the landscape around them. "I used to follow my town's Healer all over, looking for plants and mosses and bugs. He taught me a little. And I know what I have bad reactions to."

Kella raised her chin, and her reply was flat. "I see."

That was not the response Teig had hoped for, but something *had* changed in the way the other woman held herself. Her shoulders seemed less stiff. That could mean a dozen things, but at least it was an easing change. "Come on. This is the spot marked on the map. Keep your eyes open. There might only be a few of them."

She shifted the big pack as she scanned the ground for pink-mottled white flowers. Something tugged again at the back of her mind—either something from when she was small or something from the smeared pages of the book.

She didn't see any flowers among the patches of snow. What if they didn't find it? Well, that didn't bear considering until they had actually looked. Teig moved slowly across the hilltop, careful where she stepped, lest she crush the very thing they sought.

The others spread out around her, expanding the search.

All over the rocky ground they looked, among patches of dried grasses, between rocks, behind logs, until Calth's happy shout echoed from the west side of the hill, where the land began to slope steeply up again. He pointed up, and Teig when came to his side, she laughed.

There was the flower all right, but it wasn't growing on the ground. Instead, it bloomed in tight clusters atop a huge shrub that towered over her head by a good two arm spans. It was half as big in diameter as the wagons they had driven here, and the blossoms were so far atop the plant that not even the tallest among them would be able to just reach up and pluck them.

Teig laughed again as she realized a small section of the slope before her was covered by the tall, tight-growing plants. She looked around. This slope and only this slope. Well, the book said it only grew in one place.

She studied the angle of the hill. This wasn't going to be easy. But surely a special Gift wasn't needed just because the plant was tall? Well, that wasn't her problem. They had found the flower, and the rest was up to the Healers and their abilities.

She moved out of the way to let them work.

Everyone set down their packs and bags and began preparing themselves. Kella organized the group in the order of skills she had prepared them to use. Starting with Calth, one after the other, they each tested their skill against the bush.

Calth, a skilled Fetcher, tried time and again to pluck a blossom and pull it into his hand. Time and again, the flower failed to come to him. And when at last he managed to get one to respond, it landed in his palm, but immediately withered into brown dust. Then the remaining flowers in the cluster from which he had drawn speckled, crumbled, and died.

Kella gasped and took a step back. "Enough, Calth," she said to the now exhausted man. "Time to try something else."

Teig, watching, frowned deeper by the moment as the failures continued. From healing spells to negotiating skills to even delightful and persuasive songs, the flowers failed to survive being coaxed from their perch.

At last, Kella used a snapping energy usually reserved for setting out-of-place bones. She cast it at an entire bunch, and the effort yielded a bright cluster that fell from its narrow branch. Kella rushed forward and caught it before it hit the ground. Triumphant, she carried it back to the group, which gathered around and congratulated her, laughing with relief.

Teig shook her head in surprise. It wasn't that special a spell, and the book had said *most special*. But perhaps this skill had been rare when the thing was written . . . Even before she completed the thought, the flowers crumbled in Kella's hands. The Healer's face went stark.

Oh, no . . . Kella's was the last of the Gifts among the group.

A last resort. Failure upon failure ruled the day. The Healer looked as if she would either cry or shout, either of which could turn to full rage if frustration became too great. It was a reaction Teig knew too well from her own experience.

"Most special of gifts . . . Most definitely need . . ." The strange spear in the margins . . . *Never assume* . . . Could it be she had guessed correctly? Teig pulled open her bulging pack and pulled out two lengths of wood, each with a metal collar at one end. Quickly, she screwed them together, forming one long length. Then she dug a chunk of metal out of the bag and attached it to one end. Getting to her feet, she walked over and joined the deflated group of Healers.

"Kella—if I may. In preparation for our journey, I found the book on harvest instructions in the library. There was a tiny drawing . . . I thought it might be . . ." She held out the spade. "What if something like *this* was what it said would be definitely needed? What if *not even the most special of Gifts* would be useful?"

Kella stared at Teig, and a dozen emotions warred on her face, but she eventually dropped her gaze to the object. Then her expression became thoughtful. "It doesn't give us much time when we take the blooms. But taking the whole plant . . . if we had everything we needed ready in the greenhouse to transplant it . . . We might have enough time."

"Maybe?" Teig said. "But if we need to take the whole plant, why doesn't the Collegium already have one?"

"Uhhh . . ." Calth ventured. "I think we used to."

Kella looked at him and then, to Teig's surprise, choked out a small laugh. "I remember now—a plant that looked like this in the herb house when I was a girl. It was ancient, and died several years ago. No one even knew what it was for!" She raised both eyebrows, looked at Teig. "All this way with a dozen Gifted, and all we needed was a country girl with a shovel?"

Teig shrugged. "Us country folk are used to doing things the hard way. But sometimes practical is more useful than clever." It sounded funny to her ears as she said it, especially given how often she'd gotten herself in trouble for being anything *but* sensible. *Never assume.*

Maybe Kella wasn't the only one who needed to learn a lesson. Teig smiled. "It seems the joke is on both of us. I thought I was being punished by being sent on this trip. But it looks like you really did need me. And I think I needed to remember that not all my skills are in wild thinking."

For several moments, Kella said nothing, just looked at the tool, then at Teig, then around the group. At last, she grunted. If she'd learned something in the moment, she didn't say it. But she also didn't delegate. She rolled up her sleeves, reached for the shovel, and climbed up the slope to start digging.

Maybe, just maybe, it was a start to admitting she didn't know everything, and that she didn't need to.

Teig watched her. Time would tell, once they made it back to Haven with the shrub. She glanced at Calth, who was staring at Kella, mouth open. Regardless, one thing seemed likely—none of this group would ever make a long trip without a shovel again.

She shrugged. "Come on, Calth. We need to go rearrange things in the wagons so we've got room for this." She started heading back down the hill. After a moment, she heard his footsteps behind her.

"Teig," he said as he came up beside her. "I'd heard you always have wild ideas, but this one seems almost too simple."

She grinned at him. "For me, simple *is* a wild idea." She glanced back at Kella, hard at work digging in the nearly frozen ground. "Maybe for more than one of us. And that's not a bad thing to learn at all."

Once a Bandit
Brigid Collins

Even after almost a full year of living in Haven, Kimfer couldn't say he felt comfortable with it. He didn't belong in the fancy quarters he shared with Herald Marli, his lifebonded, and their adopted daughter Lillia. Nothing made that more abundantly clear than the odd looks he still got from the Heralds and their strange white witch-horses as they came and went on their Circuits or taught the various students at the Collegium whose sacred grounds he was currently despoiling merely by existing.

But he hated going down to the city just as much. Seeing so many people who needed things—food, clean water, clothes for the coming winter, money—and couldn't get them no matter how or what they tried made him sick deep inside. Yes, the Princess and her new husband were working to rectify what they could, but Kimfer's few visits to places like Exile's Gate had left him with a sense of desperation he'd never felt before, even in his time living as a bandit.

At least back then, he would have been able to hunt wild game if he was hungry, find a stream if he was thirsty, or steal the warm winter coat off the back of some rich merchant who could afford to buy another one if he was cold.

But Kimfer couldn't exactly turn to his old habits of banditry whilst he was living on Palace grounds, not even to help someone else. Not only would it get him kicked out—which he didn't mind so much for his own sake—but it would reflect poorly on Marli, too. Again, not really so important to Kimfer.

No, what would truly dig at him was how it would take little

Lillia away from her schooling. That girl was his reason for living these days, and with the trouble her witch-gift of Past-sight was giving her, she needed all the teaching she could get.

Still, Kimfer was hoping Marli might get assigned to a Circuit sometime soon, which was a sign of how much he hated it here. He and Marli got along like water and oil at the best of times, but sometimes he'd rather be traversing the wilds with her and her demon horse snipping at him than suffer one more day at the Collegium.

:You're not much good company yourself,: said Taren.

Kimfer ground his teeth and forced himself not to jump. He would never get used to the way the demon horse—Marli's *Companion*—could drop words into his mind anytime he pleased. Taren didn't speak to him often, but when he did, he invariably chose moments when Kimfer was most wishing to be left alone.

"Stop doing that," he hissed under his breath as he continued through the hallways that would bring him to those fancy rooms he and his little "family" shared. "Aren't you supposed to only bother your own Herald?"

Taren's answering laugh echoed against the inside of Kimfer's skull.

Kimfer squeezed his eyes shut, as if that would make the noise stop. Marli assured him there were ways to close a Companion's words out, but Kimfer had no witch powers. Even attempting such things was a fool's errand, and it always left him with a headache to boot.

:It's because you try too hard. You should take lessons from Lillia, if you can't stomach learning from Marli.:

"Leave me alone, you stupid—"

As he rounded the corner, eyes still closed, Kimfer ran straight into another person hard enough to send a bolt of pain through his shoulder.

The other person crashed to the floor with a sharp cry of anger. "I beg your pardon!" he said in tones that made it clear he was doing neither begging nor pardoning.

Kimfer, brushing his own shoulder off, took in the man's fine velvet robes, jeweled rings, and haughty bearing and sighed. He thought he even recognized the man. He'd seen him from a distance here in the Palace. *Husband to one of the ladies who served on the King's council,* Kimfer thought. *Lord Hargen, maybe?*

:*Better play nice,:* Taren said.

Kimfer held out a hand to the fallen noble. "I apologize, milord. Let me help you up." There, he'd even said it without sounding like he was imagining holding the man up for all his gold and jewels.

Not that Lord Hargen appreciated Kimfer's effort. He scowled up at Kimfer until the light of recognition flared in his eyes. Then the scowl transformed into a sneer. Even from the floor, he managed to make Kimfer feel as though he was being looked down upon.

"The Heralds' pet bandit. You'd love a chance to pick my pockets, wouldn't you? If you haven't already!"

Kimfer bit back another sigh as the man scrambled to his feet unassisted. "I swear I haven't touched your pockets, milord. I'm on my way to see Herald Marli."

"Likely," said Lord Hargen with a sniff. "Though I'm sure there are better places for you."

:*He means a prison cell,:* said Taren, unhelpfully.

"I know what he means," Kimfer said.

Lord Hargen frowned. "Don't get smart, boy. I'll have you know, I—"

"Papa Kimfer!"

Lillia's high voice broke through Lord Hargen's grousing, and a moment later she appeared, rounding the corner from the hallway that led to their rooms. A bright smile lit her face, and her dark hair curled where it was coming loose from the braids Kimfer had carefully pleated that morning.

Despite Lord Hargen's odious presence, Kimfer smiled to see her.

"Lady Callia helped me with my lessons today, and I managed to see the boy who reshelves books in the archives without showing him to anyone else this time!"

"Bard Callia," Kimfer corrected automatically as he opened his arms to the little girl. "And that's very good news. Congratulations."

He didn't understand the first thing about how any of the witch powers the Heralds and Bards and even the Healers of Valdemar used worked, but Lillia had always struggled to keep from projecting the things she saw from the past onto other people in her vicinity. It had gotten her into trouble more than once already.

Lord Hargen made a disgruntled noise. "People like you ought to be kept away from children."

Kimfer stiffened but, not wanting to frighten Lillia, held himself back from any outburst. His blood had turned to ice in his veins, though.

He lifted Lillia into his arms, grunting with the effort. She was growing faster than a weed, and soon enough he wouldn't be able to pick her up so easily.

But for now, her weight provided a reasonable excuse for turning to face Lord Hargen with his jaw tight.

"Good day, milord," he said through clenched teeth. "My girl and I must get to our rooms."

He stepped past the still-scowling lord without even inclining his head. Despite his best efforts, he knew he was crushing Lillia too tightly, but the girl made no complaint. She was smart, and didn't take kindly to those who insulted her papa.

Her small arms tightening around his neck were a reassurance.

His blood began to thaw as he continued down the wood-paneled hall. Their rooms were three doors further down. As soon as he reached them, they could step inside and be out of Lord Snot's reach.

Behind them, Lord Hargen let out a sudden squawk. "Thief! Robbery! Stop right there, boy!"

His voice rose as he carried on, until the hallway rang with his accusations. Doors opened up and down the length of it, and curious Heralds poked their heads out to see what all the fuss was about.

"Someone seize that man!" Lord Hargen demanded. "He's stolen my heirloom emerald ring!"

Lillia wriggled in Kimfer's arms. "He did not!"

"I never touched any of your filthy jewels," Kimfer said, struggling to keep his hold on her. The last thing he needed was for his charge to attack a well-respected noble in front of so many Heralds.

A pair of Heralds approached him, both strong men who looked as though they could pin Kimfer if they wanted. They wore matching stern expressions. One clapped a hand on Kimfer's shoulder. "A charge of theft within Palace grounds is serious enough to warrant a Truth Spell. Do you consent?"

Kimfer fought the urge to writhe out from under the strong grip. The thought of letting the Heralds touch him with their witch powers was terrifying, even if he hadn't done anything wrong. But if he refused, they'd be even more suspicious of him.

Carefully, he set Lillia down with a quiet admonishment to keep still. She scowled up at him, then turned that scowl on the Heralds and Lord Hargen.

"My papa Kimfer didn't steal anything," she said, crossing her arms. "You don't have to Truth Spell him. I can prove it."

Before anyone could respond, she marched up to Lord Hargen, one hand out as if to grab hold of his velvet robes. Her face was screwed up in concentration.

"Here, now," said Lord Hargen, jerking his robes out of her reach. He looked at her as if she were a mangy dog he'd like to kick away.

"Lillia," Kimfer said. "Come back here."

But Lillia continued to approach. Beads of sweat popped up on her brow, and she gritted her teeth in effort.

Moments passed. The Heralds shifted in discomfort, one still gripping Kimfer's shoulder. Kimfer's heart thudded in his throat. If Lord Hargen took it into his mind to punish a little girl, who would stop him?

Finally, Lillia let out a gasp, then sagged to the floor with a cry of frustration. "I can't see what happened," she said. "I always see things when I don't want to! Why can't I make it happen when I *do* want to?"

Though Kimfer hated to see her upset, he was secretly relieved she hadn't been able to prove Lord Hargen a liar. He didn't need her intervening on his behalf and earning a lord's ire in the process.

"It's all right," he said as she swiped tears from her cheeks and scowled even harder at Hargen. "I'll consent to a Truth Spell."

The words felt like slime coming out his mouth, but he kept from shuddering. All this time he'd spent living amongst the Heralds, feeling the proximity of their witch powers crawling over his skin like ants. But he'd never yet had one actually apply their magic to him.

Lord Hargen sniffed. "Be quick about it, then."

The Herald who held Kimfer nodded to the other, who lifted a hand.

Kimfer swallowed.

"*I'll* apply the Truth Spell," said a quiet voice.

Herald Marli stepped up to the group, her Whites sporting stains from working in the Salle, from which she'd just come. Her brown eyes were hard as she turned them from Lord Hargen to her fellow Heralds, and finally to Kimfer.

Kimfer's relief at her arrival warred with his shame at having her see him in such a situation. He couldn't deny he trusted her to be quick and efficient with her witch powers. She was too kind not to be. But this was one more event in a string of them that dragged his unfitness to be partnered with her out into the harsh light of day.

No matter how much time he put between himself and his time living as a bandit, it would never be enough.

Lord Hargen spluttered as the other Heralds deferred to Marli. "This is a travesty! He's her lifebonded, isn't he? She'll fake the Truth Spell to make him look innocent!"

"On the contrary," said one of the Heralds. "It'll make her more likely to be absolutely fair."

As he spoke, Marli came up to Kimfer. She pressed the cool tips of two fingers to his forehead, looking right into his eyes the entire time.

He didn't truly feel anything as she laid the spell over him, but he knew it was there. He suppressed a shudder as she withdrew her fingers.

"Did you steal Lord Hargen's emerald ring, Kimfer?" she asked. Her voice was so soft and calm, she might have been asking him if he had the meat rolls at lunch today.

Kimfer shook his head, then swallowed against the tightness in his throat. "I didn't."

He stifled the impulse to remind her of his promise. When they'd come to live together, he'd told her he would never steal again. And in truth, he didn't think she'd forgotten it.

She nodded, quirked her full lips into a smile just for him, then turned to the other Heralds. "That's settled, then. I didn't see any glow of falsehood on him."

The other Heralds agreed, but, unsurprisingly, Lord Hargen did not.

"That doesn't change the fact that my emerald is still missing," he said as the Heralds subtly herded him down the hallway. "I tell you, he's no better than a common rat, and the only way to stop an infestation is to exterminate the first one you see!"

"But even rats deserve to live," said Lillia as the nobleman disappeared around the corner. "Papa Kimfer, I don't think you're a rat."

Kimfer let out a laugh that was almost a sob. "Thanks, sweetling."

Marli, still looking down the corridor, shook her head in disapproval. Then she turned a bright smile on Lillia.

"Come on, you two. Let's get home and hear all about your lessons with Bard Callia."

As he followed them to the safety of their rooms, Kimfer wished he could put things behind him so easily as the rest of his little family.

He knew the burn of Lord Hargen's accusations—and the suspicion in those other Heralds' eyes before Marli had laid her spell on him—would keep him awake all night.

It was not the last time Lord Hargen accused him of thievery. Two days later, a pair of Heralds—different from the two he'd encountered in the hallway—came to collect him while he was working some drills in the training yards outside the Salle. He might not be living as a bandit any longer, but that was no reason to let his muscles atrophy or his skills degrade. One day, Marli might go out on Circuit again, and if he intended to come along, he'd need to be at his best.

The Heralds cut in on him as he was pulling out of a roll, which meant they had him when his face was full of dust.

"Lord Hargen claims you broke into his chambers last night and made off with some valuable statuettes," said the one on his left. "You can submit to a Truth Spell, or to a search of your person and chambers."

Kimfer rose to his feet, his fingers tight around the wooden practice knives. "Do you really think I'd hide stolen goods in a room I share with one of your fellow witch-riders?" He was almost more insulted to have such a flashy stunt laid at his feet. No bandit worth his skin would do something so obvious. That was asking to be caught and hanged.

"No one ever called a thief smart," said the other Herald with a half grin as he held one gloved hand out in silent demand.

Kimfer had to let someone other than Marli lay a Truth Spell on him that time. Though he still physically felt nothing as the second Herald cast his magic over him, his stomach writhed in discomfort. This Herald did not have Marli's compassion, either. He drew out his questioning until he, his partner, and—grudgingly—Lord Hargen were satisfied.

By the time Kimfer was allowed to return to his drills, he was too exhausted to do more than trudge home. Anger crackled beneath his skin, though.

The anger soon drove him back out of his rooms and down

into the city. He needed to be around regular people, folks who would understand him even if all he did was nurse a mug of ale in a corner.

The tavern he slipped into was full of such. Stable boys, carpenters, ash sweepers, shop girls. The bartender and his trio of daughters working the room with knowing smirks or a sympathetic tip of the head. The four grizzled men playing dice at the big table.

His lordship's stupid baubles would do a sight more good amongst this lot than they do dangling about his soft flesh.

Not that any fence in Haven would take such easily tracked goods. Kimfer snorted into his ale at the very thought.

Which raised the question: who *had* fleeced the mark? Kimfer had to admit, there wasn't anyone else living on Palace grounds who fit the bill so nicely as himself. If he could find the real culprit . . . but then, he wasn't interested in pointing the finger at anyone who stole, even if they did deserve a knock upside the head for their showy ways.

For all he knew, nobody had stolen from Lord Hargen. It was far more likely, at this point, that the nobleman was afflicted with the memory of an infant babe. Perhaps if he ever took the time to shake his pockets out, he'd find his missing emerald ring, and his statuettes, and the coin he ought to hand to the porters who carried his things in and out of his chambers with every move between them and his fancy town house.

Then again, finding the things would make it harder to tack a crime on Kimfer.

Kimfer tipped the last of his ale down his throat, savoring its rough flavor, as well as the equally rough atmosphere of the tavern. The coarseness of regular, down-to-earth folk set his mind on steady ground.

The more he turned the idea over in his head, the more he realized it had to be true. There was no thief, because no thief would be stupid enough to pull such a stunt. But the Heralds would never think of a thing like that, not with their righteous ways and their witch powers to lean on.

But if Kimfer didn't do something now, he knew Lord Hargen would keep losing his precious baubles, and the losses would keep getting pinned on him until something stuck.

He didn't know if he could prove his innocence if multiple instances of Truth Spell hadn't been enough to convince the Heralds. But he could, if he was willing to be a little ruthless, convince Hargen he'd be better off if he stopped his little game.

Luckily, he was perfectly happy to take the kid gloves off. And, as he swirled the dregs of his ale around his mouth, the first pieces of a plan came together.

Lord Hargen was about to learn how *real* bandits worked.

Companion's Field was top of Kimfer's list of Palace landmarks to avoid. The white horse-creatures made him nervous, especially the ones that hadn't yet Chosen someone to be their rider. He didn't like the way their blue eyes shimmered. They always looked like they were laughing at him and whispering the joke amongst themselves.

Kimfer hated being the butt of a joke.

But being framed for theft was the bigger insult, and thus, here he was, approaching the fence that surrounded the grassy field right as the stars were coming out. It was the best time to find the place empty of Heralds or Trainees, while they were all at dinner.

A smattering of Companions stood out in the field, looking more like silvery-gray ghosts than pure white horses. One or two tilted their graceful heads toward him. Their eyes glowed like an owl's.

His hands shook as he placed them atop the wooden fence beam. With a low growl, he forced the trembling to stop.

"Demon Horse," he said through gritted teeth. "I need to talk to you."

He knew he didn't have to specify which demon horse he meant. They'd know. They always knew.

Taren appeared out of the evening gloom, trotting until he could arch his graceful neck over the fence to come nose to nose with Kimfer.

:You are having trouble with the sparkly lord,: he said in

Kimfer's mind. To his credit, he didn't sound smug. He sounded more like Marli, actually, as if he understood what it was costing Kimfer to initiate this conversation.

Kimfer drew in a breath. He kept his voice lower than a whisper. He couldn't respond with his mind like he knew most Heralds did, but he didn't want anyone to overhear him. "I have to put a stop to this nonsense, or eventually it'll affect Lillia. And Marli, I suppose, though she can handle herself."

:She can. But I see what you mean about Lillia. She is young, and her past still pains her. You have something in mind.:

It wasn't a question. Kimfer nodded. "Can you keep Marli busy elsewhere? Just so she doesn't get involved. I need to do this on my own. If my lifebonded Herald steps in, people will think I can't fight my own battles."

Taren blew a warm snort that ruffled Kimfer's hair. *:Plus, you think she won't approve of the methods you intend to employ. But I agree with you. Marli can do with another lesson on letting people work things out for themselves. Have no worries, bandit-man. I will keep her occupied.:*

"Thank you," Kimfer said. He was surprised to find he genuinely meant it. The relationship between former bandit and demon horse was even pricklier than between him and Marli, if it was possible.

Hesitantly, Kimfer let his hand drift upward until his fingertips brushed the underside of Taren's jaw. The Companion's uncanny eyes drifted closed as Kimfer scratched him.

:Don't take too long,: he said, his voice sounding drowsy in Kimfer's head. *:My Chosen is hard to distract when she senses injustice around those she loves.:*

Kimfer tried to stifle the bloom of pleasure that thought evoked. But as he walked away from Companion's Field, the little fire inside his heart flickered steadily.

The dark of full night cloaked him as he dropped into the manicured gardens that separated Lord Hargen's stately town house from the other fine homes in the upper district of Haven. A cool bit of metal rested in his curled fingers, ready to lend some weight to his fists once he made it inside that gilded dwelling and was face to face with his tormentor.

Not that he intended to hurt Lord Hargen. He only needed to look like he would, if pressed too far.

A cool rush of satisfaction flowed through him now, lending lightness to his steps as he moved through the gardens. Only a few more paces, and he could be looking at the end of his harassment—if not a formal apology—by sunrise.

His foot fell on an unraked pile of gravel. Tiny stones clattered as they tumbled against each other.

Overhead, a window flew open, and Lord Hargen's pale head poked out.

Kimfer froze, his once-honed bandit reflexes warring with the bolt of adrenaline coursing through his veins. The man had been waiting up! Had he known Kimfer would strike tonight?

Lord Hargen bared his teeth in a death's head's grin. "I've got you now, little rat. Guards! Thief! Robbery! Don't let him get away!"

As lights flared in the neighboring houses and the hue and cry rose out on the street, Kimfer ran.

Demon Horse, don't fail me now, he thought as he dashed through the garden and into the thin alleyways between gaudy homes. He couldn't bear it if Marli used her Farsight to look in on him right as he found himself in hot water.

The sounds of pursuit bounced around the stone and wood buildings differently than they had in the forests where he'd survived for so long. Were the City Guard ahead of him, ready to cut him off? Or were they coming up on him from behind? He cursed his lack of practice in such close quarters. He should have spent more time walking the city streets, no matter how uncomfortable they made him.

There: movement at the end of the alley drew his eye. He turned back the way he'd come, meaning to loop back through Lord Hargen's garden.

He ran smack into the City Guard who'd come up behind

him. In the dark of night, the guard's blue uniform looked as black as a cat burglar's getup.

The man caught Kimfer up in a firm hold and called to his fellows.

Kimfer made himself relax as the guard brought him out onto the street. No sense in wasting his energy with struggling. But his heart thudded in his throat as more guards arrived with torches blazing. Would these city men give him a fair trial? Or would they see he was bandit material and hang him at once, the way they did in the border towns he was so familiar with?

Lord Hargen glided out of his house, looking somehow both regal and harassed in his disheveled night robe. He approached Kimfer, eyes narrowed.

A gleam of cunning shone in those eyes. He came so close Kimfer could smell the roast meat he'd had for dinner on his breath.

"This man has stolen from me time and time again," he said in a voice that carried through the whole street. "Now I've finally caught him red-handed. Take him away."

He made as if to turn on his thin-slippered heel.

"Wait a minute, milord," said the guard who held Kimfer. "A man skulkin' about a garden is one thing, an' a man breakin' an' enterin' is another. Have you proof of his crime?"

Lord Hargen sniffed disdainfully. "Search him."

Kimfer held himself still and silent as the guards ran their hands over him, dipping into pockets and along the cuffs of his collar and sleeves. He kept his gaze trained on Lord Hargen, not even blinking as the search went on. He'd tossed the bit of metal aside when the chase began; they wouldn't be able to pin that on him.

One of the guards exclaimed as he pulled something from Kimfer's left pocket.

A single ruby ear stud glimmered in his palm, reflecting the torchlight.

Kimfer's body went numb at the sight. Trying to mask his disbelief, he looked back at Lord Hargen. A slim, satisfied smile was unfurling itself across his lordship's face.

"My wife's treasured ruby earrings," he said, tutting. "She'll be relieved to know I've saved them in time."

Kimfer's throat was tight, not with fear, but with rage. Somehow, Lord Hargen had gotten a step ahead of him.

Or, at least, he thought he had.

But Kimfer, like any good bandit, had more than one trap laid for his mark.

"Truth Spell," he croaked. "Call a Herald."

Lord Hargen laughed. "Oh, no, I don't think so. You've found some way to hoodwink the thing, haven't you? I'll not give you the chance to weasel out of your due punishment this time, rat."

Kimfer suppressed a smile. He knew he had his mark now.

"I never set foot inside that house, and you and I both know it. If you don't want to bring a Truth Spell into it, then have the Guard search the place for signs of forced entry. Who knows? Maybe they'll find your misplaced emerald and statuettes while they're there. And then you can tell everyone how you slipped this ruby stud into my pocket just now."

Hargen's face darkened. "Lies! Guards, take him away and lock him in the deepest cell you've got."

But the guards made no move.

"His story is plausible, Lordship," said one. A badge on his uniform marked him as a captain. "We could easily rule it out with the search he suggests."

"He's bluffing, you fools!" said Hargen. But from the slight panic on his face, even he could see the Guard weren't buying it.

"We don't muck about with the fancy stuff Heralds use if we don't need it," said the captain, almost conversationally, to Kimfer. "Good, plain, hard evidence, now, that's the stuff to put things to rights."

Hargen spluttered, but, backed into a corner, had little choice but to consent to a search of his house.

Kimfer, Hargen, and the Guard captain, as well as the guard still holding Kimfer captive, remained out on the street as the search progressed. Kimfer tried not to look too pleased, but as the candlemarks went past, Hargen looked more and more ruffled.

Finally, the guards emerged. Each one reported the same thing.

"No signs of forced entry anywhere, sir. Everything in its place and neat as a pin."

"Fancy that," said the captain. "And how are Mullery and Thamo getting on?"

"Here, sir," came a voice from inside.

Two more guards appeared, but they weren't empty-handed. A lovely set of statuettes and a heavy ring set with a large emerald caught the torchlight.

"Right in the strongbox, they was, Captain."

"How interesting," said the captain. "It seems they weren't stolen after all."

Lord Hargen exploded. "This is preposterous! Can't you see this criminal has clearly placed the things he stole back here to make himself look innocent?"

"But there was no forced entry, milord," said the captain. He gestured to the guard holding Kimfer. A moment later, Kimfer stood free, rubbing feeling back into his elbow.

"He's clever enough to get in without leaving marks, then, or your men are too stupid to find them. I tell you, he's a danger to all decent people. You can't let him free to wreak havoc! I'll bring this before the King if I must, Captain. I'll see you stripped of your office!"

Hargen's eyes flashed, wild with anger, and Kimfer went still. His instincts told him to leave off when a mark got like this. It was too dangerous to push someone who became unpredictable or fought back.

But if he didn't clinch this now, he'd lose the advantage he and the Guard captain had gained.

The captain cast an uncomfortable look at Kimfer, one that said their partnership was on rocky ground. "Well-l-l-l, it's true, a particularly skilled thief could hide his tracks. It may be an issue for the courts to decide."

A sound like bells broke the tension, and a moment later, Taren came cantering into the gathering. His blue eyes sparkled hard as diamond.

Kimfer's stab of betrayal twisted to surprise when he realized the person astride the Companion was not Marli.

"Lillia?" he said. He met Taren's eye, incredulous.

:She was quite insistent. And I never promised to keep her out of your little ambush.:

"Did you *tell* her what was going on?"

Taren shook his mane. *:I, too, am stubborn when it comes to the people I love. And Lillia is becoming her mother's daughter as much as her father's.:*

The little girl slid down from Taren's back as gracefully as if she'd been born doing it. Her small face was full of anger, which she turned on Lord Hargen.

"I'll show you my papa Kimfer is innocent. I figured out why I couldn't see before."

She stomped over to the guard who held the emerald ring and plucked it from his palm, ignoring the little squeak of protest the man made and the growl from Lord Hargen.

"It's because I can't see what happened to a thing in the past if the thing isn't there for me to look at now. It wasn't even *there*, Papa Kimfer."

She held the jewel up, and a vision filled the street.

An ornate office appeared, with Lord Hargen standing in it. A large window had its curtains open, showing the motley flags of the Midsummer Festivals, which had occurred over three months ago. The image of Hargen was putting his treasures into the strongbox set in the office wall.

Then the image sped up. The weather outside the window flickered through sunny days and the first rainstorms of autumn. The strongbox lay untouched the whole time.

Untouched, until the image slowed to a nighttime scene, when two City Guards entered the office, searched it and its window for signs of entry, and finally used the key from the drawer to open the strongbox.

The valuables were, of course, waiting for them, as they had been since Midsummer.

"Well," said the Guard captain. "I'd say that about settles it."

"I can't believe you didn't tell me what you were planning, Kimfer!"

Kimfer watched from his reclined position as Marli paced the length of their sitting room. "Would you have let me go forward with it if I'd told you?"

"Of course not! You could have ended up arrested—or worse, killed! Not to mention the King is not happy to have to try one of his nobles for framing you."

Kimfer snorted. "He should be happy to have a dangerous criminal rooted out of his den."

"That's not funny."

"No, it's not. Look, Marli, I had to put a stop to his nonsense myself, or I'd never have earned anyone's trust around here."

Marli spun on her heel and opened her mouth to protest, but Kimfer held up a hand.

"Not everything can be solved with your witch powers. You know as well as I do that your fellow Heralds were perfectly ready to suspect me of something if the right evidence came about. Two Truth Spells weren't enough to stop that."

"Well, we didn't ever put a full Truth Spell on you," she mused. "And Lillia still came in to rescue you in the end. Not that I'm happy about that, either."

"Neither am I! But you can take that one up with your demon horse, not me. I would have been fine on my own. The Guard captain knew I was innocent. I told him he'd find those jewels in the strongbox unmolested myself."

Marli let out a gusty breath and collapsed into the nearby armchair. "Bright Lady, you are vexing."

Kimfer bit down on a wry smile. "Vexing, yes, but not a thief. I promised you, remember?"

Marli's smile was a light in the dark. "I remember. And I never suspected you. But you're right about the other Heralds." She sighed. "Kimfer, I'm sorry. I thought we should stay here so Lillia could get training. But I think we'd both be better off if I went back out on Circuit. You could be out in the wilds again."

Kimfer sat up and shook his head. "Lillia's come far already, and if she needs more schooling, you're not such a bad teacher, failed attempts at teaching me to block your demon horse's mind-talking out notwithstanding. I'm a fair bad student, is all."

He had to squint, but he thought he caught a dusting of pink across Marli's cheeks. He rather liked that.

"What about the reparations you're due from Lord Hargen?" she said, obviously changing the subject.

"Oh, them? That's already sorted. I told him to sell his precious baubles and give the money to them that live in Exile's Gate. I'd rather see folks eating proper than one man with too much flash about him. Likely to draw thievin' sorts, that is, and we wouldn't want any of that in the Palace."

Kimfer even dared to wink at her.

Who knew? Maybe he'd be happy to return to Haven in another year. But he wasn't in such a rush to get out into the wilds just yet.

He had a feeling the place was going to feel a bit more welcoming from now on.

Wooden Horses
Rosemary Edghill

Jing.

Hamlin was ordinary. He had been born in Haven, to a family that built and painted sets and props for masques and plays. He asked nothing better out of life than to do as they did, and so, when he was old enough, Hamlin attached himself to a company of traveling players, there to repair old sets and build new ones.

The players were not a first-rate company or even third; they were forced to take the least lucrative routes, playing to tiny towns no one else would. It suited Hamlin, who wanted to see the world.

The troupe's most popular play—*everyone's* most popular play, as the captain of the troupe told Hamlin—was *The Founding of Valdemar*, a play that required no less than one dozen life-sized silhouettes of white horses with silver hooves and silver bells and blue velvet tack. (Or at least paper made to look like velvet.) It was a piece difficult to stage even in a well-equipped playhouse, what with all the horses moving at once and most of the actors in front of them declaiming speeches about how Baron Valdemar had led them all to safe haven, but the troupe's captain was ambitious as well as audacious. He dreamed of dazzled nobility and rich purses, of praise from all his peers, though he'd find little of any of that out here in the back of beyond.

The show played well, thanks to Hamlin's talents. Everyone said he could easily find work with a more established company as soon as they returned home, one that would travel a better circuit and offer better wages.

But Hamlin found he wasn't very interested in the prospect of more money and easier work. In his travels, he had seen things he had never suspected existed. In the borderlands and the hill towns he saw ground-down poverty, fear of border raiders, real suffering and real problems. And Haven and the Heralds of Valdemar were very far away. Or they didn't know. Or they didn't care. Or they couldn't do anything. Hamlin didn't know which answer he liked least. None of them seemed fair.

So when the troupe's circuit was done, and the players parted ways just north of Haven, scattering to homes and families and other engagements, Hamlin took his paints and his tools and headed back north.

Alone.

Jing-a-jing.

On the eastern side of the border, north of Lake Evendim, the crops were tin and iron. The foothills were a place nobody wanted, even the Valdemarans, because there the Terilee widened and the hills would be impossible to hold and nothing could grow there anyway. Hard and careless men set up temporary camps there to pull the metal out of the soil by any convenient means.

It was just easier that way.

Pit mines were open to the sky, gaping craters where the valuable ore was pried out of the earth with picks and hammers and human sweat. Placer mines separated the valuable from the worthless using water, carried bucket by bucket from a nearby stream.

But when tin was found, a shaft mine was sunk, for tin lay pure and deep in its long black galleries far underground. The lower the cost to bring it to the surface, the more profit could be had. A wide shaft, or a wide face, was expensive to open or to mine.

Children could fit their bodies into narrow spaces. And they were cheap.

So when the mines ran dry—when the workers were used up—the hard men moved on.

On his long walk north, Hamlin turned over ideas in his mind. The best one, he thought, required something he didn't already have to make it work, but he thought he could find it here, so once he got past the lake, each time he stopped at an inn or a public house (often paying for his food and shelter with some juggling and dancing and a few simple tricks he'd learned from the players he'd traveled with), he asked if anyone had seen any children. Perhaps looking for work.

Some simply said "no." Others said "no" and added that they were runaways, and thieves, and dirty, and ought to be put on work gangs. Some pretended they hadn't heard him at all.

In a place like the last one, Hamlin was eating his supper when a boy sat down across from him at the table. His age looked to be twelve or thirteen. He pulled Hamlin's wooden cider mug toward him and drained it, then reached for his half-finished plate.

Hamlin's automatic protest was stopped by the boy's words. "They said in the kitchen. Why're you looking for one of the mine kids?"

Hamlin took a closer look. There was little meat on the boy's bones, and the way he enthusiastically gobbled up the rest of Hamlin's dinner without reaching for a utensil suggested he had been hungry for a very long time. Hamlin signaled the landlord for two more meat pies.

"I need advice," Hamlin said, and the boy snorted. "I need to know what the camps are like inside."

The boy stared at him for a long moment before he spoke. "Why?"

"Because children don't belong in work camps," Hamlin said. "And because if I can get them back to Valdemar, they won't be."

"There's a number of people who will fill you full of arrows if you try."

"Well," Hamlin said, "I think I have a plan that will work. I just need someone to tell me how these mining camps are run and how the children are kept."

The pies arrived. The boy pulled both to himself, clearly not intending to share. "Call me Rat," he said. "If you're looking for kids, you're looking for tin. Did you have a specific place in mind?"

"I was with a troupe of traveling players one night when we played a place called Beauteous Salvation. Is that—?"

"Unless you brought an army with you, that op's too big to take on," Rat said with certainty. "Start small."

"But I want—" Hamlin said.

"—to save the world," Rat finished. "So who are you, World Saver? And what do you want with someone like me?" He drew breath to say more when he was suddenly wracked by a spasm of coughing. Even listening to it was painful. He covered his mouth with a grimy rag, and Hamlin could hear his gasping attempts to breathe between coughs.

"Where were we?" Rat said brightly, as soon as he could speak.

"You're sick!" Hamlin exclaimed.

"I'm *dying*," Rat answered. "And not of anything you could catch, so you don't have to worry. It's just that it's dusty down there in the mines. That's probably why they have to replace workers so often."

"'Probably'?" Hamlin said. "Don't you know?"

Rat shrugged. "Don't know much. Just that you're crazy."

Hamlin thought hard about whether he'd been called crazy before. No, not yet. "You asked who I am. I was about to tell you that I'm not particularly interesting. I'm a sign painter. I'd been traveling with a theater company when—"

"And a sign painter wants to go over the border to rescue a bunch of kids nobody will miss?" Rat interrupted.

"If I can," Hamlin said steadily.

"Kids vanish all the time. What's it to you, World Saver?"

"It's something that shouldn't be allowed to happen. And if you're going to insult me, you might as well call me Hamlin."

"You're crazy, and we're going to die," Rat announced. "Let me explain reality to you."

Hamlin ordered a pitcher of honeyed cider, and Rat (who was older than Hamlin thought; nearly fifteen) told him how things worked in the hill country.

Once someone found and opened a mine, it was worked. Children were easy enough to get. Sold by their families, sole survivors, burned out, loot from raids, runaways—

"Always more where we all came from."

Rat had been born in a little village back in the hills. They'd worked the mines, even copper, like everyone else, but for themselves, and sold what they didn't use to the larger operations. Rat's parents had indentured him to the mining operation, assuming he'd be home at the end of seven years.

Rat soon realized that was not the plan.

"So I waited for a chance and ran on home—took me a while—" He sighed and rubbed his forehead. "Town was gone. Seam ran out, I guess. Didn't want to go back to mining. Not as a runaway. Figured one of these inns could use a kitchen boy, maybe."

He paused to cough again, and Hamlin pushed the jug of cider over to him. "Drink. Why not head straight to Haven? There are Heralds there. Healers, too."

"Neither of whom would give a cat's—a cat's *ass* about me, Sign Painter. And anyway, who says I'm not? I might be," Rat said belligerently.

"They'd care more than you think," Hamlin said.

"Have you been listening to me? I wasn't born in Valdemar, and I broke my indentures. I stole food from the dying. *I'm* the bad guy, not them."

"They'd care," Hamlin said firmly. "In Valdemar, a lot of people care about what's good and right."

Rat stared at Hamlin as if he had just grown a second head, then shook himself as if throwing off a heavy drench of water. "You're madder than I thought. Never mind. Here's how the smaller operations work."

Half the workers were in the mines while the other half were locked in the barracks. The workers were fed on bread and water and worked until they dropped. And when that day came—it was almost always *when*—the bodies were taken and disposed of far enough away from the workings that animals wouldn't be drawn into the camp.

Rat had survived three camps by stealing food from the sick and the dying. He managed to get himself moved from mine to mine as a shift leader. He said the smaller workings only took on a few new workers at a time, "employing" two dozen at most. Tin or iron was like anything else stolen—you sold it on and went back to get more.

Even if every other sentence contained an insult, Hamlin had never met anyone whose mind interlocked with his like this. He felt as if Rat *understood*—when you saw something, you judged it for yourself and decided whether it was good or bad. Even if you had a good reason to not do anything, you didn't just pretend something was good when it was bad.

He knew Rat was going to take more convincing to help, especially given the nature of Hamlin's plan, and the boys argued into the night, each trying to convince the other. When the serving girl swept the floor and banked the fire for morning, neither had budged.

"It's stupid," said Rat.

"It's unexpected," said Hamlin.

"It's unexpectedly stupid," said Rat.

"It has the element of surprise," Hamlin urged.

"And you'll be the one who's surprised, City Boy. You'd best give me a letter to take to your parents," Rat said. "It's the least I can do."

That afternoon, Hamlin and Rat continued northwest, still arguing.

They chose their target, and spent a few days watching it. Rat slipped in between shift changes to make sure there would be no surprises from the other children—they couldn't be trusted not to betray their hopeful rescuers, nor not to panic when rescue arrived. Then Rat and Hamlin planned where they would meet up afterward and where they would go.

Hamlin was waiting for the full moon. Rat had wanted to attack in the dark. That had been one of the things they'd argued about most of the way here.

"Just so you know," Rat said to Hamlin, "I still think this is a really stupid plan and we're both going to die."

"It's better than doing nothing," Hamlin said, and since Rat agreed with that much of the plan, he didn't answer.

Jing-a. Jing-a-Jing. Jing!

In the night, the moon and stars overhead gave a fanciful brightness to the ground below. But even surrounded by mist and illusion, the dancing figure shone.

It was an impossible sight. Ghostly-white, its long, domed body made to suggest a horse but not actually resemble one. Its tail was a thing of rags and ribbons, and as it moved, it danced, spinning first one way then another, twirling and bowing. The bells along its skirt rang and jingled, and its huge white head seemed to nod in agreement with the bells. If there were legs beneath the hobbyhorse's basketwork skirt, they were invisible in the darkness, as must be the head and arms beneath its gigantic neck with its wooden head. The body was held up by straps that fitted over Hamlin's shoulders, and the fierce wooden head sat atop his own like a fabulous knightly helm.

Sometimes the hobby's muzzle pointed skyward and its teeth clacked, but there was no one to see, for once it was past the outer perimeter there was no one guarding the mine or its barracks. Even those who might see it wouldn't report it. What could they say?

Hamlin danced onward.

This was his third trip to the mining camp. The first had been to make sure he could evade the guards. The second was to scout the barracks itself and make sure Rat would have secure hiding places.

He'd hoped this would be easier—as much, he imagined, as

his former master had hoped for fame and coin. There were nearly two dozen children here, but only half were above ground at any one time. The other half toiled in the sunless dark of the mine shafts, and there were guards at the mine head to send them to the barracks and guards to bring the second shift out. He'd have to unbolt the barracks door first thing, then catch up to the children who were leaving the mine. The guards wouldn't see him as a menace. And neither would the children.

And then they'd all run away.

That was the heart of Hamlin's plan. Run away, run back to Valdemar, run to safety. The children would be more likely to follow a hobby than another strange adult, and the guards wouldn't know what to make of him at all. Even Hamlin had to admit it wasn't much of a plan, but it *might* work. And he couldn't just sit back and do nothing. Ever since he'd found out about these mining camps they had preyed upon his mind.

It all depended on two things.

How far the mine guards would chase them.

And how fast the children could run.

Jing. Jing-a-Jing. Jing. Jing. Jing! Jing! Jing!

It was perhaps an hour before dawn when Hamlin took up his position and settled himself to watch the mine head. Rat had already gone down and snuck into the mine shaft so he could ready the others to run.

Jing a Jingity. Jing. Jing. Jing. Jingity! Jingity! Jing-a-Jing!

The first children to come up out of the pit were sad, sorry little things, covered in rock dust and blinking even in the wan light. They stopped dead at the sight of Hamlin for a precious second, then ran for the barracks. The children from the barracks were already running back the other way, to seize their counterparts and drag them toward the river.

"Run! Fire! Goats! Mad cows! Perjury! Lightning!" Hamlin stepped between them and the guards. It didn't matter what he shouted, so long as he was loud. He waved his arms and clacked the hobby's jaw. "Doom! *Doooooom!* Matching china! Inclement weather! Hurry!" Hamlin howled.

The mine guards, who had *not* been warned that anyone was going to be rescued today, simply stared at him as precious seconds ticked by, until one said: "Get the horses! I'll get the loony!"

There was a clatter of retreating feet as the bad-mannered one advanced upon Hamlin, arms spread wide and a cudgel in one hand. He grinned, obviously thinking Hamlin would be an easy mark.

Hamlin pivoted as if to run, then spun back, a large rock in his hand. He struck his assailant upon the jaw. The man fell unconscious to the ground. Hamlin arranged the skirts of the hobbyhorse over the body and squatted down. Now his former assailant was hidden completely.

Seconds to get to the stables. Seconds to saddle the horses. Seconds to return. Precious, precious time in which children led by Rat could run and hide.

The men returned on horseback, one of them leading a saddled, riderless horse. The horses regarded the motionless white figure nervously.

"Where's Jorik?" someone asked.

"Eeee-yow!" the hobbyhorse shrieked, leaping to its feet. It rushed at the riderless horse, which promptly bolted. Hamlin spun and capered, singing an off-key—but very loud—song about missing socks.

The horses had never seen anything like this in their lives. The hobbyhorse rushed at them, clacking its wooden teeth, and the horses reared and bolted. The fear spread among the beasts like a bad smell, and soon every single one of them had turned to run either to their home stables, or just *away*.

Their riders, not wanting to be thrown in the midst of spooked horses, had prudently decided to remain in their saddles as the horses took them elsewhere.

Hamlin turned and trotted back after the children. Rat was shepherding them along, laughing so hard he kept coughing. *"Matching china?"* he demanded. "How terrifying is that?"

"The horses didn't seem to like it. Come along now," Hamlin said, pointing the hobby's head eastward. "Once we're over the border we'll be safe. Safer," he corrected himself, because Hamlin didn't like to lie. "There's judges and magistrates and sheriffs and even Heralds there. They'll protect you."

"Aren't *you* a Herald?" one of the boys asked.

"I am nothing more than a man with a hobbyhorse," Hamlin said. "Off we go."

"Still a stupid plan," Rat murmured in his ear.

Jing. Jing-a-Jing-a-Jing-a-Jing-a-Jingity. Jing!

The sun rose fully as the little party scurried eastward. Now they were in a green-needle forest. Hamlin pushed them to go as fast as they could, but the children—especially the ones from the night shift in the mines—were tired, and pleas for rest stops grew frequent.

Hamlin knew as well as Rat did that they had only a halfmark to perhaps a doublemark's lead. The guards weren't simply going to let their stolen workforce go running off either. Did they keep remounts? How long would it take them to catch or calm the spooked horses? Horses could stay skittish for hours. When they chased the children, would it be on fresh horses or tired ones? What about the man he'd hit? Would they leave men behind to care for him?

How many people would be coming after them?

As they walked, Hamlin kept the children's spirits up as best he could, spinning and dancing and bowing for them just like the real hobbyhorses he'd seen at fairs. Anything to keep the children following him. Rat kept a sharp eye on the ground they crossed, on the lookout for smooth egg-shaped stones. Each time he found one, he gave it to one of the children to hold, until nearly everyone was carrying one or two.

At last Hamlin could see his painter's cart up ahead, with one of the Companion figures from *The Founding of Valdemar* leaning against it. It might remind their pursuers what risks they were taking. Its presence meant they were near the border now, after all.

Not near enough.

"They're coming," Rat hissed.

Hamlin whipped around, but there was nothing to see yet, just a faint sound of hoofbeats behind them. "Get up into the trees," he said quietly.

All the children stopped, staring at him hesitantly. He gestured, because voices carried. At last they began to move, scurrying up into the green-needle trees and doing their best to vanish among the branches.

"You too," Hamlin said, and Rat disappeared into a tree.

It was only two horsemen, one with a bundle of shackles across his pommel, the other with a crossbow. The man with the shackles seemed to be the man Hamlin had hit earlier that day. Hamlin ran toward them, waving his hands and whooping hoarsely. The bowman fired, and the whoops turned to screams as Hamlin fell to the ground. It was all for show, of course: he had warned the children that any screaming or yelling he did was part of the show, and in fact the quarrel was stuck somewhere inside the hobby's skirts nowhere near him.

Then the rain of stones began. Many throws didn't have a lot of force, but all were thrown with a great deal of sincerity, and most hit their mark. The horses shied. The riders tried to control them and only succeeded because the animals were, in fact, tired. The bowman dropped his weapon.

It was what Rat had been waiting for. He sprang from his hiding place and pounced on it.

"I have a crossbow and you don't!" he sang out gleefully as Hamlin got to his feet to reassure the children he was well.

"I have a sword!" cried Jorik.

"Do you?" Rat said. "Well, throw it down to the ground, because we have plenty of rocks left and you don't want to walk home."

"You'll let us keep the horses?" the bowman asked.

"If they're pointed in the right direction," Hamlin said. "But we'll keep the saddles and the tack—for now."

The men dismounted and removed saddles and bridles from their horses under Rat's watchful gaze. Rat collected the sword and passed it to Hamlin, who hung it around the hobbyhorse's neck. Some of the trees giggled.

Then the little band of escapees went on their way as the two miners found out that it was very hard to catch and bridle two horses that were tired and completely fed up.

Jing.

At least now there was a cart people could take turns riding in, and at last, Hamlin was grateful to see a toppled and rain-worn marker stone indicating that they were back over the border of Valdemar. It didn't mean they were safe, but it meant they were safer. There was a difference between picking up children a few at a time from no one knew where and swooping down on a company of obviously maltreated orphans.

Still.

Hamlin, who had never thought much about Heralds one way or another, thought it would be nice if one showed up right about now.

And one did.

He and his ragged little army had just crested the ridge, and Wildwold could be seen in the distance. In front of the inn was a Companion with their rider.

"Heralds ride Circuits, you know, City Boy," Rat murmured seraphically. "That's who I was waiting for at the tavern."

"You go ahead," Hamlin said. "I want to do something first."

Davos stopped at Wildwold mostly as a courtesy to its mistress, and because he could take the few missives that accumulated there with him and save the postal rider the extra distance. Wildwold was listed on the maps and in the books as a town, but in reality the tavern was all there was. (Who drank there would remain forever a mystery.) It was in the middle of no-where, surrounded by nothing, and populated by no one except the five members of the tavern's staff. In the morning, Davos and Heleganth would turn and ride southward, along their twining snake-simple route, until orders came, or someone needed them.

On the other hand, maybe he didn't have that long to wait.

A tide, a swarm, a host (if a very small and dirty one) of

children came running toward Davos. Their captain seemed to be the only one of their number who was slightly clean. He looked familiar.

"You're the boy who wanted Valdemar to start a war with pirate miners without a shred of evidence," Davos said.

"Here's your evidence," Rat answered. He made an expansive gesture. "Tricked, stolen, worked to death—and lied to, first to last. What are you going to do now?"

"Feed them and clothe them," Davos replied. "Anything else will be up to the Queen. If we did—"

At that moment there was a sound of bells.

"Actors," Rat said. "Always wanting to make an entrance. He may say he isn't, but he is."

The hobbyhorse surged over the little hill, ribbons flying and bells jingling. Even Heleganth stared.

"*This* is how you got them out?" Davos said after a long pause.

"The mine guards are probably off reporting to whoever their boss is right now," Hamlin said. "What he's going to say when they tell him a hobbyhorse stole his children, I don't know."

"Now *you're* going to go with Herald Davos," Hamlin said to the children. "He's going to take care of you while *I* am going back up into those hills."

"Twenty children?" Davos said faintly.

"Upright is just south of here," Rat said. "You can find nursemaids there. I'm going to have my hands full keeping City Boy here alive."

"You're coming with me? Who told me he was dying?" Hamlin demanded.

"The sooner you go, the sooner I can start regretting most of my life's choices," Davos said.

"But we want to say goodbye!" one of the little girls piped up. Several of the children stepped forward, and Hamlin knelt down to receive them.

But it was the hobbyhorse, not the boy, whom the children hugged and kissed.

Intrigue in Althor
Jeanne Adams

The carriage rocked and swayed along the rutted road. Demarra and her maid were both feeling battered after five days
of travel. Winters along the borders were harsh, but Demarra
had never seen it this bad. Her muff dog Pia whined, sensing
her unease.

"Shhh now, I'm fine." She stroked Pia's silky fur. She wasn't
fine, but she would pretend she was. She owed that to King's
Own Amily and Herald Mags and to Lady Dia and Lord Jor-
thun. Only for them, and for the Handmaidens, would she
come back to this Havens-forsaken place.

The carriage slowed and her mastiff, Burgher, rose. Demarra
caught the soft sound of bridle bells. Her lady's maid, Daisy,
opened the window when Herald Joss and his Companion Lilliard stopped coach-side. The cold wind swirled in, bringing the
scent of snow and smoke.

"Everything all right?" Demarra forced her voice to steadi-
ness, cloaking her inner trepidation.

"Lady Demarra, we've seen neither guard nor scout." The
Herald's frown was ferocious. Whoever had shirked that duty
was going to get a dressing down. "The fences are damaged."
He gestured to a nearby pasture, usually populated with Dolan
sheep, those with the finest, most valuable wool. Not a single
animal dotted the field.

"Things may be more dire than we expected." Demarra
peered out of the opposite window. Not far into the second

pasture a scorched area scarred the earth. "Look, a burn pile. It's still smoking."

Joss and Lilliard trotted round the carriage for a better look. She'd only seen that kind of thing one other time, after a skirmish with bandits.

Worry for Althor replaced Demarra's personal anxiety. She straightened her spine, both physically and metaphorically. She was no longer a hapless bride, starry-eyed and naive. She wasn't a beaten-down, barren, and cast-off wife either. Fenman of Althor's cowering spouse was gone. In her place was the competent, capable Handmaiden, the Dowager Countess of Althor. Demarra nearly laughed over that moniker, given that she was but eight and twenty.

Nevertheless, she was a Queen's Handmaiden, trained by the best in Haven. She had useful, even dangerous, skills. Over the past three years, Demarra had earned her place. She wouldn't let returning to Althor destroy her hard-won confidence.

"Looks like bandits," Joss said, when he and Lilliard returned.

Althor was the last southwestern bastion of Valdemar, at the conjunction of the borders with Rethwellan and Menmellith. Between those two countries lay lands and townships no country claimed. The bandits usually hit those borderland towns, not highly protected Althor.

Worry had her nibbling her thumbnail. When she realized it, she stroked Burgher's wide head instead.

"They got the sheep in." The winter grass would have shown the slaughter if the sheep were caught in the raid. Demarra shivered at the thought.

"Captain Costern sent two guards ahead." Herald Joss shaded his eyes. "Ah, here they come."

Where were the Althor guards? There should be forward sentries as well. That shouldn't have changed. When anxiety stabbed again, Demarra reminded herself that King Stefan had provided Herald Joss, Captain Costern, and the small troop for just such contingencies.

A stronger gust rocked the carriage. In the opposite seat,

Daisy pulled her cloak tight against the draft. The wind held the heavy, damp tang that presaged serious weather. Storm days in Althor had been horrific, locked in the manor with no escape from Fenman.

"Milady. Herald Joss," the Guard captain called as he trotted up. "Bandit raid three days ago. Everyone's retreated inside the walls." Captain Costern scowled. "Half of Althor's guard's injured, three killed along with the Healer. Add to it, their guard captain's missin'. Saved the woolies though, and kept them in 'cause they're expectin' a whollipin' big snow."

"Lady Nesta?" Demarra gripped the window's edge.

Costern shifted in the saddle. "Down with fever, milady. Somehow them bandits breached the manor. The Healer was killed protecting Lady Nesta."

"We should make haste to Althor."

"Very good, milady." Costern and Herald Joss pivoted to lead the way.

When they resumed their bumpy progress, Daisy broke the silence. "How old is the little? Is it a birthing fever, d'y'reckon?"

"No, Ilysa is a year old." Demarra had sent a birthing gift the previous spring.

As they rattled along, Demarra returned to her worries. Bandits raiding? Not unheard of. Bandits in the manor itself? That hadn't happened in any history she'd read.

"Reckon we'll need the herb kit first, aye, milady?"

"Yes, good thinking." Handmaidens trained with an herb Healer and had a kit of basic herbs, though Demarra had seldom used it.

Their party attracted significant attention as they rolled through the main gates. The houses and shops of the town's smallholders and craftspeople were warmly familiar. She realized she'd missed that bit of Althor. A child waved, and she waved back.

"Is that Lady Demarra?"

Demarra's heart jumped. She hadn't expected anyone to remember her. Moments later, another voice called, "Welcome back, lady!"

News apparently traveled faster than her carriage. It was so strange to be welcomed. Then again, interacting with the merchants was one of the few pleasures she'd found in Althor.

Fenman's grandfather had turned Althor's border fortress into a prosperous trading town. He'd brought in the Dolans, which in turn brought excellent weavers. His rare fruit orchards thrived in Althor's moist, mountainous climate, producing sought-after varietals.

Fenman hadn't expanded Althor's wealth, but he'd kept it in a firm grip. However, after three wives and no heir, the king had ordered Fenman to name one. He'd chosen Tiran Chern, a distant cousin.

During Demarra's musings, they'd pulled up through the manor's gates.

"Milady." The Herald helped her alight into the familiar cobbled courtyard.

"Hopefully Missus Partridge, the housekeeper, is still here," she told Joss, Lilliard, and Costern. "With the Healer dead, Brother Gasper of the temple of Thenoth will likely be tending the wounded here as well."

"Milady!" a familiar voice called out from the manor's doors. An apple-round, silver-haired woman trotted down the wide stairs to bob a curtsy.

"Missus Partridge, so good to see you." Demarra set Pia down so she could lean in and hug the newcomer. Cinnamon and savory spices tickled her senses, calling up a few more good memories of Althor. "You're well?" she managed through a tight throat.

"I am, though many's not," Missus Partridge replied. She bent to coo over Pia, perhaps to hide her own emotions. She patted Burgher as well. "You've come at a dire time, milady."

"I'm sorry for that." To bridge the awkwardness, Demarra introduced the Herald, his Companion, and Captain Costern. "This is Missus Partridge."

Introductions done, she asked the housekeeper, "Are the snow walls up?"

"Some. Nawt enough though, milady." The woman twisted

her apron. "And us with injured guard an' Lady Nesta so ill. Nawt enough t'do it."

"With Vernian missing, who's in command of the Althor guard and watch?"

"That's the blacksmith's boy, Carter. A good lad. Far and away better than that Vernian, he is." She nearly spat in disgust but stopped herself with a glance at the Herald.

Demarra turned to Captain Costern. "Captain, if you'd find Carter? We'll need to integrate our guards with Althor's and bridge any gaps. Bandits notwithstanding, the most important task is erecting the remaining snow walls before the storm hits. Carter can explain what they need."

"Aye, milady." He shot her a salute. "Ma'am." He tipped his cap to Missus Partridge.

"Missus Partridge, where are the wounded?"

"In t'lower hall. Brother Gasper's helping there since Healer Derth was killed."

Thenoth's priests were called to serve animals rather than people. With Althor's fortunes resting on so many specialty breeds, Fenman had tithed his portion there. Oddly, it was Brother Gasper, Thenoth's priest, who'd done his best to ease Demarra's way.

As they headed into the manor, Demarra turned to Herald Joss. "If you could find Gasper and get me a headcount of the wounded?"

"Of course."

"Daisy, please find those medicinal herbs and meet me in Lady Nesta's rooms."

"Aye, milady." Daisy turned back to the coach as the supply wagon rolled up.

Inside, Demarra climbed the stairs to the second floor, Demarra's guts clenching with each step. She wanted to run from the rooms where her maidenly dreams had shattered.

Not your rooms. Not your life. You're a Handmaiden now.

Forcing herself forward, she stepped in. A maid she vaguely remembered jumped up, her face wreathed in shock. "Milady!

It really *is* you! I didn't believe . . ." The woman stumbled to a stop. "Welcome home."

"Thank you, Millie." To her own surprise, Demarra dredged up the young woman's name. "How is Lady Nesta?"

"Poorly, milady."

The smell alone told that story. How did the maid stand it?

Millie hurried forward, neatly pressed apron swishing crisply against her skirts. "I'll take that to your rooms, milady." Millie seized Demarra's heavy cloak and scurried down the hall. When she darted around the corridor's odd, angled turn, Demarra heard a man's hail, but not Millie's response.

Dismissing them, she washed well at the basin and brushed any debris off her clothes before going to Nesta's bedside. The young countess was shivering despite the overwhelming warmth of the room. Her hair was tangled with sweat, and the bedclothes were stained and sour.

"This is criminal," Demarra stated, hands on hips.

Daisy trotted into the room with the herb kit and stopped short.

"O-Oh, my," she stammered. "This won't do."

"Absolutely correct. Everything must be cleaned, then we must get Healer Bear's fever tea into her."

It took them more than a candlemark, but they got Nesta bathed and the bedding replaced. Dribble by dribble, they fed her the healing tea.

"She already looks better," Daisy said.

When the long-absent Millie finally returned with broth, Demarra was too tired to scold her. Few housemaids had any nursing training, especially not in Althor. "Give her another dose of this tea within the candlemark," she ordered. "We must break the fever's hold."

"Yes, milady." Millie's eyes glittered with tears. "Thank you, milady."

"Daisy will relieve you after dinner."

Daisy frowned at that, but Demarra shot her a look.

"Oh, there's no need—"

"There's every need. You must be very tired, and we're here to help."

They left Millie to her charge. "You want a watch on Lady Nesta, aye?" Daisy's words were quiet but her scorn was obvious.

"Yes. That was abominable." Demarra felt foul from the necessary cleaning. "I want to see Ilysa before dinner." She hoped the heir wasn't in the same shape as her mother. "I need to get a sense of things as fast as I can."

"Of course, milady."

They'd just found their rooms, the dark blue, velvet curtains drawn against the cold, when Missus Partridge bustled in. She hurried to stir the fire.

"You've seen Nesta then? Young Millie is very protective. I've hardly been in there."

Not wanting to rock the boat, Demarra replied with a noncommittal "Hmmmm."

Daisy changed her own soiled garments, then helped Demarra into a deceptively simple, black wool gown. Its ornamentation was demure, but it fit Demarra with exceptional grace. While she didn't need fashion for a blizzard in Althor, it was incredibly warm, and it gave her courage.

"Missus Partridge, what happened here?" Demarra asked as Daisy brushed Demarra's disheveled hair.

The housekeeper all but moaned. "Milady, it's been one terrible thing after t'other. First Lord Fenman's death, and Lord Tiran . . ." She hesitated. "When the Herald brought the news, Tiran took charge."

"I'm sure he did." Demarra would have bet a copper he'd taken charge the minute Fenman left the manor. Tiran had happily stranded her in Haven. He had authorized Fenman's remaining travel funds to be turned over to her, but firmly declared she need never return to Althor.

"Lord Tiran married Lady Nesta in his mourning clothes," the housekeeper continued, oblivious to Demarra's wandering thoughts. "She hails from Ellistown, 'cross the border. She weren't never what I'd call . . . strong."

"I understand." Fenman had raged that Demarra wasn't a proper woman. He expected her to be like Nesta and catch fever and die, as any good wife should when she couldn't produce a child. Instead, Demarra had survived *him*.

Burgher leaned against her knee just then, and she was glad to stroke his wide head and feel the heat of his strong body against her legs. She forced herself to relax. Her assignment was to protect Nesta, the baby heir, and Althor in that order, not slog through bad memories.

Sensing her distress, Pia trotted over, nosed her way under Demarra's skirts, and curled up on her cold feet. The reassuring presence of both dogs reminded her of who she was. She could do this.

"Anyway," Missus Partridge continued the tale, "Lady Nesta was quickly with child. Sick from the first day, she was. Couldn't hardly keep nothing down."

"And Ilysa?"

"Healthy as a hog in a wallow." The housekeeper beamed. "That little is as sturdy as her mother is frail."

"I'm glad." Demarra started to ask about Millie, but let it go. Althor was obviously short staffed. Then again, as many people as could be spared, now augmented by Costern's troop, were likely fighting against time to build snow walls.

While Daisy set to unpacking, Demarra headed to the nursery, Burgher and Pia at her heels.

"She's a good child, Lady Demarra," Rhea, Ilysa's nanny declared.

"I see that." Demarra knelt down to introduce Ilysa to the dogs. The child was captivated by them. Chortling, she toddled after Burgher. When Pia finally jumped into Demarra's lap to rest, Ilysa gripped Demarra's skirts.

"Up! Up!" she demanded. Within minutes, Ilysa had curled up with the dog, her head on Demarra's lap. She was asleep in a blink. Demarra's heart turned to absolute mush.

She could've sat for hours stroking Ilysa's back, but Rhea

expertly bundled the cherubic child into an ornately carved cradle, tucking a soft dolly under her blanket.

"She sleeps well?" Demarra whispered.

"Very," Rhea said in a normal voice. "Once she's down, there's no waking her. No need to whisper."

Demarra smiled. She'd reportedly been much the same. It wasn't until Fenman that she'd learned to sleep lightly. "I won't keep you from your dinner, then. I'll be back in the morning."

"Yes, milady."

Demarra called the dogs and stepped into the shadowy hall. There was a soft swish of fabric, and Burgher's menacing bark filled the empty space. His growl and Pia's rumbled a dangerous threat into the silence.

"Who's there?" Burgher's growl increased.

"'Tis only me, milady." Millie materialized from the shadows carrying a meal. Demarra smelled good ale and a rich beef stew.

"No ale while you're watching Nesta," Demarra snapped. She regretted the sharp tone, but the girl had frightened her. Burgher still rumbled softly at her side. As to the ale, Millie should have known better. "Nursing Nesta is vital, Millie. You need your wits about you."

"Oh." Millie looked blankly at the tankard. "Of course, milady. I didn't think."

Unacceptable. Since Demarra didn't trust the woman, she took the ale.

"Sorry, milady."

Demarra's nod was curt. She'd caught the sharp look of annoyance, despite Millie's demure words. "Daisy will relieve you after dinner."

"Yes, milady." Demarra followed her to Nesta's rooms, then made her way downstairs.

Crates and boxes from the wagon lined the foyer. Large hams, casks of pickled beets, and straw-packed winter apples were stacked along the walls. Burgher sniffed the hams, and tiny Pia pranced next to him, barking defiantly at the barrels.

The door opened in a rush of cold air as two footmen brought in more crates. The dogs retreated to her side.

"Take this down t'the kitchen, lads," Missus Partridge directed as she hurried in.

"Yes'm." They headed off, and Demarra pulled the housekeeper aside.

She had intended to complain about Millie, but instead asked, "What can you tell me about the missing guard captain?"

The housekeeper narrowed her eyes. "That one? A rotten apple, if'n you ask me. He's been eyein' Lady Nesta, *that* way. An' her not well enough to sit up."

"How unpleasant." It reminded her of Fenman, so she changed the subject. "When did you get word from the weather worker in Persfall?"

"Four'r so days ago," Missus Partridge affirmed. "At least that layabout Vernian started snow preparations—notified the farms and sent supplies. Guard started piling bales for the snow paths and pulling the posts from storage. Then the bandits hit. They's no match for our Guard, but somehow they got in!" Missus Partridge was as affronted as Captain Costern.

"Unprecedented," Demarra agreed.

"They stole provisions right out'n the kitchen, and sommut tried to get to Nesta." The older woman wrung her hands. "I didn't sleep a wink that night."

A shuffling sound had Demarra pivoting. "Gasper!" As she hurried to greet him, Burgher and Pia bounced over to sniff his thick brown robe. "It's good to see you."

"You too, Lady Demarra," he said, bowing over his withered right arm, which he held stiffly across his stomach. By contrast, Gasper's left side was robust and well-muscled. "You've come in a bad hour, I'm afraid."

"Or, perhaps, just in time to help," she countered, and straightened her back.

Gasper shot her a sharp, assessing look.

"We're always glad of your help, Lady Demarra." He smiled at the dogs. "Those are wonderful specimens. Mastiff and muff dog, is it?"

"Yes. This is Burgher." She ordered the mastiff to sit. Burgher offered Gasper a paw, which Gasper shook with grave courtesy while Pia happily danced at his feet. "He and Pia were gifts from a friend."

"A queenly gift." Gasper ruffled Pia's ears before looking up. "Herald Joss and your Captain Costern are in the parlor."

"Ah. Will you join us?"

With a last pat to Burgher's head, he demurred. "The storm is almost upon us. I must see to the injured, as well as my novices, Lady. My apologies." With a bow and a warm smile, he left her.

How odd. She turned back to the housekeeper. "What is the state of the kitchens, Missus Partridge? Are we storm-ready?"

"Not like we should be, milady." The housekeeper's exasperation showed. "We've had two mild winters. Lord Tiran felt we could keep fewer supplies on hand."

"Idiot," Demarra huffed. "The storms always return. Better to be prepared."

"Too right. I'm mortal grateful you brought provisions. I'll have an accounting for you in t'morning. Join your lads in the parlor and I'll send supper in. If'n your dogs'll go with me, I'll see them fed."

"They will, if I tell them to." Which she did.

The housekeeper smiled. "It's good to have you home, Lady Demarra." The housekeeper bobbed another curtsy, but stopped at the doorway, giving Demarra an oblique look. "You learned a lot in Haven."

"Oh, of a certainty, I did." If they only knew how much . . .

Laughing at Demarra's wry response, Missus Partridge headed for the kitchens, dogs at her heels.

Demarra stood alone in the great foyer. As in the nursery hall, only half the torches were lit, and shadows and memories loomed. Fenman had hauled her up those stairs by her hair more than once, despite her protests. His first wife had died of fever, his second of a fall, and Demarra was certain he'd tried to kill her more than once after that first, unproductive year. But she'd survived.

"And I'm going to keep surviving," she declared.

A soft, evil laugh echoed from above, shocking her into the

present. Demarra spun to look upward, pulling the blade she kept hidden in her pocket. "Who's there?"

After a moment with no other sound, she put the blade away. Embarrassed, she muttered, "Nothing but shadows and pain."

"Herald, Captain, we have a serious problem." After five days on the road with these men, Demarra felt she could speak plainly.

"How can we help?" Herald Joss leaned onto the table, mug in hand. They'd finished dinner and now sat with cheese and fruit.

"We need Belhaven's Healer. Joss, there's a slim chance you and Companion Lilliard could get there and back before the storm."

"I wish I could Fetch her," he quipped. He'd complained that his Fetching gift wasn't much help out on Circuit. "But we'll have to do it the regular way. Is Lady Nesta that bad?"

"Yes, plus three of the Guard, as you noted. Even with the medicines I brought, we may lose them." She swallowed her distress, focusing on the work.

Joss folded two pieces of cheese onto a slice of winter apple as he rose. "With your permission, Lady Demarra, I'll leave now. May I take these two apples for Lilliard?"

"Absolutely. Herald Joss, if the storm comes on too fast, don't risk yourself, Lilliard, or the Healer. We'll make it." She forced a smile. "We always do, here in Althor."

"I'll return as soon as I can, milady." Joss popped the cheese and apple into his mouth and headed for the door. Demarra and Costern returned to the vellum they'd unrolled onto the table.

"How did you find young Carter?"

Costern grunted. "Green as grass, but eager as a pup. He'll do."

"What about the bandits?"

"Young Carter says they took a toll on them ruffians." He jerked his head toward the door. "You saw the burn patch. Don't reckon they'll be a bother."

"That's a relief. And the snow walls?"

"We're working our men together right enough, putting up them walls. Right smart idea, that is," he said with a firm nod. "But it's slow going."

"Althor is a maze." Demarra pointed to the lines marking various shops coloring the map. "With the shops' overhanging eaves, the snow walls let people move along the shopfronts even in deep snow. While that's important, reinforcing the sheep enclosure is vital. We *must* get those walls up."

"We're almost done there," Costern reported. "The shopkeepers and shepherds started on their own." Costern pointed to a section on the map. "They've put the wooden poles in place, at least."

"Good." Demarra fought panic. She felt the storm's pressure changes in her bones. "Thankfully the storm warning came in time. Provisions went out to the upper farms, and the Dolans are already penned into the city enclosures." They couldn't lose the sheep.

"Young Carter says things've been bad." Costern grimaced. "That missing one, Vernian, started intimidating the shopkeepers. Lady Nesta, bein' widowed and sick and all, had no way to curb him." His lips thinned into a tight line.

"So, Vernian had free rein. No one would think to take Althor's troubles to Brother Gasper or Missus Partridge." They'd been the only other authority figures in Althor.

"E'zactly." Costern's frown deepened. "Only good news I kin see is his bullies is what died in the bandit raid."

"One less problem. I'll take it and be thankful." She thought for a minute. "We need to feed these workers. Will you accompany me to the shops in the morning, Captain?"

"Absolutely."

The morning dawned colder, with sullen clouds topping the western hills. Demarra and her dogs met Costern in front of the manor for the walk to the bakery.

The shop bells jingled, and Pia poked out of Demarra's muff.

"Just a moment!" a voice called. A man bustled around the

edge of the wall, then stopped short. "Milady Demarra! It's good to see you!"

Walking to Dalkeith's had been one of her few pleasures. "Thank you, Dalkeith. How are you? How are Sara, Hans, and Berta?"

"All well!" He was obviously curious about her return, but he only asked, "How can I serve you?"

"I've been appointed regent for Althor until Lady Nesta regains her strength." It wasn't that simple, but close enough. Dalkeith would make sure that got around. "Dalkeith, the snow paths aren't ready, and the storm will be here before nightfall."

"Aye, 'tis already snowin'," Dalkeith said. "Hans is out helpin' get the sheep enclosure secured. He's sweet on a weaver gal."

"Oh, that's so nice." She started to ask more, then forced herself to focus. "Althor's strong, but this will test it."

"Aye," Dalkeith agreed.

"But it won't best us," she insisted. "After the storm, I want to hear all about Hans and his weaver, but for now, I have two requests. We need every hand. Can you spare Sara or Berta?"

When he looked surprised, she added, "They know where everything is, and people respect them."

"Yes." He called the women from the back. They exclaimed over Demarra in much the same fashion, but she cut that short.

"Do you have enough rolls to pair with sausage from Samiel's shop? We'll need meals for the extra guardsmen I brought from Haven. By feeding them and any able-bodied person who can pitch in, we have a slim chance to get the snow paths done."

She set a gold piece on the counter. "Will you help?"

"We've got rolls started and can make more," Dalkeith declared, slipping the coin into his apron pocket.

"I'll start a new batch," Sara added. "Then join the work party. Berta, fetch Karim, Elodie, and Bertram from their temple lessons. Get any others who can be spared. Make sure they know it's Milady Demarra's request."

"Yes'm. Milady. Sir." Berta had been delighting Pia with pets, but she dropped a curtsy and hurried out the door.

They repeated the task at the sausage maker's shop and at

the inn. "Old Bert," she exclaimed to the innkeeper. "Didn't you retire to Seven Springs with your youngest?"

"Aye, but my eldest had twins, so here I am back again. It's right good to see you, milady."

"Thank you. We've got to finish getting the sheep protected." She stated the obvious. "Dalkeith and Samiel will feed them, but I need your cider."

Bert looked dubious until she set a gold coin on his counter. "Without shelter for the sheep, we'll lose people and their livelihoods. We can't afford that." He nodded. A slow, deliberate agreement as he eyed the mastiff sitting quietly by her side.

"I'm no help on the ropes." She was a great deal stronger now, but not quite that strong. "But Althor can support its people."

Old Bert folded his arms. He glanced at the coin, then back to her. "Fenman wouldn't'a done it, nor that Tiran either. Why're you?"

"Because Althor matters. To me, and to the King. Besides," she managed a smile. "People will work harder for your good cider."

Old Bert met her gaze. That look seemed to say he knew too much about her, and about what had happened when Fenman was alive. Given he supplied the town and the manor with spirits, he probably did. "Why'd you come back?"

"Because my King asked me to." Her insides shook, but she boldly met his gaze. "His majesty knows I care about Althor, and its people."

Costern spoke for the first time. "King Stefan has every faith in her."

"Hmmmpf," Old Bert grunted, but picked up the coin. He gave her another uncomfortably long assessment. "It'll be ready, milady."

When they came out of the inn, Costern bowed. "I'll join the work, milady."

"Thank you. I'll be back at nuncheon."

Walking back to the manor, she was hailed several times. She waved but kept walking. She needed to check on Nesta and Ilysa.

Burgher, trotting at her side, suddenly stopped. He stared into the space between the metalsmith and the glassblower's shops with a menacing growl.

Unease gripped her. "Come, Burgher."

The dog followed, but he continued to growl and look back, so she picked up the pace. Burgher settled when they reached the manor, but she trusted him. Someone in Althor meant her harm.

Ilysa was as delighted with Pia and Burgher as she'd been the previous day, and Demarra and Rhea enjoyed their antics for nearly a candlemark.

Demarra jumped when a knock sounded at the door, and Burgher put himself between Demarra and any danger.

"That'll be Ilysa's nuncheon," Rhea said as she opened the nursery door.

"My cue to get to my own work as well," Demarra declared. Much as she wanted the reassurance of Burgher's presence, the temperature had dropped even more. "Rhea, may I leave the dogs with you? Their coats aren't made for this cold, much less the snow."

"I'd be delighted, milady."

Demarra bundled up and joined the luncheon lines, passing out sausage rolls and cider to hardworking guardsmen and townsfolk. Most thanked her before returning to the vital task of finishing the snow walls.

As the afternoon advanced, Daisy came to spell her. "Milady. I've been with Lady Nesta all morning," she reported. "That Millie's not shown up at all."

"Unacceptable." Demarra carried her irritation back to the manor, which held off any of the morning's unease.

When she got to Nesta's room with more herbal tea, Nesta was alone. Though she hated to do it, she rang for Missus Partridge. "Do you know where Millie's gotten to?"

"No, milady." Missus Partridge's terse tone boded no good for the woman when she turned up. "I'll have Cassie come—"

A youngster burst in. "Milady, can you come?" the boy panted. "It's the storm."

"Go, I'll handle this," the housekeeper declared.

Demarra hurried after the boy. Minutes later they climbed the guard tower as the rising wind tried to claw them off. Black clouds boiled over the hills. The fluffy, graceful flakes from the morning were gone, replaced with a thick, steady fall.

"Close the gates, Captain Costern." She had to shout against the wind's roar. "The Herald won't make it in this. We're on our own."

"Yes, milady. He'll get here on the trot when it clears, I'm sure."

She nodded. "Until then, we'll do what we can with what we have."

"Walls're up," he reported. "With the townsfolk helpin' we got it done. Took near everything we had, though." He let out a sigh of relief when the gates banged shut and the bar dropped behind them. "Got lines strung to the manor and gatehouses for patrols too, once things settle."

"That's all we can do." She shivered. "Missus Partridge assured me there's a good meal waiting in the barracks. It'll be snug, with both your people and the town guard."

"Aye, but it'll be warm." They descended and, using the ropes, he saw her to the manor doors.

She'd just hung her cloak to dry when she heard screams. Demarra rushed upstairs to find Missus Partridge cradling a bleeding housemaid. "Someone attacked Lady Nesta! Cassie tried to stop them."

"Trying to get to her under the cover of the storm . . ." They'd missed. What would they . . . Demarra connected the dots. "Ilysa!"

"Oh no!"

Demarra raced down the hall only to find the nursery door barred. "Rhea!?"

"Milady?" came a frantic voice from within. "Is it you?" The door opened a crack, revealing a disheveled Rhea, poker in hand, growling dogs by her side.

"I heard screams, so I locked the door like Lady Nesta told me. Your dogs set t'barking and drove 'em away."

"Lock the door again," she urged, signaling Burgher to come. "Don't let in anyone but me or Missus Partridge."

She raced back to Nesta's room. She'd barely cleared the door when someone grabbed her arm. She twisted away, just as she'd been taught. A knife whistled through the space she'd been in. Before she could counter, Burgher leaped in with furious, guttural snarls.

His teeth flashed, laying Millie's arm open to the bone. Demarra straightened, only to have an arm jerk across her neck, pinning her against a hard, male body. A knife pricked her throat.

"Call off the dog, bitch," the man snapped.

"Burgher, cease." The dog disengaged, his fangs dripping red.

"Kill her!" Millie moaned in pain. "Kill her now!"

"Don't take orders from you, bitch."

Rousing slightly from the fever, Nesta groaned. Missus Partridge, still cradling Cassie, peeked over the bed. "Vernian?"

It was the distraction Demarra needed. She snapped her head back, crunching her attacker's nose even as she forced his arm from her throat. She dropped down, slamming her elbow back into his privates with every iota of fear and fury boiling in her veins. Burgher leapt back at Millie.

Vernian folded, clutching his groin. But he wasn't down. Someone screamed as Demarra brought her fisted hands down on the back of her attacker's neck and kicked out his knee for good measure.

"Burgher, cease," she croaked. That's when she realized she'd been the one screaming.

Millie collapsed the minute the dog released.

Footsteps thundered up the stairs. Daisy and the two footmen stopped dead in their tracks. "Holy Havens."

Seeing Demarra, Daisy rushed over. "My lady!"

Demarra nearly collapsed in her arms. "Well," she muttered. "That elbow thing works just like the weaponsmaster said it would."

Daisy's near-hysterical giggle helped. "Good to know."

Demarra repressed a giggle of her own. If she laughed, if she made any other sound, she'd burst into tears.

"Tie them up, please," she rasped, poking her assailant's body with her shoe. "See to his wounds, and hers too."

The footmen rushed to comply. None too gently, either.

"Keep them alive," she ordered. "We need answers."

Missus Partridge staggered up, her eyes narrowed to furious slits. "That little minx was in on it." She pointed to Millie. "People *died*. I'll see to *her!*"

Though Demarra appreciated the sentiment, she shook her head. "Herald Joss will deal with this."

"I can't wait," Daisy muttered.

"Millie swore she was Fenman's daughter, and thus his rightful heir," Herald Joss began. His audience gaped at him. Joss had returned with the Belhaven Healer five days after the storm subsided. Now he'd finally seen the captives, and Demarra, Gasper, and Missus Partridge were gathered to hear what the Truth Spell had revealed.

"Millie killed twice to gain access and become Nesta's maid."

Missus Partridge shook her head over that. "Poor dear things."

"Once Tiran died," Joss continued. "Millie enlisted Vernian, but he planned to double-cross her and marry Nesta, thereby seizing Althor. The baby would then have had a convenient accident. Lady Demarra's arrival meant she too had to die."

"Goodness, that's . . ." Demarra paused. "Bloodthirsty." She was grateful for Pia's presence, warming her feet as they talked of murder.

"She wasn't Fenman's get," Gasper interjected, looking mildly embarrassed. "My predecessor believed Fenman unable to sire children. A childhood injury."

He very carefully didn't look Demarra's way.

"How did Vernian disappear?" That was something Demarra couldn't parse out.

"Millie," Joss replied. "Vernian used the bandit raid as cover. She wrecked the kitchen and stole supplies, while he went for Nesta. He killed Nesta's guards, his own men." The Herald rubbed his forehead, his features a study in disgust. "Millie hid him in the manor, waiting for another chance."

"So . . ." Demarra summed it up. "Under the cover of the storm, he planned to kill me, and probably Millie, marry Nesta, and secure his hold on Althor?"

"Pretty much." Joss poured more spiced cider. "It wouldn't've stood. King Stefan frowns on murderous coups."

"A good policy," Gasper's dry rejoinder brought a much-needed laugh. "What now?"

"Lady Demarra's authority remains until Lady Nesta is healthy." Herald Joss bowed Demarra's way.

Demarra took up the narrative. "Lady Nesta is recovering, thanks to the Healer, as are the injured guardsmen. It's to Gasper's credit that they lived through the storm."

Gasper smiled. "Thank you, Lady Demarra."

Herald Joss looked absent for a moment. "Lilliard informs me that the Crown extends its thanks, Lady Demarra, for foiling this plot."

"They *should* be grateful," Missus Partridge stoutly chimed in as she rose. "Althor's always run best under Lady Demarra's care." She accorded them all a brisk nod, and headed for the kitchen.

Two days later, when Herald Joss came to take his leave, he offered her a packet of letters. "From your friends." She must've looked shocked. "My gift *is* Fetching," he reminded her, then cocked his head. "Lady Nesta will be months in recovering. Will you stay?"

Thinking of Gasper, of Missus Partridge and the townspeople who'd remembered her, Demarra's decision was easy.

"Of course."

A Day's Work
Charlotte E. English

At fifteen, and undersized, Trick still had a roar on her that wouldn't have disgraced a soldier twice her height.

"*MAK!*"

The name, uttered at shattering volume, caused its owner to jump guiltily: his head snapped up. He'd parked himself right in the center of their cellar hideout, spilling a handful of something that glittered over Trick's campaigning table, and crowing fit to bust his lungs.

Trick knew trouble when she saw it.

"Trick, they'll hear you halfway across Haven," said Pinto from behind her, but she ignored him; she couldn't worry about that now.

"What've you done?" she demanded, and Mak flushed, running a nervous hand over what was left of his black hair (Trick had cropped it herself, a week ago, when the lice got too bad).

"Nothing!" he protested, his thin face a study in self-pity. He always had been the weak link in her little band. "I done nothing wrong! I was give it, the whole lot."

Trick stared, shaking her head. There they lay, a sparkling indictment of Mak's morals: eight or ten jewels, shining dully blue and yellow in the light of their lone lamp. Oh, not diamonds, or anything fancy like that. Topaz, maybe, or some such; Trick didn't know. She knew they cost, though. Cost quite a bit.

"You know the rules," she said, quietly now, but they all knew to fear Trick more when she was quiet than when she was loud.

She advanced on Mak; he shrank away from her. "No stealing. You *know* what comes of them as steals, Mak. You think I'll let you get yerself caught—and the rest of us with you?"

"I din't steal 'em," Mak sniveled. "I *earned* them."

"Do you take me for a fool? What could a kid like you possibly do to earn a haul like this?" Mak was twelve, if he was that old, and runty, and didn't have much in his upper story. Trick had taken him in because Ashleen had begged, though if the truth were known, she wouldn't have turned him away anyway. Kid'd get himself killed out there without a gang at his back.

She regretted it, sometimes.

"Was a job, Trick, like you tell us to do," Mak whined. "Foller this cove, find out where he goes, an' they give me the jools. And there's more where they came from. I'm goin' back tomorrer. Feed us for months, Trick, won't it?"

He was whining again, gazing at the both of them with that pitiful, hangdog look—thought he was keeping up with the rest of them at last. He wanted a pat on the head, like he was a dog himself.

Trick couldn't.

"You got paid *all that* for an easy job, and you din't think there was nothing wrong with that?" Trick's fingers found their way into her messy braids and tugged. She could smash something when she felt like this. Didn't do to let it get the better of her, though. "Mak, someone's made a mark of you. They're playing you for a fool."

Shaking his head, still, because he didn't want to believe she was right. Like he could make it go his way just by shutting his ears to what she said.

Trick slammed a small fist on the tabletop, but when she spoke she was deadly quiet. "Tell me what happened," she ordered. "Tell me every little thing, Mak."

The story had come tumbling out of the kid all confused, bits of the tale all mixed up with irrelevances; Trick'd had him go through it twice to make sure she'd got it.

She'd left that room still more uneasy. Bad enough some

knave was pushing stolen goods on a kid like Mak—oh, it wasn't hard to guess those jewels never legally changed hands, if you had a brain in your head—but the errand he'd been set wasn't merely an excuse to send him away red-handed with compromising goods. They wanted a scapegoat, right enough. If Trick tried to sell Mak's pretty trinkets, she'd be done for the theft before she could turn around.

But they'd sent Mak after a real target. And Trick didn't like the sound of that, at *all*.

"Rich cove," Mak had told her, describing the man he'd spent half the day tailing about. "Taller'n Pinto, dark hair like yours. Not fat, but been living soft. Frowns a lot, like he's got a lot on his mind. And he wears a red cloak made outta that plushy stuff. Velvet. Shone in the sun, like."

For all Mak's flaws, he had skills as well. He saw a lot, and he remembered. And she doubted this soft-living courtier had any idea he was being tailed; Mak could be nigh invisible, when he chose to be.

Not so for everyone. "Weren't just me," Mak had rushed to tell her. "I saw two of Pigeon's boys lurking round him, and Straw Annie, and another girl I din't know. Must be new."

It was that, more than anything else, that had turned Trick cold with horror. Three different gangs he'd named, plus the newcomer: whoever wanted this man watched wasn't going easy. What was the ploy?

That he came out of the Palace wasn't in question. Mak had followed him almost to the gates himself—if the noble's attire hadn't been enough of a giveaway. Someone interested in Palace business, then. But that was as far as Trick could get with Mak's information. She needed more.

Well, that was easy enough. They wanted a lotta kids on this job, did they? Trick took herself out to the north corner of the market, right where Madgie hawked those pies of hers that smelled so good, and made sure she was seen. This was where Mak'd been yesterday, where he had got himself hired.

Didn't take long before someone approached Trick.

Wasn't an adult, though, to her surprise. A girl came sidling up before Trick had stood there more than ten minutes, and she wasn't your typical street waif. She had muscle on her, like she'd been eating well, and she was a head taller than Trick.

"Look like you could use a job," she said without preamble, and jerked her chin at Trick, looking her over with eyes that took in every jutting bone on the younger girl's skinny frame.

It wasn't that Trick didn't get to eat. She and Pinto and Ashleen and Mak, they got by just fine. She was just thin, that was all.

Still. Wouldn't hurt to play the starveling for a bit. "What's it to you?" Trick answered, with just the right hint of belligerence.

The girl thrust a hand at Trick, opened her fingers for a split second: a clear blue jewel glittered in the light, and vanished again. Clumsy, and ham-handed. Pushy. Whoever was behind this mess wanted it done fast.

Trick folded her arms. "All right. I'm interested."

The girl smirked. "Come along wi' me, then."

Trick followed her out of the market, didn't so much as turn her head once. She didn't need to check that Pinto had seen, that he was still on her tail. He had her back, no matter what.

They'd set up in one of the old tumbledowns out past the market: hovels, to look at them. They weren't much, all weathered stone and leaking roofs, and the folk living there didn't have much except pride. Dirt poor, but respectable, didn't cause trouble with the Watch. Didn't steal. With nothing to offer and nothing they were taking, the city passed them by, and *that* made this a perfect spot to stir up trouble. Made Trick mad again with them, that they'd risk the peace of these folks with their nonsense.

She also filed away that nugget of information: somebody knew Haven very well indeed—or they'd been well advised by someone who did.

Trick strolled along with the girl like she didn't have a care in the world, but every sense was alert as they went under the low frame of one of those shabby old doors and into a cottage with nothing to recommend it save its very lack of appeal. There was a room at the front, living space, sparsely furnished but scrupulously clean; a narrow staircase leading to a bed-chamber above; and at the back, a cramped kitchen space with a large fireplace and a pot hanging over it, though the coals were cold. Trick's quarry stood at a gaping window, shutters open just enough to let some light in.

He wasn't so tall, to Trick's surprise: a compact, slight figure draped in a dark cloak like he was the villain in some street play. He had the hood drawn up to cover his hair—in fact, Trick couldn't even tell if it *was* a he, or a she. Could've been anybody under there.

The girl didn't say his name, to her disappointment, only made a soft sound of greeting, or alert. Before the figure even turned, Trick was getting it: bit of a bad feeling, like she'd wandered into a story and it was one of the stupid ones.

"You got to be kidding me," she said flatly, and stared her contempt for this fool of a boy. For it was a boy: only three-quarters grown, dancing about in his silly cloak and fancying himself some kind of spy or something.

He turned to show Trick a face about her own age, maybe younger, all pinched up with worry, and *that* was stupid, for sure. Nobody trusted you if you didn't look like you had it all figured out. He had mouse-brown hair, closely cropped, and a glimpse of color at the neck of his cloak that told her he wore livery of some sort.

He cleared his throat, straightened his stupid, skinny shoulders, and said, pitching his voice deep, "Ah, and who've you brought me?" Talked like they did up at the palace. Likely a page, or some such person, and what were Court folk doing down in the city, spying on each other?

"You can call me Trick," she said, "if you've got time to call me anything, which I don't reckon you do." She turned to go.

"Wait," called the boy in the cloak, and his friend, the girl, darted quick as a flash to block the door. Trick glared at her, cold as stone, and the girl flinched. *Ha.*

Trick turned that glare on the boy, and waited.

"You look like you know your way around the streets," he said.

Trick looked him up and down. "You don't."

"Well, exactly. That is why I need your help. And your friends', too, if you'll bring them to me. I am paying well." He held out a hand, and there were more of those jewels like Mak had brought, shining like pools of sunlight in the palm of his hand.

"Palace boy you may be, but I don't suppose those are yours for all that," Trick informed him. "Steal them, did you?"

He flushed, and bridled. "It's none of your business where they came from. They are yours, if you—"

"It's my business if I'm caught with stolen jewels. What do you want with that fat man in the velvet that's so important?"

It was his turn to stare, and he looked spooked—good. "How do you—"

"Because you dragged one of my boys into your mess, so now it's my mess, too. The worse for you."

"He's a traitor."

Pinto materialized at Trick's elbow, silent as always. He didn't say anything, just stood shoulder to shoulder with Trick while the boy babbled accusations.

"Oh, he is?" Trick said. "You got any proof of that?"

"No. That is what I'm *doing*. I heard him talking—he is selling secrets, I *know* he is, but it's my word against his and he is a—well, I need proof."

Trick's glare faded, her quick mind racing through the disparate parts of this odd story. He was right about proof; few adults would take the word of a child over that of another adult, nor would anybody believe a low-ranking Palace boy over that of a fully fledged noble. Which was as it should be, in this instance; an accusation of treason was as serious as it got.

She'd be inclined to scoff, save that earnestness rolled off him like water. She doubted he could lie to save his life.

And she had Mak's testimony, too. Whatever that man was doing skulking about Haven all on his own, it was something he couldn't send another to do. Something he didn't want known. And that was odd, for his sort always had servants to run their errands for them.

"Put them things away," she said, when he tried again to offer her jewels. "It en't right to steal, and if we're helping you, then they're going back where they came from."

"It's a just cause—"

"No cause is just enough." Trick spoke bluntly, with finality. "Those are the terms."

"All right." The jewels were pocketed, and forgotten. He turned back to Trick with alacrity, and relief. "Thank you."

"Don't thank me yet. You don't have a clue what you've got into."

He was called Roald, Trick discovered, though he was cagey about giving any more of his names. That was fine with her. Only Pinto had ever learned her real name, and that was how she liked it. Names were dangerous.

By the time she'd got the whole story out of him, her skepticism was turning into a grudging respect. Most people would've called it none of their business and shut their eyes, let it be. And maybe Roald should have, too, if he knew what was good for him. He was lucky he hadn't run into Vander's gang; they'd have stripped him of everything he owned and dropped him down a well. Trick had to shake her head at it. Innocence and a sense of responsibility: dangerous combination. Sort of thing that got a boy killed.

Within two hours, she had all the details, Roald's implicit trust, and Ashleen, Pinto, and Mak on board—as well as Kress, the girl who'd towed Trick out of the market. Six against one. Decent odds.

She also had the beginnings of a plan. "We need to know more," she decided. She'd taken them out of the cottage—Roald claimed he knew who lived there, had their consent to use it, but Trick thought that was dafter than ever, you didn't get your friends involved in treasonous plots if you could help it—and brought them back to her own cellar hideaway, rather against

Pinto's judgement. Trick shrugged this off. She did her best thinking at home, over her campaigning table, and if they wanted a plan, a *good* plan, then the cellar it must be. "Roald, what have your eyes and ears brought you? If this man—"

"Lord Kalgan," Roald interrupted.

"If this Lord Kalgan's selling secrets and he don't want anyone to know, then he's down here meeting someone. Either the person's who's paying for information, or some lackey of theirs. And he don't want any of that taking place up near the Palace, where he's more like to be recognized."

Roald nodded at this and interjected eagerly, "Annie tracked him to a tavern out on the edge of the city. He met someone, but she could tell little about him, for he had a hood and scarf, and never stepped out of the shadows. She heard him speak, though, a little, and his accent was not from Valdemar."

Ashleen spoke up, not without a touch of rancor; she didn't like Roald, nor any part of his story. She was littler even than Trick, younger than Roald, but spiky enough for the both of them put together. "Lots of people got funny accents," she said pugnaciously, her flat blue eyes glinting like stones. "Most of 'em ain't buying state secrets."

"And most of them are not hiding their names and faces, and meeting displaced lords in dark taverns," Roald returned.

Ashleen tried her best to find fault with this: Trick watched the play of emotions over her face, settling at last on annoyed resignation. He was right.

"Well," said Trick. "So we know where to find them. But watching ain't enough, nor's eavesdropping. Still our word against his lordship's, that way. We got to be cleverer than that."

Pinto said nothing, only watched her with steady attention and a faint smile: he knew her, knew she wouldn't have said so much if she didn't already have a plan in mind.

Ashleen scowled; it was Roald who said, "I know, but I have no—I thought if I just got enough information, somehow a solution would—present itself."

Trick shook her head at him, sad-like. "Only the rich got

time to sit and wait for fortune to show up. You're at the other end of the city, now. We make our own luck."

Roald looked dubious. "Does that mean you have a plan?"

Trick grinned. "Course I've got a plan."

Trick liked certainty. Leaving too much to chance got a person in trouble, and you were like to make mistakes when you weren't sure. So she sent Mak and Kress out first, asking questions and listening in: at the nicer taverns nearer the Palace, where those that served the nobility sometimes lingered; at the hostlers, and the tailors, and even a jeweler the Court folk liked. Apprentices weren't sorry to talk, as a rule, and nor were servants and seamstresses—within a few hours, Trick had all the word she wanted on Lord Kalgan.

It didn't look pretty. He was a man as had fancy tastes and a greed for finery, with an expensive wife to boot. And he'd come down some in the world of nobles: he had bills all over town he hadn't paid, and the traders were growing impatient with him.

Fallen on hard times, then, the velvet cloak notwithstanding. And he had a temper on him. He'd knocked about a stable boy one time, and there were more tales like that, too many more. Greed and viciousness. Trick didn't feel so much like maybe they could be wrong about Lord Kalgan. If someone had offered him cash for information, well, he had the need for it, and no sense of justice to set him against it.

Right, then.

His lordship skulked about at night, on the whole, like most people up to no good. By evenfall, Trick and her people were scattered over the rooftops of Haven, eyes peeled for the approach of Lord Kalgan—or his shadowy contact. Mak had clocked Kalgan's route near enough, and he could be trusted to play lookout.

Ash and Roald were already at the tavern, the one waiting tables, the other drinking quietly in a corner ("But what if he recognizes me?" Roald had said in a panic, and Trick'd had to laugh at that. Like any lord would even look twice at a lackey.)

Kalgan was prompt. *Probably feeling the holes in his pockets,* Trick thought as Mak's whistle sounded. She didn't wait to confirm the evidence of Mak's eyes—the kid might be a flake, but his gaze was sharp. She slipped soundlessly down into the narrow alley behind Kalgan's chosen drinking hole and slid inside, hoping hard to see their other quarry already inside and waiting.

There he was. Couldn't miss him: only one man in there with his face hidden, which weren't clever, really. Best way to stand out Trick knew of: try too hard to look like you wanted to hide. He'd taken the darkest corner, too, sat there by himself with a tankard he wasn't touching. Trick waited for him to reach for it, something, so she could see his hands, but he didn't.

Roald sat clear on the other side of the noisy taproom, several ale-soaked tables between him and Kalgan's contact. Smart of him. He didn't so much as glance up, seemed absorbed in his own thoughts and his own tankard. Good.

She found Pinto by the back door, silent as the moon. He had a stillness about him, and it'd come in handy many a time. Your eye slid past him, fixed on other, more interesting targets; soon you forgot he'd ever been standing there. "Give me good news," she hissed in an undertone.

"It's on him."

A wave of relief silenced Trick's tongue for a moment. "Right," she said. "Almost time."

Even as she spoke, the door swung open and in came Lord Kalgan. His quick, sharp glance took in the crowded tables and rowdy patrons, traveled to the rear corner. Suspicion or fear relaxed out of his face, replaced with impatience. He shoved his way to the unoccupied seat opposite the cloaked man, and sank into it, already talking.

Trick made no move to overhear what his traitorous lordship was saying; she didn't care. Didn't need to. Here came Ashleen, weaving through tables light as a feather; she swiped a pair of tankards on her way past, mostly full, and thunked the both of them down before Lord Kalgan and his companion. "Here," she said, like she was serving, and made sure to slam them down hard enough to send half the ale slopping over the table in a pungent tide.

Lord Kalgan cursed her with a foul tongue, but it was the other man Trick watched. He jerked back and half-stood, letting the ale wash over the side of the table and onto the floor. His hands'd come up, and that was what she wanted: could see the fancy bracelet on him from here, the way it caught the light. Annie had clocked it with the eye of a born thief, and she was right: looked like gold, with red jewels in it. Worth a bit, and distinctive.

Ashleen produced a rag and swiped futilely at the mess; when she stamped away again, the gold glitter was gone from the cloaked man's wrist.

Didn't take him long to notice.

"What—" he said, loud enough for half the tavern to hear him. He was groping at his arm, like the bracelet might be there after all. It wasn't.

Lord Kalgan's brows snapped together. Trick saw his mouth form the words, "What is it, man?"

The kerfuffle after that unfolded like a street play, all big gestures and shouting. For even Lord Kalgan couldn't deny that his companion's expensive gold bracelet had somehow got onto his own wrist, pushed up under his sleeve, as if to hide it.

"You're a *thief*!" shouted the man in the cloak, and he was furious enough that the scarf slipped off his face and hung there, unheeded. He weren't from Valdemar, that was for sure. Karse, most like.

And here came the tavern keeper, a rotund man with solid shoulders on him; he'd want to prevent the kind of brawl that led to broken chairs and broken heads. "Fetch the Watch," he was saying, and gesturing; two people went off at a run.

Trick slunk closer. Close enough to feel the rage pouring off Kalgan and his crony; close enough to hear his lordship beginning to bluster, "I am a lord of this realm! Do you dare to accuse *me* of stealing?"

"Oh, a lord, is it?" said the tavern keep, folding his splendidly muscled arms: he was like a wall between Kalgan and freedom, just as he should be. "And what would a *lord* be doing in my tavern of a nightfall, drinking ale and filching my customers' possessions?" His eye fell on the disputed property, and his frown deepened. That, too, was out of place in a tavern like his, and he cast a swift, suspicious look at Kalgan's companion. Trick could practically hear the thoughts unscrolling behind his eyes: didn't seem likely as there'd be a lord down here, but these folk were in jewels and velvet, right enough; but *Karse*, now? Lords had no business meeting such folk as *that* in a dark tavern at night—

"I can vouch for this man," came a young, clear voice, pitched to carry over the bustle and chatter. Roald stood up and came striding over, tall as he could manage to be, and looked the tavern keeper steady in the eye. "This is Lord Kalgan." He said the name loud and clear, too, made sure everyone in the tavern knew that Lord Kalgan had been spotted somewhere right odd that night.

The tavern keeper seemed at a loss; Trick couldn't blame him. You couldn't just haul a Lord Kalgan up for stealing—but *something* fishy was afoot, no doubt about that.

The man from Karse wasn't that stupid, after all. The rage faded off him, turned to wariness. He'd made a scene, and he shouldn't have. In two strides he was halfway to the door—but Pinto was there, blocking him. "Get out of my way!" he raged.

Pinto, with a false show of concern, didn't budge. "But surely, sir, your property—if you'll just wait a moment for the Watch, you'll have it back in a trice."

He was swift enough to dodge the blow aimed at him—and after that the Watch was in, and it was all over.

Nothing was heard from Roald for some time thereafter; long enough that Trick began to wonder if she'd been used after all.

"Told you," Ashleen muttered more than once. "Weren't our business getting involved, and what have we got to show for it?"

What indeed. Trick had retrieved the three jewels from Mak, to the younger boy's disgust, and returned them to Roald, which meant nobody got paid. She could allow for Ashleen's disgust, and let it pass.

Still, when Roald finally showed up at Trick's cellar, nearly a full month after Lord Kalgan's arrest, she felt a degree of relief unusual for her. She didn't like to think she'd been played, least of all by a wide-eyed Palace boy.

Pinto admitted him, wariness in his every gesture; he'd been almost as suspicious as Ashleen, after a while. Roald came up to the campaigning table under escort, almost under guard.

"I'm sorry," he said immediately. "Everything took longer than I thought it would, and I thought I ought not send a messenger down here."

That was thoughtful. Trick and her crew hadn't stuck around to watch the end of their trick on Lord Kalgan; nobody wanted to answer awkward questions from the Watch, not with them all looking like the street waifs they were. People assumed things. She didn't want any Palace folk wandering into her cellar, either—except Roald.

He'd produced a pouch of something from under his tunic, and it bulged enticingly. Best of all, it made a metallic *clunking* sound as it fell onto the tabletop: Ashleen, tearing it open, spilled coins everywhere. The sort they could use, even, nothing too valuable. There were a lot of them.

"It worked like a dream," Roald was saying, grinning. "That man Kalgan was meeting? Known to the Spymaster. He had some awfully difficult questions put to him, and no good answers he could come up with. Once I'd told my tale, well, investigations were made, and his lordship removed. It's done."

"Told your tale?" Ashleen, mollified by the money, stiffened into wariness again. "Not *all* of it?"

"I didn't mention you," Roald rushed to assure her. "Not in detail. I told them I had help, which was true, and this was the reward they gave me." He gestured at the money.

Trick wondered if he'd kept any of it for himself, but decided not to ask. Not her business. And anyway, he'd earned it.

Roald fell silent, stood there looking desperately out of place in his good cloak and boots. It was raining outside: a trickle of water ran merrily down the back wall and plip-plopped into a hole in the stone floor.

It was Pinto who said: "Thank you, Roald, but you shouldn't hang about."

"Ain't your place," Ashleen put in.

Nor was it, indeed, but Trick felt a momentary sadness as Roald's face fell. He wasn't a bad sort, for Palace folk, and he'd played his part in Trick's plan to perfection. She could use someone like him on her crew.

He hesitated, and she thought he was an instant away from saying something he might regret. She watched a brief flash of hope die out of his face, and he sighed. "Maybe I'll see you around," he said, like it was a joke.

Trick didn't laugh. "Maybe," she said, and grinned at him. "You never know."

Old Wounds
Terry O'Brien

Life was so much easier in the military, thought Baron—formerly Sergeant-Master—Tokran as the cluster of stern-faced women walked into his home. At least *there* he didn't have to deal with civilians.

Specifically, one civilian, the self-appointed "voice of the village," Mother Evanari. Mother Evanari and several other women of the village of Valleywood had just arrived at the door of the ramshackle old inn that was now his official residence. They were trailed by Aidan and Landin, two of "his men" who had retired along with him from King Tremane's service.

Tokran invited her and the others into the inn's common room. He sat on his canvas camp chair behind his desk as Mother Evanari stood facing him in the center, while the other women sat on split-log benches around the walls. Aidan and Landin stood in the doorway.

Mother Evanari didn't waste time; she never did when it came to demonstrating her smug, supposed superiority over Tokran. She had been the first person to question his authority as the new baron of this little village and the surrounding lands, and probably the last one to accept it, if she even had. "We have a problem. Pigs."

"Pigs." The only thing Baron Tokran knew about pigs was that they were herded in one end of the Imperial slaughter-houses and were rolled out the other end in barrels, like the ones in the storeroom behind him.

She smirked a little. "Our best sow escaped before that last big Storm. We all thought she'd died in it, but now we see she's been hiding in the forest, killing and eating just about anything there."

Aidan and Landin nodded in unison. "Wild pigs are the meanest critters in the forest. They'll attack anything, even Change-creatures."

"If you skewer one, they'll run up the shaft of the spear, just to get to you."

"Farm pigs gone wild are the worst. They're not afraid of people, not at all."

Tokran couldn't tell which one of the twins said what; the only way to tell them apart was that one parted their blond hair on the left, and the other parted it on the right, but right now, both their heads were warmly hooded.

Mother Evanari glared at the twins for interrupting her. "We've seen the signs." The other women all nodded and muttered confirmations. "Tracks in the snow, gouges in the trees."

Tokran had been around the village long enough to know that meant someone was sneaking down the steep trail to the forest in the valley below, against his orders and against all common sense, probably hunting mushrooms, or maybe gathering evergreen branches for Midwinter decorations. Probably Mother Evanari's only child, her pretty—and pretty willful—daughter Loomira.

Mother Evanari pointed at one of the women. "One of Milly's lambs got loose last night. We just found what was left, not that far down the trail. She didn't even eat it all. Sooner or later, she'll come hunting us."

Mother Evanari was long on problems, but very short on solutions, which is why she loved to throw the problems to Tokran. Fortunately, past problems had required minimal effort to solve, just the organized assistance of several other people. This one, however, was an exception.

"Then we have to hunt it down first." Whether it hunted the villagers or hunted the livestock that fed and clothed the village, it was a threat and needed to be dealt with, and the sooner, the better, especially before the mild winter weather turned, as it usually did right around Midwinter.

Mother Evanari replied with that patronizing tone that reminded Tokran of every Imperial officer fresh from the Academies. "Back when I was just a sprout, there was a boar we called Ironhide. Left a trail of kills from here to the forest. Swear it laughed at our arrows. The old Baron had to come hunt it down. He brought a whole army of retainers, his own personal mage, and a couple of Healers, and they needed all of them to finish the beast off."

By this time, the rest of "his men" were outside the doorway, peering over or between Aidan and Landin's shoulders. "This, then, it appears . . . is going to take an army." He considered the village's inhabitants, after Ancar's recruitment gangs stripped Valleywood of every man or boy who could hold a sword or a bow, or anyone Gifted or possibly Gifted: the older women who really ran the village, the young women who did all the chores, the few young boys that were barely considered men, the even fewer older men, then the five men who had retired alongside him. "This . . . isn't an army. But I know where we can find one."

"No!" Mother Evanari knew exactly what Baron Tokran meant. "Absolutely not!" She continued ranting, not noticing the other women turning their heads away in embarrassment.

Tokran had expected this; her opinions about their neighbors across the valley were well known throughout the village. He waited until she paused to take a breath, then he grabbed his cane and levered himself erect, a full head shorter than Mother Evanari.

"Enough!"

Very rarely did he use his parade ground–covering voice, but now was the time. He pounded the bronze tip of his wooden cane on the wooden floor for emphasis, punctuating every pause with another loud pounding. *"I* am the baron here. It is *my* decision, *my* authority, and *my* responsibility."

Mother Evanari's face froze in a pop-eyed, indignant scowl. She turned to glare at the other women, looking for support, but they all refused to make eye contact. Instead, she threw her dangling scarf about her neck and stalked out of the room, the men in the doorway parting before her, most of the rest of the women slowly following after.

Findoran, another of "his men," eyed Mother Evanari with a slight scowl as she left. When she was gone, he turned to Tokran and nodded; he knew exactly what Tokran meant. "We'll have everything arranged for you before dawn, sir."

Tokran didn't sleep well that night—these days, he rarely did. Instead, he remembered what King Tremane had told him about the land he was to oversee: "The biggest problem, Baron Tokran, is that the border with Hardorn there is . . . unnatural."

The problem was a recent development. Long ago, a wide, fast-flowing river meandered through the densely packed evergreen forest that overflowed the valley between the village and the Imperial border post on the opposite ridge. Long ago, Hardorn and Imperial mapmakers drew a line on a map, following the river, and that was the border. But the river dried up, not-so-long ago, and the forest reclaimed the riverbed. The far-off mapmakers never changed their maps, but without the river, the locals treated the forest itself as the border. It was a particularly porous border: there were no official roads through the forest, no official bridges across the river, but long ago and not-so-long ago, there was a path through the forest, if you knew where to find it.

All that changed when the Change-Circle appeared in the middle of the forest one night, followed shortly thereafter by the last Storm: all the familiar animal sounds and bird calls within the forest were replaced by stranger sounds, thorns and thistles and strange fungi overwhelmed the underbrush, and strange lights flickered in the shadows under the trees. The cautious locals shunned the forest, for good reason, and the forest became a border more secure than the highest, widest wall.

In other words, it was unnatural. Therefore, it was a problem, and King Tremane did not like problems in his kingdom, which is why he made one of his most trusted aides the Baron of this particular village.

Tokran's first priority was to secure the village; it was standard military protocol to establish a secure base of operations before any campaign. He *had* intended to wait out the winter and begin the campaign to investigate the problem come spring. He had no taste for winter campaigns, no military man did.

But now, it seemed, the campaign came to him.

Dawn came late to the village. Dawn came even later to the forest, deep in the valley; it would take most of the minimal daylight hours for the party to cross to the other side.

People were awake before dawn, preparing in the inn's common room. Tokran re-wrapped the ugly red burned patch on his arm before putting on his patchwork fleece overcoat while Findoran's wife Angwen fussed with tying his knee-high fleece boots. Dour Sodan simply shrugged the backpack frame that was almost as tall and wide as he was into a more comfortable position across his broad shoulders, while his wife Dorada tied his boots. Aidan examined his bow and the contents of his quiver with a critical eye.

The rest of his men were elsewhere. Findoran was asleep, after spending all night scouring his treasured collection of Imperial Army manuals. Jomari was scurrying around the village, rummaging through every bit of scrap metal and lumber for anything that might be made into more boar spears than the two old ones left behind after Ancar's gangs carried off the rest. Landin was in the old firewatch tower, signaling the firewatch tower in the Imperial border post across the valley.

Tokran regarded it all with a proud yet rueful eye. Imperial military discipline at its best. Each one of the men, and the women, too, went about their jobs without orders or interference from him. Now it was finally time to start doing *his* part.

Dawn was barely lighting the twisting path down the slope to the valley below. There was a large boulder that obscured the overgrown path into the forest from casual eyes. Instead of taking it, however, Aidan slipped between a pair of trees barely wide enough for Sodan to pass as he broke a path through the choked underbrush. The thick, thorny berry bushes were the hardest to pass, even as Aidan wielded his machete with silent but brutal efficiency, every slash an attack on an old memory. It was hard and heavy work, and Tokran called for frequent rest stops so Aidan could check their progress, for fear of getting lost.

The Change-Circle was barely visible through the trees when Tokran called for another break. Sodan slipped his backpack frame off his shoulders with a relieved sigh. Aidan leaned against a tree, pulled the waterskin out from under his coat, and took a long drink. Tokran slipped his left arm out of his coat and was adjusting the bandage when Aidan whispered to the others, "Don't move, just look left."

Tokran glanced in that direction to see a dark shape moving in the shadows between the trees from the direction of the Change-Circle, until it emerged into a shaft of sunlight, sniffing the air with a sharp, wheezing sound. "By the Hundred Little Gods, it's *huge*."

Larger than a bull cow, too big to fit between the densely packed tree trunks between them, the sow glared at them with palpable fury, and did its red eyes seem to *glow*?

Tokran and the massive sow locked eyes for several seconds before the breeze turned and it turned and plowed through the underbrush deeper into the forest. Tokran saw several old scars and more than a few broken arrows and quarrels embedded in its thick hide as it rambled away. By their color bands, Tokran recognized the shafts as Imperial make.

Aidan took a deep breath to steady himself. "We'd best be moving, sir. We can still just make the fort by early dusk."

The Empire had one overriding rule: *nothing* escaped the jaws of the Wolf. It never retreated. It never surrendered in battle, and it never surrendered land. For the Empire to abandon even the smallest border fort was unthinkable.

But when Emperor Charliss abandoned Grand Duke Tremane, that rule was torn asunder. The Empire, itself, might be torn asunder, but, as far as anyone could tell, looking at the border fort overlooking the Imperial side of the valley from the firewatch tower, the Empire still lived. The fort was still being maintained according to strict Imperial regulations. The dark brown log palisade was clean of any growing vines, the slippery gray flagstones on the steep rise below the palisade were clean of any grass growing between the stones, and the Imperial banners still flew proudly over the walls.

Yet as he approached the fort, Tokran could see something was not quite right. The flags were tattered and faded: the brilliant Imperial wolf's head in gold and silver thread on grayish black, the Third Army's pale red crossed triple swords on pale yellow, and the Fifth Regiment's grayish white badger against the pallid green background.

There were tracks in the snow, footprints and others, some gouged down into the hard-packed soil, leading all the way up the ramp around the fort, coming and going. Aidan knelt and measured the gouges against his outstretched hand, then shook his head in that slow motion that always meant bad news, while Sodan shifted his double-handed grip on the haft of his stonemason's hammer.

As Tokran and his men walked over the rise, they encountered a small squad of men, standing at rest in a precise row some distance away, all dressed in familiar dark blue Imperial Army woolen winter overcoats. The one in the center had officer's gold braid on his shoulders. "This is Imperial land. State your name and business."

"I am Baron Tokran, master of the village of Valleywood. I would have conference with your commander on an issue of mutual importance." Tokran saw the reaction to his choice of words: unofficially, yet importantly, leaders of import had "conferences" on "issues of mutual importance" with outpost commanders.

"Sub-Commander Freylin." Freylin placed his right fist over his heart, the standard Imperial Army salute to any member of nobility outside of his chain of command. "I am in command of this outpost."

Tokran responded in kind. The crisp display was better than he had hoped; these isolated border outposts were sometimes used as punishment details, usually for lack of discipline. He nodded toward the fort.

Freylin took the hint. "Shall we discuss this in my office?"

Tokran nodded again.

The fort's interior was familiar ground, a fortified manor house, standardized across the Empire: the surrounding palisade higher than four men; the square observation towers at the four corners of the palisade, with the firewatch tower another two man-heights higher than the rest; the elevated walkways around the palisade connecting the towers; the three-story command building against the palisade along the side away from the border; the two-story storehouse opposite the command building; the neatly maintained gray stone paving in the courtyard.

Freylin led everyone into the command building and into the commander's office on the ground floor. He took the seat behind the commander's desk, and the four men with him stood at attention against the side wall. Tokran sat on one of the chairs in front of the desk, and Aidan and Sodan took their positions behind Tokran.

"Where is the commander?"

"Commander Idiris went to the regimental headquarters to bring back supplies. Then a Storm struck the area, and they never made it back. I've been in charge ever since. Now, your conference."

"We have a problem, and I believe you are aware of it. Pigs, or, in specific, one very large and possibly Changed sow."

Freylin was obviously *not* surprised.

"Then you know something must be done about it." Tokran noticed Freylin and his men sharing looks, heads downturned, avoiding his gaze. Guilty looks. "You *are* doing something about it." That explained *a lot*, especially about its improbable survival. "You're *feeding* it!" Tokran almost gave in to his urge to leap across the desk and wrap his hands around Freylin's throat, and only the touch of village peacemaker Sodan's hand on his shoulder prevented it.

"Yes, we *were* feeding it. We had *no choice*. We *couldn't stop it*." Freylin leaned over the desk, fists clenched. "We cornered it in an arroyo just down the hill from the fort. It shrugged off our arrows and quarrels, plowed through our barriers, took down anyone who tried to get close. We lost three good men then; I buried them the next day. After that, five men went over the wall within the next two weeks, and I couldn't blame them. That left just us, barely half a squad to hold this fort. We do what we can to maintain it, but we couldn't hold it.

"There are several farms less than a candlemark further inland. Good grazing land, plenty of cattle and sheep, very few people left to raise them. The manager of the nearest and biggest farm invited us to come and settle in. Thought we'd seen the last of it." Freylin pounded the desk with his fist, once. "But *It* followed us.

"Once it started attacking the herds, we *had* to do something. That meant feeding it, out here, near the fort, to keep it away from the farms. We spread the toll around to the other farms so everyone shared the cost. Except things have been hard on everyone lately. No one would give us even a chicken or two.

"This morning, *It* approached our farm, but we managed to get every piece of stock tucked away and safe, but even then they were spooked. One herd almost broke out. It roamed around the yard for too long, then sniffed the air and rumbled back toward the fort. We followed, until it went down into the forest. We waited to see if it would come back. We *were* about to head back when we saw you come out of the forest."

"You are in a bad position. Were you able to contact your superiors?"

"We tried to contact Regimental, and the farm manager tried to contact their regional supervisor, but we never heard anything back. I don't know what's all going on around the rest of the Empire, but, around here, we're all alone."

That sounded all too familiar to Tokran. The nearest royal signal tower was five days away, seven or eight in winter weather, and help would be weeks or months in coming. "Why didn't you come and ask Valleywood for help?"

Freylin snorted. "What kind of help? Valleywood lost all its men to Ancar's recruitment gangs. Who's left? A bunch of old women and young kids." The classic young Imperial officer disrespect for civilians, especially women and children, was evident in his voice.

Tokran nodded, slightly—he wasn't wrong, by much. "Did you try poison?"

"Didn't work. Turned its nose up at it. It likes its food alive and squealing."

Tokran closed his eyes for a moment and shook his head. "Given the circumstances, I can't say I would have done anything different. Come close to it a couple of times, under the Grand Duke, a long time ago."

Tokran looked up and saw a questioning look pass between Freylin and his men. He decided to take a big risk here, depending on what this lonely border fort had heard about the Grand Duke. "I am, or was, Sergeant-Master Arrs Tokran."

He stood and unbuttoned the front of his heavy coat. The unmistakable dark blue of the standard Imperial Army winter uniform stood out against the pale wool fleece. He didn't know why he kept it, nor why he wore it today, but he was now glad he did. "Fourth Army, First Regiment, Sixth Division." Grand Duke Tremane's army, the command regiment, and the training division. "Thirty years, honorable retirement."

Sub-Commander Freylin looked back to his men, who all nodded in agreement. "Word came down *officially* from Regimental about how the Grand Duke betrayed the Emperor and the Empire, then word came down *unofficially* about how he and his men were gutted and left to bleed out dry by the Emperor himself. Didn't blame him, not one bit."

Tokran breathed a sigh of relief as he sat down. "Just so you know, then, that I know what I'm talking about. You probably heard the stories of the Fifth Regiment from your old sergeants. The best monster hunters in the Empire. Basilisks, dire wolves, *wyrsa*, the Fifth hunted them all. The most honored regiment in the whole Third Army. I heard those stories, starting my first day of training. 'Be good, and you might be assigned to the Fifth.'

"But something happened. We all heard the stories, official and unofficial. *Officially*, the Fifth failed, and failed badly. *Unofficially*, the Fifth was the scapegoat for someone higher up. Didn't matter, which: the Fifth was demoted to border duty and another regiment took its place."

"We heard the stories, too. So what?"

"What I'm offering you is the opportunity to reclaim some of Fifth's honor and reputation. And, possibly, some revenge."

Freylin checked the rest of his men, who were all nodding, even if he wasn't. "All well and good, but words are just air. You can't build a castle out of air. Do you have an actual *plan*?"

Tokran reached under his uniform jacket and produced a pair of brown, dog-eared manuals with the Fifth's regimental insignia on the covers. "Got one, but first off, do you have a mage? A Healer?"

"No Healers, they ran off with Commander Idiris, likewise most of the mages, worthless maggots. The farms lost all theirs about the same time. Our last mage's mind went Beyond about a day before the last Storm. He was raving about blood and iron for hours, then bolted out into the height of the Storm. We found what was left of him a couple of days later, a dry husk of a body, looking like something sucked the life right out of him."

"Was he one of the mages you were warned about? Told to keep an eye on? Strictly on the quiet?"

"One of them, yes." Freylin nodded. "Commander Idiris told me it came from Regimental, but he also said it probably came from much higher. *Much* higher."

Tremane had two such mages, and they both suffered the same fate. Tremane kept that fate a closely held secret. The only reason Tokran knew was that he was one of the people tasked by Tremane to "keep an eye on them" for some reason Tremane wouldn't say out loud, but with a knowing glance in the direction of the Imperial portrait on the wall of his office, long before the Hardorn campaign started.

"Then we do this the hard way." Tokran held up the pamphlets. "A company of the Fifth were hunting some *wyrsa*. They used a place the locals called Drunken Timbers. It was a large clearing where a big windstorm had knocked over several young trees. The *wyrsa* were lured into the clearing, where the company caught them in a crossfire. We're going to do something like that."

"You mean to catch it in the Change-Circle?"

Tokran nodded. "What all do you know about the Change-Circle?"

"It was a big bowl of salt water, shallow, like a lake. Scouts said there were things in the water, like fish, but not. I ordered a watch, but I pulled them back when the last Storm hit the area.

"After the Storm, it all dried up. The things in the water were dead; some looked like they'd been chewed on. It left a layer of salt, but nobody wanted to touch it. One man tried it, on a dare, said it tasted funny. Didn't seem to hurt him, though.

"Now, nothing grows there. The Circle cut a couple of trees in half, and the salt killed the rest of the trees and undergrowth around the bowl. Trees all collapsed into the bowl after that big windstorm last spring. Left a tumbled ring of bare earth around the edge."

Tokran smiled. "All the better."

Tokran's knees ached as he slowly hobbled down the stairs of the firewatch tower alongside Aidan. Fortunately, there was enough oil in the signal lamp for Aidan to signal Landin in the opposite tower that they had arrived, and to lead the small party of villagers through the forest at first light. Landin's reply was equally brief, with a final series of flashes that set Aidan chuckling.

"He said some folks complained that this will disrupt the Midwinter celebrations."

"He meant Mother Evanari complained." Tokran shook his head. "There will be plenty to celebrate if this all works."

"Landin also said she'll be coming tomorrow."

"To complain in person, no doubt. No matter—her medicinal skills could be of assistance."

Aidan chuckled, then stopped suddenly. "Hear that, sir?"

Tokran stopped, listening. It was faint at first, but gradually got louder, a familiar sharp, wheezing bellows sound. They looked out over the palisade in the growing twilight to see the sow moving slowly up the trail from the forest. "What's it doing here?"

"Sir, may I?" Aidan rolled up Tokran's coat sleeve, exposing the lamb's-wool bandage on his left arm. Almost immediately, the sow started sniffing directly toward the fort. Aidan unwrapped the bandage, then wiped the sweet, grassy-smelling lamb's-wool oil from the burns on his arm before wadding it into a ball and throwing it to the ground a little ways away from the sow. It took the sow several more moments before it turned around and ambled toward the ball of wool. It nosed it several times, turning it over and over, unwrapping the clumsy wad.

"Do you see what I see, sir?"

Tokran did. "By the Hundred Little Gods, it's *blind*!"

"Thought so, sir, when I spotted its eyes this noon. Seen it before, in some of the monsters we hunted." Aidan and Landin had volunteered for several such hunting parties. "Hunts by smell, not sight. Pigs got the best noses in the forest."

Before Tokran could stop him, Aidan stepped past Tokran over to the heavy crossbow on its swivel in the center of the walkway around the palisade and started to pull the string back. The mere sound of the crossbow startled the sow, and it fled back into the safety of the forest. "Good hearing, too."

Tokran noted the sow's reactions. "Go back up and signal Landin. We'll need a different lure."

Tokran, Freylin, and Sodan spent the next morning moving the heavy crossbows from the palisades into the courtyard. Aidan was up in the fort's firewatch tower, watching for any sign of the sow and to track the people from the village on their way through the forest. One of Freylin's men was detailed to report to the farm manager, and try to bring back one or two capable men from the farms to assist, and the others went to the other nearby farms to ask for help.

By midday, two crossbows were assembled in the courtyard, with the other two from the palisades and the two still-functional replacements from the storehouse neatly disassembled for transport. Several small bound bundles of the two-foot-long barbed quarrels and the coils of finely braided rope were neatly stacked next to them, apart from the more untidy pile of quarrels that were tossed aside upon close inspection—these far-flung border outposts were sometimes also used as the dumping grounds for inferior or out-of-date equipment.

Landin and the people from the village arrived midafternoon, as did Freylin's men, bringing a pair of husky farm hands, Jodry and Big Thom, to assist. The other farms couldn't send men, but, together, the men loaded a wagon with enough preserved food to feed everyone. Tokran made a mental note to petition King Tremane to repay the farms for their assistance; he was already planning to send them some of the barrels of salt pork from his storeroom. After today, he didn't even want to *think* about pork.

Two targets were set up at the far side of the courtyard, and Freylin drilled *everyone* relentlessly on the setup and operation of the crossbows until after sunset, arranging and rearranging teams until all six were fully operational. Strong arms, steady hands, and keen eyes were needed: cranking the winch to draw back the bowstring and lock it, then triggering the release smoothly for an accurate shot against the tension of the bowstring was hard, and aiming the quarrel was even harder. More than one quarrel not only missed the target, it missed the wall behind it entirely, soaring over the palisade. More bounced off the stone flags of the courtyard.

But as the afternoon wore on, more and more quarrels hit the targets.

After dinner, Tokran gathered everyone in the torch-lit courtyard.

"Tomorrow, we will kill a Change-creature, and we will do it together!" He punctuated every pause in that one statement by pounding stone flags of the courtyard with the metal base of his walking stick. "Just us. No mages, no Healers, just . . . *us*."

"Hear, hear!" Tokran was pleased to see that even the Imperial soldiers were cheering. Even Mother Evanari was faintly nodding.

"We all know our assigned duties, our assigned teams: I will be commanding the operation; Sub-Commander Freylin will be my deputy.

"We will be using a strategy that the best monster-hunting regiment of the Imperial Army has used successfully several times in the past. We lure the target into an open space, immobilize it, then eliminate it. We have all the tools necessary, right here, and you are the most important ones of all."

That set off another round of cheers from everyone except Mother Evanari. "We lure it in, get it tied down, then what? Who's going to run up and kill the beast before it manages to break free? Or, how?"

Freylin shook his head. "Boar spears won't work; its hide was too tough. We found that out the hard way."

"That will be my responsibility. Have any of you ever delivered a mercy blow?" A couple of the villagers started nodding, and one of the two farmhands shyly raised his hand, but they stopped when Tokran slowly shook his head. "This isn't like slaughtering a sheep or a cow. It's staring into the eyes of a friend, or an enemy—" *or a fatally wounded or sick animal,* "—and knowing this is a mercy. It's knowing *exactly* how to do it, knowing you may have only *one chance* to do it. Not many people can do that."

Tokran produced his short sword and ran his thumbnail along the edge: good Imperial steel, honed and sharpened to a fine edge, finer even than his own razor. "Fortunately—" *or, unfortunately,* "—I have."

It was shortly after midday, and Tokran's hands were cramped from nervously clutching his walking stick. It had been a harrowing morning: a line of laden people slipping into the forest in the false dawn, everyone glancing from side to side, everyone freezing at the sound of snowdrifts falling from overloaded branches.

Everybody knew their duty, when they reached the edge of the clearing around the Change-Circle. Freylin directed three teams to the opposite side of the clearing, circling the depression. Tokran did the same with the three teams on this side. Another group carrying additional quarrels and ropes, including Mother Evanari and Loomira, stayed well back from the Circle. The crossbows were designed to be set up quickly, and the six crews were ready in better time than their best yesterday, always with one eye looking over their shoulder.

When the crossbows were armed and ready, Tokran pointed at Landin. He went down into the shallow center depression of the Change-Circle, untied an oiled canvas bag, removed a dirty white bundle, and placed it on the ground. As he withdrew, he let out a series of bleats that more or less sounded like a lamb in distress.

The crossbowman beside Tokran, one of Freylin's soldiers, muttered something incredulous under his breath.

"You were expecting a bloody carcass? It's the smell of the wool and the greasy stuff on it, the sound of prey in distress, that draws the sow's attention, not blood."

The soldier just shrugged his answer.

"Now, we wait."

It was a long wait, long enough for Tokran to consider withdrawing overnight, when he spotted one of the teams waving and pointing toward the path into the Change-Circle.

He heard it before he saw it, that same unhealthy wheezing as it emerged into the Change-Circle. Tokran held the red banner over his head, almost dropping it because of his hand cramps, and every team crouched low, tracking the sow.

The massive beast nosed the wool bundle, turned it over with its nose, then flung it into the air. Tokran dropped the banner, and each bowman yanked the release to fire the quarrels. One of the quarrels sailed right over the sow's back and embedded itself in a downed tree trunk. One hit the sow's shoulder on an angle and skidded away. Another struck the sow and stayed, but the knot had gotten loose, and the rope trailed out barely halfway to the target. The other three struck home, with the ropes still slack.

Tokran waved the red banner back and forth, and the teams cranked the strings back and reloaded as the sow turned about wildly, almost tangling itself in the ropes, hunting for the insects stinging it. He waited until someone from every team waved in response before dropping the banner again.

Landin had just finished waving, and was turning back to signal the soldier standing ready to release the crossbow, when the opposite tip of the bow broke with a loud *crack*. The stressed bowstring lashed back, striking him in the chest. He doubled over in pain, and the sow turned for a moment in his direction. That caused two more quarrels to bounce off or miss entirely, but the other three stuck and held.

Tokran circled the banner and the teams pulled the ropes tight, wrapping them around the nearby tree trunks. One of the quarrels came free as the sow fought back, but the rest of the arrowheads were embedded deeply into the beast's abnormally thick hide, and the lines attached to the barbed arrowheads were pulled taut. It thrashed and heaved, but its hooves didn't seem to get any traction.

Tokran circled the banner again. Aidan ran out, carrying both looped ropes, slowing when he got near the sow. He stayed toward its side, not in front, until he darted in and cast one loop, then another, around the sow's neck. Sodan looped the trailing rope over his fists, and the mismatched pair of farm hands looped the rope around their waists, and all three tugged hard.

Now it was his turn. Tokran slipped his arm out of its sling, drew his short sword and tightened the attached cord around his wrist, and approached the sow, slowly, quietly. It hadn't noticed him yet; it threw its head up, sniffing the air, sniffing for those stinging insects, not paying any attention to him.

Tokran was now so close he could just see the paler patch of fur just below the throat, where the hide was probably the thinnest. He took one more step, lifting his left foot over the downed branch before him, then shifted his balance before taking another step—

He had just one moment to react before his left foot slid out from underneath him and he toppled onto his back, knocking the wind out of him. His head slammed into the frozen ground, and stars and darkness clouded his vision and mind for several moments.

Tokran reached out to try to push himself up, but his gloved hand slipped as it brushed away the snow to reveal a sheet of ice underneath him. His other hand tugged on the cord to his short sword, only to find it tangled in a broken limb. He tugged at it twice more, finally pulling it free. He tried to untangle his leg out from underneath him: he gritted his teeth in a failed attempt to keep from groaning from the stabbing pain down close to his foot in his right leg. Through the stars and darkness he glimpsed the sow moving her head quickly and deliberately, trying to catch the faintest sound or scent, moving too fast for a clean, quick thrust.

Then he saw Sodan's heavy boots next to him in the snow. He must have tied off his rope to a nearby tree. Sodan the architect, Sodan the village peacemaker, Sodan the regimental wrestling champion who swore never to wrestle again after what happened in his last match. "I have this." Sodan took his stance, smiled a feral grin, wrapped his arms around the sow's thick neck.

"*We* have this." Jodri and Big Thom added their strength and weight, and all three slowly began to raise the sow's head to reveal the throat as its clattering back legs kept losing traction on the sheet of ice.

The words from Ballasteros, the old sergeant who first put a blade in his hand and taught him how to perform a mercy kill, ran though his mind: *"Make it quick. Make it clean. Make it count."*

It wasn't very quick, it wasn't very clean, but, in the end, it did count.

Sodan and Jomari rigged a fulcrum and lever to roll the carcass over and away from Tokran. Sodan helped Tokran stand, then casually lifted him when he gasped upon accidentally putting weight on his bad leg.

Self-proclaimed "healer of the village" Mother Evanari pulled off his boot and pulled up his leggings, then ran her fingers over his leg with surprising tenderness. "No blood, not his. That's a good sign." A *very* good sign, since the bloody kind of broken bone she meant required either a Healer's immediate attention or an immediate amputation. "Simple fracture. All you'll need is binding and a splint. It will heal naturally, *if* you let it, Baron."

Tokran smiled in reply. He had the sudden feeling that everyone in the village was going to ensure that happened, *especially* Mother Evanari. At that moment, he didn't care; this was the first time Mother Evanari had ever called him "Baron."

What he *did* care about was how everyone *else* was doing. Sodan was actually, honestly, smiling. Jomari and Findoran were measuring the sow with a knotted piece of string for the report. Loomira was fussing over a bemused Landin, while an even more bemused Aidan stood by. Freylin and his men were disassembling the crossbows for transport; they were already talking about other monsters, other hunts. They'd best hurry— a big, wet snowflake landed on Tokran's cheek. He looked up: iron gray clouds were rolling in from the west, bringing the promise of the first heavy winter snowfall by nightfall.

Tokran looked at Sodan and Mother Evanari. "Let's go home. We have a Midwinter celebration tonight." And he had a *very* long supplement to his domesday report to write in the morning.

Anything, With Nothing
Mercedes Lackey

Herald Tadeus lay in his bunk in the tiny Guardhouse in the equally tiny hamlet of Hob's Rest on the very northernmost border of the very young Kingdom of Valdemar. Only three kings so far: old Valdemar the founder, then his son Restil, then his grandson Hakkon. Not so long ago that there weren't a couple of ancient grannies who swore they remembered seeing King Valdemar himself as a babe in arms, but long enough ago that the Guard was *mostly* stationed now outside of Haven in small, fortified Guardhouses, while the City Watch patrolled the streets of the city itself. The only guards inside Haven now were the ones assigned to Palace duty.

Tad was from Haven, as were most Heralds, but he'd been brought up as part of the Watch in the unpopular part of town where the dyers and tanners were, where the Watchhouse barely held four, because who with any sense would steal what lay in the tannery, or touch what lay in the dye vats? Finished fabric, thread, and leather always went straight out the door to the warehouses at the end of the day; stuff half-processed and wet, heavy, and possibly stinky was in no danger of being lifted. No one was going to buy half-tanned leather, and undyed fabric and thread and yarn were locked up in storage sheds, and too bulky to be worth taking.

Tad had been mustered into the Watch as soon as he showed interest and basic mastery of the pike, did well in training, and to everyone's surprise, insisted on taking his duty in the Tannery Watchhouse alongside his da, his granther, and his nuncle.

He had tried to explain when the Watch Commanders told him, "You're too good for that post." He tried to point out how different the tanners and dyers were from other people—how carefully they reused as much of their potentially dangerous colors and all, and how exactly they broke down the stuff that could not be reused until it was pure enough to drink. How careful they were of their environment, and how touchy they were about anyone else that might come in and carelessly ruin their spotless records. That was on account of those ghostly Hawkbrothers, of course, who had made it a condition of bringing then-Baron Valdemar's escape group here and granting them the use of their land. No one had seen any since King Restil's time, but everyone knew about Hawkbrothers: if you annoyed them, you'd only know it when the arrow or bolt of magic hit you.

But in the end, he couldn't make them understand that the people of this quarter *needed* watchmen that knew them, knew their craft enough to appreciate it, knew what all their quirks were. So he just shrugged and said, "Got used to it, 'specially for the extra pay." Because working the Watchhouse in the Tannery certainly did bring in extra hazard and unpleasantness pay, even if the house itself often got the short end of supplies. That pay allowed a man to set up a nice house and family in a part of town upwind from the Tannery.

He never expected to rise beyond Chief Watchman, and that contented him. He certainly never expected to hear the chime of bells, look out of the Watchhouse door at the sound of high commotion, and open it to see an incandescent wonder standing on the step, surrounded by what looked like at least half the neighborhood.

Well, that was that.

But that was also where something went . . . well, not the way you'd expect. Oh, Tad had Mindspeech all right, just as expected, but when checked for anything else, he'd tested as having almost nothing. Just a tiny, bare little squib of a power. Just enough to light a small flame and produce a mage-light.

King's Own Polety had given him a very odd look, as if

unsure how to break it to him. He'd laughed. "Pish-tush, what *are* you training Heralds for now? You told me yourself it's not magic or Mind-magic that matters, it's how you help sort out the problems of people out there, the ones we can't see from Haven! That ain't too different from what the Watch does, mostly."

Polety had blinked at that. "But I was just trying to make you feel better!" he blurted.

Tad snorted. "Remember where I come from." Then he snickered. "After all, I worked Tannery Quarter."

As if that was worse, when it came to the real job and not the general stink. The job was essentially the same, of course, and there were times he wished he was back in the old Watchhouse about to start a night shift. But then—

:*You wouldn't have me,:* teased Jocile in his head. :*I will love you forever, but not enough to live in the Tannery Quarter.:*

It was just a tease, and they both knew it. But there was no need for Heralds in the Tannery Quarter—or, indeed, for anything in Haven itself, except being on call for the law courts of the city.

The Herald-Mages, and those with great Mind-magic—*those* went out to the big Guardhouses, or patrolled the border themselves or in pairs, because great powers like that were worth an entire Guardhouse full of guards. Meanwhile Tad and his fellows, of which there were only a handful at the moment, went out to patrol the *people*. See to their concerns and their needs. Be an impartial voice with the authority of the very Crown. Oh, there were a hundred things plain old common sense was needed for, and sure, an ordinary guard might be able to sort things out, but not quickly, and a guard wouldn't be backed by that authority to make people stop arguing and settle down.

This was good, solid, steady work—work he was good at. He didn't mind people getting a little mad at him to get a problem solved, and he was good-natured enough that the anger didn't last. Truth to tell, Tad didn't really feel comfortable with the idea of playing around with big magics like that; it made him itch inside, like the person that was thinking about meddling with such power wasn't really *him*.

Sometimes he got a little tired of attitude—"You're just a squib-Herald, not a real Herald-Mage." But there was a sure cure for that. Granther's present to him when he'd left to take up his duty and learn his new job. A copy of the Tannery House motto that had been laminated under a sheet of horn on the wall since forever. The copy Granther had given him had been laboriously burned into a thin sheet of veneer he'd attached to the wall of his room in a similar fashion to the original.

We the willing
Led by the unwitting
Are doing the impossible
For the ungrateful.
We have done so much
For so long
With so little
That we are now capable
Of doing anything
With nothing.

It was true, too. Tad was very proud of his record out here so far. Quarrels solved, legal issues clarified, tiny wrongs righted, justice served, and all of it done in such a way that most of the time when compromises were required, everyone was a little bit discontented, which was how a compromise should end up. But not unhappy, when they saw everyone else was also a little bit discontented.

Like the other Heralds who tended to the people out here, he had a territory he was expected to travel through at least three times a year, visiting even individual farms to make sure all was well. And it took about four moons to properly do that, especially when there was bad weather. Mostly he was able to go out, spend about three days on a loop centered on Hob's Rest, and return for a rest and resupply before going out on another loop, so that his thrice-yearly route looked like a daisy with crooked petals, centered on the village. A few loops were longer than others. Hob's Rest was not the biggest village in the

Circuit—there were entire towns out here—but it had the distinct advantage of being right in the center.

He was halfway into his first year, and aside from not being back home with his kin, he was about as happy with his work as he'd ever been in his life. Although this was right on the border, this Circuit was comprised of sleepy agricultural villages and market towns that didn't specialize in anything valuable, except one thing.

A specific area, roughly centered around Hob's Rest, grew and pressed the richest oilseed in the entire Kingdom. That same area produced a mouthwateringly sweet plum that almost instantly fermented before you could get it off the tree, and as a consequence, thanks to a double-distillation process, made brandywine strong enough to take the top off an unwary man's head. These two products were stored (in the case of the brandy, aged) in identical barrels branded on the head with their contents—a standardized brand of a plum or an oilseed burned into the wood.

Almost all of both were sold out of the area at harvest time. Dealers came around with small caravans of wagons, went from village to village, and bought the aged brandy and new oil until they ran out of money or room in their wagons. And part of Tad's job at harvest had turned out to be keeping track of where the dealers were going so no one got left out of selling what they needed to. On Jocile, who could (if unburdened by everything but her Herald) could cover three days' travel by horse in half a day. It might have bored other people, but Tad took it seriously, and this year no one had gotten left out of the selling. This had eased a whole lot of any lingering resentment left over from some of his decisions.

He shared this Guardhouse with four guardsfolk who probably could have been mustered out due to age or injuries, but who wanted to keep serving, and really knew no other life. A truly impressive palisade protected the village itself, and there was room enough inside for everyone from the farms outside to shelter in an emergency. The villagers had spent a lot of time and effort on that palisade, making the four guards who lived here far more effective than they would have been otherwise. It was only logs and stone—logs on the outside, with a stone wall on the inside—but a regular work crew saw to it every single day with inspections and small repairs, so it never needed big repairs. This, it seemed, had been going on as long as the village had had the palisade. He wondered who had browbeaten everyone in the village to participate, because even the littles did their part, but no one remembered. "Allus done it that way," was the response. There were times when an answer like that was a sensible one, and this was one of those times.

The more time Tad spent out here, the better he liked these people.

The people out here had often proved to be more like his tanners and dyers than he would have imagined. Particularly in their attitude toward him.

There was indeed a bit of ingratitude toward him and his "keep." Basically, "You an' that horse both eatin' yer heads off, doin' nothin'." Apparently riding around constantly wasn't "real work." Nor was interpreting new laws for them, nor settling disputes, nor making sure everyone on the Circuit got a fair shake at selling their disposable products at a good price. They weren't actually mean about it, but they never lost a chance to remind him about how little "real work" he did in Hob's Rest, usually with a little smugness.

And in that, too, they were not unlike his old tanners and dyers.

Tad was more like his nuncle than either his da or his granther. He was, generally, more amused by this attitude than anything. It was absolutely understandable in his old place; tanners and dyers were looked down on by most of the skilled workers in Haven, so they *needed* someone they, in turn, could look down on. He and the rest of the Watch, with their extra pay that allowed them to live outside the district, out of the stink, were a logical choice for scorn.

Here, well, he supposed he represented the "effete city man," who didn't know how to do a proper day's work. They didn't really mean anything by it, and he was disposed not to take

offense. The powerful, magic-wiclding Heralds who were actively defending the border, *those* they understood. A squib like
him was just a sort of guard with a fancier uniform. Or more
like guard and judge combined, but until he had made enough
sound decisions to make them think he warranted the authority
of the Crown, they were going to be skeptical. And he might be
dead before that happened! They didn't really understand what
Companions were . . . but at least they knew a Companion was
a magical thing, a gift of the gods, and gave them the respect
they might not give the Heralds.

Well, maybe he resented it a little. But only a little. And
never for long.

And he wasn't above lending a physical hand to anyone, or
suggesting an improvement, then pitching in to help build it—
like the sort of roof around the inside of the palisade that would
protect people near the wall from stones or arrows or other
missiles shot over the top. They liked that idea. He liked it for
another reason that might or might not be obvious depending
on if that roof was ever needed.

It was turning colder, the harvest was in, the crops were all
sold, and it was going to get a lot harder to make his loops. He'd
probably be staying in barns a lot, or better still, on kitchen
floors, under the table to avoid being stepped on. Had to be
done, though. This near the border there was no telling what
might come over it. And there was one thing about this fall he
did not like.

It was dry.

The harvests were in. That meant for people on the other
side of the border, too. That meant a leader with a mind to mischief who had a cadre of tough farmers to take raiding into
Valdemar would be able to do so until the snow started, on
good hard roads, with plenty of browse for horses still available,
and grain stored in barns to steal. No, he did not like this year,
and as bad as it would be to go on Circuit in snow, that snow
was his friend.

In fact—

His skin prickled before he consciously picked up that there were faint noises, growing nearer, screaming and shouting noises, the pounding of hooves—

:Trouble!:

:I know!: Tad jammed on both boots, threw a tough leather armor-coat over his white uniform, and ran out the door, grabbing his bow and quiver from their peg beside the door on the way.

Farm carts full of people poured in the front gate—"poured" being relative, since there were only about twelve farms between the Rest and the border. Shouting, screaming, crying—but organized. Tad allowed himself a tiny smile. That was the work of the four guardsfolk here—particularly that of Sergeant Heavyweld, who'd been a supply sergeant. She'd talked those farmers into three-times-yearly drills to evacuate for the past three years, so when the time actually came to flee behind the safety of the palisade, there were no stray children or forgetful grannies left behind. She'd succeeded mostly because she made a competition out of it, with a feast out of the Guardhouse supplies and a prize for the family that made it to shelter fastest and with all their needed things. The last thing the sergeant wanted was for a toddler to go running back home for her corn-dolly.

BOOM!

Even as he strapped his quiver to his side, the gates slammed shut. The carts and horses were already under the shelter of that roof he'd had built, which meant no flaming arrows would land in flammable carts, and no horses would be hurt. Every family had one person responsible for getting the larger livestock into hiding, and hopefully they all had good places out there in the farmlands where they would not be discovered. Chickens and ducks and geese were on their own.

The farmers hustled under the roofs of friends. The four guards were at prime positions on the palisade. Tad scurried quickly over to the stone wall inside the log one and climbed up to where the sergeant peered through a chink in the logs.

"Well," she said flatly, "they're here. I'd hoped this would never come."

Tad found another spyhole nearby and looked through it. "Wasn't this going to happen eventually?" he asked. "That's what you told me when I arrived."

The sergeant grunted. "I allowed the boundless optimism of you Moving Targets to persuade me it was possible the folk on the other side of the border might decide they liked what they saw and ask for alliance instead of deciding to raid us. Silly me."

"Well . . ." he began, then shrugged. "So far they've done what you thought they would."

"Let's see if we can't get them to do more of that."

From where he crouched, through a crack between two logs as thick as his arm, the view left a lot to be desired. It seemed to feature a lot of pikemen, probably a lot of bowmen, not much in the way of horse or heavy armor. Definitely a small army—but more than enough to take this place.

:According to what I've gotten back, the fastest help can get here is in three days,: said his Companion. *:There's a Herald-Mage coming north, and a troop of Guard heading out this moment from Barrowith.:*

"Three days," he said to the sergeant, who nodded. "Could be worse."

She whistled, and a scarecrow poked up in front of her in the space between the stone wall and the sloping roof. A second one popped up beside Tad, and he seized it, drawing it up beside himself but keeping it out of sight past the logs. This had been *his* idea, and he hoped it was going to work, because if it did, he'd never let Heavyweld hear the end of it.

Relative silence fell.

He peeked out the hole again. The lines of approaching men had stopped. Probably just out of bowshot. There was not a lot of noise from over there; some shuffling of feet, a little muttering, but on the whole, it was the sound of an organized group of armed men who knew what they were doing.

:So do we,: his Companion reminded him.

The villagers that had volunteered to expose themselves to danger and whom he and the Guard had drilled were creeping silently out of their houses with their bows and arrows and taking up positions on the top of the stone wall. Some had scare-crows, some had poles for pushing ladders away from the palisade. But hopefully, there wouldn't be any need for them. No plan ever survived getting punched in the face, but . . . Tad didn't want to see those men get any closer than bowshot.

:Heyla.: There was a snort below and he looked down through the gap to see Jocile peering one intensely blue eye up at him. *:I'm going out now, before they figure out we have a back gate too. Stick to the plan. Anything with nothing.:*

:I love you too. Be safe out there.:

She whisked down the lane and out of sight, but he knew the moment she'd been slipped out the tiny back gate, because it was all playing inside his head, and always would, unless either of them muted what they got from the other. "An unpreced-ented bond," some had murmured dubiously, and a couple had predicted dire fates, but he and Jocile had, from their very first moment, been able to instinctively keep themselves bound-yet-separate, constantly in motion around each other, like a flaw-less pair of dancers.

So he was fully aware of her slipping into a tree line and disappearing, exactly as he was fully aware of himself crouched down with a half-scarecrow on the wall beside him.

And now came the hardest part of the plan.

Waiting.

Farmers are patient people, and most of the folk who had volunteered to fill out the guards were farmers. But was it the right kind of patience? The kind that can weather the candle-marks of waiting, enduring a looming danger that is very much present, but not *there,* not *now,* not *yet?*

Everything Tad could count on depended on it, that no one would snap, pop up from behind the logs, and receive many pointed objections from their foes.

Not that it was much better for him. Despite being on the Watch most of his life, plus now being a Herald, he'd never ser-iously hurt a man, much less killed one. And this waiting—this wasn't what the Watch did. The Watch, when they had to move with force, did so silently and swiftly, and got the problem over with before the problem even knew they were there. The point wasn't to have a brawl. The point was to keep the streets safe and quiet.

He kept putting his eye to that crack. The men out there didn't move. *:No horse,:* Jocile told him. *:There's a couple carts. No long-term supplies. They didn't expect a siege. They were waiting until the merchants cleared out, and they were here for the harvest money and anything light and portable.:*

In a whisper, Tad repeated this to Heavyweld, who pursed her lips. "Didn't expect *that*. Expected they'd come looking for winter supplies one day, not just a hit-and-run raid for money."

"If they'd done that, they wouldn't have been able to move as fast as they did," he pointed out. "They must have bypassed every farm except the ones on their path."

"Good news for us. That'll give people time to close themselves up and get their stock into hiding."

He nodded, but his gut knotted up and he felt as if he might be sick. It was so quiet out there! Was that because the raiders were surprised, or because they'd expected this?

:They're spreading into a thin ring all around the village. Good thing I got out when I did.:

"They're surrounding us," he told Heavyweld.

"So now they're settling in for a siege. They think they surprised us. They think we have no way to get word out."

"They don't know about Jocile," he said flatly.

"Likely not," Heavyweld agreed. "Most likely there aren't many that understand what Companions really are. Even those that do would expect Jocile to stay locked up safe in here with us and not risk herself outside."

Tad felt his lips curling in a little smile. "They don't know Companions."

The silence continued, although there was distant muttering coming from their besiegers. He tried to parse out what they were *feeling* rather than to try to make sense of their words. Unease? Maybe? They'd expected to come running up to a disorganized village, gates still wide open, farmers and their panicked families clogging the lanes. Instead, they'd seen the gates snap shut behind a loosely organized retreat to cover, and then—nothing. No sound. No one stirring. It was cold, sitting here motionless. His nose was freezing. So was his back. Was it worse out there, on the exposed meadow?

Their officers surrounded us, and now they don't know what to do.

Was the moment right? How cold and impatient were they? They sounded restless. It felt right. "Let's give them something to do before they start cutting down trees for rams and climbing poles," he said.

Heavyweld winked, and whistled a green-jay call, which carried right across the entire village.

Tad took his scarecrow and slowly, carefully, as if it was a living head, poked it just barely above the top of the palisade.

And pulled it back down again as a hailstorm of arrows rained on his position. Most thudded into the logs and dirt at the foot of the palisade. Two hit the top. Two flew over the top onto the roof behind him.

On the other side of the village someone else did the same, with what sounded like the same result.

A single barked order came from somewhere within the besiegers. As one, the men took what sounded like three steps forward—which should be just enough to put them within range of the palisade now. Heavyweld eased her scarecrow up and brought it back down again. This time most of the arrows made it to the roof behind them, some skidding off it to land in the lane. He grinned at Heavyweld, who shrugged and grinned back at him. He'd bet her he could make any enemy virtually *give* them a supply of arrows with this tactic. However long this lasted, they were already a few dozen arrows ahead of where they had been a moment ago. He'd gotten the idea from back when there'd been an apprentice riot down in Tannery. He and the rest had simply let the apprentices hole up in one of the drying yards and throw things. They'd kept showing themselves and dodging into cover until the apprentices were tired, hot, thirsty, and had run out of things to throw.

"So now, if I'm the commander, after a few more volleys, I'll

send out a foraging party. Nearest farm is Amaran's." He
pursed his lips. "That might give us . . ." He paused. "I don't
want to promise anything . . . but Amaran has four full years of
brandywine aging in his storehouse."

Heavyweld nodded. "So he does."

"So we'll see what they do with that and what we can make
out of what they do. Meanwhile, we wait."

After a while, the volleys of arrows stopped altogether, regardless of the provocation. Tad decided to give them incentive to
start again. He picked himself a target through the slit, popped
up with the pikeman still in his sight, loosed an arrow, and
dropped down. A shout followed his appearance, a scream rang
out as he dropped down, and a fresh and furious volley rattled
down onto the roof and thudded into the logs.

The sergeant nodded and whistled a wood-dove call. This
meant *only* the guards were to expose themselves. They had
helms and armor, the villagers didn't.

:They're sending a foraging party out,: reported Jocile. *:With
a wagon. Toward Amaran's place. Individuals are bringing
back wood. They look like they each have a couple days of
dried meat and other basic rations, one waterskin per man, and
a bedroll. If they don't want to half-freeze tonight, they'll have
to have fires. And those men will gobble everything down and
still want more. They need more food, too.:*

*:Let me know what they bring back and how it gets distrib-
uted.:*

He nodded at the sergeant, who uttered the *prrrt* of a wren,
which was repeated all down the village at irregular intervals.
This marked people turning around and using their sticks or
scarecrows to shove the arrows off the roof. Beneath the roof,
villagers with rakes pulled the arrows in under cover, and sorted
them into quivers, or at least into bundles. There were more
arrows in the lanes, and even some that had made it into or onto
cottages, but they weren't desperate enough to go after them yet.

*We should have thought about the possibility that a raid
would come looking for actual money. It was obvious—*

But at the time, something like this made no sense. The village wasn't heavily guarded, but it was fortified, and the kind of bandit raiding party that would attempt such a thing would normally pick off individual farms. It wouldn't, shouldn't have been an actual (small) army. Much less one like this—obviously force-marched quickly across the border, without a supply line, in winter.

Unless this is meant to be an occupying force, and bringing them here this way means whoever is commanding them has put them in a position where they have *to take the village or die.*

:*Jocile, is it ethical for us to insert suggestions in—*:

:*Is it ethical for a Herald-Mage to use illusions?*:

He smiled. :*That's what I thought. And for all I know, all we will be doing is merely telling them the truth.*:

His projective Mindspeech was not at all bad, and receptive was more than adequate for the job. So as they continued to tease volleys of (fewer and fewer) arrows out of their besiegers, he would seek out, not so much thoughts, as feelings. Fear was good, but not as good as mistrust, suspicion, doubt. He quickly got the impression these men had been told they'd virtually be able to rush the gate and Hob's Rest would be theirs and everything in it for the taking. Now they were starting to question that. He encouraged those questions, and more, encouraged them to doubt their fellows. What had the others been promised? It was every man for himself, after all.

Jocile was doing the same, but with more finesse than he was.

:*You're a little busy.*:

Well, yes, he was. So far he'd been pretty lucky with his shots; every one of them had hit *something,* and he was hoping to wound, to be honest. For pragmatic reasons as well as compassionate ones. One wounded man ties up two more—and if you put all your wounded in one place, with a force spread as thin as this one, you create a weak point in the line.

But these men were starting to settle in now. They retreated out of bowshot, started fires, went out foraging on foot. And just as the sun was about a hands-breadth above the horizon, the wagon returned, and as Tad had hoped, it was loaded precariously with as many barrels of brandywine as could possibly be fastened to it. The poor horses groaned as they literally collapsed in their harness. Trailing the wagon were four cows that looked just as bad.

Going to be worse than shoe leather, Tad thought. But then he and Jocile let loose a barrage of random thoughts on their besiegers, all centered on one thing.

Wine!

Tad could do what Jocile could not: he invoked his many memories of drinking that deceptively sweet and smooth potion, concentrating entirely on the taste, smell, and intoxication. *She* took those memories and infected the besiegers with them.

Then they both turned the thoughts dark. No one was going to get any! Only the officers were going to get some! Got to get my share! *My share! Now!*

Before whatever passed for officers could even say a word, the men nearest the wagon pounced on it and began bringing down the barrels. The infection spread, and soon the ring-camp was all but deserted except for where the men were fighting over the wine.

They were so preoccupied over it that they didn't even notice all the heads cautiously peering over the palisade in the growing twilight. Then again, it was probably too dim for any of their besiegers to make out heads against the dark logs.

"Should we—" Heavyweld said hesitantly.

"No, no, we do nothing yet. Tell people they can probably make supper, but try and keep lights dim. Right now, we're ghosts to them; they're distracted, and they don't know what to make of us. Let's keep it that way." Tad was able to pick out officers now; they'd given up any fight to save the wine and now were just trying to get it evenly distributed across the ring so fights wouldn't break out. The men were just bashing in the tops of the barrels and dipping out cups full, shouting, singing, outwardly cheerful—

But he *felt* Jocile's mind-thread weaving through everything going on over there. *Got to get my share. Got to get MY share!*

I haven't had MY share yet! And in the drunken gluttony going on over there, "my share" was always going to be "more than I've been able to drink yet."

Tad and Heavyweld put their backs to the palisade and slid down it to sit on the top of the rock wall. It was definitely colder. "You clever little man!" exclaimed Heavyweld, though she kept her voice low. "You and your partner out there are egging them on to drink! You planned this all along?"

"Yes, we are, and no, I didn't. I *hoped,* but—" He sneezed. It really was getting awfully cold. And a lot of those men were going to fall down and probably not wake up again in the morning. They thought it was wine . . . and were drinking it like wine.

"Well, I say me and the lads go sortie out there when the ruckus dies down and give anyone who's still awake a nice little nap?" She started it as a statement, but ended it as a question. "Then in the morning we all go out before they wake up, take all their weapons, and secure them?"

He thought about that. Then thought about what they were going to do with a group of nominally "captured" fighters who absolutely outnumbered the villagers. Even if half of them died tonight from poisoning themselves from drink or the cold, there were still too many to handle.

"No," he said instead. "How are we supposed to control them? We're safe in here. Tomorrow the ones that live through the night will be in no shape to do anything, then there's only two days, maybe less, before help comes. We remain ghosts. If they're still here when the Guard shows up, then they become the responsibility of the Crown. The more mysterious we can be, the less likely they'll try this again."

Heavyweld shook her head, but in admiration. "Well, we could take everything but their clothes, including their boots—"

"And then we are responsible if they die of exposure," he pointed out. "Don't want killing an unarmed fool on my conscience, don't think you want one on yours, either."

There was singing going on over there. *The ones that live through the night are going to wish they hadn't.*

Heavyweld sighed, and took her helmet off. "Well . . . no."

:Please can you come let me in?: Jocile asked plaintively. *:They're starting to wander off in random directions to vomit.:*

:I'm coming,: Tad said, getting to his feet.

"Pretty lady afraid of puke on her pretty silver hooves?" Heavyweld chuckled as the sound of someone trying to throw his stomach as far away from himself as possible drifted over the logs.

"Something like that. Just make sure anyone who wanders toward the palisade gets a pointed reminder why that's a bad idea."

"Yes, sir, Herald," Heavyweld replied. And Tad suddenly realized she was not mocking him. Not the least little bit. "Damn if you two aren't exactly what we need out here. You can take nothing and make anything out of it!"

"Only with the help of everyone else, Sergeant," he replied, feeling warmer than he had since this day started. And for the first time, he did not regret, not the least little bit, that he was not back in the Watchhouse in Haven.

:Come let me in now*!:*

:Yes, Majesty.: Tad laughed as he trotted down the dark lane to the postern gate.

About the Authors

Jeanne Adams has been a full-time writer for ten years, and has loved every minute of it. She lives in Washington, DC, with a fabulous family and three ridiculously silly, big dogs. She also writes thrilling suspense novels, full of action, adventure, and romance. Her first suspense novel was *Dead Run*, with more on the way. Find her at www.JeanneAdams.com, @JeanneAdams on Twitter, and JeanneAdamsAuthor on Facebook.

Dylan Birtolo is a writer, game designer, and professional sword-swinger. He's published multiple novels, novellas, and short stories both in established universes and worlds of his own creation. Some of the universes that he's created stories in are *Shadowrun*, *Exalted*, *BattleTech*, *Freeport*, and *Pathfinder*. On the gaming side, he's the lead designer at Lynnvander Studios and has created multiple games including Pathfinder's *Level 20*, Starfinder's *Pirates of Skydock*, *Evil Dead 2*, and many more to come. He trains with the Seattle Knights, an acting troupe that focuses on stage combat, and has performed in live shows, videos, and movies. He's had the honor of jousting, and yes, the armor is real.

Jennifer Brozek is a multi-talented, award-winning author, editor, and media tie-in writer. She is the author of *Never Let Me Sleep* and *The Last Days of Salton Academy*, both of which were nominated for the Bram Stoker Award. Her *BattleTech* tie-in novel, *The Nellus Academy Incident*, won a Scribe Award.

Her editing work has earned her nominations for the British Fantasy Award, the Bram Stoker Award, and the Hugo Award. Jennifer's short-form work has appeared in Apex Publications, *Uncanny Magazine*, *Daily Science Fiction*, and in anthologies set in the worlds of *Valdemar*, *Shadowrun*, *V-Wars*, *Masters of Orion*, and *Predator*. She has been a freelance author and editor for over fifteen years after leaving a high-paying tech job, and has never been happier. She shares her husband, Jeff, with several cats, and often uses him as a sounding board for story ideas. Visit Jennifer's worlds at jenniferbrozek.com.

Paige L. Christie is originally from Maine, and now lives in the North Carolina mountains. While she is best known for her *Legacies of Arnan* fantasy series (#1 *Draigon Weather*), her work can also be found in several anthologies, including *Galactic Stew*, *Witches Warriors & Wise Women*, *Passages* (Valdemar #14), and *Boundaries* (Valdemar #15). When she isn't writing, Paige runs a nonprofit soup kitchen and food pantry, walks her dog too early in the morning, and is teaching herself to crochet (badly). She is a proud, founding member of the Blazing Lioness Writers. Website: PaigeLChristie.com

Brigid Collins is a fantasy and science fiction writer living in Michigan. Her fantasy series *The Songbird River Chronicles* and *Winter's Consort,* her fun middle-grade hijinks series *The Sugimori Sisters*, and her dark fairy-tale novella *Thorn and Thimble* are available wherever books are sold. Her short stories have appeared in *Fiction River, Feyland Tales*, and Mercedes Lackey's *Valdemar* anthologies. Sign up for her newsletter at www.brigidcollinsbooks.com/newsletter-sign-up/ and get a free copy of *Strength & Chaos, Mischief & Poise: Four Cat Tales*, exclusively available to her subscribers!

Ron Collins is a bestselling science fiction and dark fantasy author who writes across the spectrum of speculative fiction. With his daughter, Brigid, he edited the anthology *Face the*

Strange. His short fiction has received a Writers of the Future prize. His short story "The White Game" was nominated for the Short Mystery Fiction Society's 2016 Derringer Award. He holds a degree in mechanical engineering and has worked to develop avionics systems, electronics, and information technology before chucking it all to write full time.

Brenda Cooper writes science fiction, fantasy, and the occasional poem. She also works in technology and writes and talks about the future. She has won multiple regional writing awards and her stories have often appeared in *Year's Best* anthologies. She lives and works in the Pacific Northwest with her wife and multiple border collies, and can sometimes be found biking around Seattle.

Dayle A. Dermatis is the author or coauthor of many novels (including snarky urban fantasy *Ghosted* and YA lesbian romance *Beautiful Beast*) and more than a hundred short stories in multiple genres, appearing in such venues as *Fiction River*, *Alfred Hitchcock's Mystery Magazine*, and DAW Books. Called the mastermind behind the Uncollected Anthology project, she also edits anthologies, and her own short fiction has been lauded in many Year's Best anthologies in erotica, mystery, and horror. She lives in a historic English-style cottage with a tangled and fae back garden, in the wild greenscapes of the Pacific Northwest. In her spare time she follows Styx around the country and travels the world, which inspires her writing. She'd love to have you over for a virtual cup of tea or glass of wine at DayleDermatis.com, where you can also sign up for her newsletter and support her on Patreon.

Rosemary Edghill (who also writes as eluki bes shahar) is a *New York Times*–bestselling, multiple-award-winning author. She has won the Cauldron Award, given by *Marion Zimmer Bradley's Fantasy Magazine,* numerous times. Her first professional sales were to the black and white comics of the late

1970s, so she can truthfully state on her resume that she once killed vampires for a living. She is also the author of more than sixty novels and several dozen short stories in genres ranging from Regency romance to space opera, making all local stops in between. She has collaborated with authors such as the late Marion Zimmer Bradley and SF Grand Master Andre Norton, worked as an SF editor for a major New York publisher, as a freelance book designer, and as a professional book reviewer. One of her short stories was nominated for the Rhysling Award, which is given for SFnal poetry, and she has been a Philip K. Dick Award judge and survived. She has written a number of short stories set in the world of Valdemar.

English both by name and nationality, **Charlotte E. English** hasn't permitted emigration to the Netherlands to change her essential Britishness (much). She writes (mostly) feelgood fantasy over copious quantities of tea, and rarely misses an opportunity to apologize for something. She loves few things so much as peace and quiet, long walks, and really good cake. Her whimsical works include the *House of Werth* series, the *Wonder Tales,* and *Modern Magick.*

Terry O'Brien is a dual-classed bard/engineer who writes elegant software in several languages and crafts compelling stories and characters in several formats. He currently combines his creative and technical talents behind a camera, in the control room, or at an edit station as a member of multiple audio and video production teams for several clients, employers, and venues. His creative work can be viewed on his website: www.terryobrien.me.

Fiona Patton was born in Calgary, Alberta, and now lives in rural Ontario with her wife, Tanya Huff, an assortment of cats, and two wonderful dogs. She has written seven fantasy novels published by DAW Books and close to forty short stories. "Look to Your Houses" is her seventeenth story in the Valdemar anthologies, and the fifteenth to feature the Dann family.

Diana L. Paxson is the author of twenty-nine novels, including the *Westria* series and the *Avalon* novels; nonfiction on goddesses, trancework, and the runes; and more than ninety short stories. Many of her novels have historical settings, a good preparation for writing about Valdemar. Her next book will be a nonfiction study of the Norse god Odin. She also engages in occasional craftwork, costuming, and playing the harp. She lives in the multi-generational, multi-talented household called Greyhaven in Berkeley.

Cat Rambo's 250+ fiction publications include stories in *Asimov's*, *Clarkesworld Magazine*, and *The Magazine of Fantasy and Science Fiction*. In 2020 they won the Nebula Award for fantasy novelette *Carpe Glitter*. They are a former two-term President of the Science Fiction and Fantasy Writers of America (SFWA). Their most recent works are space opera *You Sexy Thing* (Tor Macmillan) and an anthology, *The Reinvented Heart* (Arc Manor), co-edited with Jennifer Brozek.

Kristin Schwengel lives with her husband near Milwaukee, Wisconsin, along with the obligatory writer's cat (named Gandalf, of course), a Darwinian garden in which only the strong survive, and an ever-growing collection of knitting and spinning supplies. Her writing has appeared in several previous Valdemar anthologies, among others. An avid foodie, she thought it would be fun to play around with the power of food and its associations.

Stephanie Shaver lives with her family in Washington state, where she is gainfully employed by Wizards of the Coast, working on Magic Arena. With this story she finally gets to spend some time with Khaari, who is finding her way back to Wil and company. You can find more about Steph at sdshaver.com, along with random snapshots of life and the food she's made along the way.

Dee Shull has an MA in Communication, and doesn't get to use it nearly as much as they'd like, either in or out of their job.

In their spare time they read for fun, noodle around with other stories and universes, and very much want to find a stable table-top roleplaying group. They currently live with their partner near Denver, Colorado, though they've been yearning for the ocean ever since moving out of California.

A lover of local history and fantastical possibilities, **Louisa Swann** spins tales that span multiple genres, including fantasy, science fiction, mystery, and steampunk. Her short stories have appeared in Mercedes Lackey's Elemental Magic and Valdemar anthologies (which she's thrilled to participate in!); Esther Friesner's *Chicks and Balances;* and several Fiction River anthologies, including *No Humans Allowed* and *Reader's Choice.* Her steampunk/weird west series, The Peculiar Adventures of Miss Abigail Crumb, is available at your favorite etailer. Keep an eye out for her new fantasy adventure series featuring an ex-soldier betrayed by his king, a child witch tasked with saving the world, and a rabbit-size creature who claims he's a god! Find out more at louisaswann.com or friend her on Facebook @SwannWriter.

Elisabeth Waters sold her first short story in 1980 to Marion Zimmer Bradley for *The Keeper's Price.* Her first novel, a fantasy called *Changing Fate*, was awarded the 1989 Gryphon Award. She also edited many of the *Sword & Sorceress* anthologies. Her favorite real place to get away is an Episcopal convent, while her favorite imaginary place is the Temple of Thenoth.

Phaedra Weldon grew up in the thick, atmospheric land of South Georgia. Most nights, especially those in October, were spent on the back of pickup trucks in the center of cornfields, telling ghost stories, or in friends' homes playing RPGs. She got her start writing in shared worlds (*Eureka!, Star Trek, Battle-Tech, Shadowrun*), selling original short stories to DAW anthologies, and sold her first urban fantasy series to traditional publishing. Currently she is working on the paranormal women's fiction series *Ravenwood Hills*, as well as researching a new era in *BattleTech*. See more at phaedraweldon.com.

About the Editor

Mercedes Lackey is a full-time writer and has published numerous novels and works of short fiction, including the bestselling Heralds of Valdemar series. She is also a professional lyricist and a licensed wild bird rehabilitator. She lives in Oklahoma with her husband and collaborator, artist Larry Dixon, and their flock of parrots.